Melanie Milburne read h[er] novel at the age of sevente[en ... studying] for her final exams. After c[ompleting a Master's] degree in education she decided to write a novel, and thus her career as a romance author was born. Melanie is an ambassador for the Australian Childhood Foundation and a keen dog-lover and trainer. She enjoys long walks in the Tasmanian bush. In 2015 Melanie won the HOLT Medallion, a prestigious award honouring outstanding literary talent.

When **Kali Anthony** read her first romance novel at fourteen she realised two truths: that there can never be too many happy endings, and that one day she would write them herself. After marrying her own tall, dark and handsome hero, in a perfect friends-to-lovers romance, Kali took the plunge and penned her first story. Writing has been a love affair ever since. If she isn't battling her cat for access to the keyboard, you can find Kali playing dress-up in vintage clothes, gardening, or bushwalking with her husband and three children in the rainforests of South-East Queensland.

Also by Melanie Milburne

Illicit Italian Nights

Weddings Worth Billions miniseries

Cinderella's Invitation to Greece
Nine Months After That Night
Forbidden Until Their Snowbound Night

Also by Kali Anthony

Awoken by Revenge

Behind the Palace Doors… miniseries

The Marriage That Made Her Queen
Engaged to London's Wildest Billionaire
Crowned for Her Royal Secret

Royal House of Halrovia miniseries

Royal Fiancée Required

Discover more at millsandboon.co.uk.

BILLION-DOLLAR TEMPTATIONS

MELANIE MILBURNE

KALI ANTHONY

MILLS & BOON

All rights reserved including the right of reproduction in whole or in part in any form. This edition is published by arrangement with Harlequin Enterprises ULC.

This is a work of fiction. Names, characters, places, locations and incidents are purely fictional and bear no relationship to any real life individuals, living or dead, or to any actual places, business establishments, locations, events or incidents. Any resemblance is entirely coincidental.

Without limiting the author's and publisher's exclusive rights, any unauthorised use of this publication to train generative artificial intelligence (AI) technologies is expressly prohibited. HarperCollins also exercise their rights under Article 4(3) of the Digital Single Market Directive 2019/790 and expressly reserve this publication from the text and data mining exception.

® and TM are trademarks owned and used by the trademark owner and/or its licensee. Trademarks marked with ® are registered with the United Kingdom Patent Office and/or the Office for Harmonisation in the Internal Market and in other countries.

First published in Great Britain 2025
by Mills & Boon, an imprint of HarperCollins*Publishers* Ltd,
1 London Bridge Street, London, SE1 9GF

www.harpercollins.co.uk

HarperCollins*Publishers*, Macken House, 39/40 Mayor Street Upper, Dublin 1, D01 C9W8, Ireland

Billion-Dollar Temptations © 2025 Harlequin Enterprises ULC

Fake Engagement Arrangement © 2025 Melanie Milburne

Prince She Shouldn't Crave © 2025 Kali Anthony

ISBN: 978-0-263-34477-6

08/25

This book contains FSC™ certified paper
and other controlled sources to ensure responsible forest management.

For more information visit www.harpercollins.co.uk/green.

Printed and Bound in the UK using 100% Renewable Electricity
at CPI Group (UK) Ltd, Croydon, CR0 4YY

FAKE ENGAGEMENT ARRANGEMENT

MELANIE MILBURNE

MILLS & BOON

In loving memory of my dearest and oldest friend Ina Shepherd.

We became firm friends from the first time I arrived in Tasmania as a lonely young mum starting from scratch all over again when my husband moved around the globe for his surgical career.

I was so blessed to have known you and loved and been loved by you for so long.

Rest in peace. Xxxx

CHAPTER ONE

MOLLIE WAS AT the reception desk at the beauty clinic, looking at the latest cancellation on the computer diary. This was the third cancellation this week, and it was only Wednesday. And all of them were her clients. The economy was suffering, and as a result so was she. But wasn't that the story of her life.

It could have been so different if you had married Jago Wilde...

The thought drifted into her head, and she quickly shoved it away, like slamming a door on an unwelcome guest. Too many times that wayward thought would catch her off guard, torturing her with what could have been. Two years had passed, and still, every day she thought of Jago. Every day and every night. She still found herself reaching for him in her bed. No one had taken his place and she wondered if anyone ever would. She was trying to break herself of the habit of thinking of him, but her dire financial circumstances kept reminding her of what she could have had if she hadn't jilted him. Money. Security. Safety. A sense of connection she had never felt in her life before him.

The salon door opened, and Mollie looked up from the computer with a welcoming smile, hoping it was a walk-in client to fill her empty hour, only for her smile to freeze on her face like a wax model. Her blood chilled to ice in her veins, her hands trembled, her heart thumped, and her breath halted.

It couldn't be him. It couldn't be real. She must be hallucinating. Was it really Jago Wilde standing there? Was it a trick of her brain, an apparition brought on by the stress she was under with her worries over her younger brother? She opened and closed her mouth but couldn't get her voice to work. It was rare for her to be lost for words. Rare for her not to be able to stand up for herself, but the circumstances surrounding her break-up with Jago brought hot shame ripening on her cheeks like blood red apples. How could she face him without triggering the feelings she had tried to smother with work and responsibilities? How could she see him without breaking her agreement with his powerful grandfather?

Jago gave a cynical twist of his mouth that passed for a smile, his dark blue eyes scanning her like a laser beam. 'Got a minute for a chat?' His deep, mellifluous voice stroked down her spine like the caress of his warm, broad-spanned hand. Oh, how she had missed his voice. That gorgeous baritone with its crisp English accent that spoke of wealth and privilege from the cradle. The way his voice matched his appearance and yet *tall, dark and handsome* was an understatement. His movie star good looks were beyond traffic-stopping: he could stop a meteor mid-descent. The way he carried himself with confidence, assurance of his place in the world, and yes, even a generous dose of the legendary Wilde arrogance was etched in the landscape of his features. The jet-black hair, the slash of prominent eyebrows, the deep-set, intelligent eyes that could melt stone. The sculptured lips that could break into an easy smile that could make a marble statue's legs tremble, let alone Mollie's.

But Jago wasn't smiling at her now. The cynical slant on his mouth didn't reach his eyes, and it made her stomach clench like a fist.

Mollie was relieved her boss wasn't in that day because Shelagh discouraged personal visits at the clinic. Mollie's job was already hanging by a gossamer thread because of all the days she had taken off to rescue her brother Eliot from yet another disaster. She couldn't lose her job over Jago Wilde—that would be the ultimate humiliation.

'I have back-to-back clients,' Mollie said, holding his gaze with an effort. 'I'm expecting my next one any minute now.' Turns out she was a stellar liar. Years of being shunted from foster home to foster home had honed her skills in mendacity to the point where sometimes she even convinced herself she was telling the truth. Like that she no longer loved Jago Wilde. She didn't miss him or want him any more. That she didn't regret signing that wretched agreement written by his autocratic grandfather, Maxwell Wilde, who had been keen to get her out of his grandson's life before she soiled it and the Wilde name with her trailer trash background. If she hadn't thought there was truth in what Maxwell believed, that she would indeed taint the man she had loved, she would have fought and fought hard. She wasn't a quitter, hence the years of chasing after her brother, searching for him in dark, shadowy, murderous alleyways, paying off his drug debts to keep him out of prison or worse. Holding the basin while he was hideously ill after an all-night bender. Doing all she could to make up for what she had failed to do when they were children.

Jago's eyes penetrated hers like a powerful searchlight, an inscrutable glint showing in his. 'Have a drink with me after work.'

It was typical that Jago commanded rather than asked, and it was also typical Mollie was tempted to obey his command. Just to see what he had to say. Just to spend a few minutes in his company to prove to herself she was finally over him. That she could be in his presence for half an hour and not want him feverishly. He was standing on the other side of the reception counter, close enough for her to see the midnight blue of his eyes and the ink-black lashes that framed them. His eyes had always fascinated, captivated and entranced her. They were an unusual navy shade reminding her of a deep ocean with unknowable depths. She could pick up the exotic spice and woodsy notes of his aftershave, and she had to stop her nostrils from flaring to take in more of his addictive smell. Her eyes moved from his to glance at his mouth. Big mistake. His mouth was her kryptonite. One kiss from his lips when they first met had made her stomach somersault and her pulse race out of control. She had never been able to resist those tantalising and skilful lips. She had felt them on every inch of her body, and being in his presence again triggered a storm of need in her flesh, and she had a feeling he knew it. His mouth was sensually contoured with evenly full lips and a well-defined philtrum ridge like he had been designed by a master sculptor. He hadn't shaved in a couple of days, and she suppressed a shiver as she remembered how those sexy bristles felt against her soft skin.

But his face had changed since they had parted. He now had a deep line carved between his prominent brows as if he had spent a lot of time frowning over the last two years. And his thick black hair was longer than it used to be and brushed back from his face in a careless manner, as if he had run his fingers through it recently.

Mollie gripped the counter that divided them in an effort to control her hands from reaching out to touch him, to see if the electric energy was still there when they touched skin-on-skin. But she could feel it anyway—the tightening of the atmosphere as if all the oxygen particles had shifted. A galaxy of dust motes of desire circling between them. A palpable current in the air that made it almost impossible for her to hide the affect he was having on her.

But hide it she did.

Mollie gave him an arch look. 'A drink? Is that all you want, Jago?'

His eyes darkened to pools of blue ink, glinting, measuring, unwavering. 'I have a proposal for you.'

Her brows rose in a haughty manner. 'Not another one?'

A dark gleam shone in his eyes as they held hers. 'This one you would be a fool not to accept.' There was a hard edge to his voice that hinted at the bitterness that still simmered in his veins. Bitterness her actions had caused.

In spite of her misgivings about spending any more time in his company, Mollie was tempted to hear him out. What sort of proposal did he have in mind? And what would happen if his elderly grandfather found out they had met up again? The agreement she had signed with Maxwell Wilde had forbidden her from ever contacting Jago and from ever explaining to him why she had jilted him the day before their wedding. Forbidden her from speaking to the press for a tell-all interview. Forbidden her to tell Jago about the AI-generated sextortion she was a victim of and how Jago's grandfather had presented her with an ultimatum to make it all go away. Maxwell could make the AI images of her disappear, but she had to disappear too. She had been paid handsomely to go away, and go away she had—all the way to Scotland. She would have gone farther if not for her brother. But of course, the money had eventually run out due to her brother's chronic addiction and mental health issues, and she was starting to wonder if any amount of money would save him from the same self-destruction of their mother. But Eliot was her only living relative, and she would do anything and everything in her power to save him. He was currently on another long stint in a rehab centre, and it had drained every penny from her bank account to keep him there. She couldn't remember the last time she had eaten a proper meal. Beans on toast or instant noodles had been her only source of nutrition and would be until her next pay cheque…if her boss didn't let her go due to the downturn in business.

'How did you find me?' Mollie asked in a cool tone that belied the tumult of her emotions.

'I've always known where you were.'

Mollie tried not to show her stunned reaction, but even so her eyes widened in shock. He had known for two years that she was living and working in the suburbs of Edinburgh? She moistened her talcum powder-dry lips and schooled her features back into some semblance of neutrality. She couldn't imagine Maxwell Wilde would have told him, but who else knew? No one. 'Who told you?'

Something passed across Jago's face like a faint ripple across a calm body of water. But his jaw tightened as if he was biting down on his molars. His diamond-hard look drilled into her gaze. 'It wasn't my grandfather. The only thing he told me was what a lucky escape I had when you jilted me.'

Mollie disguised a swallow and let go of the counter, opening and closing her stiff fingers. She kept her expression impassive, but her stomach was churning enough to make butter for every supplier of shortbread in the country. Possibly even the world. 'And no doubt you agree with him?'

'There are some things my grandfather and I do not see eye to eye on,' Jago said with an unreadable look. 'What time do you finish work?'

'I don't think it's a good idea if we—'

'Meet me at my hotel at six this evening. I'll be waiting in the bar.'

He slipped his hand inside his jacket pocket and took out a business card and, taking a pen from the counter, scrawled the address of his hotel on the back and then handed it to her. She looked at it like it was a hand grenade that could blow up in her face. But then again, it could. A meeting with her ex-fiancé, in public, was flirting with danger.

Terrifying, but tempting danger.

Jago sat slowly sipping a single malt whisky and kept his eyes trained on the entrance to the stylish bar of his Edinburgh hotel. He was taking a gamble Mollie would show up, but he was determined to talk to her in private. A hotel bar was hardly private, but if he could get her to agree to take their discussion to his suite, then even better. Seeing her again had triggered things in him he didn't want triggered: anger, bitterness, humiliation at what she had done. And yes, those other feelings he didn't want to think too deeply about. The feelings Mollie had stirred in him from the moment he met her. The connection with her had been instant and intense, reminding him of how his father must have felt about his mother and vice versa. Was it love? He had never acknowledged it, but he had a worrying sense it could well have been something close to it. But Mollie's jilting of him had blown it out like a flickering match stick in a stiff breeze. The flame was gone, but the match head was still warm. He had to make sure it wasn't in any danger of being reignited. He would have kept his distance, like he had doggedly done for the last two years, mostly out of stubborn pride. But since his grandmother's recent fall, which the doctors were worried she might not fully recover from, he needed Mollie's help, and he was prepared to pay for it. Besides, she had accepted money before, so he was confident she would accept it again, especially the eye-watering amount he was offering.

Jago leaned forward and put his whisky glass down

on the table in front of him, his eyes catching sight of a brunette head outside the hotel. His pulse leapt, his blood throbbed, and his anger and bitterness boiled. Mollie was no longer dressed in her white beauty-clinic uniform with its grey trim but in a simple long-sleeved black dress that clung to her slim body in all the right places. Places he had caressed with his lips and tongue and hands. A shiver went down his spine like a streak of lightning, and he drew in a harsh breath to remind himself to keep on task. This was not the time to think of the red-hot lust that brought them together from day one in a cataclysmic storm. It was not the time to recall how his body had possessed the tight, wet, silky warmth of hers until he lost all conscious thought. She had been his most exciting lover, and no one had ever come close to measuring up to her. Which only made him all the more furious and intent on drawing a final line under their relationship once his grandmother's health situation was sorted one way or the other.

Jago stood as she approached and waved his hand to a deep velvet chair close to his. 'Take a seat. What would you like to drink?'

'Water is fine, thank you.' Mollie sat and elegantly crossed her slim legs, her hands clasping her evening purse with tense fingers. But as if she sensed his glance at her hands, she loosened her hold on the purse and then released a long, steadying breath like someone about to start a yoga session after a stressful day. Even though her expression was as blank as an unpainted canvas, there was a flicker of tension in her eyes. A barely perceptible movement like a stagehand covertly shifting the set pieces around out of sight of the audience.

Jago waited until the waiter had served Mollie a tall glass of ice-water and moved away again before he spoke. 'Busy day at the clinic?' He raised his own glass to his lips and kept his eyes on hers as he took a sip.

'Busy enough.' Her mouth tightened and her gaze shifted, focusing on the open neck of his business shirt. He saw her throat move up and down, a telltale sign of nervousness she was clearly at great pains to hide. She glanced around the bar then turned back to face him, another flicker of worry passing through her gaze.

'Relax, Mollie,' Jago said, leaning back in his seat and putting his glass down beside him. 'There are no paps around to document this auspicious moment.'

A frown tugged at her brow, and she shifted in her seat as if there were marbles beneath her. Then she tossed the mane of her light brown hair over her shoulders, her expression masked. 'What did you want to speak to me about? You mentioned a proposal. I'm guessing it's not a marriage one like the last time.' Her tone was cool with a hint of mockery that ignited his anger all over again. And that was what he wanted ignited—anger, not those other feelings.

'My grandmother is unwell.' He kept his gaze locked on her so he could gauge her reaction.

Mollie blinked and swept her tongue over her lips, her eyes showing compassion rather than the cool indifference he was expecting. 'I'm sorry to hear that. Is she in hospital?'

'She has been but is now at Wildewood Manor. She had a fall and has broken her arm and suffered a concussion.'

'I'm sorry. It must be so difficult for her.'

'That's not the worst of it.' Jago kept his gaze trained on hers. 'Gran has some memory issues as a result of the fall.' He waited a beat and continued. 'She thinks we are still engaged to be married.'

Mollie's eyes widened for a fraction of a second before she adopted a bland expression once more. 'That must be quite inconvenient for you having to explain that we are no longer—'

'I have chosen not to explain that to her.'

Mollie stiffened like a ventriloquist's puppet suddenly jerked upright. 'What?' Her shocked voice rang with a note of panic.

Jago eyeballed her, a grimly determined set to his mouth. 'I want you to come with me to her eighty-fifth birthday party this weekend. As my fiancée.'

Mollie looked as if he had asked her to fly to the moon and back and pick up a souvenir satellite on the way. Her mouth opened and closed, her hands tightened around her glass, and then she placed it down on the table beside her, the surface of the water shivering slightly. 'There's no way I can do that, Jago. It's unfair of you to ask me to.'

'I'm not asking you. I'm telling you.'

Her grey-blue eyes challenged his, and his blood pulsed and leapt in excitement. He had always found her strong-willed spirit a turn-on. It was one of the things he had missed about her since she'd walked out on him—the fiery spats that always ended up in bed. The sun never went down on their anger; he made sure of it. The combustion of their lust for each other had been cataclysmic, and even though he did everything in his power to erase those sensational sensual sessions from his mind, nothing worked. Mollie was branded on his body, his brain, in his blood. He could feel it now: the heat, the throb, the tightening of his flesh. The hunger. The raw raging need nothing would satisfy but her.

'What does your grandfather think of this...plan of yours?' she asked with a cautious look cast in his direction without fully meeting his gaze.

'I haven't told him yet. I thought I'd surprise him.'

The colour leached from her face like a cartoon character, and her gaze snapped back to his. 'I seem to recall your grandfather isn't one for surprises.'

'People can change.'

She gave a snort and reached for her water with a not-quite-steady hand. 'I haven't yet seen a leopard prowling around without its spots.' The bitterness in her tone didn't surprise Jago. His grandfather wasn't known for his charm, but he was legendary at cutting insults and masterful manipulation. Jago and his brothers had been on the receiving end of Maxwell Wilde's vicious tongue too many times to count. But since his grandfather's stroke a year ago, the old man was not as powerful as he liked to think he was. And Jago was going to use it to his advantage. The press so far had not been privy to how much less powerful Maxwell currently was, and Jago was making the most of it.

Jago leaned back in his chair, one ankle crossing over his knee in a casual fashion, his finger idly flicking the toggle on the zipper of his Italian leather ankle boot. 'Of course it goes without saying I'll pay you for your time.'

Twin spots of colour came flooding back into her cheeks, and her mouth flattened. 'How much?'

'Double what my grandfather paid you.'

Mollie gaped at him, her eyes as wide as a cornered animal. 'He told you about that?' Her voice came out as a shocked thread of sound that was barely audible.

Jago slanted his lips in a cynical smile. 'Don't act so surprised, my love. I made it my business to find out what price had induced you to make a fool of me.'

Mollie looked down at her hands in her lap, her fingers gripping her purse like it was a lifeline. 'Please don't say that. We both know you didn't love me.' Her voice was strained and her colour high.

'There are much worse things I could say, so you should be thankful I chose that.'

Jago was still confused about his feelings for her, back then and now. So many emotions had thundered through him when she'd jilted him. Shock, humiliation, anger, rage, despair, a deep, burning sense of betrayal—the list was endless. How could he have been so easily hoodwinked by her? She was a consummate actor, able to play the role of devoted fiancée for four months while all the time waiting for her chance to grab the money and run. As sums of money went, especially given his family's wealth, it hadn't been that huge an amount. But clearly it had been enough for her to make a new life for herself, without him. It infuriated Jago he had genuinely believed she had fallen in love with him. He wasn't the sort of guy to be easily deceived, and yet she had done it and done it convincingly. He knew Hollywood actors who couldn't have done a better job of fooling him. He knew he should direct most of his anger at his grandfather for paying her such a sum, but he couldn't find it in himself to forgive Mollie for taking it. Why had she done it? If she had needed money, he would have gladly given it to her. He still had trouble accepting she was a gold-digger, but all the evidence pointed to it. What other interpretation could he have? She chose to humiliate him by pretending to be madly in love with him for months on end, sharing his bed, wearing his specially designed engagement ring, looking up at him adoringly. How had he not seen through it? Jago used to pride himself on being able to spot a gold-digger from afar, but in Mollie's case he had got it so wrong. She had made a fool out of him in front of the world, and that he would *never* forgive.

But now, all Jago felt was a need to protect his grandmother, and if he had to bribe Mollie to play a little game of make-believe with him, then so be it.

CHAPTER TWO

MOLLIE WAS TRYING to control her reaction to Jago's outrageous offer. He was willing to pay her a jaw dropping amount of money to pretend she was still his fiancée for his grandmother's sake. How could she accept? She mentally pictured the paltry balance in her bank account. How could she *not* accept? Did she even have a choice? It didn't appear so by the steely light of determination in Jago's eyes as he watched her like a hawk about to swoop down to collect its much-prized prey.

Besides, there was Eliot to consider.

There was always her brother to consider. His issues had consumed her life to the point that she wondered if she would ever be free of the burden of worry she carried around like a backpack of boulders. Eliot needed long-term rehabilitation and therapy, but those things did not come cheaply. She had already spent every penny Maxwell Wilde had given her on getting help for her brother. Help that had failed time and time again, because no sooner would Eliot be clean for a day or even a week or two, his demons from the past would come back to haunt him like cruel, taunting ghosts.

Mollie let go of her purse and picked up her water-glass for something to do with her hands. The cold glass with its cubes of ice bobbing inside it reminded her of the ice around Jago's heart. He hated her. She could see it reflected back at her in those impossibly blue eyes. It pained her to see how much he loathed her when once he'd looked at her with eyes gleaming with passion and respect.

Who in her life had ever looked at her that way?

No one.

Mollie hadn't told him anything of her background, and she wondered now if that had been a mistake on her part. But she had spent her life trying to forget about the chaos of her childhood. She had made up a new version so she didn't have to suffer the retelling of a terrible tale of neglect and abuse and deadly violence. She hadn't even told Jago she had a younger half-brother. It was easier to edit Eliot out of her backstory so she didn't have to explain the tragic circumstances that had made Eliot such a train wreck. Circumstances she should have protected him from but had failed to do so. That was another burden she carried through life: the guilt of not protecting her younger brother from a vile predator.

Mollie took a sip of water to relieve the dryness of her mouth then put the glass back down. She straightened in her seat, forcing herself to meet Jago's gaze. 'What's your grandfather going to say when I suddenly appear by your side?' The thought of facing Maxwell Wilde was almost as daunting as seeing Jago again. Would Maxwell sue her for breach of contract? He was a powerful man with contacts and connections in the upper echelons of society.

'He won't be happy about it, but he's not the one I'm concerned about right now. Gran is my focus.'

Mollie knew Jago and his brothers Jonas and Jack had never been close to their overbearing grandfather, but they each adored their gentle grandmother, Elsie. Orphaned when young children, they had been raised by their grandparents. Jago had always been reluctant to talk about his childhood, she assumed because of the grief of losing his parents when he was only five years old, which had made it easier for her not to talk about hers. His grandmother had always been lovely towards Mollie on the handful of occasions she had seen her, and she had often thought of her in the two years that had passed. But Mollie had never warmed to Maxwell Wilde because she had met his type so many times before. A wonderful friend but a dangerous enemy. Charming on the surface but manipulative and conniving if you fell out of favour with him. Which unfortunately Mollie had by not being considered good enough for his middle grandson. Maxwell had done a background check on her and uncovered some of the dark secrets she had so desperately tried to keep hidden. Eliot's time in youth detention; her run-in with the police as a teenager when she stole a jacket from a store because she was cold and didn't have the money to buy one.

But there was one new dark mark against Mollie's name which she only found out via Maxwell Wilde the day before her wedding to Jago. While doing research on her, Maxwell had discovered an extortion plot and presented her with a solution to her dilemma. Suddenly finding herself the victim of an AI sextortion turned her world upside down and inside out. The horror and shock of seeing those explicit images of her about to be uploaded to a popular porn site had made her sick to her stomach. The panic. The dread. The drumbeat of fear that if her brother saw those ghastly images, it would send him into another downward spiral, from which he might not recover. There hadn't been time to even talk to Jago about it because he had flown to New York for a meeting and couldn't be contacted. She thought of how those sickening images might destroy his reputation as well as hers, which was why when Maxwell Wilde swooped in and assured her he could make it all go away by paying off the extortionist, she had agreed to his terms.

Those terrible, heartbreaking but totally necessary terms.

How could she face Maxwell now? Those terms had demanded she disappear from Jago's life and never return. Mollie didn't know if or what Maxwell had told Jago about her and her brother's history. She didn't know if Jago knew about the sextortion that had come close to destroying her life and, by association, perhaps his. But hadn't it already destroyed her life? Her hopes and dreams for a better life—a life where she didn't have to worry about her brother or try and scrape enough money together to help him—had been part of why she'd wanted to marry Jago. She had loved him, yes, although she had never heard him say those words back to her. It hadn't mattered to her back then. She hadn't allowed it to matter. She had only whispered those words once to him while he was sleeping. She had loved him and wanted to be his wife and pretend her old life belonged to someone else. But of course, her past came back to haunt her, and it was particularly humiliating that it was Jago's grandfather who had uncovered her secrets and lies.

'I heard your grandfather had a stroke a year ago,' Mollie said to fill the silence. 'Is he doing okay?' Mollie wasn't a vengeful person, but she couldn't help feeling there had been a bit of karma at play when she read the news report of Maxwell Wilde's stroke. He'd survived it but was now confined to a wheelchair and was working doggedly at his rehabilitation. Whether it had been a success or not hadn't thus far been reported.

Jago picked up his whisky glass and twirled the amber contents for a moment, his expression inscrutable. 'He's found the limitations thrust upon him hard to accept, and he's made my grandmother's life difficult as a result.' He put the glass down again and uncrossed his ankle, his eyes hard as they held hers. 'So will you agree to my offer?'

Mollie rolled her lips together, trying her best to resist the outrageous sum he was offering for a weekend of playing pretend. This was her chance, quite possibly her only chance, of getting Eliot the help he needed. The drugs he was hooked on had done so much damage to him, but there was a possibility that he could recover with long-term rehab and psychotherapy. What other way was open to her to raise that amount of money? Winning the lottery, but what were the chances of that? Wouldn't it be better to accept Jago's offer, for his grandmother's sake as well as Mollie's brother's?

'How long do you want me for?' As soon as Mollie uttered the words, she wished she had chosen different ones. She could feel betraying warmth stealing into her cheeks and reached for her glass of water to take a sip, lowering her gaze from the steely glint of his.

'That depends.'

She glanced at him again, her hand tightening around her drink. The cold from the glass was seeping through her skin into her body. In spite of the flickering warmth of the fireplace nearby, she shivered. 'On what?'

'My grandmother is quite unwell. The doctors aren't willing to give us any certainty on whether or not she will recover her memory. But we will start with her birthday party weekend and see how it goes from there.'

Mollie put her glass down and then began to absently rub the knuckle of her empty ring finger. She had loved the ring Jago had chosen for her and was surprised Maxwell hadn't insisted on her handing it back when he paid her to go away. She had offered it to him, but he'd shaken his head, his faded blue eyes cold. It was as if he thought the priceless ring was already tainted by her wearing it. Mollie had planned to post it back to Jago, but then remembering the terms of the non-disclosure agreement Maxwell had insisted she sign, that option was off the table. She was not to contact Jago under any circumstances. She'd held on to the ring for weeks, taking it out and looking at it as a reminder of what her engagement to Jago had represented: a chance to change her life for the better and help Eliot finally slay his demons. To believe in love conquering all. But one day when she'd opened the drawer where she kept the ring, she found it was gone. Sold by her brother to pay off a drug debt. It confirmed to Mollie the hopelessness of her dream. Happily-ever-afters didn't happen to people like her. Dreams didn't get a chance to fly. Hope could only hold out so long, no matter how driven and determined you were.

There had been an element of compromise about Mollie accepting Jago's marriage proposal after only four months of dating, but she had loved him and hoped his feelings would grow for her. He had certainly acted like a man in love. He was an attentive and considerate lover. He had patiently listened when she'd vented about a difficult client or when she'd told him of some new skin product she was excited about using. She had fooled herself—like a lot of women did—that one day he would say those magical three little words. He hadn't, and now he never would. Not after what she had done. He hated her. He loathed her. He thought her a gold-digger. And if she told him the truth, there was a chance he wouldn't believe her.

No one had ever told Mollie they loved her, not even her brother.

'What did you do with my engagement ring?' Jago asked, glancing at her left hand. 'Sell it?'

Mollie stilled her hands and wished she could slow down the rapid thump-thump-thump of her heart. 'I… lost it.' She regretted hesitating over the choice of word to use, but she didn't want to implicate her brother. Not that Jago even knew she had a brother.

'Lost it or sold it?' Jago looked at her with a penetrating gaze she found a trifle unsettling. Suspicion lurked in his eyes, and it pained her to see it. She had lost his respect, and it stung. Oh, how it stung like acid poured into an open wound, her pride shrivelling, scarring.

Mollie had chosen not to tell Jago about her brother,

not because she was ashamed of Eliot but because she had so skilfully whitewashed her background, simplifying it to make it less likely to trip over a lie. She had told Jago she was an only child, which was partially true—she was the only child of her mother and her scumbag of a father who hadn't bothered waiting around long enough for Mollie to be born. Eliot was her half-brother, the son of her mother and her mother's abusive partner, but to Mollie, there was nothing half about her love and concern for Eliot. He was her only living relative, and she was the only person he could rely on. Mollie had told Jago she was an orphan, which had created a connection with him at the time. The orphan bit wasn't a lie: her mother and her partner had both had drug and alcohol issues and ended their days in squalor, leaving two wild-eyed terrified children sitting with their decomposing bodies for three days before someone found them.

Mollie was no longer that pitiful six-year-old who hadn't been able to undo the deadbolt on the front door or open the painted-over latches on the windows. She was no longer without agency or control over her circumstances.

But Eliot...

Her heart tightened like it was in a cruel vice. Mollie hated thinking about how it had impacted his young brain, the neglect, the starvation, the drugs her mother's partner had given him to stop him crying... It seemed to her a betrayal of Eliot's privacy to tell everyone what had happened to him. Even he hadn't told her about the sexual abuse that had occurred in foster care until he was an adult. When Mollie started dating

Jago, she'd realised his high profile would draw unwanted attention to her and then Eliot, if his existence became known. Who didn't love reading a salacious rags-to-riches story? It was clickbait on steroids. The headlines had flashed across her brain then, and they did so again now.

Impoverished Girl from the Wrong Side of the Tracks Engaged to Handsome Playboy Billionaire Jago Wilde

Drug-addicted Half-Brother with a Criminal Record Joins the Wealthy Wilde Family through Marriage

It was gut-churning to think of the damage it could have done—and still could do—to Eliot if he was exposed to unprincipled journalists hunting for a juicy story.

Mollie forced herself to hold Jago's laser beam gaze. 'I genuinely lost it. I have no idea where it is. I always intended to send it back to you. I'm sorry. I know it cost you a fortune and—'

'You're damn right it cost a fortune.' The bitterness in his voice was unmistakable, the scepticism in his gaze excoriating.

His vision of her as a gold-digger was understandable, but how could she change it without revealing her dark secrets? Secrets she wanted to keep hidden for her own benefit as well as Eliot's. Once she had reached the age of eighteen, she had changed her name to avoid being linked to that lice-infested, malnourished little girl with red welts on her legs from the savage beatings she had endured. She had distanced herself from little Margaret Green and become Mollie Cassidy.

Jago continued to look at her with his marble-hard gaze. 'I've already taken the liberty of purchasing a replacement ring. A fake one just in case you have any idea about—' he held up his fingers in air quotes '—*losing* it.'

Pride brought her chin up, and she held his gaze with gritty determination. 'I never asked you to buy me such a ridiculously expensive ring. It was a waste of money when there are homeless people on the streets.' Mollie knew she wasn't exactly following the gold-digger's handbook right now, but his distrust of her was so irritating. Fine for him with his mouthful of silver spoon to call her out on losing his priceless engagement ring.

But then to her horror, he reached inside his jacket pocket and took out a velvet ring box and set it on the table between them. He leaned back in his chair and surveyed her features with an inscrutable expression.

Mollie stared at the blue box, noticing it was almost the same colour as his eyes. She longed to reach for it but instead curled her fingers into her palms until she could feel the curve of her nails leaving crescent moon impressions in her skin.

'Go on. Take it. See if I got the size right.'

Mollie took a bracing breath and leaned forward to pick up the ring box. She waited a moment before lifting the lid, only just managing to block the rush of air that threatened to come past her lips in a hurricane gasp. It looked exactly the same as her lost ring. Only a jewellery expert would be able to prove it wasn't. The sapphire-and-diamond ring glittered at her, and she had trouble keeping her hand steady as she gazed at it with a host of memories flashing through her brain like a flicker tape movie. Jago's unexpected but romantic proposal the night he gave it to her. For someone who for most of her childhood had rarely received anything but charity shop gifts, Jago's choice of ring more than made up for it...or so she'd thought at the time. She remembered him sliding it over her knuckle, his fingers warm and gentle as they held her hand. She remembered his gaze focused on her with an intensity she hadn't seen in it before. And she remembered the overwhelming sense of joy, of feeling safe and secure for the first time in her life. She would have liked him to declare his love for her, but she'd fooled herself his proposal, his commitment, was enough. But of course, it wasn't. How could it have been?

'It won't bite your finger off if you put it on.' Jago's sardonic tone broke through her painful reverie.

Mollie flicked him a churlish glance and then took the ring out of the box, holding it up to the light to watch the diamonds catch the light from the chandelier overhead. 'It's a very convincing fake.'

'That's the plan—for you and the ring to be convincing fakes.'

Mollie still hadn't put the ring on but was holding it, wanting to accept his fake ring and fake fiancée offer but worried about the consequences; for there would be consequences, of that she was certain. Apart from facing Maxwell Wilde when he had banished her from his grandson's life forever, how could she spend a weekend in Jago's company without him tempting her all over again? She could feel the magnetic pull of him even now. He was the only man who had ever treated her with respect. His touch had sent tingles along her skin from the first moment they met. He had worshipped her body, taking it to heights it had never experienced before. Her skin came alive, her senses went into freefall, her need for him a powerful passionate drive she hadn't known she possessed until he'd awakened it in her.

'So you haven't told your grandfather of this plan of yours?'

'No.'

'But surely me suddenly turning up would be a terrible shock for him, wouldn't it?' Mollie had to be so careful with her words, so careful not to compromise the rules his grandfather had set down.

Jago gave a dismissive shrug of one broad shoulder. 'As I said before, he's not my primary concern right now, my grandmother is. She will be delighted to see you.' His eyes hardened a fraction, and he continued. 'She was heartbroken when our wedding was cancelled. I suspect that's why she doesn't remember it since her concussion—it was too painful for her.'

Mollie could feel the heat pooling in her cheeks and looked back down at the ring in the palm of her hand. It seemed to sit there mocking her with its glittering diamond eyes so like its giver. Daring her to put it on.

Come on. Do it. You know you want to.

She did want to, which was deeply troubling. She would be entering enemy territory, but she didn't know what Jago's grandfather would do. Would he accept her presence for the sake of his elderly and frail wife? Surely, he wouldn't be so cruel as to expose her past to

Jago? But what about the AI-generated images? Maxwell had promised the images of her would go away, and since then two years had passed and she had begun to feel a tenuous sense of safety. He had stayed true to his word, so what would happen if she didn't keep her end of the deal? Maxwell had paid for her silence. He had paid her to go away. He had paid the blackmailer... She frowned and looked at the ring again, her thoughts spinning like clothes in a tumble dryer. Blackmailers didn't usually go away. They usually wanted more money once the first ransom was paid. They upped the ante, bleeding their victim to breaking point.

How had Maxwell Wilde got rid of them with a single payment? Or had he paid them more than he said? If so, it was even more brazen of her to reappear in his grandson's life. Mollie knew Jago wasn't close to his grandfather, but she also knew that blood was thicker than water and Wilde blood thicker than most because of their enormous wealth. Jago might well believe his grandfather over her version of events, and given how many lies she had told in the past, she could hardly blame him. She hadn't seen Jago the day she jilted him. He had been on his way back from New York, which made her look even more of a gold-digger for not having the decency to end their relationship in person. But Maxwell had insisted she leave before Jago got back. He had said it would be easier on everyone if she left, especially as the extortionist was threatening to make those wretched images go viral if the ransom wasn't paid within twelve hours. That looming deadline had made it impossible for Mollie to think things through with any sense of rationality. She had become almost like an automaton, a mindless puppet, doing everything Maxwell Wilde insisted she do. It made sense to her in her distressed and overwrought state to take up Maxwell's offer. It was an escape hatch she desperately needed. The money was not the only reason she left, although it was a part of it. A big part of it. She didn't want to bring shame on the man she loved. She didn't want to taint Jago with the dramas and traumas of her past. And she wanted to protect her brother who had no one else batting for him, believing in him that he could, with the right help, make something of his life before it was too late.

'Are you waiting for me to get down on bended knee or something?' Jago's voice had a note of mockery in it that stung like a slap.

Mollie flicked her gaze to his, doing everything in her power to keep her expression cool and composed. 'Do you really think I'd be such a fool to accept a second time?'

A flash of incendiary heat lit Jago's gaze, and his mouth thinned. 'Who knows what you'd do if you could work it to your advantage? Why are you working in that clinic? I thought your dream was to set up your own luxury spa?'

Mollie had to control every muscle in her face so he didn't see how affected she was by the mention of her failed dream. She had fought so hard for so long, worked punishingly long hours and taken numerous courses to get the qualifications she needed to run her own day spa. But because of her brother's constant draining of her resources, she had been like Sisyphus pushing the ball up a steep hill, only to get within sight of the top for it to come rolling back down again, crushing her hopes and dreams. 'I still intend to open my own spa. It's taking a little longer than I planned, but I will hopefully get there in the end.'

Jago kept his gaze trained on hers. 'If you accept my offer, you can do it sooner rather than later.'

Mollie had already done the numbers in her head. With the amount Jago was offering, she could open her own spa and get Eliot the help he needed. She could achieve her life's dream, but by pretending to be engaged to Jago Wilde, she would have to live her worst nightmare. 'I need more time to think about this. It's a big decision and—'

'I want your answer now.' The implacable edge in his tone reminded her she was the one with the most at stake. She wasn't in the position to bargain, to draw things out, to delay or stall to get time to measure the risks. Jago wanted a commitment now, and she would have to give it to him or lose this chance, this only chance, to save Eliot.

Mollie ran the tip of her tongue over the parched terrain of her lips. The supposed engagement ring she was holding in her palm was digging into her skin. Her stomach was churning with nerves, with dread, but also with a strange sense of excitement. The electric energy Jago generated in her made her think of how his hands had touched her, how his mouth had kissed her, how his body had entered her and taken her to paradise time and time again.

He was paying an exorbitant sum for her to pretend for the weekend of his grandmother's birthday, but would he expect more? Dare she ask what his intentions were? They would be in close contact, pretending to be the lovers they once were. How tempting would it be to slip into his arms, to reach for him, to consent to his earth-shattering lovemaking? Too tempting. Outrageously tempting. Every fibre of her being would have to fight the instinct, the raw and earthy drive to crush her mouth to his, to feel the sexy stroke of his tongue against hers, to wind her arms around his trim waist and pull his hardness against her softness. Thinking about it created a tumult of need in her lower body, her feminine core moistening with greedy want for the hard presence of his.

Jago's dark blue gaze glinted, and his sensual mouth lifted at the edges in a mercurial smile as if he was reading her mind as easily as reading an X-ray. 'If you're finding the prospect of sharing my room a little distasteful, let me assure you I will not lay a finger on you.'

Mollie swallowed a gasp of raw hurt that he no longer wanted her. Disappointment washed through her like a poison, making her fingertips fizz and her heart contract. But what else did she expect? She had jilted him the day before their wedding. She had not even explained why she had done it—she had left that to his grandfather. Jago no longer desired her; he now hated her and was intent on punishing her by making her play by his rules.

She wanted to reject his offer.

She wanted to stand up and throw her glass of water in his too handsome face.

She wanted to fist her hand in his crisp white shirt and pull his head down to press her mouth on his sensual one. To ignite the fire that was still smouldering between them. Flickers and flares of lust licked across her skin, blood pulsed and pounded in her feminine core, molten heat travelled to all her secret places simply by being in Jago Wilde's presence.

Mollie wanted him, and worst of all, she suspected he knew it.

Mollie decided to act like the gold-digger he believed her to be. It was born out of a perverse desire to retaliate, to hurt him as he had hurt her. She knew it was petty and immature of her, but she needed to shift the balance of power. For the sake of her pride, she couldn't allow him to toy with her like a string puppet, making her dance to whatever tune he chose to play. She would make him perform for her. And she knew exactly how to do it.

She knew her sensual power for he had awakened it in her, and it had bloomed and blossomed and blistered into an inferno. The heat between them still sparked in the atmosphere. She could see it reflected in the midnight blue of his gaze, could sense the tension in his toned body, could feel it thrumming in her own. A primitive beat of need that had not gone away in spite of her jilting him. He might say he wasn't interested in sleeping with her, but she knew his body. She knew the signs. She knew his taste, his touch, his smell, his wild and passionate need.

Mollie smiled to herself and crossed one slim leg over the other, holding his gaze without flinching. She would enjoy every moment of bringing Jago Wilde to his knees.

'All right, I accept your offer,' Mollie said.

If Jago was relieved she'd finally agreed to his plan, he didn't show any sign of it on his aristocratic features.

Mollie tried not to think about how little time she had to get herself prepared. She wouldn't only be seeing Elsie again but also Maxwell as well as Jago's brothers. They must all hate her by now. How could they not? She had embarrassed and humiliated their brother. She was a runaway bride, and even worse, she had accepted a significant sum of money to go away. She was reasonably sure Maxwell hadn't told the Wilde brothers the truth about why she had jilted Jago. Jago hadn't mentioned anything about the blackmailer and the AI images, so she assumed that was a detail about her deal with his grandfather he was not aware of, and hopefully it would stay that way. But blackmailers and money deals aside, Jago's brothers would be as appalled by her cowardly behaviour as she would be if the situation was reversed.

'Will your brothers be there?' Mollie asked, glancing at him.

Something moved at the back of Jago's eyes, a shadow, a flicker, a frozen nanosecond of internal thought before his vision cleared to its cold assessment of her. 'It will be a small gathering due to the fragile state of my grandmother's health. Jack will be there, but unfortunately Jonas can't be.'

'Oh, why not?'

'He's...abroad at present, working on an important project.' His slight hesitation before he explained his brother's absence made her sense something wasn't quite right.

'But I thought you told me once that Jonas is the closest of all of you to your grandmother? Why wouldn't he make the time to come and be with her, especially as you said her health is so fragile right now?'

Jago's expression became masked like curtains closing over a stage. 'My grandmother will be disappointed, of course, but not offended by him not being there. She understands Jonas's work takes him abroad for months at a time. Besides, having you there with me will more than compensate for his absence. Her dream is to see at least one of her grandsons settled down before she passes.'

Mollie slid the ring over her finger, eyeing it like she was measuring its worth, but inside she was thinking *Can I really do this? Can I act convincingly enough?*

'There's another thing I need to stipulate,' Jago said. 'There is to be no talking to the press. I don't care how much you're offered for a tell-all interview, I forbid you to speak to them about our relationship, why it ended and why it's back on again.'

Mollie arched her eyebrows and lowered her hand to her lap. 'But it isn't back on again, is it? We're just pretending. Or do have plans to seduce me to get back at me for jilting you?'

A devilish glint appeared in his gaze. 'Now, there's a thought.' His eyes roved over her in a leisurely manner, causing her body to flare with molten heat.

Mollie knew he was thinking of all the times he had stripped her naked, all the times he had kissed her body from head to toe. All the times he had possessed her, gently, roughly, urgently, passionately. She wasn't one to blush readily, but she could feel the hot bloom of colour flowing into her cheeks once more as each erotic memory flooded her brain. Blood flowed to her inner core, making her feminine folds swell with wicked want. How could she control this driving need for him? Was it because she had been celibate for two years? Even her breasts tingled inside the lace of her cheap bra, as if anticipating the roll of his tongue, the warm, wet suck of his mouth, the sexy scrape of his teeth and the rasp of his stubble on her soft flesh. He could unravel her senses, blow her mind and her body just by looking at her. She would have to be careful how she handled him this coming weekend. It had broken her heart to give him up two years ago; she wasn't sure she would survive a second time.

Mollie challenged him with her gaze, using every bit of acting talent she had gained over the years of her crazy, chaotic life. 'If you put one finger on me, Jago Wilde, I will make you regret it.'

Jago gave a mocking laugh that grated on her already shredded nerves. Then he leaned forward, his forearms resting on his muscular thighs, his eyes nailing hers. Even though there was a coffee table between them, it seemed like no distance at all. This close, she could see the individual pinpricks of his dark stubble that liberally peppered his jaw. Her fingers itched to run over his skin, to feel the abrasion of his growth on her softer skin. She suppressed a tiny shiver and tried to stop thinking of what it had been like to have his head between her legs, his tongue playing her like a maestro plays a priceless instrument. Why couldn't she forget all the times he had touched her? The memories were burned, seared, scorched into her flesh like a brand.

'We will have to act like lovers while we're at Wildewood Manor. You will have to accept my touch, even my kisses, or the deal is off. Understood?' His voice was deep and gravel-rough and underlined with the implacability she knew was an essential part of his personality.

Feminist she might be, but his unshakable authority sent a delicate frisson over her flesh. She had locked horns with him in the past, and it had always been resolved with smoking-hot sex. Make-up sex. But there was no way Jago would ever forgive her for jilting him, so any sex between them now would be revenge sex.

Could she allow her body to be used that way? But her body still craved him, so how would it be anything but a mutual explosion of the senses? Jago wanted her on his terms, but she had terms of her own and she would insist on them.

Mollie ground her teeth behind her painted smile. 'I want to be paid up-front.'

Cynicism burned in his gaze like a laser beam. 'That can be arranged, but it comes with conditions.'

A feather of unease danced up and down her spine. 'What conditions?'

'You've run away from me before. I am not letting it happen again.'

'I promise you I won't—'

'Your promises mean nothing to me. They are worthless,' Jago said in a harsh tone that lashed her like the flick of a whip. His eyes were so dark they were almost blue-black, and his jaw was tight as a clamp.

And yet again, her traitorous body revelled in his commanding manner. It made every cell of her body tingle with awareness and every inch of her skin tighten. Even though he clearly hated her, Mollie knew without a doubt he still wanted her. It was written in his features, it pulsed like electricity in the atmosphere, it circled back and forth between them like a fizzing current. It gave her a fraction of power in their relationship as it stood now. Physical power she could use to her advantage. And she would use it. She would be as ruthless as she needed to be to survive being around him again.

'It's only Wednesday,' Mollie pointed out. 'You can hardly keep me chained to your side until Friday.'

One black brow arched up in a satirical manner. 'Can't I?'

Another frisson of excitement coursed. He was ruthless enough to do whatever it took to get what he wanted, especially now. He was a Wilde, and the name was synonymous with *ruthlessness*.

What Wilde men wanted, they got.

'I'll come with you Friday, but I need time to prepare myself,' Mollie said. 'We've spent two years apart. It won't be easy to slip back into the role of your fiancée.'

Jago leaned back in his chair, one of his hands scraping his hair back from his face, leaving deep fingertip grooves in the thick black strands. How many times had she lain draped across his naked body, her fingers doing the very same thing to his hair? Was he remembering it? Remembering how it felt to hold her, to possess her?

She studied his expression, searching for a clue to what he was feeling, but all she could see was bitterness and distrust etched in his handsome features. It pained her to think of what their relationship could have been if it hadn't been for those dreadful photos of her.

They might have even had a baby by now...

They hadn't discussed having children in much detail, but she knew it was Jago's grandmother's yearning desire to hold a great-grandchild in her arms before she died. Neither of Jago's brothers were settled down, although Mollie had seen a gossip article about Jonas and his girlfriend, Tessa Macclesfield, who he had dated for a couple of months. Coincidentally, Tessa was the wedding cake designer who had designed Mollie and Jago's spectacular wedding cake. Mollie had always wanted to call on Tessa and apologise in person at her shop in Notting Hill, but there hadn't been time before she'd left to move to Scotland to get Eliot into a private rehab clinic in Glasgow. He had left after four months, which had been heartbreaking for her. Heartbreaking to have a glimpse of hope only for it to be snatched away again. But he had agreed to try it again and had been there six months so far this time. But it was expensive. Hideously, terrifyingly expensive for someone in Mollie's dire financial position. The money Jago was offering would not only pay for a whole year or more of private rehab but could also get her started in her own health and beauty spa. To have her brother healed as well as her career on track was like wishing for the moon and stars and the International Space Station, but she refused to give up hope. If she gave up on her dream, then she would have failed herself as well as her brother.

'I have a few business things to see to in Edinburgh tomorrow, but we will fly down to London early on Friday then drive to Wildewood,' Jago said. 'Give me your address so I can pick you up on Friday.' He took out his phone in preparation to type in her current address.

Mollie gave him a quizzical look. 'But surely you must already know it. I mean, you found my clinic easily enough. Did you engage the services of a private investigator to track me down?'

Jago lowered his phone to look at her. 'You once mentioned you'd always wanted to visit Scotland. I did a little research and found out a young woman matching your description was working in a beauty clinic here.'

Mollie wouldn't put it past him to have engaged MI5 to track her down. There were numerous beauty clinics in Edinburgh and its surrounds. But then, Jago had connections most people could only dream about. Wilde money opened doors and created opportunities way out of reach for the general population. But it was a little unnerving to think it hadn't taken Jago long to find her. She wondered if he already knew about her awful little bedsit and was only asking for her address as a formality. Again, it made her think of how she could have been living in the lap of luxury if she hadn't jilted him two years ago. She certainly wouldn't be living in a cramped and mould-ridden studio on the basement floor of a rundown tenement house.

Mollie told him her address, keeping her expression masked as he typed it in his phone. She looked at his long fingers as he entered her address, her imagination taking her places she knew she shouldn't be going. Those fingers had touched her, stroked her, tantalised her in places no one else had touched. She could not imagine wanting anyone else to touch her now even though two long, lonely years had passed. Her body was branded by his touch, her mouth craved only his taste, and she couldn't see it changing anytime soon.

Jago Wilde, damn him, had quite literally ruined her for anyone else.

CHAPTER THREE

JAGO WAS RELUCTANT to let Mollie out of his sight, but short of kidnapping her, there was nothing he could do but escort her home and hope she didn't do a runner before Friday. Being with her again stirred up so many emotions, none of which he wanted to acknowledge. He had never considered himself a jealous man, but since meeting Mollie, he had seen the way other men looked at her. With her long light brown hair and grey-blue eyes, she could easily have graced the cover of a high fashion magazine. She moved with a ballerina's grace, floating, gliding, ethereal. Her face was a neat oval, her nose a ski slope, her mouth… Oh God, why did he have to keep looking at her mouth? His own lips tingled with the memory of the softness of her lips against his. His lower body turned to steel as he recalled those lips sucking on him. Even their first kiss had detonated something inside him, sending him wild with need. A need that had reawakened by being in her presence. Since their break-up, he had not rushed into a new relationship but left it for close to a year before he ventured back to his playboy lifestyle. Strangely, it hadn't satisfied him the way it had before, which he was reluctant to admit to anyone, including himself.

The press made a big deal about his enviable lifestyle—wealthy, privileged, with his choice of women to entertain him as he pleased.

But since Mollie had left him, no one pleased him.

Jago had accumulated even more wealth in the two years since the cancelled wedding, but he didn't take any pride or satisfaction in the extra millions in his bank account and property and investment portfolio. He didn't feel any sense of pride in what he had achieved. Instead, he felt a sense of niggling failure that the one person he wanted had got away. Had got away because she had valued money over him.

That was something he could not forgive.

Jago looked across at Mollie sitting with a cool and untouchable expression on her face. She could be so animated when they discussed something she was passionate about, and yet at other times, she could shut down her features in a blink of her eyes, effectively locking him out like a window shutter. Like any couple, they had had their differences of opinion at times, but their electric physical chemistry had always ironed out those differences with a distracting lovemaking session. And they had been spectacularly distracting. So distracting, he still could not erase them from his mind. If he allowed himself, he would think about her skin against his every day. He had never been the type of man to obsess over a lover. He had flings, so many flings he had trouble recalling faces, let alone names. When a fling was over, it was over. Never had he ruminated on a break-up like his with Mollie. But then, he hadn't broken up with her—she had done it to him and in the most humiliating way of all.

But in spite of all that, Mollie had somehow burrowed her way into his brain and body to the point he was nearly always thinking about her, and that *had* to change. He had to move on, and his grandmother's recent memory loss had given him the perfect way to do it.

It occurred to him he didn't know how to reach Mollie other than physically. That had been their language, their communication. A look, a kiss, a stroke of a finger, a hand down the other's face or arm had spoken volumes. His body pounding into her welcoming silky wetness had told him all he needed to know...back then.

Now, with her sitting coldly and closed off from him with a coffee table as a barrier between them, Jago realised he knew nothing of her life over the last two years. What had she done with the money his grandfather had paid her to go away? It was a significant sum and yet she was working in a rundown suburb in a beauty clinic that looked like it needed more of a makeover than its clients. He had only found out about the money in the last few months as he had taken over more and more of his grandfather's business affairs. His grandfather's stroke a year ago had not just affected his physical mobility, but Maxwell no longer had the sharpness of intellect one needed to run a multi-arm corporation. Jago had his own property development business to run, but at least he had the skills and mental acuity to juggle both businesses, although it was tough right now with his younger brother, Jonas, out of the country for an unspecified time. While Jonas occasionally went off-grid to work as a naval architect on top-secret missions, his sudden departure seven months ago had been a little unusual. Not that Jago was close with either of his brothers—their grandfather had seen to that—but Jonas was the closest to their grandmother. Jago hadn't even been able to get a message through to him about their gran's health crisis. Jonas had simply disappeared, leaving instructions that no one was to contact him, including the young woman he had been dating. But that was his younger brother's personal business. Jago had his own to sort out.

'So what have you been doing with yourself the last two years?' Jago asked to break the silence because it was becoming obvious to him Mollie was not going to.

Mollie's eyes dipped to the glass she was holding, the ice cubes rattling against the sides. 'Working.'

'Because you want to or you need to?'

Mollie gave him an unreadable glance. 'Both.'

He had trouble controlling the urge to curl his lip. 'It didn't take you long to get rid of the money my grandfather paid you. What did you do with it?'

Her small chin came up, and her eyes flashed like a struck match. 'I am not going to discuss my financial affairs with you.' Her tone could have clipped a yew hedge.

Jago held her gaze with iron determination. 'Ah yes, the non-disclosure agreement.' It was a guess on his part, but Jago knew enough about his grandfather to realise Maxwell would never leave himself open for exploitation. No way would he pay someone off without making sure they never told anyone about it. For as long as Jago could remember, the press had feasted on stories of the Wilde brothers. Jago's grandfather was, in his halcyon days, a savvy businessman who had used every means in the book to build his wealth, not necessarily for his family but for the sake of his ego and overblown pride. But since his stroke, his grandfather had had to rely on Jago to take over more and more responsibility, a situation Maxwell did not accept with grace or gratitude but with criticism and grumpiness.

Mollie's eyes flared for the briefest moment at the mention of the non-disclosure agreement, but she didn't respond. She swirled the contents of her glass, then lifted it to her lips and took a measured sip. He got the sense she was trying to find her way through a verbal minefield, careful in what she said and how she said it. She put the glass back on the table between them with almost exaggerated precision, then sat back and met his gaze with a cool stare that made him all the more determined to get under her fortresslike guard.

'I know what my grandfather is capable of,' Jago said into the throbbing silence. 'He's ruthless and manipulative and will stop at nothing to get what he wants.'

Mollie's neat eyebrows rose ever so slightly, and her mouth slanted at a cynical angle. 'You could easily be describing yourself, coming all this way with offers of money to get me to do what you want.'

Jago had to stop himself from clenching his jaw out of frustration. Of course he was prepared to be ruthless. He had to be to get her to come to his grandmother's birthday, and he would do whatever it took to achieve it. He didn't trust her not to do another runner on him, so he had to find a way to keep her close, as dangerous as that was. Dangerous because of the sexual chemistry that still thrummed in the air between them. He could feel it in his body—the stirring of his blood, the swelling and tightening of his flesh as he recalled the way she'd welcomed him into her body in the past. Had she really wanted him back then, or had it all been an act? She had been so damned convincing he had fallen for it. Fallen hard. Not in love, but in lust. Red-hot and flaming. Lust so powerfully addictive he had never wanted it to end, thus the marriage proposal. It was the one thing he prided himself on—that he hadn't told her he loved her.

She had said those three little words, albeit in a whisper one night after making love, but he hadn't said them back. He had pretended to be asleep, for saying those words were difficult for him because the last time he told someone he loved them—his parents—they didn't come back. Not that he truly believed he had been in love with her anyway, or at least he didn't want to think he had been that foolish to fall in love with someone who threw him over for money. It was physical attraction that had bound him to her back then. Their connection had reminded him of his parents' strong physical bond: they had been so happy with each other until fate stepped in and ruined everything.

'Money seems to be the only thing that appeals to you,' Jago said, nailing her with his gaze.

'Money has universal appeal, does it not?' Her voice was straight out of the gold-digger's playbook but something about her eyes reminded him of a wrong note played in a performance.

Jago reached into his jacket pocket for a single-sheet document. He unfolded it and handed it to her.

'What's that?'

'A contract.'

She stared at it for a moment before taking it with a hand that was not quite steady. She drew it closer and scanned it with her gaze, her teeth momentarily snagging her lower lip. Then she released her lower lip and looked at him in a guarded manner. 'You want me to sign this?'

'Of course.'

She glanced back at the sheet of paper in her hand, but he had a feeling it wasn't to reread the contract written there but rather as a way to avoid his gaze. Her jaw worked for a moment like she was clenching her jaw to control her emotions. Then she lifted her gaze back to his, her mouth in a line so tight her lips were almost white. 'You're way more like your grandfather than I thought.'

Jago acknowledged her comment with a wry smile. 'I'm not sure he would agree with you. He's made it his life's work to toughen my brothers and me up.'

'It's clearly worked.' There was a stinging note to her voice, and it pleased him to have got under her skin.

Jago lifted one shoulder in a careless shrug. 'I'm tough when I need to be.' He took out his gold pen and handed it to her. 'Sign the contract between us. I'll get the money to you first thing tomorrow.'

Mollie took the pen from him with another gelid glare. 'I'm not signing until I have the money.'

Jago ground his back teeth and mentally apologised to his dentist for the damage he was probably doing. 'I'm not handing over a penny until you sign. Take it or leave it.'

Mollie flicked the pen back and forth between her

fingers, looking as if she'd rather use it as a weapon. 'You don't trust me, do you?'

'Nope.'

If she was wounded by his response she didn't show it. Instead, she leaned forward to put the paper on the coffee table, then signed the contract with a flourish, before handing both the pen and paper back to him. 'You can transfer the funds into my back account right here and now. I'll text you the details.' She sat back and took her phone out of her purse and texted him her details.

Jago's phone pinged a few seconds later, and he swiped the screen open to view her message. 'I'll give you half now and the rest at the end of the weekend.'

'But you said you'd—'

'It's in the contract you just signed.'

Mollie gestured with her fingers for him to hand the contract back to her. He did so, and she scrutinised it like a forensic detective. Her mouth tightened, and her gaze blazed, and she handed the contract back. 'Fine. Half now, the rest later.'

Jago opened his banking app on his phone and transferred the funds. There was no way he was going to let her out of his sight, contract or not. He pushed back his sleeve to glance at his watch then brought his gaze back to hers. 'It's getting late.' He stood and, scooping the now empty ring box off the coffee table, handed it to her. She took it with a scowl and opened her purse and dropped it inside, clicking it shut with a snap.

'Come on,' he said. 'I'll escort you home.'

Mollie rose to her feet with regal grace, but her eyes

were on still on fire. 'That is totally unnecessary. I can find my own way home.'

'I'm sure you can, but I have a burning desire to see where you live.' He had another burning desire, one he wished he could switch off, but his body wouldn't obey the rational commands of his brain. It had its own agenda, and it was making it hard for him to imagine getting through the next few minutes without touching her, let alone sharing a bedroom at Wildewood Manor this coming weekend.

Mollie had no choice but to do as Jago commanded. Even she could see the sense in Jago making sure he knew where she lived since he had just handed over a veritable fortune. But allowing him to see her ghastly little bedsit was the ultimate in humiliation, especially when he knew she had already been given a large sum of money by his grandfather. Still, she was supposed to be playing the gold-digger, so she would have to act like a pro to get through it. She followed Jago out of the swish hotel bar and stood by his side as he used a rideshare app. Normally, she walked or caught public transport, but it had started raining, and even though it was spring, the Edinburgh air was bracing to say the least. She tucked her evening purse under one arm and cupped her elbows with her hands in an effort to keep warm. She had lived in Edinburgh long enough to know how capricious the weather could be. But the only warm coat she possessed was so old and unfashionable she had decided against bringing it with her.

'You're shivering.'

'I'm n-not.'

Jago shrugged himself out his jacket and then draped it across her shoulders. The warmth of his jacket suddenly enveloped her, intoxicating her with his body heat as well as his spicy cologne. Her nostrils flared to take in more of that alluring smell evoking such sizzling erotic memories that even the ice-cold rain couldn't cool down.

Mollie glanced up at him. 'Aren't you cold?'

He gave a crooked smile that sent a dart to her heart. 'I'm tough, remember?'

The rideshare pulled up in front of them at that moment, which saved Mollie the necessary brainpower to think of a witty reply. He opened the door for her and she got in, sweeping the skirt of her dress inside the car with her hand. He closed the door and got in the other side, greeting the driver with a polite exchange of words, before clipping his seatbelt in place.

Jago met her gaze, and she watched as his eyes drifted to her mouth. 'Thawed out yet?'

'Getting there.' Mollie wasn't entirely sure he was talking about the weather. She knew she had to pretend to be engaged to him in front of his grandmother, which meant she could hardly act cold and indifferent towards him. Her eyes went to his mouth seemingly of their own volition, and her heart skipped a beat. How was she going to act cold and indifferent when he looked at her like that? His eyes darkened to the colour of the night sky. The focus in them was intense as if he was imagining the press of her lips against his and the meeting of their tongues. She shivered and hugged his jacket closer, forcing her gaze to look in the direction of travel.

Mollie had always known Jago was tough, but he definitely seemed even tougher now. More ruthless. More determined to get his way. Had she done that to him by jilting him? He hadn't been in love with her, so it wasn't as if she had broken his heart. She had dented his pride more than anything else. But now her pride was at stake as the rideshare took them closer to her bedsit. Her heart rate increased as the car rumbled over every cobblestone on the back streets that looked even more dismal and dangerous in the growing darkness and driving rain.

A short time later, the driver pulled up outside her address. Jago got out and came around to her side of the car before she had even undone her seatbelt. Something with small, pointed teeth was nibbling at her stomach lining, and her heart was pumping like she had just run up the steps of the Scott Monument.

Jago opened her door and did his best to shield her from the pelting rain. He thanked the driver and then closed the car door. Mollie held his jacket over her head and dashed to the steps that led to her lower-ground flat. She didn't need to look at Jago's face to witness his disgust at her accommodation as he followed her down the stone steps. She summoned up the remnants of her pride and took out her keys from her purse and unlocked the door, stepping inside and handing him back his jacket. 'I'm sorry it's so wet. Thank you for the lift home.'

He took the jacket from her and hung it on a hook on the back of the door then closed it. He turned and gave the room an assessing sweep with his gaze, his mouth tightening. 'This is your home?' His incredulous tone was another dent to her pride, the derision in his gaze making her cheeks burn.

Mollie raised her chin, determined to stand her ground with him. She had lived in worse. Much worse. 'Careful, Jago, you'll wake the neighbours speaking with all those silver spoons dangling from your mouth.'

He rolled his eyes at her attempt at humour, but his mouth was still in a tight line. 'How long have you been living here?' His ink-black eyebrows were drawn into a severe frown making him look intimidating but concerned at the same time.

'I've only been here a few months.' Mollie shook back her hair, determined not to show how embarrassed she was at him seeing how far she had fallen. She had had so few choices when it came to accommodation after Eliot's rehabilitation deposit took the rest of her savings. She had missed meals and turned off the heating in order to get through. It certainly wasn't how she'd expected her life to turn out. She had done everything possible to avoid living in the same squalor as her mother and stepfather, but Eliot's problems made it difficult for her to get ahead. She was unfortunately casually employed at the clinic, which meant she could be told by her employer to stay home if not enough clients had booked in on any particular day. She literally did not know from one week to the next how much money she might earn.

But you have plenty of money now.

Mollie was tempted to open her banking app on her phone just to see the money in her account that Jago had transferred earlier. If she could get through the coming weekend with him at his grandmother's birthday party, she wouldn't need to return to the beauty clinic at all. She could set up her own business in a nicer area. Her flagging dream took in a deep lungful of air, inflating Mollie's hopes to the point where she began to feel lightheaded and giddy with the possibility of success at last.

Jago proceeded to do an inspection of her flat like he was some sort of structural engineer. His expression grew all the more thunderous as he tapped against the walls and turned the tiny kitchen's taps on and off. Mollie folded her arms and watched him with a bored teenager look on her face.

Finally, he turned and faced her. 'You're not staying here another minute.'

She arched her brows in an imperious manner. 'Excuse me?'

He blew out an impatient breath—one with a thick curse word attached on its backdraft. 'You can't possibly live like this. It's practically a hovel.'

'I've lived in far worse.' Mollie could have bitten off her tongue as soon as the words were out. She had told Jago nothing of her chaotic and disadvantaged childhood. She had removed all trace of her past, changing her name and her accent in order to take herself as far away from it as possible. And she had mostly done so… except Eliot kept pulling her back like a towrope she could not and would not sever.

Jago's blue eyes narrowed, his frown forming two deep pleats between his eyebrows. 'Worse?' His voice had a probing quality to it. He reminded Mollie of a detective who had picked up a significant detail of evidence everyone else had missed.

'Not everyone grows up in an Elizabethan manor

house with its own country park, Jago. Not everyone flies in private jets for their holidays or has chauffeurs driving them to and from boarding school each term,' Mollie said with scorn dripping from every word. Or maybe it was jealousy. Who wouldn't be jealous of the Wilde lifestyle?

'Yeah, and not everyone loses their parents in a plane crash when they're five years old,' Jago said with a thickness in his voice she had never heard in it before. 'No amount of money or property can compensate for that.'

There was a silence so intense only the sound of the kitchen tap's leak could be heard. *Plop... Plop... Plop...*

Mollie had never heard him mention his parents before. She had read about the light-plane crash that had tragically killed his father and mother, but she had never heard Jago refer to them. Not once, even though she had been engaged to him, shared his bed, his life, his world. She hadn't pushed him to talk about them because she had ghosts of her own she preferred to keep well hidden.

But it was her scornful words now that had triggered him to speak of his heartbreaking loss, and she was ashamed of herself. Deeply ashamed. It was a cheap shot and cruel of her, given all she knew about being an orphan. Yes, he'd been fortunate enough to have grandparents to step in and raise him and his brothers, but Mollie had good cause to wonder if Maxwell Wilde had been an ideal parent substitute. She thought of Jago, the middle of the Wilde brothers, only five years old. Old enough to know what had happened and to feel gut-wrenching grief and despair, and yet so young, so terribly young.

Mollie swallowed against a stricture in her throat. 'I'm sorry…' She moistened her dry lips and continued in a scratchy voice. 'You're absolutely right. No amount of money could ever make up for such a tragic loss.'

Jago moved back to the kitchen sink and tightened the tap until there were no more drips. 'That should stop it for now.'

So there was to be no acknowledgement of her apology and no further conversation about his parents. But Mollie could sense the tension in him, the tightness of his expression and the shadows in his eyes hinting at deeply suppressed emotions.

'But I won't be able to turn it on again,' Mollie said, glancing at the tap he had just tightened.

An implacable look came into his eyes. 'You won't be turning that tap on again. You're coming with me. Now.'

Mollie's eyes widened in alarm. 'Now?'

'Go pack a bag. There's no way I'm allowing you to come back here. Not even after the weekend.'

'But I have a lease that's—'

'I'll sort out the lease.'

Mollie's pride brought her chin up to a defiant height. 'What gives you the right to tell me where I can live?'

He took her left hand in his and held it up so the fake engagement ring glinted. 'This.'

Mollie snatched in a breath at the feel of his fingers wrapped around hers. His hold was gentle, and yet she suspected if she pulled away, he would tighten his grip. But strangely, she didn't want to pull away. She was a tiny iron filing, and he was a powerful magnet, drawing her closer, closer, closer. She could feel her heart rate pick up, a hectic pace that made her feel dizzy. Or maybe that was because she was only a few centimetres from his rock-hard chest and strongly muscled thighs. The desire to close the gap was almost unbearable, every muscle and sinew in her body wanted to feel him against her. All of him. Her body recognised him, the heat and smell of him, the strength and power of him an aphrodisiac she had no immunity against.

'We both know that's just a fake ring,' Mollie said, trying but failing to stop from glancing at his mouth.

His mouth kicked up at one corner in a wry smile, his eyes sexily hooded as his gaze drifted to her lips. 'That may not be real, but this is, isn't it?' And his mouth came down to just above hers, hovering there as if he knew every cell in her body was throbbing with the need to feel his lips against hers.

'I don't know what you're talking about.' Mollie tried to keep her voice even but her increasing breathing rate betrayed her. It was so damn hard to resist him. Her lips were tingling with anticipation, her legs feeling as if the bones had turned to liquid. She still hadn't pulled her hand out of his, still hadn't stepped back from the scorching temptation of his masculine body that called out to her with a primitive energy she could feel in her most feminine flesh.

'I think you do.' His mouth came even closer, his warm minty breath wafting across her lips, making them tingle all the more. 'You want me to kiss you, to see if the magic is still there.'

Ironic that he should speak of magic for Mollie's eyelids lowered like she was being cast under a spell. Her senses were intoxicated by his proximity, every cell of her body aching for him to crush her mouth beneath his. She swept the tip of her tongue over her lips, her heart kicking like a wild animal against her breastbone, her body tilting towards him as if she had no power to stop it. But then she didn't. Jago Wilde was her kryptonite: he could get her to do anything with the sensual power he had over her. She gave him an upwards glance to see the glinting intent in his midnight blue gaze. Something tilted sideways in her stomach like a bowl of liquid threatening to spill over. Moist heat throbbed between her thighs, and she closed the distance between their bodies, her breasts pushed up against his chest, her free hand going to the front of his shirt, fisting in it to bring his mouth down to hers.

CHAPTER FOUR

MOLLIE DIDN'T CARE THAT she had let him win by making her reveal her desire for him. Right then, all she cared about was the feel of his lips moving on hers with such explosive sensual heat. His mouth was firm and yet gentle, cajoling her into joining a dance as old as time itself.

But this was *their* dance, the sexy tango that she had only ever experienced with this degree of pleasure with Jago. His lips moulded to hers as if they had been crafted for exactly this purpose, to tease hers into sensual play and transport her to another place, a place where nothing mattered but the molten heat that fizzed and flashed and fired between them. Their chemistry hadn't changed: if anything, there was a new quality to it. A desperate clawing sort of hunger because they both knew this was not going to last forever. By the end of the weekend, they would return to their separate lives. Somehow that made their kiss all the more passionate, even poignant.

Jago's hands went to her hips, holding her against his hardened body, his mouth moving with mind-blowing expertise on hers. He made a guttural sound and deepened the kiss with a bold stroke of his tongue. Mollie couldn't hold back her own sounds of pleasure and encouragement, her tongue dancing with his in an erotic choreography that sent tingles racing up and down her spine. How had she gone without Jago's kisses for two years? How had she denied herself the sensual pleasure of being hotly wanted, urgently desired by a full-blooded man? But what other man could ever make her feel this way? Jago was the only man who had ever made her feel this level of arousal, this level of enjoyment, this level of delight.

Jago finally lifted his mouth off hers and looked down at her with desire shining like a bright light in his eyes. His hands were still on her hips, his arousal pressing against her stomach. Her own arousal was pulsing away in silky secrecy, a throbbing ache, a sense of being left hanging. But she tried not to show it in her face. She didn't want him to know how close she was to begging him to make love to her here and now. To satisfy the ache, to ease the burning fire of her longing. She was conscious of his gaze scanning her face, his expression inscrutable all except for the glitter of unrelieved desire in his eyes.

Mollie moved out of his hold and smoothed her dress over her hips, giving him a worldly glance that was a million miles from what she was really feeling. 'If you kiss me like that in public, people will think you're madly in love with me.'

'Don't go confusing lust with love,' he said with one of his trademark cynical smiles.

'I'm not going to make that mistake twice,' Mollie said with an edge of bitterness she couldn't eradicate in time. 'You weren't in love with me, so why you asked me to marry you in the first place is a total mystery to me.'

His features hardened like fast-setting concrete. 'There's no mystery about why you said *yes*, though, is there? You would never have accepted my proposal if I'd been some regular guy with a basic income. You saw money and fell in love with that, not me.'

Mollie held his stony look with enormous self-possession, a skill she had perfected since childhood. 'I think it's time you left.'

'Not without you.' Thunder rumbled in his voice, and lightning flashed in his gaze.

She arched her brows and folded her arms in an intractable pose. 'You're not the boss of me.' She knew she sounded like a recalcitrant child, but his overbearing manner was getting her riled up. That was another power he had over her: he could make her lose control of her carefully crafted self-possession in a heartbeat.

Jago drew in a slow breath and released it in a steady stream. His shoulders loosened, and his features softened as if he was trying to calm himself down. He moved over to the other side of the room and sat on the worn sofa, his left arm draped languidly across the back. 'I'll wait here until you pack what you need for the next two nights and the weekend.'

Mollie wanted to argue the point with him, but she thought of the huge sum of money he had already paid her and the remaining balance she would receive at the end of the weekend. She would be every type of fool not to do as he said. She hated her bedsit anyway. Why make such a big deal out of something she would gladly escape for a few days? She, too, blew out a long breath and dropped her tense shoulders. 'I'm not sleeping with you. I want to make that clear right here and now.' Mollie was saying it more for her own benefit than his. She had to resist him. She had to find a way to break his powerful, sensual spell over her.

'You're under no obligation to sleep with me. We do, however, have to appear in public as if we are an engaged couple, so that will require some display of affection from time to time.'

Mollie steeled her spine, holding his unreadable gaze with an effort. 'There's one thing that concerns me…' She unfolded her arms and let out another breath, wondering if she should risk mentioning his grandfather. She dared not reveal the reason why she took the money and ran, but she was concerned about seeing Maxwell when he had expressly told her never to contact Jago again. To turn up at Wildewood Manor newly reunited with Jago was going to cause a mountain of a trouble she could do without. What if Maxwell decided to punish her by leaking the images of her for reneging on their deal? But then Mollie thought of Elsie, Jago's grandmother who, because of her memory loss, still believed her grandson was engaged. And then there was the money Jago had paid her to pretend to be his fiancée. She could not do without that money because it was her last chance to help her brother. She might never get another opportunity to get Eliot the help he so desperately needed. She had failed him before; she would not do so again. If she had to risk a scandal if those deepfakes were released, then so be it. Jago knew she had been paid to go away, but as far as she could tell, he didn't know why she had accepted the payment.

He assumed she was a gold-digger and had planned the whole thing, to pretend to fall in love with him and run away as soon as she got a payout.

'If you're worried about my grandfather, don't be,' Jago said. 'He doesn't have the power he used to have. He'll grumble and insult you like he does everyone, but he can't force you to stay away. Anyway, we're only going to be there two nights.'

Mollie scratched at the inside of her wrist, a nervous habit she had when stressed. 'But what if your grandmother doesn't get her memory back? Won't you have to tell her we're not engaged then?'

Jago rose from the sofa in one fluid movement, his hand raking through the thick pelt of his hair, a frown pulling at his brow. 'She's very frail since the fall. The doctors aren't giving any guarantees about her prognosis. She may live weeks or months, no one knows. My grandfather's stroke last year put extra stress on her, even though we employed help with his care. She tried to take care of him herself, and he, of course, has not been an easy patient.'

'It must be hard facing the prospect of losing your grandmother. I mean, she raised you and your brothers since your parents' death.'

There was a cavernous silence.

Jago's jaw worked for a moment, his eyes moving away from hers to look past her left shoulder as if he was looking into the past, remembering the day of the plane crash and how the news was broken to him. Mollie could see the flickering emotions going through his gaze like a reel of memories. But then he blinked a couple of times and met her eyes again. 'I'll give you ten minutes to pack your bag. We'll spend tonight at my hotel and then travel to Wildewood tomorrow instead of Friday. I think it's best if we get down there sooner rather than later.'

'But I have to tell my boss I'm not coming in and—'

'Is it your dream job?'

'No.'

'Do you like your boss?'

Mollie grimaced. 'Not particularly.'

'Then, you can hand in your notice by email or phone call. The money I gave you will tide you over for a year without having to work.'

But it won't tide me over when most of it is going towards getting help for Eliot.

Of course, she didn't tell Jago that. 'I have clients booked in for tomorrow,' Mollie said, even though she only had one the last time she'd looked, and they might well have cancelled by now anyway. But she had to find a chance to talk to Eliot in private to tell him she was going away for the weekend. She only hoped he would stay at the rehab clinic long enough for his cycle of addiction to be broken.

'Fine,' Jago said. 'But as soon as you're finished, I'll pick you up, and we'll head straight to the airport.'

Mollie left him to go and pack her bag, her thoughts in turmoil. Being in proximity with Jago for the next few days would test her resolve in ways it had never been tested before. She had to resist the temptation to fall into bed with him, but their kiss had shown her how weak her defences were. His kiss had reawakened her desire for him, the driving need that had drawn her to him two years ago. Lust was the way he described his feelings for her, but she knew deep in her bones that it was more than that for her. She had developed feelings for him in the few short months they had dated and become engaged. She would not have agreed to marry him unless she had genuinely loved him. She had spent the last two years trying to forget about him, trying to fool herself she no longer loved him, but that passionate kiss had shown her what dangerous territory she was venturing into again. Her heart had never quite healed from having to jilt him. To turn her back on the future she had dreamed of with him had cost her dearly emotionally. But what else could she have done? If those ghastly images had gone viral, she would have been publicly shamed and vilified, not to mention humiliated beyond imagination. Jago's reputation, too, would have been sullied by his association with her. Maxwell Wilde might well be a hard-nosed businessman with a ruthless streak wider than the English Channel, but she knew he would do anything and everything to protect the Wilde name. Mollie had no idea how Maxwell was going to react when he saw her with Jago this coming weekend. Jago didn't seem to be too concerned, but how much did he know? If his grandfather had told him about the images, surely Jago wouldn't be inviting her back into his life, even if it was only for a weekend of playing at being engaged?

Jago paced the floor in Mollie's bedsit like a lion in a cat carrier. Why was she living in such a rundown place? The money she had been paid by his grandfather should have been enough to set her up better than this. She could have bought a nice apartment, even a nice house in a genteel suburb. What had she done with the money? Did she have a gambling problem? Did she do drugs? It seemed highly unlikely for she didn't even drink alcohol. But there was so much he didn't know about her. He knew every inch of her skin; he could picture every fleck in her grey-blue eyes and recall every contour of her beautiful full-lipped mouth. He knew what it felt like to be inside her body, but he couldn't get inside her head. He reflected back on their relationship and realised it had been mostly about the sex. They had fallen in lust, smoking-hot lust that had consumed both of them into its spellbinding vortex. And kissing her a few minutes ago had proved their lust for each other had not died. It had smouldered for two years like long, spreading tree roots underground, just waiting for a spark to reignite an inferno.

Jago looked around the pathetic bedsit for any signs of Mollie's private life, but there no were photos of her family and friends. He frowned and thought back to the wedding planner asking Mollie who she wanted to invite to the wedding. He hadn't thought much of it at the time, but now it seemed glaringly obvious that Mollie had had no intention of going through with the wedding. There were so many red flags he hadn't seen or had chosen not to see, which made him even more furious with himself. Had he been so blind with lust he couldn't see she had set him up right from the start? Mollie had said her parents were dead and that all her other relatives such as uncles and aunts and cousins were living abroad and couldn't make it to the wedding. He hadn't met a single one of her friends, although she had mentioned going out with them for coffee or yoga and Pilates classes. That in itself should have alerted him to something. Who didn't introduce their partner to their friends? And when the wedding planner had asked if Mollie wanted someone to walk her up the aisle and give her away as per tradition, Mollie had said she didn't believe in such outdated nonsense. She had kept insisting on a small wedding, but of course his grandmother was having none of that. If one of her playboy grandsons was finally going to settle down, Elsie had wanted all the bells and whistles of a big, white wedding. Jago still had the blasted wedding cake and Mollie's wedding dress. He had them in one of the spare rooms at his London house like he was a male version of Miss Havisham from Dickens's *Great Expectations*. He'd kept it to remind himself to never let his guard down again. To never be so blindsided by lust that he proposed marriage. To never feel so deeply for anyone that gave them the power to hurt him.

Before Jago met Mollie, he'd had no intention of settling down. He wasn't the eldest, so Jack had more pressure on him to marry and produce an heir than either he or Jonas had. But one date had turned into two, then three, then weeks had gone by and he'd found himself more and more in lust with Mollie. He couldn't get enough of her. He decided to ask her to marry him, not on a whim or impulsively. He'd thought about it for weeks before he decided it was the right thing to do. He'd wanted the commitment from her, the security of marriage that would guarantee she was his and his alone. Their connection was so like the passionate one of his parents. He had wanted to be with her all the time just as his parents had adored being in each other's company. Jago didn't believe himself to be in love, but sometimes he wondered if he had got scarily close to it. But he had been duped by Mollie right from the beginning. And yet when he kissed her earlier, he could not find it in himself to hate her for jilting him. Did that make him a lust-driven fool?

Jago ground his teeth, annoyed with himself for not putting the pieces together until now. Two years ago, he had been thinking with his hormones instead of his head. His lust for Mollie had blurred his judgement, opening him up to ridicule as a jilted groom when she bolted. He hated thinking about that day and all those that followed. Cynicism was in his blood, hardwired into his personality, and yet he had not seen the signs that were so obvious in hindsight.

But this time would be different. He was paying her to act the role of his fiancée. Yes, they might kiss and hold hands in front of his family, but he would take it no further.

But you still want her. Badly.

Jago dismissed the voice of his conscience. He wasn't going to allow his hormones to override his common sense. Not again.

CHAPTER FIVE

MOLLIE PACKED A few necessities in her weekend bag, but most of her clothes were not up to the standard of a Wilde gathering, especially for Jago's grandmother's birthday party. Mollie wore a uniform for work and casual clothes in her free time. She did not go out to dinner or on dates, and apart from the little black dress she was wearing, the only other glamorous outfit she possessed was one Jago had bought her two years ago. She located it in the back of her small wardrobe and took it out and held it up for inspection. It was still wrapped in drycleaner's plastic, but she knew it was the dress to wear. The baby-blue silk made her eyes pop and clung to her figure in all the right places. She took it off the hanger and rolled it up, plastic wrapping in place and packed it along with a pair of heels and a matching slimline evening purse.

A short time later, Mollie joined Jago in the combined kitchen and sitting room. He was pacing the floor with a frown on his face and turned to face her. 'Got what you need?'

'I think so.'

He strode over to take the bag for her. 'Let's go.'

A few minutes later, Jago led Mollie into his luxurious hotel suite. The difference from her bedsit was stark and reminded her of the different worlds they occupied. Jago was used to having the best of everything. He had never had to miss a meal in order to pay a bill. He not only had savings, but he also had investments—properties and share portfolios and who knew what else. All Mollie had was debt, despair and dread over what might happen to her brother if she didn't succeed in getting him the help he needed.

But this weekend was the solution to helping Eliot. She wouldn't have accepted a penny from Jago if it wasn't for her brother. Being with Jago in any context, real or pretend, was dangerous. Didn't their kiss prove it? Her mouth was still tingling from the passionate pressure of his. His kiss had awakened her ongoing desire for him, and as much as she wished she could turn it off, she knew it was impossible.

'Nice room,' Mollie said, sweeping her gaze around the suite, which was larger than any place she had ever lived in. She tried not to look at the king-size bed, but her gaze was drawn to it regardless. The snow-white sheets and artfully arranged pillows and the cashmere throw rug were of the highest quality. The soft lighting in the suite gave an intimate atmosphere to the space which was soothing, and the soft carpet under her feet threatened to swallow her up to the ankles. The stress and emotional roller-coaster events of the day suddenly caught up with Mollie, and she couldn't hold back a yawn.

'Time for bed?' Jago said.

Mollie gave the bed a sideways glance. 'Where are you going to sleep?'

He shrugged himself out of his jacket and hung it over the back of a chair. 'We've shared a bed before.'

Mollie swallowed a gulp but made sure her expression revealed nothing of her inner turmoil. 'Yes, but that was before, and this is now.'

One of his black brows rose in a sardonic arc. 'Don't you trust me to keep to my side of the bed?'

The problem was Mollie didn't trust herself. What if she reached for him during the night? What if she called out his name as she dreamed of him as she so often did? What if her body sensed him there and acted on instinct, moving to entwine her legs with his, to stroke his manhood to steel? She was getting hot and bothered just thinking about it.

Mollie affected a cool expression, but her lower body was already on fire. 'You told me you wouldn't lay a finger on me and yet you kissed me.'

'We kissed each other, Mollie.'

He was right. It had been entirely mutual, and it had actually been Mollie who had closed the gap between their mouths.

'You had every opportunity to tell me to back off, but you didn't,' Jago said. 'Why was that, hmm?'

Mollie wasn't sure she knew the answer to that, or at least none she wanted to share with him. Why had she allowed him to kiss her? And more to the point, why had she kissed him back so enthusiastically? Had her self-control vaporised the moment he strode back into her life?

She gave a careless shrug of her shoulders and placed her tote bag on the chair where he had hung his jacket.

'You always were a good kisser. I guess I wanted to see if you had got better or stayed the same.'

'And your assessment is…?'

Mollie gave him a flinty look. 'I don't think your robustly healthy ego needs any stroking from me.'

His eyes gleamed, and his mouth tilted in a smile that made her lower spine loosen. 'Do you want to have a shower before bed?'

She tried not to think of all the times they had showered together. Was he thinking of those sexy times too? The warm water cascading over their bodies, his erection thick and potent inside her, his deep thrusts and the clever caressing of his fingers tipping her over the edge time and time again. No one had ever made her feel the level of ecstasy that Jago Wilde had. No one had ever sent her senses into such a tailspin, leaving her body tingling for hours afterwards. Two years on and a frisson danced through her when she thought of him making love to her. It was one of the reasons she hadn't ventured back into dating. She wanted to hold those memories of him for as long as she could.

Mollie sent him a frosty look that was at total odds to the fire burning in her lower body. 'Just in case you get any funny ideas, I'll be locking the door.'

'Good idea.' His smile was faintly mocking as if he knew how tempted she was to ask him to join her.

Mollie turned and rummaged in her bag for her evening skin products and the sleepwear she had brought. The two-piece pyjama set was hardly what one would describe as *sexy*, but it was comfortable and modest. Right now, modesty seemed the right way to go.

The bathroom was a glass-and-marble wonderland

with brass taps and underfloor heating. There was a walk-in shower as well as a deep claw-foot bath and twin basins set in front of a large gilt-edged mirror. There were gloriously soft towels and luxury soaps and hair and beauty products to choose from. Mollie put her own things on the marble counter and then went back to the door and locked it. She stood stock-still for a moment, listening for any sound of Jago on the other side of the door, but she couldn't hear a thing.

After a relaxing shower, Mollie turban-wrapped her hair in a towel and then dressed in her cotton pyjamas. She did her evening skin care routine and then unwound the towel on her head to let her hair fall about her shoulders. There was a top-quality hair dryer in a drawer below the basins, so she gave her hair a quick blast to remove the excess moisture.

She looked at herself in the mirror and not for the first time wondered why Jago had been attracted to her. She saw herself as average, not stunning, but she had the advantage of being trained in beauty therapy, so she knew how to make the most of her assets. But without the professional mask of her make-up, she looked a lot younger and far more vulnerable than she wanted to. There was a haunted look in her eyes that she took great pains to hide when not alone. The constant worry of her brother's welfare wore her down to the point where she felt older than she was. In two years, she would be thirty, and for more than half her life she had tried to keep Eliot out of harm's way. What if she failed? What if, after every sacrifice and effort she had made, her brother didn't make it? Mollie knew the statistics on long-term drug and alcohol addiction. She could already see the negative effects on her younger brother's health. The chronic diseases that could only be managed, not cured. As hard as it was to be in Jago's company, she had to see this through for her brother's sake.

There was a light knock at the door. 'Are you finished in there?' Jago asked.

Mollie blinked away the ghosts in her eyes. 'Yep.' She took a deep breath and pushed herself away from the marble counter, hung up her used towels on the warming rail then went over to unlock the door.

Jago was no longer standing close to the bathroom door but was sitting on one of the plush velvet armchairs, scrolling through his phone. He glanced up as she came into the room, his eyes running over her dove-grey pyjamas. 'Feel better?'

'Much.'

He rose from the chair and slipped his phone in his trouser pocket. 'Go to bed. You look exhausted.'

Mollie shook out her still slightly damp hair. 'Yes, well, it's been quite a day.'

Jago came up close to her, his expression serious. 'I meant it when I said I don't expect you to sleep with me as part of the deal.'

Mollie swept the tip of her tongue over her lips, her gaze lowering to his mouth as if drawn by a powerful magnet. His mouth was set in a firm line, but she knew how quickly it could soften with one press of her lips to his. She brought her gaze back to his, her heart pounding unevenly in her chest. She fought with herself to remain strong, resolute in not caving in to her body's desire for him, but it still pulsed and throbbed in her blood regardless. 'If you think I would sleep with you for money, you are seriously mistaken.'

Jago's features tensed, and his gaze heated. 'Then, what was our past relationship all about, if not money?'

Mollie compressed her lips into a tight line, her spine ramrod stiff. 'I know someone as cynical as you won't believe it, but I did genuinely have feelings for you.'

'Love?' He said the word so mockingly she could feel a blush staining her cheeks. 'If that's how love acts, then I want no part of it.'

'I'm sorry I hurt you, but at the time I had no other choice.'

His expression was scathing. 'Your choice was to fill your bank account with money and make a fool of me in the process. But did you ever consider what your actions did to other members of my family? My grandmother, for instance?'

Back then, Mollie had had no time to think about anything but keeping those images out of circulation. It was only much later that she thought of Jago's grandmother, who was so excited about her middle grandson finally settling down. Elsie must have been so bitterly disappointed and sad for her grandson, falsely believing him to be in love with his runaway fiancée. Mollie had briefly thought of his brothers too, but she had only met them a handful of times, and while she knew they would abhor what she had done to Jago, she didn't think they would give her another thought. Out of sight, out of mind.

As for Maxwell Wilde...well, Mollie tried not to think about him at all. But even so, she often found herself wondering why it had been Maxwell who had been approached by the blackmailer and not Jago. As her fiancé, surely Jago should have been the target for blackmail? He had wealth equal to if not greater than that of his grandfather.

'I can only imagine how upset your grandmother must have been,' Mollie said then added with a note of bitterness, 'As for your grandfather, I'm sure he was glad to see the back of me. He never liked me. He never considered me good enough.'

'No one is ever good enough for my grandfather including, at times, his wife and grandsons.' Jago's tone was as bitter as hers had been, his frown deep.

Mollie had always wondered what Jago's childhood had been like growing up with such an overbearing grandfather as his guardian. Jago was only five when his parents were killed. It was such a young age to lose his primary caregivers, but to be then raised by an impossible-to-please grandfather must have added another level of trauma.

'Was your father good enough for him?' It was bold of her to ask such a question when Mollie already knew he had refused to talk about his parents on every occasion she had raised the topic.

There was a beat or two of weighted silence.

Jago let out a rough-edged sigh and stepped away from her. 'Just go to bed, Mollie. I need to shower and shave.' He turned and entered the bathroom, closing the door with a click that was like a full stop. End of conversation.

Mollie released a long breath and glanced at the bed again. Jago expected her to share the bed with her, but he didn't want to share anything about his parents. They had died nearly thirty years ago, and yet Jago refused to tell her anything about what he had gone through in being bereaved at such a tender age. While she had her own reasons for not talking about her parents, Mollie longed for Jago to trust her enough to tell her about his. She had done some research of her own and found images of his parents online. His father had been a striking man with the Wilde jet-black hair and chiselled jaw and deep-set blue eyes and aristocratic bearing. Jago's mother had been like a supermodel in looks: a gorgeous brunette with a wide smile, sparkling brown eyes and a willowy build. They had died in a small-plane crash on their way to a weekend away together. Several of the press articles had mentioned that tragic as the crash was, it was fortunate the three Wilde boys were not with their parents in the aircraft. One article had shown a photo of the boys standing outside the front of Wildewood Manor the month before they lost their parents. Jack, the eldest was standing beside Jago with a cheeky smile. Jago's smile had looked genuine enough, but Jonas, the youngest, had not been smiling at all, as if he saw the world through a more serious lens than his two older brothers.

Mollie sighed and brought herself back to the present by listening to the sound of Jago showering. She knew so much about his body, had explored every inch of it in detail, and yet he had not given her access to his past. It was a cordoned-off area, a do-not-go-there place she could only speculate about because of his point-blank refusal to speak of it.

Just like you.

Mollie knew it was hardly fair of her to badger Jago

to reveal all about his childhood when she had told him nothing but lies about her own. But she hated talking about her childhood. It was something she wanted to erase from her memory, to keep the pain and distress out of her mind. Talking about it stirred up memories and flashbacks that gave her nightmares.

Mollie heard the shower stop, and she quickly dived into the bed and brought the covers up to her chin. She turned on her side, facing away from the bathroom, and closed her eyes, willing herself to sleep. But she was aware of every sound Jago made, and her body refused to relax enough to get anywhere near sleeping, even though she was tired from the events of the day. She curled up a bit more, adjusting the pillow under her head, breathing in the clean, fresh smell of the bed linen. Jago seemed to be taking an inordinately long time, so she tried some other relaxation techniques to get her body and her mind to relax, until finally she found herself sinking into the cloud of the mattress and the softness of the pillow, and her mile-a-minute brain slowed…slowed…and shut down…

Jago came out of the bathroom with a towel slung around his hips. Mollie's slim form was facing away from him, and she was curled up like a comma. Her breathing was slow and even, which meant she was asleep or doing an excellent job of pretending to be. He moved to the other side of the bed, glancing at her face to see if she responded to his presence, but her eyelids remained closed. He had to stop himself leaning down to press a kiss to her cheek and gently run his fingers through the fragrant silk of her hair. He had to stop himself thinking about all the times he had slipped in between the sheets with her and engaged in bed-wrecking sex. He had to find some way of resisting the magnetic pull of her. He could have saved himself this agony by booking separate rooms, but he didn't trust her enough not to disappear again.

Jago sighed and took off the towel and stepped into a pair of boxer shorts. He usually slept naked, but he decided a layer of fabric was called for to keep himself in check. He turned back to his side of the bed and got in, glancing at Mollie to see if she was aware of his presence, but she remained in the same relaxed position, her bee-stung mouth slightly parted as she slept. He turned on his side and watched her for endless minutes, fighting the urge to stroke his hand down the satinlike skin of her shoulder. He couldn't take his eyes off her mouth, remembering how soft and pliable it had felt beneath his. One kiss was never going to be enough, and yet he had to keep his distance to avoid being sucked into her sensual force field.

He clenched his hand into a fist and turned onto his back, his body throbbing with the raw need she triggered in him. He let out another sigh and turned to switch off the bedside table light, cloaking the suite in darkness. He lay there for what felt like hours, unable to sleep, unable to stop thinking about her lying within touching distance.

Mollie made a soft murmuring sound and moved closer, her eyes still shut in sleep. One of her legs brushed against his, and his blood surged to his groin.

This was your idea, buddy.

His conscience gave him a mocking prod. Yes, it had

been Jago's idea to keep Mollie with him, not just to stop her running away again but to prove to himself he could resist her. But kissing her had stirred his blood to fever pitch, and he wanted her more than ever. No other lover turned him on the way Mollie did. She only had to look at him a certain way and he was hot and hard and ready. The chemistry between them was as electrifying as before, if not more so. He had promised himself he wouldn't act on it unless she wanted him to.

Jago closed his eyes, but he could still smell her, the shampoo she used, the lotions and potions combined with her own natural scent. It was like a drug to him. He wanted to breathe more of her in. Would there ever be a time when he didn't want her any more? He had spent the last two years thinking of her, dreaming of her, aching for her. It had to stop. Mollie was a fraud, a gold-digger who had royally screwed him over. He had to remember he had been completely taken in by her, and he couldn't let it happen again. He would have to have an even tighter rein on his emotions to make sure she didn't get under his guard like the last time. He hated thinking about that day before the wedding when he came back, excited about getting married the following day. Mollie hadn't responded to a single call or text, but he reassured himself she was preoccupied with wedding preparations. But then he'd arrived at Wildewood to find the place in an uproar. His grandfather had taken him aside to tell him Mollie had left.

'She's gone. She's bolted. She's not coming back. Get over it.'

He still remembered the sound of his grandfather's

voice, the deep timbre of it reminiscent of when he had delivered the tragic news of Jago's parents' death.

'They've gone. They're not coming back. Get over it.'

Was that why Jago was having so much trouble getting over her? Moving on with his life? He had a problem with processing grief, but then, who wouldn't after losing their parents so young? Not that he talked about it, even with his brothers. His friends were as casual as his lovers. He didn't allow people to get close, which was why Mollie had been such an exception. He *felt* close to her even though he hadn't told her everything about his past. There was a meaningful connection with her, an invisible bond he had only ever felt with his parents. He had trouble believing she was a gold-digger, as his grandfather had insisted she was. He still had trouble believing it, but how could her behaviour be explained any other way? He wished now he had not let his pride prevent him from finding her and asking her what the hell had gone wrong. Why hadn't he stood up for her? A niggle of worry began to wind its way through his brain. If Mollie was the gold-digger his family believed her to be, why wasn't he accepting it? Why did one tiny flicker of hope burn in his chest that there was some other explanation for her actions? But she had sold his specially designed engagement ring. He had asked a jewellery expert to keep a look out for it, hoping he would be proved wrong, but it had turned up in a pawn shop, and he'd had to accept she had sold it. Could he forgive her for it? The disposal of his ring had felt like another savage jab to his heart.

Mollie shifted again in her sleep, her movements not so relaxed this time. She flung one of her arms out, almost clocking him on the chin. Her face screwed up like she was having some sort of nightmare. 'No, no, no,' she cried and began to thrash her limbs.

Jago gathered her closer, guiding her head to his chest, his hand gently stroking the back of her head to settle her. 'Shhh, Mollie. Relax, babe. I'm here.'

She moved against him with a soft whisper. 'Eliot?'

Jago stiffened like he had been snap-frozen. His gut tightened like someone was clenching his intestines in a brutal blood-blocking grip. His heart cramped like someone had punched him in the chest.

Who the freaking hell was Eliot?

He glanced down at Mollie draped across his chest, but her eyes were still closed, and her breathing rate had slowed down. Two years had passed since she'd jilted him. She could have had any number of lovers since him. Why was he feeling such strong emotions about it? He had nothing to be jealous about: he had slept with other people too. Not as many as the press had made out, but enough to try and erase Mollie from his muscle memory. Not that it had worked, but still. He had no right to judge her for moving on with her life, other than she had taken his grandfather's money to do it and then sold the ring Jago had designed for her. It suited him to allow Mollie to think she was wearing a replica of his ring when in fact it was the original she had sold. The irony of it amused him: she was pretending to be his fiancée, believing the engagement ring to be as fake as their current relationship. There was a risk she might sell the ring again if she realised it was genuine, but it was a risk he was prepared to take. Although it was an expensive ring by most people's standards, he had enough money to bear the loss.

The only thing that niggled at him was there was nothing fake about the desire he still felt for her, and that was a problem he had yet to solve. As were those indefinable feelings that lingered in his heart which he was not ready or willing to examine too closely.

CHAPTER SIX

MOLLIE WOKE EARLY to find herself alone in the bed. The space beside her was crumpled, as was the pillow, so she assumed Jago had spent some of the night with her, although not reaching for her as he had done so often in the past. She sat upright and pushed the tangle of her hair out of her eyes then found Jago seated in one of the velvet chairs in the suite, his forearms resting on his knees and his midnight blue gaze trained on her.

She noted the dark shadows beneath his eyes and his tousled hair, which if anything made him look even more broodingly attractive, like a Gothic hero from the classics. 'You look like you didn't sleep too well.'

Jago leaned back and dragged a hand down his face, the rasp of his morning stubble against his skin sounding overly loud in the silence. 'Turns out you're right.' He pushed himself out of the chair and came over to stand beside her side of the bed, still with his gaze locked on hers. 'Pleasant dreams?' His tone had a sour note to it that made the hairs on the back of her neck stand up like miniature soldiers.

Mollie frowned at him, not sure how to handle him in this mood. 'Stop towering over me and looking at me like that. It's not my fault you didn't sleep well.'

'I beg to differ.'

'You were the one who insisted on us sharing a room,' she pointed out.

There was a pulsing beat of silence.

'Who is Eliot?'

Mollie stiffened, her gaze wary as it held his penetrating one. She took a steadying breath and fashioned her features into a cool mask. 'None of your damn business, that's who.'

His expression tightened, and his mouth went into a flat line. 'Have there been many lovers since you called off our wedding? Or was this Eliot guy in the picture before we got together?'

Mollie tossed the bed covers aside and got out of bed, furious with him for thinking she might have had a lover on the side while engaged to him. But how else could she explain without telling him about her brother? 'How many lovers have you had?' she shot back with a scalding look.

'Five.'

'Only five?' She coughed up a laugh that had not an ounce of humour in it. 'You surprise me. I thought it would be closer to fifty.'

Something glittered in his eyes that reminded her of unreachable stars in the night sky. 'I seem to recall I told you when we first met, you shouldn't take as gospel everything that is reported about me or my brothers in the press.'

Mollie was still trying to contain her shock at his number of lovers. Only five? Even if the press got it wrong occasionally, she knew enough about his strong sex drive to find such a low number of lovers surprising. Jago Wilde was a man in the prime of his life, full-blooded and virile and rich and handsome beyond belief. Why hadn't he gone back to his profligate playboy ways? He would have had numerous opportunities to do so over the last two years; women swarmed around him like bees to exotic pollen.

'You still haven't answered my question,' Jago said. 'Who is Eliot?'

Mollie compressed her lips, torn between wanting to keep her private life private but feeling a strange need to share her burden with someone. Someone who would understand and not judge her for her hardscrabble origins and the damage that had been caused to her and her brother as a result. Was Jago that person? But how could someone from such a wealthy and privileged background ever understand what she and her brother had gone through? But then, she wondered if by sharing a little of her background, Jago might lower his guard and talk about the loss of his parents. She decided to take a chance. 'Eliot is my brother, my half-brother really. We don't share the same father.'

Jago's frown deepened. 'I thought you said you were an only child?'

Mollie folded her arms across her body. 'I'm not. I may well have other half-siblings for all I know. I've never met my biological father. Eliot and I share a mother.'

'You told me you were an orphan. So that was a lie too?' Jago was standing with his hands on his hips, looking down at her with a glimmer of hurt in his gaze that made her heart contract.

'I don't know if my biological father is alive or not,

but I know for sure my mother is dead.' Mollie decided against telling him the rest of that ghastly story. Revisiting that time in her life was too traumatising.

Jago turned away from her and paced the floor like he was trying to maintain control of himself. He finally turned to face her once more, his expression still cast in lines of confusion, hurt and anger all mixed together. 'Why did you lie to me?'

Mollie gave a dismissive shrug of her shoulders. 'I try to distance myself from my upbringing. The only way I could find to do it successfully was to pretend it hadn't happened. I made up a backstory for myself that was easier to live with.'

Jago's frown was so severe his brows met over his eyes. 'But I was your fiancé, Mollie. Surely, I deserved to know the truth about the woman I intended to marry.'

Mollie reached for a hotel bathrobe and wrapped herself in it like she was putting on a coat of armour. She turned to face Jago again, her expression cool. 'Why were you intending to marry me? You never told me you loved me. Surely that is Marriage Proposal Protocol 101?'

Jago deftly avoided answering her question by throwing one back at her. 'Was that a lie when you told me you loved me?'

Mollie absently twirled the engagement ring on her left hand. 'I did love you, Jago.'

'You said that in the past tense.' Jago said without any trace of emotion in his voice as if he was simply making an observation, one that meant little or nothing to him. But then, why would it mean anything to him? He hadn't loved her. He hadn't said the words she'd most wanted to hear. He had proposed marriage without saying he loved her. She should never have accepted, except she had foolishly believed he would change, that he would open his heart to her. How many women made the same mistake? Too many. But she had felt wanted for the first time in her life, and it had made it impossible to say *no* to him. He had made her feel safe, secure and wanted, and it had been enough for her back then.

'That was two years ago,' Mollie said, folding her arms to stop herself playing with the ring. 'A lot of things have happened since then.'

His handsome features were now cast in guarded lines. 'So tell me about your half-brother.'

Mollie sighed and sat on the edge of the bed, her hands clasped in her lap. 'Eliot has…issues.' She began to scratch at the inside of her wrist but then stopped and glanced up at Jago who was watching her intently. 'I've been responsible for his welfare for a long time. He's three years younger than me.' She looked down at her hands again, the fake engagement ring glinting at her like an accusing eye.

You failed him. You allowed Eliot's life to be destroyed. You don't deserve to be happy.

Her inner critic was relentless in its disparagement of her failings where Eliot was concerned.

'Why did you take it upon yourself to be responsible for him?' Jago asked, still frowning darkly.

Mollie stood from the bed in one jerky movement. 'Because none of the adults in our life were up to the task.'

Concern was written large on Jago's face. 'Who took

care of you?' There was a hollow-sounding quality to his voice she had never heard in it before, as if he was picturing her as a young child trying her best to survive.

'I took care of both of us,' Mollie said. Her earliest memories were not of being cuddled or nurtured by her mother but of abuse and neglect, the gnawing pain of hunger and the cold-footed fear that tiptoed up and down her small spine on a daily basis. 'My mother and her partner were drug addicts who had no idea how to look after little kids. We were in and out of foster care, but every time we were sent back to my mother, who had supposedly cleaned up her act, it would all begin again. The drinking, the drugs, the parties, the creepy boyfriend who had brutal methods for controlling little kids who were crying with hunger.'

Jago swallowed deeply, the sound audible in the silence. 'Mollie...' There was an anguished quality to his voice and his eyes looked pained. 'Did he...hurt you?' His hands were clenched into tight fists as if he wanted to track down her mother's criminal boyfriend and deal with him then and there.

'I taught myself to go somewhere else in my head when he hit me. But Eliot was so little, and he didn't stop crying, so my mother's boyfriend used to slip him a pill to make him sleep. I think that's why Eliot has such addiction problems now, that and the abuse he suffered in foster care, which I blame myself for.'

The shock and horror on Jago's face was painful to witness. 'Why do you blame yourself?'

'Because I should have done a better job of protecting him. He was only three.'

'But you were a child, only six years old yourself.

The foster carers were supposed to be protecting you both.'

'That's not how it always works, although to be fair, there are some wonderful foster carers out there. We were mostly placed in care together, but occasionally we were separated. One of the times we were apart, I begged to be with him, and finally we were sent to another foster home. On the surface it looked like a wonderful family to be in. The foster parents were nice people, but there was an occasional visitor to the house, the brother of the foster father. He...' Mollie swallowed tightly, barely able to get the words out. 'He... Well, without going into too much detail, my little brother became a victim of his...attentions. Eliot didn't tell me about it until he was an adult. I felt so guilty because I thought the uncle was charming. I would never have left Eliot alone with him if I'd realised.' Mollie knew deep down she wasn't really to blame for her brother's abuse—it was the perpetrator who was responsible and should be shouldering the blame—but her sense of failure haunted her regardless.

Jago came over to her and took her hands in his. Concern shone in his eyes. 'You must stop blaming yourself. Men like that groom not just their victim but the whole family, even whole communities.'

'I can never forgive myself,' Mollie said. 'Eliot is a train wreck but I can't give up on him. He's been in and out of rehab, but he doesn't stay long enough for it to take any effect.'

Jago put his arms around her and drew her close in a hug. Mollie leaned into his solid warmth and let out a heavy sigh. He stroked her back in a soothing fashion, and her tight muscles slowly unclenched until she melted against him. This was why she'd fallen in love with him in the first place. He'd made her feel safe for the first time in her life. She was a little bobbing boat in a wildly unpredictable ocean, and he was a lighthouse, a safe harbour, an anchor to hold her steady.

'Where is Eliot now?' Jago's voice rumbled against her left ear.

'In a very expensive rehabilitation clinic in Glasgow. He's been there six months, but he needs to stay for a whole year for it to be effective.'

There was a silence that Mollie measured with the slow steady thump-thump-thump of Jago's heartbeat next to her ear.

After a long moment, he held her a little apart from him so he could look down at her. His expression was contorted with so many emotions, they flickered through his gaze as if he was thinking back over their relationship and their break-up and putting things together in his mind. 'You took the money my grandfather offered you to help your brother.' It was a statement, not a question, as if he had come to a final conclusion about her actions.

Mollie grimaced. 'I'm sorry I can't tell you anything...'

'Because of the NDA?'

She gave a tiny nod, her lips pressed together before she spilled any more of the horrid secrets she carried. Heavy and burdensome secrets that had weighed her down for so long.

Jago picked up her hands again and gave them a gentle squeeze. 'Why didn't you come to me for help?

I could have paid for Eliot's rehab.' There was a gruff edge to his voice, a side note of hurt that she hadn't considered him as her go-to person.

Mollie was tempted to tell him about the deepfakes, but she couldn't risk it, not until she saw Maxwell Wilde's reaction to her being back in Jago's life, albeit temporarily. She pulled her hands out of Jago's with a strained smile. 'Hindsight is a beautiful thing, is it not? There are so many things I would do differently if I could.'

Jago was looking at her as if he were seeing her for the first time. The real her, not the made-up version. It made her feel exposed and vulnerable, and yet there was a part of her that was relieved she had told him about her brother. She felt like she was no longer carrying that emotional burden on her own.

'Mollie...' Jago scraped his hair back with his hand then dropped it back down to his side. 'I think we need to get to Wildewood Manor as soon as possible. You need to call your boss and tell her you're not coming in. In fact, tell her you're not coming back.'

Mollie stared at him, not sure whether to be annoyed at his taking command of her employment situation or relieved he was rescuing her from a job she had grown to loathe. The clients she loved; it was her boss that was the problem. 'But—'

'I'll cover any expenses you have until you find another job.'

'You're making me sound like a kept woman or, even worse, a gold-digger.'

Jago twisted his mouth in a rueful manner. 'I can see you're not going to forgive me for that, are you? I can't forgive myself for ever believing it.'

'I'm not a vengeful person, Jago.'

He came back over to her and lifted her chin with the tip of his index finger, locking her gaze with his. His eyes were so dark a blue they reminded her of a bottomless ocean. An ocean she wanted to dive into and explore those hidden depths. His eyes lowered to her mouth, lingering there for so long she could feel her lips tingling in anticipation of the descent of his mouth.

'If I kiss you,' he said, 'it will delay our departure.'

'How long a kiss are you thinking?' Mollie's voice was just a whisper of sound, liberally laced with longing.

He lifted both hands up to frame her face, his eyes holding hers. 'Longer than I anticipated when I first approached you about this weekend.' His thumbs moved like twin metronomes, slowly stroking her cheeks in a tender but blood-heating manner.

Mollie was finding it hard to remember to breathe. Her heart was beating with hammer blows that threatened to shatter her rib cage. Her feminine core was stirring in response to the tempting closeness of his body. She could feel the thickening of his erection pressed against her. 'They're your rules. You can break them if you want.'

The dark intensity of his eyes sent a wave of heat through her flesh. Molten heat that left spot fires in its wake. 'Not unless you want me to break them.'

Break them. Break them. Break them.

Her blood was pounding with the chanting of her feverish need. Mollie brought her mouth closer to his until there was barely space for a puff of air. 'I want you to break them.'

Jago's mouth fused to hers in a slow and deliberate kiss that sent shock waves of delight through her body. Tingles raced up and down her spine, fireworks went off in her blood. Her body melted with the hot, moist dew of desire triggered by his tongue entering her mouth and mating with hers. Her hands wound up around his neck, her fingers delving into his hair, stroking and tugging in the way she knew he liked. He groaned against her mouth and brought her closer to the hard ridge of his erection.

'I want you so bad.'

'I want you too.'

He eased back to look at her. 'Are you sure?'

'It's only for this weekend, right?'

Something flickered in his gaze like an interruption in the transmission of a film. 'It will certainly add authenticity to our game of pretend,' he said, glancing back at her mouth as if he couldn't keep his eyes off it.

Mollie raised herself up on tiptoes, bringing her body closer to his. 'I thought you were in a rush to get to Wildewood Manor?'

He grinned at her and planted his hands on her hips, tugging her even closer. 'I have a private jet on standby. The pilot will wait until I see to some outstanding business.'

Mollie raised her brows. 'Is that how you see me?'

His mouth came down to just above hers. 'You are more along the lines of unfinished business,' he said and sealed her mouth with his.

CHAPTER SEVEN

Touching Mollie again stirred every cell in Jago's body into throbbing excitement. He ached for her with a bone-deep need that had pulsed in his flesh for two long years. His mouth devoured hers like he was unable to get enough of its sweet taste, one he had not forgotten. Her mouth was soft and pliable beneath his, her murmurs of encouragement making him as hard as stone. His hands were on her hips, holding her to his pounding need, relishing in the feel of her so close. He entered her mouth on a deep sigh of pleasure—or was it relief? He could barely get his thoughts in any sort of order. All he wanted was to lose himself in the nectar of her mouth, to feel her tongue dancing and duelling with his.

Mollie wound her arms around his neck and began to play with the ends of his hair, and a wave of electrifying pleasure flowed through him. Her touch was magic to him; he had never forgotten the way she could turn him on with a simple look or touch.

Jago deepened the kiss, groaning against her pillow-soft lips, wanting all of her. His hands moved up to gently shape her breasts, and she murmured her approval against his lips.

He eased back to look down at her. 'I want to touch you all over.'

He lowered his mouth back to hers in a lingering kiss, his hands sliding under her pyjama top, his senses going wild as he touched the gentle slopes of her breasts. Her nipples were tight buds, and he took his mouth from hers to take each in his mouth, licking, tasting, teasing her flesh into even tighter points.

Mollie's hands tugged at his trouser fastening, and his heart raced with excitement. He loved how enthusiastic she was about making love with him. In record time they were both naked, and he drank in the sight of her body, his blood pounding through his body with anticipation.

He ran his hands over her from her shoulders to her hips, tugging her closer so she could feel his need against her belly. 'You drive me to distraction. I want you like I want no one else.'

Mollie reached between their bodies and stroked his length, and he groaned in delight. He slipped his hand down to her most female of flesh, and within seconds she was falling apart, gasping and arching her spine as she orgasmed. When it was finally over, she looked at him in a dazed manner, her eyes wide, her mouth open, her breathing ragged.

'Good?' Jago asked with a smile.

'Fast and furious and fabulous,' Mollie said, her cheeks a soft rose-petal pink.

How could he not feel a measure of pride in being able to pleasure her so quickly? Her responsiveness to him was so delightful, and it heightened his pleasure. 'I need to get a condom.' He let her go just long enough to grab a condom from his wallet, applying it with haste as his need for her hummed and throbbed in his blood.

Jago took her by the hand and led her to the bed, coming down on top of her with a sigh of pure bliss. It was like coming home after a long journey. Her arms went around him, her legs opening to welcome him. He entered her with a guttural groan that sounded almost primal, the silky tightness of her wrapping around him, sending him wild. But his need for her was primal: it had driven him crazy for the last two years. He had missed her so damn much—the taste of her, the feel of her in his arms, the spine-tingling chemistry they had together. He began to thrust, slowly at first, allowing her time to get used to him again, but Mollie arched her spine and bucked her hips, making whimpering noises, urging him to speed up. He drove harder and faster, losing himself in the tight grip of her body, his senses reeling as his need for release built like a rising tide. He slipped one of his hands between their rocking bodies, teasing the swollen wet nub of her clitoris until she fell apart again. He let himself go with her, her body's contractions around him intensifying his enjoyment. Every muscle in his body tensed, then he finally exploded, spilling his essence…and then a wave of peace and calm flowed through his entire body, leaving him spent and relaxed against her.

Jago couldn't move. Didn't want to move. He was enjoying the feel of Mollie's arms around him, her soft hands stroking the small of his back and then sliding over his buttocks. It was like she was rediscovering his contours, her hands shaping him as he had shaped her. If only they could stay in this intimate bubble, where no one else could intrude. But he had to get to the manor and deal with whatever reaction his grandfather would have to him bringing home his runaway fiancée.

Jago was still putting together the complicated pieces of the puzzle that was Mollie. Her need to protect and provide for her half-brother had been the focus of her life since childhood. How had he not found out about her background before now? The truth, not what she had chosen to tell him. Mollie had locked him out of her real-life circumstances, and yet she had claimed to love him.

But you've told her nothing about your childhood.

Jago's conscience reminded him of how many times he had locked her out of any discussion about his own history. Wasn't it time to let her know a little bit of what it had been like to lose his parents? But he hated being vulnerable. Maybe he was more like his grandfather than he wanted to admit, but he had always been taught that being vulnerable was a weakness. His grandfather had drummed it into Jago and his brothers: it would give people a tool to exploit you if you showed them your feelings. So Jago had locked his away and denied or ignored them.

Jago finally eased his weight onto his elbows to look at Mollie. 'Am I too heavy for you?'

Mollie looked up at him as if she couldn't believe he was real. Her hand came up and stroked his jaw just as she used to do in the past. 'No.' She gave a soft sigh and looked at his mouth, then traced around it with her index finger, making his lips tingle and a hot shiver shimmy down his spine.

Jago brushed a strand of her hair back from her face.

Then he captured one of her hands and brought it up to his lips, pressing a soft kiss to her fingertips, his eyes holding hers. 'Forgive me for thinking you were a gold-digger. I'm annoyed at myself for insulting you like that, when all the time you were trying to take care of your brother.'

A flicker of pain went through her gaze, and her mouth twisted in a rueful fashion. 'I should have told you the truth before, but I hate talking about my childhood. It's retraumatising.'

'I get it,' Jago said, stroking his finger down the ski slope of her nose. 'I hate talking about mine too.'

Her eyes moved back and forth between each of his like she was searching for the real him. Like she could see right into his soul. Like she could see every painful feeling he had locked away inside himself.

'Do you ever talk to your brothers about your parents?' Her voice was soft, tiptoe soft as if she knew she was treading on territory that was intensely painful for him.

Jago laced his fingers with hers. 'Rarely, if ever. Our grandfather forbade us as children to talk about them. He thought it would make us stronger if we just accepted that they were gone and moved on with our lives.'

'So you weren't allowed to grieve?'

'Nope.'

'Did you go to the funeral?'

'Only Jack and I went. Jonas was considered too young at only three. But once the wake was over, we were forbidden to talk about our parents to each other, our grandmother or anyone.'

'Not even to your grandmother?' Shock rippled through her tone.

'My grandfather told us it would upset her too much, but looking back now, I think she would have benefited from talking about them. She, like us, was unable to grieve the way she needed to. She had a mental breakdown a couple of years later. She didn't leave the house for months.'

'Your grandfather has lot to answer for.' There was a hard edge to Mollie's voice, and a frown pulled at her forehead.

'He's got his faults, certainly, but I suspect he was so grief-stricken himself, allowing us to talk about our parents would have made it harder for him to carry on,' Jago said. 'He had to suddenly raise his grandchildren, comfort his wife and take over my father's business as well as his own.'

'You're very forgiving. What you've described is emotional abuse.'

Jago grimaced at the uncomfortable truth of her observation. 'I know, but it was a different time back then, and now that I've been overseeing his business affairs, I realise he was under an enormous amount of pressure.' He moved away so he could dispose of the condom, then standing beside the bed, held out a hand to her. 'We need to get a move on.'

Mollie put her hand in his, and he pulled her to her feet. Jago couldn't resist wrapping his arms around her and holding her close. He breathed in the scent of her hair, the fragrance of her skin, his lower body thickening all over again. Would he ever stop wanting her? His body still tingled from making love with her, his blood running feverishly hot as her pert breasts pushed against his chest.

'Jago?'

He gently stroked the back of her head. 'Mm?'

Mollie leaned back to look up at him, longing shining in her eyes. 'Do we have time for one more kiss?'

Jago smiled and brought her even closer to the pounding need of his body. 'Just the one.' And he lowered his head and covered her mouth with his.

An hour or so later, Mollie was sitting beside Jago on his private jet flying down to London. Her body was still tingling from his lovemaking, her heart rejoicing that he had finally talked a little about his childhood. It was like a nailed-up door had been opened a fraction between them, bringing them a little bit closer, not just physically but emotionally. She hadn't told him much more about her past, but being able to share about her worries over her brother was an enormous relief. It was so reassuring that Jago didn't believe she was responsible for her brother's issues. She had known it intellectually, but emotionally she had found it hard not to blame herself. But Mollie was uncomfortably aware of her other dark secret and couldn't imagine telling Jago the real reason she had taken his grandfather's payout and left. For now, it was easier to let Jago think it was all about helping to get Eliot into long-term rehab.

Jago was sitting beside her and reached for her hand, his dark blue gaze searching as it meshed with hers. 'There's something I'd like to understand a bit better. Why did my grandfather offer you money? Did you ask him for help?'

Mollie couldn't hold his gaze and instead looked at their joined hands. The fake engagement ring on her left hand glittered from the sunlight slanting in from the jet's window. 'I can't talk about it, Jago.'

'Can't or won't?'

She pressed her lips together for a moment before responding. 'Your grandfather is a very powerful man.'

'He can't do anything to hurt you, Mollie. I won't let him.' He squeezed her hand in a gesture of reassurance.

Mollie gave a scornful laugh. 'I told you before. He didn't think I was worthy of you. And given the circumstances of my childhood, he was probably right.'

Jago frowned. 'Look, he might be a grumpy old bigot, but it was my decision who to marry, not his. I still can't understand why you didn't tell me you needed money.'

'You were in New York signing off on that big property deal,' Mollie said. 'Your grandfather…found out I wasn't who I said I was, and—'

'What do you mean?' His voice had a sharp edge to it, his gaze piercing.

Mollie let out a stuttering sigh. 'My real name is Margaret Green. I changed my name when I turned eighteen. He must have done some sort of background check on me, and suffice it to say, my criminal past was anathema to him.' She figured sticking to some of the truth was better than telling Jago the whole truth. He had asked her to marry him without really knowing who she was.

Jago's frown was so deep it made him look intimidating. 'What crime did you commit?'

'Shoplifting.'

'How old were you?'

'Fifteen.'

'Wouldn't that have gone through the juvenile justice system? You don't usually get a conviction recorded when you're under eighteen unless it's for a more serious crime.'

'I know, but apparently your grandfather has contacts everywhere and uncovered my dirty little secret,' Mollie said. 'Wouldn't the press have loved to run that story? *Jago Wilde's Fiancée Was a Teenage Shoplifter.* Think of the shame I would have brought on your family.'

Jago's features were set in tense lines. 'So you took the money and ran.'

'It was for the best, Jago. Surely you see that now?' Mollie said, pulling her hand out of his. 'You weren't in love with me. We came from such different worlds. Do you really think we would have lasted the distance? We might well have been divorced or at least separated by now if we had married.'

His jaw worked for a moment, and his eyes glittered darkly. 'Are there any other things I should know about you?'

Mollie could feel heat pooling in her cheeks and had to look away to stare at the fluffy clouds outside the private jet. 'Everyone has things they don't want others to know about, even someone as perfect as you.'

Jago made a scoffing noise. 'I'm the last person to consider myself faultless. But I would appreciate it if you'd be honest and open with me. I don't want any more nasty surprises.'

Mollie's spine chilled to the marrow. What nastier

surprise could there be than the one she was desperately hoping would stay secret? 'Will the press be at your grandmother's party?' she asked after a moment.

'No, we're keeping things quiet for Gran's sake. She isn't supposed to have too much stimulation while she recovers from the concussion. There will only be handful of family and close friends.'

Mollie let out a sigh of relief. It would be hard enough facing Maxwell Wilde and Jago's older brother Jack, let alone the press. 'I guess she'd be even more confused if the press made a big deal about us being together again, especially when she thinks we never parted in the first place.'

Jago took Mollie's hand again and began to absently stroke the back of it with his thumb. His touch sent a wave of heat through her body, making her wonder how she was going to face the rest of her life without it. Her role as his fake fiancée was for the weekend and the weekend only.

'I've thought about that too, but I want her to have this weekend surrounded by those who love her. If there's a press leak, then I'll deal with it.' Jago gave her hand a reassuring squeeze.

Mollie did her best to smile at him, but her worries about the upcoming weekend were like tiny mice nibbling at the wainscoting of her mind. Returning to Wildewood Manor as Jago's fiancée was fraught with danger, but she couldn't back out now. On the way to the airport, she had briefly spoken to Eliot and his clinic doctor and been reassured Eliot was making slow but steady progress. Mollie had also informed her boss she wouldn't be returning to work. The money Jago had given her would tide her over for months, but she really wanted to open her own beauty clinic concentrating on skin care. Being her own boss was her goal. She wanted the security of knowing she was in control of her career, not at the mercy of someone else.

It wasn't long before they were off the plane and driving down to Wildewood Manor in the Cotswolds. As they got closer, Mollie's nerves became more agitated. The scenery was as picturesque as ever in early spring—bright egg-yolk daffodils everywhere, fresh green leaves unfurling on the trees, lush pastures, and even though there were light showers of rain, by the time Jago pulled into the grounds of the estate, the sun broke through and cast the manor in a golden light.

The imposing Elizabethan mansion was softened by its verdant surroundings. The garden leading to the front entrance was set along formal lines, with neatly trimmed yew hedges of different heights and shapes on either side of the flat, soft lawns that divided the wide stone pathway leading to the front door of the four-storey structure.

Jago drove around to the back where the family usually entered the building. He parked the car on the gravelled area that overlooked the rear gardens with a central fountain. There was a kitchen garden as well as a cottage-style one and, farther afield, a wild garden and a meadow beyond that leading to a lake and a densely wooded area in the distance.

Jago came around to open Mollie's door before she had undone her seatbelt, so engrossed was she in looking at Jago's childhood home again. It was undisputedly a beautiful property, but she wondered if all those rooms and gardens and meadows and woods had provided a cosy and nurturing environment for three grieving young children. Was there any amount of wealth and privilege that could compensate for such a heartbreaking loss?

Mollie unclipped her belt with a hand that wasn't as steady as she would have liked. She stepped out of the car, and Jago closed the door for her then held his hand out to her.

'Ready?' He was still wearing his sunglasses so she couldn't read his expression apart from the tight smile on his lips.

Mollie slipped her hand into his, her stomach tilting when his strong fingers wrapped around hers. 'I think so.' She took a deep breath and walked with him to the back door.

CHAPTER EIGHT

MOLLIE STEPPED OVER the threshold, still holding Jago's hand, her heart thumping like she had run all the way from London. One of the many servants who worked at Wildewood Manor greeted her with a welcoming smile. Obviously, Jago had briefed the staff beforehand about his plan to pretend they were still engaged.

'Welcome, Miss Mollie,' Harriet said. 'So lovely to see you again. Lady Wilde will be so pleased to see you.' She turned and addressed Jago. 'I've told young Jim to take your bags to your room. I'll serve afternoon tea in the Green Room in half an hour.'

'Thank you, Harriet,' Jago said. 'We'll freshen up and then go up and see Gran. Has there been any change?'

Harriet shook her head, her expression sombre. 'She sleeps a lot and is still confused.'

'And my grandfather?'

'He's in the study. Would you like me to get one of the maids to inform him you're here?' she offered.

'That won't be necessary,' Jago said in a wry tone. 'I'm sure he already knows.'

A short time later, Jago led Mollie to the room they had once shared on their occasional visits to Wildewood. Mollie stepped inside the commodious room, a host of memories assailing her. Not much had changed in the two years since she had jilted Jago. The decor was much the same, making her feel like she was stepping back in time. She went over to the windows to look at the stunning view outside. A shower of rain had recently fallen, and a rainbow stretched from one side of the wildflower-dotted meadow to the other.

Jago came up behind her and placed his hands on her shoulders. She could not stop herself from leaning back against him, relishing in the feel of his hard toned body against hers. Feeling that sense of safety she had never felt with anyone else. He turned her in his arms and looked down at her with a serious expression.

'I know I'm asking a lot of you to do this.'

'You're paying me a lot to do this,' Mollie reminded him.

His eyes moved back and forth between hers then dipped to her mouth. As if in slow motion, his head came down, and his lips briefly brushed hers. He pulled back but then gave a low, deep groan and lowered his mouth to hers again, kissing her lingeringly, deeply, passionately. Mollie wound her arms around his neck, standing on tiptoe so her hungry body could press against the tempting hardness of his. He groaned again then ran his hands down the sides of her body, cupping her bottom, holding her to his swollen length.

'I shouldn't be doing this,' Jago said against her mouth.

'Why not? We're engaged, aren't we?'

He framed her face in his hands, looking at her intently. 'I don't think I've ever wanted anyone as much as I want you.'

'I want you too.' More than she should given the circumstances. This game of pretend had some elements to it that were starting to feel frighteningly real. Her feelings, for instance. They had never disappeared but lain deep inside her like a dormant plant in winter. But spring had arrived, and the tiny buds of her feelings for Jago were popping up each time he kissed her. Every stroke of his hand, every incidental touch poured rich fertiliser on her feelings for him. The longer she spent with him, the stronger her love became. Why had she let him reawaken the fire? One kiss had blown her willpower to smithereens, and the irony was she had been the one who had allowed it. How could she stop this from getting any more serious? He had not known the real her when he'd asked her to marry him, but he was getting to know her now. He was closer to her than she had allowed anyone, and yet this was for this weekend only. How could she protect herself from further heartbreak? Or was the pleasure of his touch worth it? Silly question. Of course it was worth it. To feel wanted and desired, to feel alive in a way she hadn't for two long years.

Jago brought his mouth back down to hers in a kiss that was hot, sweet, sexy and tender at the same time. His hands gently skimmed over her, exploring her in exquisite detail, ramping up her desire like a match to dry tinder. He peeled away her top as she worked on the buttons of his shirt, desperate to be skin-on-skin with him. Jago kissed his way down from the soft skin of her neck, taking his time to reach her breasts. He savoured each one with his lips and tongue, stirring her senses into overload. His thumbs brushed over each of her nipples and the sensitive area around them, his touch making her gasp with longing. He lowered his mouth to her puckered flesh and subjected her to the most delicious sensual attention. Every hair on her head tingled at the roots, and the nerves beneath her skin went into a frenzy of excitement, her blood thrumming, humming with the pulse of her desire.

Mollie ran her hands over his muscled chest, delighting in the lean, hard contours of his gym-toned body. He hadn't followed the trend of waxing off his chest hair, and she ran her fingers through the springy dark whorls, and then pressed her naked breasts against his chest, enjoying the sensation of his hair tickling her soft skin.

Jago covered her mouth in another deep and hungry kiss, his hands holding her by the hips to keep her against the throb of his body. Mollie went for the waistband of his trousers then pulled down his zip to shape him through his underwear. He groaned against her lips, then worked on the rest of her clothes until they were both naked.

Jago kissed his way down her body, going down on bended knee in front of her, lavishing attention on the most intimate part of her body. Mollie had never allowed any other lover—not that she had had many—to perform such an intimate act on her before. It hadn't felt right, she hadn't felt comfortable, but with Jago it was as natural as breathing…except while he was doing it, breathing was almost impossible. Her heart raced, her pulse pounded as he separated her feminine folds with his lips and tongue. He knew exactly how to pleasure her, and pleasure her he did. Spectacularly.

Earth-shatteringly. The powerful sensations took her by surprise, every nerve pulling tight before exploding in a cascade of sparks that rippled through her body in pulsating waves.

Jago moved back up her body, kissing her bellybutton, then her rib cage, her breasts and finally her mouth. He walked her backwards with his mouth still fused to hers, his hands guiding her by the hips until they landed together in a tangle of limbs on the king-size bed. He lifted his mouth from hers, looking down at her with lust-glazed eyes.

'Time to get a condom.' He sprang back off the bed and rummaged through his wallet for one.

'How many do you have in there?'

He sent her a devilish smile. 'Not enough. I'm going to have to grab some of Jack's.'

Mollie couldn't hold back a slight frown. 'You're okay with him knowing we're sleeping together this weekend?'

Jago paused in the process of unwrapping the condom he'd found. Nothing showed on his face, but she got the sense he was mulling over something in his mind. 'The only thing Jack will be concerned about is making sure Gran has a happy birthday. What you and I get up to while we're alone is our business, not his.'

'Are you close to him and Jonas?'

Jago came back to her on the bed, lying beside her, one of his hands resting on her belly, his eyes meshing with hers. 'Not as close as we might have been if our parents hadn't died.' A shadow drifted through his gaze just like the grey-tinged clouds scudding across the sky outside.

Mollie put a hand to his chiselled jaw and gently stroked it. 'I would imagine you'd be super close after experiencing such a tragic loss.'

His mouth twisted into a grimace. 'My grandfather sent us to different boarding schools so we couldn't rely on each other. It was supposed to be character-building for us.'

'That's cruel. You were so young to be left to cope on your own.'

'My grandmother was against it, but she had no say in the matter,' Jago said. 'She's of the era when women vowed to obey their husbands when they got married. I don't think I've ever seen her stand up for herself. She doesn't know how to.'

'Is it a happy marriage?'

Jago made a cynical sound at the back of his throat. 'Is any marriage happy all the time?' He blew out a long breath and continued. 'I suspect Gran realised early on that divorcing my grandfather would be an ugly battle, one she would lose in the end. She's remained faithful to him, but I don't think he's been faithful to her.'

Mollie's heart ached for his grandmother. To have spent so many years with a man who wasn't loyal to her must have chipped away at her self-confidence. 'You sound like you don't respect him much.'

'I don't. But he's too old to change now.'

Mollie chewed at her lower lip. 'I'm nervous about seeing him.'

Jago took his hand off her belly and trailed his splayed fingers through her hair, sending tingles up and down her spine. 'You don't need to be frightened of him. He can't hurt you, not while I'm around.'

He can hurt me more than you realise.

The words were on the tip of her tongue but she couldn't say them. She forced her mouth into an effigy of a smile, but inside she was quaking with fear. Fear of exposure, fear of some sort of payback from Maxwell Wilde for not abiding by the non-disclosure agreement he had insisted she sign. But she comforted herself with the knowledge that she had at least told Jago her primary reason for taking the money Maxwell had given her: to help her brother. That was one less secret to keep hidden.

Jago leaned closer to plant a soft kiss on her lips. 'Now, where was I?'

'You were about to make love to me, but I think I killed the mood,' Mollie said with a rueful grimace.

Jago took one of her hands and placed it on his swollen length. 'I'm always in the mood when it comes to you.' And he brought his mouth back down to hers to prove it.

After they both showered and changed, Jago took Mollie's hand in his to go to join his grandmother for afternoon tea. His body was still tingling from making love to Mollie both on the bed and again in the shower. He had to forcibly remind himself they were only pretending to be engaged. None of this was real, and yet he couldn't get enough of her. But asking her to consider taking this beyond the weekend was tricky. For one thing, there was the press attention their reunion would attract. He had enough trouble as it was trying to escape the intrusion of the tabloids. Secondly, if his grandmother made a full recovery, she would find out he had lied to her. Gran had spent years putting up with her husband's lies, and Jago hated to resemble his grandfather in any way, but what else could he do? He wanted what might well be his grandmother's last birthday to be happy, surrounded by her family. He wanted her to believe he was settling down at last. It would comfort her to know at least one of her three playboy grandsons was getting married. It was a pity Jonas couldn't be here to join the celebrations, but that was his brother's choice, and he had to accept it, even if it stirred a niggling worry that Jonas was not usually this long away on a mission.

Jago opened the door to the Green Room to find his grandmother sitting on a recliner near the window overlooking the garden. The tea tray hadn't yet been brought in, but he wanted his grandmother to see Mollie before the staff came in with the afternoon tea.

'Hey, Gran,' he said, leading Mollie into the room. 'Mollie is here to celebrate your birthday with you.'

Gran looked up and smiled, her eyes lighting up when her gaze rested on Mollie's beautiful face. She clasped her hands together like a young girl and exclaimed, 'Mollie, darling. How wonderful to see you. Come closer so I can kiss you. I'm afraid I'm not very mobile at present.'

Mollie came over and bent down to give his gran a gentle hug and a sweet kiss on both of her wrinkled cheeks. It made Jago's heart swell to see the enthusiasm and joy in his gran's face. And to witness what looked like the genuine affection Mollie exhibited for his grandmother.

'It's so lovely to see you too,' Mollie said, still holding on to one of the old lady's hands. 'How is your arm?'

Gran gave her arm in a cast a rolled-eye glance. 'It doesn't hurt now, but it's inconvenient, even though I'm out of the sling. I can't do the things I want to do. I feel like a doddering old fool for tripping over in the garden. Or at least that's what I've been told I did. I don't remember a thing about it. All I remember is going out to get some daffodils for the breakfast room. I love this time of year, don't you?'

'I certainly do, and daffodils are one of my favourite flowers,' Mollie said and sat on the window seat close to Elsie's chair. The filtered sunlight coming in made Mollie's hair look like spun silk, and a frisson passed over Jago's flesh as he thought of how her hair had felt as he ran his fingers through it only half an hour before.

'I love them too,' Elsie said. 'Yellow is such a bright and positive colour.'

'I'm so sorry you hurt yourself, especially so close to your birthday,' Mollie said.

The woman smiled, her eyes sparkling. 'To tell you the truth, Mollie, I'm quite enjoying being waited on hand and foot. Now, tell me about you. How are the wedding plans going?'

A panicked look crossed Mollie's face for a nanosecond, and then she glanced at Jago. *Help me*, her eyes seemed to say.

Jago came and sat beside her on the window seat, taking her hand in both of his. 'They're going well, Gran. We're just waiting for Jonas to get back from the

States. Do you remember he's over there working on a big top-secret naval project?'

Gran screwed up her face as if trying to put pieces of a complicated puzzle together in her mind. She put a hand to her right temple and then shook her head in a self-disparaging way. 'I have such gaps in my memory these days…' She lowered her hand to her lap and smiled indulgently again at them both. 'You two look very much in love. I'm so looking forward to seeing you married.' She aimed her gaze at Mollie and added, 'I always knew Jago would only ever settle for someone who loved him as he deserves to be loved.' Her expression became wistful, and she continued. 'His father was madly in love with his mother, some would say too much so, but I don't agree. How can you love someone too much?'

'I guess it's better than not loving at all,' Mollie said without glancing Jago's way, but he suspected her comment was a dig at him for not being in love with her when he had proposed to her. But marriage had seemed the right way to go. He'd wanted her, he'd enjoyed her company, and he had pictured a mostly satisfying life together. Unromantic of him, sure, but he didn't have it in him to say those three little words out loud. Maybe he was incapable of romantic love. He had avoided it for his entire adult life, settling for casual flings rather than anything permanent. Until Mollie. But his feelings about her were difficult to define. He put his attraction to her down to lust, and while that still pulsed and throbbed between them, there was a new quality to it now. An intense quality that made him feel a deeper connection to her as if their lovemaking had shifted to another level of intimacy.

'So true...' Elsie looked into the distance as if recalling her early years with Jago's grandfather. His grandparents had been married a long time, but he wasn't sure his grandfather was even capable of the love Elsie had shown him. Her loyalty and faithfulness, for one thing, had not been returned in equal measure, and Maxwell had controlled every aspect of her life to the point where she hadn't even been allowed to properly grieve her son and daughter-in-law. There were no photos of Jago's father around the manor; they had been locked away soon after the accident.

Harriet brought in the tea tray at that point, and Jago rose from the window seat to help his grandmother by placing her cup of tea and a piece of her favourite cake close to where she was sitting.

'Thank you, dear,' Elsie said, smiling up at him.

Jago handed Mollie a cup of tea, and she took it from him with a smile that faltered around the edges. 'Piece of cake? Scone?' he asked, indicating the luscious spread Harriet had prepared.

'Just the tea, thank you.' The cup rattled against the saucer in Mollie's hand, and he laid a gentle hand on her shoulder to reassure her. It was a big ask to pretend to be madly in love with him when there was so much murky water under the bridge between them, but this weekend was important, and Jago was determined to see it through. It wasn't hard to pretend to be in love with her, especially after their lovemaking earlier.

Are you pretending?

His conscience gave him a mocking nudge, but he wasn't prepared to examine his feelings too closely. He had planned this weekend on the pretext of making his grandmother happy, but he knew deep down it hadn't been his sole motivation. He had wanted to see Mollie again. That was what he had wanted for the last two painful years—to see her, to ask her what had motivated her to jilt him. To prove to himself he could move on without her in his life. But the thought of not seeing her again after this weekend was beginning to torture him. He shied away from it, tried not to imagine how lonely he would be without her in his life.

'Is my grandfather joining us?' Jago asked Harriet as she prepared to leave the room.

'No, he will see you at dinner,' Harriet said. 'He had his physical therapist here this morning so he's feeling tired.'

'Your grandfather isn't one for socialising these days,' Elsie said to Jago with a rueful grimace.

'How has he been?' Jago asked, absently stirring his sugarless cup of tea for something to do with his hands. Sitting so close to Mollie was making him distracted like a horny teenager. All he wanted to do was touch her. His blood was still thrumming with the excitement of possessing her earlier. He had to drag his eyes away from her every time she took a sip of her tea, those luscious lips around the rim of her china cup sending his pulse sky-high.

'Oh, you know your grandfather, dear,' Gran said with a sad shake of her head. 'He's finding his limitations so terribly frustrating.'

'You have limitations too, but you don't grumble about them,' Jago pointed out.

Elsie put her cup and saucer down with a sigh. 'I guess I'm used to being limited.' She turned her gaze to Mollie's and added, 'Now, let's talk about the wedding. I've forgotten all the details since my fall, but Harriet assured me that I was helping you plan it. Is the cake sorted?'

'Yep, all sorted,' Jago said, wryly thinking of the wedding cake and Mollie's dress at his London apartment.

'I can't wait to see your dress,' Gran said. 'But we mustn't talk about it in front of the groom. It's bad luck.' She leaned forward to pat Jago's hand. 'Would you mind if Mollie and I had a bit of time together catching up? You could go and check on your grandfather, take him a slice of this delicious lemon drizzle cake. But no cream. It's not good for him.'

Mollie's eyes widened a fraction at his gran's suggestion of a private tete-a-tete with her, but Jago gave her a reassuring wink and took a slice of the cake from the tea tray. He bent down and planted a kiss on Mollie's soft lips, breathing in the sweet scent of her, before lifting his mouth away. 'I'll see you at dinner, if not before.'

'You're making the poor girl blush,' Gran said with mock reproval, but there was a sparkle in her eyes all the same.

Once Jago had left the room, Mollie put her teacup and saucer on the table in front of the window seat. 'Can

I pour you another cup of tea?' she asked Elsie, to fill the sudden silence.

'No, thank you, dear,' Elsie said with a gentle smile. 'Now, how are you?' There was suddenly a piercing set to the old lady's gaze that was a little unnerving.

'I—I'm fine, thank you,' Mollie said, trying not to sound as flustered as she felt.

'Not getting wedding jitters, are we?'

Mollie swallowed tightly. 'Erm...should I be?'

Elsie gave a wistful smile. 'I was frightfully nervous before my wedding. Back in those days, of course, Maxwell and I didn't spend much time together alone, if you know what I mean.' She looked down at the rings on her left hand—a wedding, engagement and eternity ring that were probably worth more than most people earned in a lifetime. Elsie's gaze came back up to meet Mollie's once more. 'Jago is nothing like his grandfather. He might be ruthless in business, as are all three of my grandsons, but he's a good man. He'll make an excellent father. Do you want children?'

Mollie was a little blindsided by the question. 'Erm... yes, maybe one day, I guess. I wouldn't want to rush into it, though.'

Elsie put a hand on Mollie's knee and gave it a gentle pat. 'You'll be a wonderful mother, I'm sure.'

'I don't know about that,' Mollie suddenly found herself confessing. 'I didn't have the best role model in my own mother.'

Elsie looked at her with kind eyes full of compassion. 'Do you still have her?'

'No, she died when I was six.'

'And your father?'

'I've never met him. He abandoned my mother before I was born.'

Elsie sighed and placed her hand back in her lap. 'No wonder you and Jago fell in love. You have a lot in common, both losing parents so young.' She blinked a couple of times as if trying to hold back tears. Tears that were not allowed to be shed all those years ago.

'It must have been a terrible time for you when you lost your son and daughter-in-law,' Mollie said softly.

'Oh, it was,' Elsie said looking down at her hands. 'But I had three grieving little boys to take care of, so there was no time for me to dwell on things.' She looked up at Mollie again with a smile that was a little forced. 'Of course, Maxwell thinks I'm a sentimental old fool for still getting teary on James's birthday every year, but I miss him to this day. He and Alice would be so proud of their boys. They've done well for themselves in spite of...everything.'

Mollie had a feeling *everything* included how their grandfather had raised them with an iron fist and a heart of steel. 'I think you've been a wonderful grandmother to them, and they're so fortunate to have you.' Her voice came out raspy, and there was a lump in her throat.

Elsie reached for Mollie's left hand and looked down at the engagement ring glinting on her ring finger. 'Such a beautiful ring and a beautiful choice of bride. Jago has excellent taste.'

But I'm a fake, and so is the ring.

'I'm terrified I'm going to lose it,' Mollie said.

Elsie met her gaze with unwavering focus. 'Rings can be replaced, people cannot.' Then she gave Mollie's hand a gentle squeeze, and her tone lightened. 'I'm looking forward to the wedding. Ever since I woke up after my silly fall, it's all I can think about. For a horrible moment there when I woke up in the emergency room, I thought I'd missed it.' She gave a tinkling laugh and shook her head in a self-effacing manner. 'But Jago assured me I hadn't.'

Mollie disguised another tight swallow. 'No. You haven't missed it.'

Because it never happened, and now it never will.

CHAPTER NINE

Mollie was on her way back to the room she was sharing with Jago when she came to the library. As stately home libraries went, Wildewood Manor's was one of the best, but it was spoiled for her now as it was the place where Maxwell Wilde had presented her with his ultimatum two years ago. The library door was ajar, and she found herself moving towards it like an automaton, drawn to the space in spite of the memories it would evoke. She listened for any sound, but it was so quiet she could hear the soft ticking of a carriage clock in the sitting room opposite. Mollie gingerly opened the door a little farther and checked no one was in there. Finding it empty, she let out a sigh of relief and stepped over the threshold, pulling the door to behind her. The click of the lock was still faintly audible, and she stood stock-still, breathing in the scent of the ancient books that lined three walls of the cavernous room.

It was like stepping through a portal into another world, a world before phones and computers and emails. It was a dark room due to the wood panelling and floor-to-ceiling shelves and heavy brocade curtains hanging from the windows, but on this occasion, the curtains were only half-drawn to keep the afternoon light off the priceless tomes.

There was an extendable ladder set against one section of the bookshelves for gaining access to the books on the top shelves. There was a large leather-topped walnut desk to one side of the room with a leather chair set behind it. On the desk was a brass goosenecked reading lamp, a leather-bound journal of some sort, a gold fountain pen and even an old-fashioned quill, adding to the old-world atmosphere.

Mollie moved towards the desk and absently turned the swivel chair, watching as it went full circle...not unlike her, back at Wildewood Manor as Jago's fiancée. Pretending but feeling real emotions that—just like two years ago—were not returned by Jago. How could they be? Even if he had fallen in love with her, it was the other version of herself she had presented, not who she was now. But she sensed Jago was closer to her now than before, and she certainly felt closer to him, even though he had given her no guarantee of a future with him. Why would he? She had jilted him once. Would he risk it again? Unlikely.

There was a whirring sound from the shadows of the great room, and Mollie's heart leapt to her throat as Maxwell Wilde glided out into the light in his electric wheelchair.

'So you're back.' His faded blue eyes scanned her critically, his voice hard, his mouth tight, his bushy salt-and-pepper eyebrows fused in a frown of disapproval.

Mollie schooled her features into a calm facade, but inside she was quaking like a child in front of a stern schoolmaster. Her heart swung in her chest like an out-of-control pendulum, and she grasped the back of the leather chair to keep herself steady as her legs were like half-set jelly. Maxwell Wilde might be somewhat diminished since his stroke a year ago, but he still had a lot of power at his fingertips, power that could destroy her and those she loved.

'Jago insisted I came for his grandmother's birthday. I'm assuming he didn't check that was okay with you first?' She kept her voice as cool as her expression, so cool it could have frosted the windows.

Maxwell activated his chair to cross the acre of carpet, coming farther out of the shadows to glare at her. 'Since her fall, my wife has forgotten what you did to our grandson.'

Mollie ground her back teeth, fighting with every cell of her being not to be intimidated by him. 'I would never have jilted him if it hadn't been for—'

'I forbid you to speak of it.' He held up his hand like a stop sign. 'That was our agreement, was it not? It must not be mentioned again.'

Mollie flattened her lips into a tight line, staring down at him with anger pounding in her blood with hammers of hatred. 'Jago knows about the money you gave me to go away. He didn't hear it from me. He found out by himself.'

Maxwell's jaw tightened like a vice, and his eyes hardened to steel. 'You're fortunate he doesn't know why I paid you to go.' He rested his elbows on the armrests of his chair and steepled his fingers, watching her like a bird of prey.

Mollie held his gaze with gritty determination. 'Will you tell him?'

A devilish glint appeared in his eyes. 'Not unless you get any fancy ideas of becoming part of this family.'

'I can't see that happening,' Mollie said, her heart contracting. 'Jago will never forgive me for jilting him.'

'Nor should he,' Maxwell said, unlocking his fingers to grasp the armrests of his chair. 'You lied to him from the start, pretending to be someone you're not. I will not have the Wilde name polluted by the likes of you.'

Mollie stiffened her spine in pride. She had suffered from bullies since childhood and refused to be a soft target any more. She was not to blame for her circumstances of birth. It wasn't her fault her mother had not been up to the task of parenting her and her half-brother. 'I might not have the pedigree you would desire your grandson to join with in marriage, but I loved Jago will all my heart.'

Maxwell made a scoffing sound. 'If you loved him, you would have been honest with him instead of whitewashing your less than desirable background.'

Mollie gave him a challenging stare. 'You are not someone I will tolerate a lecture on honesty from.'

Maxwell's bushy brows rose in an imperious arc, but she read a mark of respect in his gaze she had never seen before. 'Ah, so you do have some spirit. Tell me, what did you do with the money I gave you?'

'I spent it on getting my half-brother into long-term rehab.'

'Did it work?'

Mollie let out a long breath, her shoulders slumping in spite of her efforts to maintain a rigid and defensive posture. 'Not yet.'

'But you refuse to give up hope?' He delivered it as a statement, not a question, his expression inscrutable.

'I figure while he is alive, there is hope. It's what keeps me going.'

'Optimistic of you.'

'Perhaps, but I can't live my life any other way.'

There was a silence measured only by the sound of a breeze that had whipped up outside, making a scratching sound from the leaves on the trees against the windows.

'Let's hope that optimism doesn't include any plans to reunite with my grandson,' Maxwell said. 'I will allow this little game of charades for Elsie's sake, but that's as far as it must go.'

'How magnanimous of you,' Mollie said with a touch of asperity. 'I'll enjoy making the most of it.'

Maxwell's eyes went to the ring on her left hand before he met her gaze once more with a cynical smile. 'Don't get too attached to that ring, will you.'

Mollie glanced down at the ring and then curled her fingers into her palm and met his gaze with a defiant glare. 'Contrary to what you believe about me, I value people, not worldly goods. Anyway, this ring is a fake, like my current relationship with Jago.'

Maxwell gave her a penetrating look as if he was reassessing her. Hardly a muscle moved on his face, and yet she got the impression he had come to a new opinion about her. One that challenged his view of her as a social-climbing gold-digger.

Mollie held his look, coming to a decision that gave her a way out of Maxwell's hold over her. She had not broken the NDA, and she now, thanks to Jago, had the money to pay Maxwell back. He could no longer control her as long as the images had been destroyed. That was a risk she would have to take, because otherwise she would never escape this nightmare. People had controlled her all her life, and she was not allowing it any more. 'I now have enough money to pay you back. You might control Elsie and your grandsons, but you are not going to control me.'

'Aren't you forgetting something?' Maxwell said with a vulpine look that chilled her to the marrow.

There was a creak as the library door opened and Jago appeared. He took in the tense tableau with an assessing glance then stepped farther into the room, coming over to Mollie and addressing his grandfather. 'What are you talking about?'

Maxwell's jaw was so tight it looked like it might crack like concrete under the pressure of old tree roots. 'Why have you brought her back here? She jilted you, for God's sake. And she's violating our agreement on the payout which, I might remind you, she grabbed with greedy gold-digging hands.'

Jago stood close to Mollie without touching her, but she drew strength from the solid warmth of his body. 'I don't believe Mollie is a gold-digger. I don't think I ever totally believed it. She put that money to good use to help her brother.'

Maxwell curled his top lip. 'A brother who is a drug addict and a drunk. I don't want our name dragged into the gutter by people who can't control their urges and obsessions.'

'I think you're the one who is obsessed,' Mollie said. 'You're obsessed with controlling everyone in your life. But there will come a day when you won't be able to do it any more.'

Maxwell glared at her like he wanted to vaporise on her the spot. 'I can still control you, and you damn well know it.'

Mollie stared him down with a source of courage she hadn't known she possessed. 'There's nothing else you can take from me. I'm not going to be manipulated again.' Then with a brief glance at Jago, she swept out of the room with stately self-possession, closing the door with a hard snick as she left.

Jago was torn between wanting to follow Mollie and wanting to find out what his grandfather had alluded to during the conversation he had overheard as he entered the library. 'Was that necessary?' he asked with a frown. 'I brought Mollie here for Gran's sake.'

'Did she ask for money to come?'

'I made her an offer, otherwise I'm sure she would never have come here.'

'She's not good for you, Jago. You were lucky to escape her, believe me. You were becoming obsessed with her. That's not something I want for you.'

Jago stared down at his grandfather. 'Isn't what I want for me more important than what you want for me? I'm no longer a child under your care—if you could call how you raised us as *care*, that is.'

'What's that supposed to mean?' Maxwell sniped with a brooding scowl. 'I provided for you. I took you boys under my own roof. I paid for your education, and you wanted for nothing.'

Except my parents...and unconditional love and acceptance.

The realisation had always been in his mind, but Jago

had stored it at the back where he couldn't think about it too much. But he hadn't been allowed to think about, much less vocalise, the trauma of losing his parents. He and his brothers had been provided for generously in a financial sense but not in terms of love, especially not from their grandfather. Their grandmother did her best while swamped in her own grief for her adored son and daughter-in-law. Jago wondered if her memory loss now was somehow related to that unresolved grief. Her mind was stuck on what was for her a rare happy time in her life: the impending marriage of her middle grandson to Mollie Cassidy.

Jago was starting to put the pieces of a complicated puzzle together, and he wasn't sure he liked what he saw. His grandfather's set against Mollie was out of all proportion. It didn't make any sense. Yes, his grandfather was an appalling snob and looked down on those less fortunate than himself, but Maxwell's treatment of Mollie begged further examination. Jago had the power now to look deeper into his grandfather's affairs to see if there was something Maxwell had over Mollie that she hadn't revealed to him. Was her continued silence because of that wretched NDA? How could he get her to open up to him? To trust him? She hadn't trusted him two years ago; instead, she had bolted after being paid to leave by his grandfather. Jago understood her commitment to her half-brother, although he wasn't particularly close to his own brothers. Their grandfather had made sure of that.

Jago looked down at his grandfather again, fighting the urge to tell him what he really thought of him. But Maxwell was old and frail and didn't have half the power he thought he had over him now. 'I'm going to Mollie. We will discuss this further at some other point.'

Maxwell gripped the arms of his chair, his bony knuckles showing white as the pebbles on the driveway outside the manor. 'Don't make a fool of yourself over that girl all over again,' he barked, his rheumy eyes flashing with barely contained rage. 'Your father was obsessed with your mother, and look how that played out.'

An echoing silence bounced off the walls of the library.

'I'm not obsessed with Mollie, nor am I in love with her,' Jago said, but something inside his chest prodded his heart like a long thin needle sending radiating pain throughout his body.

But out of habit, he ignored it.

Mollie was pacing the floor of their room upstairs, unable to settle to anything. Her emotions were in turmoil, and yet she was proud of how she had stood up to Maxwell Wilde. It would remain to be seen what he did next, but she reassured herself her brother was safe for now. She had used her phone app to repay Maxwell every penny of his disgusting payout, and in doing so a load had come off her shoulders.

Jago entered the room just as she was doing another circuit, and she swung around to face him. His expression was apologetic, and it gave her hope that some of his walls were coming down.

'I'm sorry about the way my grandfather spoke to you,' he said, raking a hand through his hair in a manner she had come to recognise as a signal of distress. 'It was unforgivable.'

'You've called me the same,' Mollie pointed out, not quite ready to let him off the hook.

'I know, and I don't expect you to forgive me, but I don't think any such thing now.' He moved across to where she was standing, not reaching for her but close enough for her to be drawn into his magnetic field. Her body craved his touch, longed for him to take her in his arms and provide the comfort and shelter she had been praying for her entire life.

Mollie couldn't take her eyes off his bottomless blue ones. They were so deep and dark like the sky on a moonless night. She ran the tip of her tongue over her lips and watched as his gaze followed its movement. The air tightened. Electric energy crackled in the atmosphere. Her body tingled from head to foot, and she stepped closer at the same time he did. Their bodies collided, his arms came around her, tightly, possessively, greedily, and his mouth came down on hers in a kiss that sent a rocket blast of lust through her flesh. He groaned something unintelligible against her lips then deepened the kiss with a commanding thrust of his tongue that mimicked the primal act she knew was coming next. She wanted him with a feverish hunger that pounded in her blood, and she could feel the same need in him as he crushed her against his thickened length.

'I want you. Now.' He said the words in an agonised way, his hands cupping her bottom to hold her even closer to his pulsing need, the same need she could feel thundering in her own body.

'I want you too,' Mollie said, tearing at his shirt like it was crepe paper. A button popped, and she heard it ping to the floor. 'Sorry, I'm ruining your expensive shirt.'

'I couldn't care less about my freaking shirt,' he growled and set to work on her clothes as she continued with his.

In a matter of seconds, they were both naked on the bed in a tangle of limbs. Jago pushed back her hair from her forehead, looking deeply into her eyes. 'When I decided to bring you here for Gran's birthday, I didn't expect this to happen between us.' He frowned and added, 'I didn't want you to feel any obligation to sleep with me.'

Mollie lifted one of her hands to his face, stroking his lean jaw, delighting in the rasp of his stubble against her softer skin. 'I told myself I wouldn't allow you to lay a finger on me, but somehow I underestimated the way your touch would make me feel.'

He gave a crooked smile and leaned closer to press a light-as-air kiss to her lips. He lifted his mouth off hers and cupped one side of her face in his broad hand, his thumb stroking back and forth in a tender caress. 'Same goes. Which brings me to the question of what we're going to do about it.'

Mollie wasn't confident enough to ask what he meant so stayed silent, watching him as he surveyed her face as if memorising every one of her features.

Jago took her chin between his thumb and index finger, holding her gaze intently. 'Do you have any suggestions?'

Mollie disguised a swallow, not sure where he was going with their relationship but aching to know. 'I'm not sure your grandfather would be happy to know we're sleeping together.'

His brows came together in a savage frown. 'Can we for once leave my grandfather out of it? He's done enough damage as it is.'

And he can do so much more.

Mollie lifted her finger to his frown and tried to smooth it away. 'Make love to me, Jago. Please?'

Jago let out a rough-edged sigh and gathered her close once more. 'With the greatest of pleasure.' And his mouth came back to hers in a kiss that sent hot shivers down her spine.

His lovemaking was fast, urgent, desperate as if he knew the clock was ticking on their relationship. Mollie responded to him with the same urgency and desperation, not wanting to think too far ahead for there, surely, lay heartbreak. Jago might say he wanted her, and he demonstrated it convincingly, but he had never told her his feelings about her. He had never mentioned the word *love*, only *lust*. Would it be enough for her to accept him on those terms, even if he only offered a temporary fling? She couldn't think about it now, not while his mouth was working its mind-blowing magic on hers. Not while his hands were touching her, shaping her, caressing her until she was panting with need.

This was always what worked between them—the sexual energy that fired between them. The intensity of it had grown, not lessened, which gave breath to her hopes, making her fall under the sensual spell of his lovemaking all over again.

CHAPTER TEN

THE BIRTHDAY PARTY for Elsie, while small by Wilde standards, was no less glamorous. Instead of using the ballroom, the garden room was set up with beautiful flower arrangements and balloons and streamers and a banner with *Happy Birthday* on the wall above the spectacular birthday cake. While the last touches were being made by the staff, Mollie went upstairs to get ready. She dressed with care, pleased with the way her blue dress hadn't dated and showcased her slim build and the grey-blue of her eyes. She put her hair up in a stylish bun, leaving a couple of tendrils to dance around her face. She was putting the finishing touches to her make-up when Jago came in.

'You look stunning,' he said coming over to drop a kiss to her bare shoulder, his eyes meeting hers in the mirror.

'So do you.' Mollie drank in his handsome features, his dress suit highlighting his tall, broad-shouldered frame and athletic build to perfection.

'I have something for you.' He opened his jacket to take out a slim rectangular jewellery box the same colour as his eyes.

Mollie took it from him, her heart skipping in her

chest. She prised open the lid to find a gorgeous sapphire pendant, surrounded by sparkling diamonds and a pair of dangling earrings to match. 'Oh…they're beautiful…' She met his gaze in the mirror once more. 'Are they…real?'

He gave a short laugh. 'Of course they're real. Here, I'll help you with the pendant.' He took the box from her and took out the necklace, placing it around her neck and fastening it. 'You'd better do the earrings yourself.' He handed her each one in turn as she put them on.

Mollie stared at herself in the mirror, feeling like Cinderella dressed for the ball. The earrings sparkled as they moved, the pendant's sapphire as dark as the ring on her left hand. 'I'll give them back once the party is over.'

'No need to,' Jago said. 'Consider it a gift.'

'But, Jago, these are so expensive. I can't possibly accept such a—'

His hands came down on her shoulders, sending shivers of reaction through her body. 'I want you to have them.' There was an implacable quality to his voice and a determined look in his eyes.

She rose from the chair she was sitting on and turned to face him. Her thoughts were tumbling like leaves in a whirlwind. 'When did you buy these?'

Something moved at the backs of his eyes. 'Why do you want to know?'

'Because it's important.'

'It's just a bit of jewellery.'

'When?' Mollie persisted.

Jago let out a rough sigh. 'I bought them two years

ago while I was in New York. They were going to be a gift for our wedding day.'

Mollie bit down on her lower lip, her heart contracting at the thought of how much she had hurt him back then. 'You kept them all this time?' Her voice came out as a scratchy whisper.

He gave a dismissive shrug. 'Who else was I going to give them to?'

'You've had those five lovers since...haven't you?'

He stepped away as if he needed some space, one of his hands raking through his hair, leaving it tousled. 'I didn't date anyone for the first year.'

Shock, surprise and relief washed over her. 'No one?'

His expression became wry. 'I shelved my playboy lifestyle for twelve months, then I began a few flings but...' He gave another shrug and went on. 'It wasn't the same. I wasn't the same.'

Mollie blinked back the moisture in her eyes. 'I don't know if this is any comfort to you, but I haven't slept with anyone since we broke up.'

Jago's eyes widened a fraction. 'No one?'

'No one.'

He came over to her and took her hands in his, drawing her closer to his body. 'Why?' His gaze was searching, a deep frown pulling at his brow.

Mollie let out a soft sigh. 'Lots of reasons. I had my brother to look after. I had to find a new job, a place to live. There's not been time for anything else.'

And I didn't want anyone but you.

She wanted to say it, but what good would it do now?

Jago lifted her chin with the tip of his finger, his gaze still locked on hers. 'We'd better not be late for Gran's party, but this conversation isn't over. My grandfather was behind you leaving me, and if you won't tell me what led you to do it, I'll have to find out some other way. It can't have just been your brother's issues.'

Mollie pressed her lips together to stop herself blurting out the truth. If she told him, she would be breaking the terms of the non-disclosure agreement and risking Maxwell retaliating by releasing the images.

The guests were still arriving as Mollie and Jago entered the party room hand in hand. Mollie could see Jack, Jago's older brother, leaning down to kiss Elsie. He straightened to his full height and glanced Mollie's way. His dark eyebrows rose a fraction, and he sauntered over with his mouth smiling with welcome, but his ice-blue eyes had a cynical glint.

'Welcome back into the Wilde fold, Mollie,' he said with a mock bow. He turned to Jago and added, 'What did the old man think of you two getting back together?'

Jago's mouth flattened into a thin line of tension. 'He's not happy, but I'm only concerned with Gran at the moment. She's thrilled to see Mollie.'

'Yeah, so I just heard.' Jack rubbed at his jaw in a thoughtful manner. 'I don't buy it, you know.'

Jago frowned. 'What do you mean?'

'I think Gran remembers more than she's letting on,' Jack said.

'You've been a lawyer way too long,' Jago said, but he was still frowning. 'Her memory is patchy, sure, but she thinks we're still planning the wedding.'

Jack's smile was as cynical as his eyes. 'And are you?'

Jago's hand tightened as it held Mollie's. 'No,' Jago said. 'This is just for the weekend.'

Jack's gaze went to the jewellery around Mollie's neck and the earrings dangling from her ears before glancing at the ring on her left hand. 'Given the amount of money you've spent, I'd be stringing it out a bit longer to get value for money.'

Jago muttered a thick curse word. 'Keep your opinions to yourself, Jack. I know what I'm doing.'

Jack gave a careless shrug, and with another mercurial smile directed at Mollie, he strolled away to speak to some of the other guests.

Jago turned to Mollie. 'I'm sorry about Jack. He's always been a bit of a pot-stirrer.'

'It's okay. I know the terms of our deal.' Mollie glanced in Elsie's direction to see her chatting with some old friends. She turned back to Jago. 'But what if your gran does remember?'

'I'll cross that bridge if and when I need to. But for now, why don't we go and get some fresh air?' He led her out through the French door that opened to the garden, taking her past a maze to a summer house enveloped in white clematis. Bees were busily buzzing, and birds were twittering, and the afternoon sunlight cast everything in a golden glow.

Jago looked back at the manor where the party was continuing without them. He was frowning when he turned to look at Mollie. 'This weekend might not be enough.'

Mollie licked her suddenly dry lips. 'What do you mean?'

'We might need to continue our relationship for a little longer than I anticipated.'

'How much longer?'

'Jack could be right about Gran. She may well remember more than we thought, but I don't want to upset her by suddenly ending our relationship when she's clearly thrilled we're back together.'

'I'm not sure your grandfather is going to be happy about that,' Mollie said, biting down on her lip.

Jago's frown carved deep into his forehead. 'Why is he anything to do with us?'

'He's everything to do with us,' she said before she could put the brakes on her tongue.

He squeezed her hands. 'Tell me everything, Mollie, please. I'm determined to find out either way, but it would be better if I heard it from you.'

'You know I can't say anything. I signed a—'

'Screw the NDA. This is about us. It's about you learning to trust me, damn it.'

Mollie pulled out of his hold as the music coming from the house signalled it was cake-cutting time. 'We'd better go back. It will look strange if we're not there to sing "Happy Birthday" to your gran.'

Jago let out a savage sigh and walked with her back to the manor in silence. The party had livened up, and people were gathering for the blowing out of the candles. Mollie put her on best party smile, but it took an effort to keep it in place. What did Jago want from her? A fling? A proper relationship? To try again? He hadn't said anything about his feelings. Their relationship was based on lust just as it had been two years ago. Wouldn't she be making the same mistake to settle for anything less than love?

***

After his grandmother blew out her candles, with some help from Jack, Maxwell rolled up to make a speech on his wife's behalf. While he was thanking all the guests for coming and being as charming as a wily fox, Jago took the opportunity to slip away to look for the answer to the question that was playing on his mind. Why did Mollie accept the payout from his grandfather to jilt him? It surely couldn't have been solely about getting help for her brother, although he knew long-term rehab was expensive and repeated sessions were not unusual. He went to his grandfather's private study which, unsurprisingly, was locked, but fortunately he knew where a spare key was planted. His grandfather resented Jago having access to his business records, but since Maxwell's stroke, Jago had made it his mission to check every detail in case of discrepancies. His grandfather wasn't as sharp as he used to be, and Jago had already found a couple of accounting mistakes that would have created a tax nightmare if not corrected in time. He logged into his grandfather's computer to access his financial transactions, searching for the payment Maxwell had made to Mollie two years ago. It wasn't the first time Jago had seen it, but this time he stared at it, his mind ticking through the possibilities. There were no records of any emails from Maxwell to Mollie, and yet he felt sure there must have been some communication other than in person. He couldn't search his grandfather's phone because he had seen Maxwell use it to read the speech he had composed for his wife. Jago rifled through the drawers of the desk, trying to be fast yet tidy in his approach. His search proved fruitless, and he leaned back in the leather chair and let out a sigh of frustration.

Then he remembered the safe hidden behind the bookshelves. It was where his grandfather kept large sums of cash and some of Gran's most valuable jewellery. Jago didn't know the combination, but on a whim, he tried his father's birthday and year of birth, and the safe opened. Inside was an astonishing amount of cash and some jewellery, and right at the back was a phone. He took it out and saw that that the battery was dead, so he hunted around for a charger. He found one in a drawer of a filing cabinet and quickly plugged it in, waiting impatiently for it to charge enough for him to access it. The minutes dragged by, and he could hear the party in the background and hoped no one would come looking for him. Finally, the phone had enough charge for Jago to turn it on. Of course, it had another code but after three tries he cracked it with Jack's birthday and year of birth.

Jago scrolled through the messages, and his eyes rounded when he saw one from his grandfather to Mollie. There were pictures attached and he clicked on them, his stomach churning when he saw the explicit images of Mollie. He had seen her naked, had made intimate love with her many times, but he had never seen her in such provocative poses. It was so out of character. The images were nothing short of pornographic. Was this part of her past she was keen to keep hidden? How had his grandfather come across them? Had he used them to get her to jilt him? Nothing made any sense…other than Mollie hadn't come to him and explained her dilemma but instead had chosen to bolt, leaving him virtually standing at the altar. That stung more than anything. She hadn't turned to him but had accepted money from his meddling grandfather to go away.

Mollie was finding it hard to make small talk with some of the guests. She felt like a fraud, pretending to be reunited with Jago when the truth was she was on borrowed time. She looked around for him, but he had disappeared during his grandfather's speech. Not that he had missed much. The words Maxwell spoke were hardly what anyone in the know would call *sincere*. But Maxwell Wilde was a showman, and he worked the room, making the small gathering of friends believe he was a devoted husband. She wanted to vomit.

Mollie made good her escape when the dancing began. She had never felt less like partying. She was on her way back to her and Jago's room when she saw him come out of his grandfather's office. There was a thunderous scowl on his face, and his eyes were dark blue flint.

'I want to talk to you. In private.' His words were clipped, his mouth set in a tense line.

'So talk.'

'Not here. Come into the library.'

Mollie followed him into the library a few doors down from the study. Once they were both inside, Jago closed the door with a resounding click then walked over to stand in front of her. 'Why didn't you tell me about the images?'

Mollie stared at him in shock, her heart beating so

heavily she could feel her hammering blood in her fingertips. 'You've seen them?' she asked without a thought for the NDA. Shame coursed through her that Jago, the man she loved, had seen her in such degrading poses. And even though strictly speaking it wasn't actually her in those pictures, it still felt like she could never escape their black mark against her.

'I found a burner phone of my grandfather's just now.'

'They're not me,' Mollie said. 'They're deepfakes. I don't know where your grandfather found them—he didn't tell me. He just told me that someone was going to release them if he didn't pay the ransom to keep them out of the press. But the deal was I had to leave and never contact you.'

Jago's frown was so deep it dug a trench between his eyes. 'But why didn't you come to me? I was about to become your husband. Why would you allow my grandfather to convince you to—'

Tears welled in Mollie's eyes, her heart aching like it was being compressed in a vice. 'I had to protect my brother, but also I was thinking of you.'

'Thinking of me?' Jago snapped back. 'By jilting me the day before the wedding? How was that in my best interests?' Bitterness laced his tone, and his gaze was as searing as a laser beam.

Mollie hugged her arms around her trembling body. 'You were negotiating that big deal in New York. I was worried if those images were released to the press, you would lose the deal and your reputation would be tarnished by me. And I was worried about Eliot. He was fragile. He still is fragile. If he saw me being humiliated in every newspaper and social media platform, it could have tipped him over the edge. I couldn't risk it. Surely you can understand that?'

Jago swung away from her and raked a hand through his hair. He dropped his hand back by his side, but she noticed both of his hands were clenched. Tension and anger rippled across his features, but behind the fury she could see a glimpse of profound hurt he was at great pains to conceal. 'You promised to marry me, Mollie. You agreed to spend your life with me, and yet you didn't come to me when you needed help. You didn't trust me. You let my grandfather rescue you, but at what price to us?'

'It wasn't about the money, although I needed it desperately for Eliot.'

'I'm not calling you a gold-digger because you're clearly not,' Jago said, some of his anger softening in his voice. 'Your love and concern for your brother are truly admirable. But I still can't see why you didn't wait for me. I was only hours away from getting back from New York.'

Mollie glared back at him out of frustration. 'Do you know how quickly those images could have been uploaded?' She snapped her fingers for emphasis. 'That's how quickly. I didn't have hours to waste, I didn't have minutes. Your grandfather promised me it would all go away, and it did. I abided by the terms of his deal, and he did too. I paid him back the money using some of the money you gave me. He has nothing over me now.'

'But he still has the images.'

Jago's statement hit her like a punch. Somehow, she

hadn't taken in everything Jago had told her about finding the images.

They still existed.

Lumps of ice chugged through her veins, and her legs shook until she wasn't sure she could stay upright. She reached blindly for the desk chair and sat down with an ungainly thump, turning her anguished face towards Jago. 'They weren't destroyed?'

'No.'

'But your grandfather assured me they would be. He said the ransom would take care of everything, that as long as I disappeared, those images would be gone.'

'He lied.'

Mollie swallowed and knotted her hands together until her fingers ached. 'So they still could be leaked?'

'Not if I can help it.' Determination underlined his tone. 'But there's one thing I don't understand. Why did the alleged blackmailer approach my grandfather and not me? I have just as much wealth and reputation to protect, and you were my fiancée.'

Mollie pushed herself out of the chair, wrapping her arms around her body once more. 'I've never understood that either, but you weren't marrying me for the right reasons, and I wonder now if your grandfather realised that.'

'All that aside, your first instinct was to lock me out, but this was your present unfolding in real time. I should have been the one to help you. You were the woman I had chosen to be my wife, for God's sake. But you left me completely in the dark.'

'You didn't love me. You never told me you loved me.'

Jago clamped down on his jaw. 'Words are not as important as actions.'

'Actions are fine, but I've never been told I was loved by anyone in my entire life.'

He drew in a rough-sounding breath, his expression locking down as if her words had triggered something painful in him. 'I can't talk about this now. I think we need to confront my grandfather to see where these images originated.'

Mollie frowned. 'Is now the best time? It's your grandmother's birthday. I don't want it ruined by an argument with your grandfather.' It occurred to her then that she was still in protection mode just as she had been all her life. Protecting herself, protecting her brother, giving up Jago to protect him two years ago, protecting his grandmother from any fallout after a confrontation with Maxwell. Mollie was twenty-eight years old and still using the same old strategies she'd used from childhood, trying to fix things and taking responsibility for others.

Jago pocketed the burner phone. 'Gran will need a rest soon anyway. I'll see if I can get my grandfather to meet us in his study in half an hour.' He held out a hand to her. 'Come here.'

Mollie stepped forward, and he captured her hand and brought it up to his lips, pressing a barely there kiss to her fingertips. 'I shouldn't have allowed my business deal to take priority so close to our wedding. It left you in the firing line, and I wasn't there to protect you.'

Plenty of people had offered to protect her and failed to do so. She herself had promised to protect her brother but had tragically failed. But it warmed her heart to think Jago would have done so two years ago if only she had asked him for help. Mollie gave him a twisted smile tinged with regret. 'I'm not used to relying on anyone for protection.'

He gathered her closer and bent his head till his mouth was close to hers. 'Maybe it's time to start.' And he kissed her tenderly, passionately, until she was incapable of thought, only feeling. Being in Jago's arms, sheltered by his embrace was like coming home after a lifetime of wandering anchorless, lost, alone. Dared she hope that he cared more for her than he was prepared to admit?

CHAPTER ELEVEN

JAGO RETURNED WITH Mollie to the party but as he had anticipated, his grandmother was tiring and ready for a rest. Jack was in the process of helping her out of her chair, tucking her arm in his and gently leading her out of the room. His brother might be a hard-nosed divorce lawyer, but there was a softer side to him not many people witnessed. There was no sign of his grandfather, but some of the guests insisted on saying goodbye to him and Mollie, which delayed his mission to confront the old man.

'Congratulations on getting back together,' one of his grandmother's friends said with a beaming smile. 'I hope you'll be very happy together. Can't wait until the wedding—that is, if I'm invited again?'

'Of course you will be,' Jago said almost mechanically. But the idea stuck in his head like a thorn on a fine fabric, leaving its mark even when he pulled away from its grip. There was nothing to stop him marrying Mollie, not now he knew what had caused their break-up. He could make up for the last two years: he had enough money to give her a comfortable life, a secure and happy future. They were a good match, not just physically. Mollie understood him in ways a lot of people didn't. She understood the loss he had experienced because she had faced her own tragic losses. He felt a connection with her he hadn't felt with anyone else. Surely that was a good basis for a long-term partnership?

Finally, the last guests left, and Jago asked Harriet where his grandfather was.

'He's out in the garden by the fountain. Jim took him out a while back for some fresh air,' she said. 'He goes out most afternoons at this time if the weather is fine.'

'Thanks,' Jago said, taking Mollie's hand in his. 'If you see Jim, ask him to wait until I've finished talking to my grandfather in private.'

'Will do, Mr Jago,' Harriet said and smiled at Mollie. 'I hope you enjoyed the party. Lady Wilde was so delighted to see you it was all she could talk about. It's given her such a boost.'

'It was a lovely party and the food was delicious,' Mollie said with a smile. 'Thank you for all your hard work.'

'It's my pleasure,' Harriet said with another smile then excusing herself went off to finish clearing the tables.

Jago led Mollie out of the room. 'Did you actually eat anything?'

'No, but the food looked delicious.'

'You're a very convincing liar.'

'Years of practice.'

They went out to the garden, and Jago spotted his grandfather in his wheelchair, facing the large fountain. Jago gripped Mollie's hand a little tighter and glanced down at her. 'Ready for a showdown?'

Her features were cast in lines of worry. 'I'm not sure any good will come out of cross-examining a fragile, old man.'

'He might be physically frail, but his mind is strong, and I won't allow him to get away with what he's done.'

Mollie didn't answer, but he heard her give a ragged sigh. Jago was not going to stop until he had answers to questions no grandson should ever have to ask a grandfather, but needs must. His and Mollie's future depended on it.

Maxwell must have heard the crunch of their footsteps on the gravel pathway for he turned his chair around to face them as they approached. 'I thought that was Jim to take me inside,' he said with a scowl.

'I want a word with you,' Jago said.

His grandfather straightened in his chair with effort, his hands gripping the armrests with white-knuckled force. 'Isn't it time you took Mollie back where she came from? You have no future with her. She's wrong for you.'

Jago clenched his jaw so tightly he thought he might crack a molar or two. 'I know about the images.'

Maxwell's bushy brows snapped together in a frown, and he aimed his flashing gaze at Mollie. 'You told him?'

'No,' Mollie said.

'I found them myself,' Jago said. 'On a burner phone in the safe. I've been thinking about it for a while now. Why did the supposed blackmailer contact you and not me? Mollie was my fiancée. I should have been the target of an extortion event, but I wasn't. Why was that?'

Maxwell's gaze lost some of its fire, and he seemed

to sink further into his chair. 'What does it matter now? I got rid of the problem.'

'The problem being me?' Mollie said with quiet dignity.

Maxwell disregarded her comment and railed at Jago. 'I couldn't allow you to end up like your father, madly obsessed with a woman who wasn't good enough for him. Their obsession with each other led to their deaths. Do you think I wanted that for you? I had to put a stop to it.'

'You orchestrated those images,' Jago said through clenched teeth. 'There was no blackmailer, was there? It was you the whole time.'

Mollie gasped. '*You* did it? Was I really that bad a choice of bride?'

'It wasn't about you personally,' Maxwell said. 'I needed to disentangle Jago from a relationship that could have led him down the same path as his father.'

'My father loved my mother,' Jago said.

'Love?' Maxwell made a scoffing sound. 'That wasn't love, it was obsession. They were more interested in themselves than anyone else. Their obsession with each other was more important than their careers, their family, their children. And it led to their deaths, making you and your brothers orphans, ruining my and your grandmother's lives in the process. I saw it happening all over again with you, history repeating itself. I had to stop you. I couldn't stop your father, but I had a moral responsibility to stop you from destroying yourself.'

'I hardly think you're the right person to lecture anyone on moral responsibility,' Jago threw back. 'Who else has those images? You're a smart man, but your computer skills are not up to the task of creating deep-fakes as professional as those.'

Maxwell glared back at him. 'I paid someone to do it, but they did it in my presence on that phone so there were no copies. I paid them in cash so there wasn't a paper trail.'

'So why did you keep the images on that phone?' Mollie asked in an anguished tone that clawed at Jago's heart.

'In case you dared to come back,' Maxwell said. 'It was my insurance policy.'

'Mollie didn't breach your damned non-disclosure agreement,' Jago said. 'I tried to get her to talk, but she refused to utter a word. Do you realise what damage you've caused? Two years of hell for both of us. How can you ever justify what you did?'

Maxwell's hands tightened even further on the arm-rests of his chair. 'Rail at me all you like, but I did it for you. Now, where's Jim? I want to go inside.'

Jago grasped Mollie's hand. 'I'll send him out for you. But first, I want to make something clear. I don't know who generated those images for you, but they belong in jail. And frankly, so do you.'

Maxwell growled like a grumpy old animal confined to a cage. 'You can delete the images, and no one will be the wiser.'

'I'll delete the images for Mollie's sake, not yours,' Jago said squeezing her hand firmly in his. 'You no longer have any hold over her or me.' He turned and led Mollie back towards the manor, desperate to get away from the evil his grandfather had wrought. He was furious he hadn't worked it out before now. He had let two years pass without searching for the ugly truth. He had blamed Mollie, believing her to be a gold-digger, when in fact his own grandfather had blackmailed her out of Jago's life. How could he forgive himself, much less his meddling grandfather?

When they got back to their room, Mollie was still trembling from Jago's interaction with Maxwell. No one had ever stood up for her before, and to witness Jago doing so sent a wave of love and admiration through her. 'Was it two years of hell for you?' she asked.

Jago scraped a hand through his hair, his expression still brooding with anger. 'He had no right to destroy your life or interfere with mine. I'm so angry right now I can barely speak.'

'Thank you for what you did for me out there.'

He turned to look at her, his anger slipping into a mask of anguish. 'What did I do for you? I believed the worst of you for two damn years. I should have gone looking earlier for answers. I shouldn't have allowed him to hoodwink me into thinking you were after money.'

'It's in the past. Let's hope it stays that way.'

Jago began to pace the floor, his strides agitated, jerky, restless. He stopped and looked at her. 'Let's go back to London. I can't stand to be anywhere near that man right now after what he's done.'

'But what about your grandmother?'

He let out a rough-edged sigh and pushed back his sleeve to glance at his watch. 'She will have gone to bed by now. I'll call her tomorrow. How soon can you pack?'

'Five minutes. I didn't bring much.' Mollie started gathering her things together, part of her relieved she didn't have to stay a minute longer and yet conscious that the weekend pretending to be Jago's fiancée was coming to an end. Would he want to continue their... whatever it was? Relationship? Fling? Something more?

The drive back to London was mostly silent. Every time Mollie glanced at Jago he was frowning, as if his mind was replaying the tense interaction near the fountain. Even his choice of music on the journey seemed to reflect his mood, the brooding Mahler symphony a perfect soundtrack for the dark emotions running under the surface.

They arrived a couple of hours later at Jago's London townhouse in Bloomsbury. As they entered the beautifully appointed house, a host of memories assailed Mollie. She remembered the first time he had brought her here. The first time they had made love. The first time they had cooked a meal together. His proposal and her eagerness in accepting, even though he hadn't told her he loved her. She had hoped he would do so in the weeks leading up to the wedding, but he hadn't. In spite of the evil meddling of Jago's grandfather, sometimes she wondered if Jago would have ever said those three little words that no one had ever said to her before.

Jago shrugged off his light jacket and hung it inside a cloak room near the entrance. 'I'll bring our bags in while you go and freshen up. Do you still know your way around? Not much has changed since you were last here.'

But everything had changed, not in terms of decor or layout, but Mollie had changed. She wasn't the same woman Jago had brought here two years ago. She was stronger now, more resilient and, ironically, more in love with Jago than ever.

Mollie used the downstairs bathroom rather than go upstairs where she knew so many poignant memories would be evoked. But Jago seemed to be taking a long time to bring in their bags, so she wandered around the house, trying not to think of all the times she had been here in the past as his real fiancée, not his fake one. She looked at the ring on her left hand and wondered how anyone could tell it wasn't real. It looked as real as the diamond-and-sapphire earrings and pendant she wore.

On her way upstairs, Mollie looked out one of the windows and saw Jago was speaking on the phone near the car. He was leaning against his car and pinching the bridge of his nose as if the conversation was not a pleasant one. Was he filling Jack in on what had happened? Or Jonas? But she didn't sense he was particularly close to either of his brothers. It occurred to her that Jago was as isolated as she was, having no one to lean on in good times or bad. She sighed and continued up the stairs until she came to his bedroom. She pushed back the door and went in, sweeping her gaze around the room. Not much had changed. The walls were still white, the bed linen of the highest quality, the bedside table lamps crystal and brass. The carpet was deep and plush, and the ensuite as luxurious as ever with a walk-in shower with a rainwater showerhead and twin basins and mirrors along the other wall. There were no feminine items on the second sink, only Jago's shaving kit and cologne on the first. Had anyone shared this space with him in the two years they had been apart? He had said he hadn't dated anyone for the first year. What did that mean? Did it mean he'd still cared for her? Missed her more than he wanted to admit? Or was she being a fool for still hoping he'd loved her when he had never articulated it? There were times both in the past and now where he acted like a man in love. Was it enough to rely on his behaviour instead of a verbal acknowledgement of his feelings? She longed for him to be the first person to say those words to her. Was it foolish of her to hope a second time around that he would?

Mollie left his bedroom and opened the door of the spare room, her eyes widening in shock when she was confronted by a wedding cake—*her* wedding cake—standing on a table out of direct sunlight. The four-tiered cake was still intact, although the frosting looked cracked in places, like old bone china. The marzipan bride and groom embracing on the top of the cake were startling lookalikes of her and Jago, which was an indication of the expertise of the wedding cake designer Tessa Macclesfield. Mollie moved closer to the cake, staring at it like it was a ghost or an apparition, a conjuring of her own imagination. She reached out a hand and touched the delicate lacework icing that bordered the top and bottom of every tier. A tiny piece came away and dropped on the table with a soft plink that made a shiver scuttle down her spine.

Jago had kept the cake.

Mollie couldn't stop looking at the cake, wondering what had motivated him to keep it. Given the circumstances, wouldn't he have got the servants at Wildewood Manor to destroy it? What else had he kept? She hadn't until this moment wondered what had happened to her wedding dress. The wedding was to have taken place in the lush gardens at Wildewood, so when she left in such a hurry, she hadn't had time to take anything but the most basic items with her. Her eyes were drawn to the wall-to-wall built-in cupboards and she moved towards them like a robot, her hand reaching for the crystal knob on the left-hand door. It opened with a soft squeak, and she gasped at her wedding dress and veil hanging there. Her heart was working its way up her throat, pounding, punching, pummelling until she could barely take a breath. She reached out her hand and touched the silk and lace and trailed it through her fingers.

There was a sound behind her, and she swung around with a gasp, putting a hand up to her throat to see Jago standing there with an inscrutable expression.

'You kept the cake and dress?' Her voice came out in a thin thread.

He walked farther into the room to stand near her but without touching. He waved his hand towards the cake and the dress. 'I know it probably confirms my grandfather's opinion of my obsession with you, but I needed these as a reminder never to propose to anyone again.'

Mollie moistened her lips that felt as dry as the cracked fondant on the cake. 'Is that your only reason?'

Jago's eyes were shuttered, but the line of his lips was thin. 'I was furious when you jilted me. I had never allowed anyone as close as I allowed you, but you left and I let my anger fester for the last two years.'

'*Close?* You held back so much from me,' Mollie said.

'At least I introduced you to my family,' Jago threw back with a frown. 'You didn't even tell me you had a brother, nor did you tell me the truth about your upbringing.'

Mollie shut the cupboard door, blocking the vision of her unworn wedding dress. It seemed to mock her, so too the wedding cake, both of them a reminder of what she had been so close to having, only to have it snatched away at the last moment. 'I told you I loved you, so I think I was much more emotionally available than you. You've only recently told me a little about your childhood, how it was to lose your parents so tragically. It's not healthy to lock that stuff away and never express your grief. Believe me, I know because I've been doing the same.'

Jago wandered over to the wedding cake, poking it with his finger, a deep frown between his hooded eyes. 'I remember everything about that day, even though I was only five years old.' He drew in a ragged breath and turned to look at her. 'My world, my safe and happy life was snatched away when the police arrived to tell my grandparents about the plane crash. I will never forget the sound of my grandmother's wailing. It went on and on and on like a siren. No one could comfort her. Jack and I did what we could, but Jonas was only three. He was too young to understand how everything had changed in the blink of an eye.'

'Oh, Jago, I'm so sorry. It must have been so dreadful, so painful...'

He made a gruff sound that was dismissive of his suffering, but she could see the shadows of pain in his dark blue gaze. Wounded eyes. Eyes that hid a world of agony behind a shield of arrogance and pride. 'My grandfather was never an emotionally available man, and losing his only child, his only son, made him even more avoidant.' He let out a raspy sigh and continued in a tone laced with sadness. 'Looking back, I suspect he sent Jack and me to boarding school within a month or two of our parents' deaths because he didn't want to be reminded of his loss. Jonas, of course, was too young, but he went to yet another boarding school when he was six.'

'That was so cruel. What about your poor grandmother? Surely having her grandchildren around would have helped her work through her grief?'

He gave her a grim look. 'Not according to my grandfather. We were forbidden to talk about our parents in case it upset our grandmother. All the photos of our parents were locked away so they didn't trigger our grandmother's grief.'

'Do you have any photos of your parents?'

'In my study.'

'May I see them?'

He hesitated for a moment, and Mollie wondered if she had pushed him too far. But then he blinked a couple of times and indicated for her to follow him downstairs.

A short time later, Jago unlocked a drawer of his desk and leaned down to take out a photo album. He placed it on the desk and pushed it towards her, the desk acting as a barrier between them. 'I managed to find these during one of my visits during the school holidays. We didn't often go to Wildewood during term breaks, as our grandfather mostly sent us to various camps and holiday programs to ease the burden of child care on our grandmother.'

Mollie opened the album to the first page where there was a wedding photo of a bride and groom, presumably Jago's parents. The couple looked at each other with such tenderness and love it brought the sting of tears to her eyes. She blinked them away and said, 'They look so in love, so happy.'

'Yes, well, my grandfather would call it *obsession*, but I believe they did genuinely love each other. I never saw them argue, and they were big on affection towards each other, embarrassingly so on occasion.' There was a hint of a wry smile in his voice.

Mollie traced her finger over the photo behind a plastic shield. 'You look like your father. So do your brothers.'

'The Wilde blue eyes, although Jack's are a lighter shade.'

Mollie turned to the next page and saw Jago's mother cuddling a newborn baby, with his proud father beaming down at his wife and child. She had light brown hair that was similar to her own, and it made her wonder if she would ever get the chance to hold a baby of her own—Jago's baby. The possibility had been there two years ago, but this was now, and their engagement was a charade, not the real deal. She turned another page or two until she got to a photo of his parents and Jago as a baby, this time being held by his father; his mother had a scowling Jack sitting on her knee. Mollie studied Jago's tiny features and his head with its sprinkling of black hair, cradled so gently by his father. 'You were a cute baby.'

Jago grunted. 'Apparently, I wasn't a great sleeper, and Jack was as jealous as hell when I came along. I often wonder why they had a third child, given what a handful we were. But they had a nanny, so I guess that helped.'

Mollie turned through some more pages of the family interacting: welcoming their third son, Jonas, then birthday parties, Christmas, holidays in exotic locations, everyone looking happy and blissfully unaware of what the future held. The last photo in the album was of Jago's parents smiling at each other with a vivid sunset behind them.

'That was the last photo taken of them,' Jago said in a sombre tone.

Mollie closed the album and pushed it back across the desk towards him. 'Why don't you get some of these framed and have them around the house?'

Jago's expression tightened as if invisible strings were tugging at his facial muscles. 'I don't need daily reminders of what I lost.'

'Then, why did you keep the cake and my dress where you can't help but see them all the time?'

A shutter came down over his features. 'I don't use that room. It's mostly locked.'

Mollie couldn't help thinking that was how he dealt with most things he didn't want to face: he locked them away, his emotions, his grief, his pain. But hadn't she done the same? Reinventing a version of herself, one that didn't contain the distressing baggage of her childhood. All those traumatic memories were locked away, never to be examined, pored over, analysed. 'Do you think it's healthy to lock your strongest emotions away?'

Jago put the album back in the drawer, shoved it closed and turned the key with a sharp click. 'I don't know any other way.'

'You could learn.'

'I'd need to be motivated, and I'm not.' There was a stubborn quality to his voice that was reflected in his gaze.

'Why did you ask me to marry you back then?'

Jago came around from behind the desk and stood next to her. 'I thought we were a good fit.'

'In bed?'

His mouth twisted, and a dark gleam shone in his eyes. 'No one came close to you in that regard.' He reached out and touched her cheek with a faint touch that sent a frisson down her spine. Longing ignited in her core, a deep pulsing ache that begged to be assuaged. 'They still don't.' His voice lowered to a deep burr, and his eyes dipped to her mouth.

Mollie drew in a wobbly breath, caught in the spell of his mesmerising gaze. Her need for him overrode her rational brain, and right now she needed to be rational, not led astray by her emotions as she was last time. 'What are you saying? That you want us to continue our pretend engagement?'

A flicker of something passed through his gaze. 'We both want each other. It makes sense to try again. Marry me, Mollie, and we can do it properly this time. No one is standing between us, no one is blackmailing you out of my life. We can be together now.'

Mollie wanted to say *yes*, but what sort of marriage was he offering? 'Are you asking me as some sort of payback to your grandfather? To thwart his plan to break us up for good?'

A frown drove a trench between his eyes. 'I'm asking you because I want you to be my wife.'

'But you haven't told me you love me. Surely that is a prerequisite for marriage?'

'Love is a fleeting emotion no one can really rely on,' Jago said. 'What you can rely on from me is financial security. That's something you craved all your life, isn't it?'

'Yes, but I also want to be loved. I don't want to be used as some sort of revenge plot against someone.'

'My grandfather has nothing to do with my proposal,' he insisted, still frowning. 'You and I make a good team. We understand each other, we have good chemistry, and this is the most practical and sensible option. To start again, to undo the damage of the last two years. I owe that to you, at the very least.'

Mollie's chest was tight with pain instead of joy. He had proposed marriage, but it wasn't the marriage she wanted. It was no different from his previous proposal. She had changed, but he hadn't. His emotions were still locked away like the photo album.

'Has anything ever been real between us?' Mollie asked, her voice cracking over the words. 'It sounds to me like you want a plus one, not a soulmate.'

'What we have is as real as that ring on your finger.'

Mollie looked down at her left hand in shock. She brought her gaze back up to his. 'It's…real?'

'I got a jewellery dealer friend of mine to track it down. He found it in a pawn shop.'

'Why did you make me think it was fake?'

'It seemed like a good idea at the time.'

'Like when you believed me to be a gold-digger, you mean?'

Jago thinned his lips. 'I apologised for that. I know you're not after my money.'

'And yet you just proposed to me using financial security as one of the benefits of marrying you,' Mollie pointed out bitterly.

'It is a huge benefit. I can give anything you want. I can provide for you and your brother. You won't have to do without a thing.'

'Except the one thing I want the most.'

Jago released a jagged sigh of frustration. 'You're asking too much.'

'And you're offering too little.'

His frown deepened, his eyes flinty. 'So you're not accepting my proposal?'

Mollie stepped back from him in case he touched her. His touch could unravel her willpower in a heartbeat. 'I don't want to end up like your grandmother, married for years to a man who doesn't see her for who she is. Who doesn't love her the way she deserves to be loved and honoured and treasured.'

Anger ignited his gaze like the strike of a match. 'Don't compare me to my grandfather. I'm nothing like him.'

'Has he ever told you he loves you?'

'No.'

'Did your parents?'

His throat moved up and down in a tight swallow. 'Yes.' The word seemed to be forced out of him, and a shadow passed through his gaze like a cloud drifting past the moon.

'Did you say it to them?'

Jago swung away from her and went back behind the desk, one of his hands raking through his hair. 'If you're not going to accept my proposal, then at least consider continuing our relationship as it stands. My grandmother is still not well enough to accept the truth.'

Mollie knew this was her chance, her only chance, of finally being true to herself. True to what she wanted, needed, deserved. Accepting his proposal would desecrate what she believed a marriage should be, one full of mutual love and respect and loyalty. That was the security she longed for, not financial comfort but emotional safety and surety.

'I can't do that, Jago.'

His expression showed no sign of disappointment. It was as if she had told him she couldn't pick up his dry-cleaning or something equally banal. 'It's your decision. I can't force your hand.'

Mollie pulled the engagement ring off her finger and held it out to him. 'You should have told me it was real. I could have lost it as it's a little big for me now.'

He ignored her outstretched hand. 'So you're running away from me a second time?'

Mollie stepped forward and laid the ring on the desk that separated them. She took off the pendant and earrings and put them beside the ring. 'This is nothing like the last time. Back then, I was running scared, terrified those images would hurt not only me but you and my brother. This time, I'm going with my head held high. I don't deserve to live the rest of my life without true love. I spent my childhood like that, and I will not settle for it in my adult life.'

His jaw worked for a moment, and he thrust his hands in his pockets as if he was trying to control the urge to reach for her. 'You're making a mistake, Mollie. I've never asked anyone else to marry me, only you.'

'So I should be honoured? Grateful?' Mollie said with an incredulous look. 'I lived in abject poverty. I was raised in filth and neglect. I was found with my half-brother beside my dead mother and stepfather three days after they overdosed. I've waited my whole life for someone to say they loved me, and you can't or won't do it, even though you claim to want to spend the rest of your life with me. Well, I'm not grateful or honoured to be your choice of bride. The job description doesn't reflect who I am now.' She turned for the door but only got three steps when his voice stopped her.

'Where will you go?'

She turned back to face him. 'I have enough money left over to find myself a place to live. I don't need or want your help.'

All I want is your love.

'At least let me find you somewhere for tonight so you can think things over,' Jago said.

'I'm a fully grown adult, Jago. I can book myself a hotel room.'

His eyes moved between each of hers as if searching for something. 'You're really saying *no*, aren't you?' His tone contained a note of disbelief as if he had never factored in her refusing him. The notorious Wilde arrogance on display once more.

'I'm really saying *no*.' And then she walked out of the study without a backward glance, although her heart cracked like the fondant on her abandoned wedding cake.

CHAPTER TWELVE

JAGO CONSIDERED RUNNING after her, begging her to change her mind, but he didn't want to acknowledge how much her rejection hurt him. He ignored the pain that seized his chest; he disregarded the ache in his belly, the bitterness and disappointment he could even taste in his mouth. He had unfinished business with Mollie, but she was done with him. He was not the type of man to beg, to weep and wail and gnash his teeth over what he couldn't have. Mollie had made her decision, and he had to accept it, but hot damn, it hurt him in ways he hadn't been expecting. He had been looking forward to continuing their relationship, to bringing it full circle to make up for the lost two years. Those two miserable years that he could not get back. Of course, most of his anger should be directed at his grandfather for thinking he was obsessed with Mollie. Maybe he was for all he could think about was her. The taste of her, the feel of her against his body, the way she smiled at him, the way she melted when he looked at her. But that was to be no longer because she wanted more than he had to offer.

Jago stared at the wedding cake, stale now and falling apart bit by bit. Why had he kept it and the dress?

What did he hope to achieve by keeping such souvenirs of a doomed relationship? Doomed not just because of his grandfather's meddling but because Mollie had kept so much from him, the stark details of her childhood, the poverty and neglect no child should suffer from. His own childhood had been marked by tragedy, but at least he and his brothers had had the love of their grandmother. But neither he nor Mollie had opened up about their painful childhoods; they had been engaged to each other but offered versions of themselves, not their true selves. Their public personas, their identities, not the essence of who they really were.

Jago closed the door, telling himself he would get his housekeeper to get rid of the cake once and for all. The wedding dress… His gut tightened at the thought of donating it to charity for someone else to wear. It had been made specially for Mollie. It belonged to her, so he would courier it to her to do with it what she wished. But then he thought of her marrying someone else, and his gut soured and cramped as if he had swallowed poison.

Maybe his grandfather was right: he was obsessed with Mollie, and it had to stop, right now.

Mollie had only just arrived back at her flat in Edinburgh when she got a call from the rehab centre to inform her that Eliot had signed himself out. Despair hit her like a punch, knocking away her hopes and dreams for a full recovery for him. Would this nightmare ever end? How much money had she already thrown at getting help for him? How much had she already sacrificed? Never had she felt so alone in the world. Even when she was in the wretched dosshouse with the dead bodies of her mother and stepfather, at least she'd had Eliot with her.

Now she was on her own.

No one knew where Eliot was. Her imagination made her crazy with horrible scenarios of him injecting a contaminated drug in some dark alley in Glasgow, and there was nothing she could do to stop it.

She had failed. Failed to keep him safe as a child and now as an adult.

Even if she had accepted Jago's proposal, no amount of money could stop Eliot destroying himself. It had to be his decision to accept a long-term commitment to help…which in a strange way was exactly what Jago needed to do. To commit to loving someone instead of avoiding opening his heart out of fear of losing that love like he had lost his parents. Mollie understood the reasons behind Jago's locked-away heart, just as she understood the choices Eliot made came from a place of deep hurt and loss, but it was not up to her to fix either of them. It had taken her a long time to realise it, but there were some things you could not control, could not repair, could not restore.

But you could rebuild, and that was what she was going to concentrate on now. Day by day, she would work at following her dreams, even though her top dream was for Jago to love her, and that was out of her control. She had other dreams that required her focus, and they would be fulfilling in a different way.

Three weeks later, Mollie attended a week-long skin care workshop in London. It was a costly affair, but attending it was a step closer to her achieving her goal of setting up her own specialised clinic. To her surprise, on booking the conference, she received a Cinderella ticket, meaning both the workshop and her hotel accommodation were fully paid for. It was just the boost of luck she needed. Her brother had finally contacted her, informing her he had moved to London and was doing well by checking in to a daily rehab centre where mentors were assigned to each client to help them on their journey to recovery. It gave Mollie another reason to attend so she could catch up with him to assure herself he was doing okay. She had met with him for lunch, and he was surprisingly sober and assured her he was staying clean. He was working with a therapist he had really clicked with and had since made considerable progress in moving forward without the need to anaesthetise himself with drugs or alcohol. Mollie had to take his word for it, but from what she had seen so far, all seemed to be going well with him.

She wished she could say the same for herself. She was lonely, sad, depressed and despairing that no one would ever love her. The only love she wanted was Jago's, but that was asking for a miracle, and she wasn't so foolish to think there would be two granted her in a lifetime. Shouldn't she be grateful for her brother's improvement? Why push her luck and dream that Jago would finally open his heart to her?

After a long day at the workshop held at a plush hotel in the centre of London, Mollie was about to take the lift to her room when she caught sight of an elderly lady being escorted into the foyer by a female companion.

Her eyes widened and her heart began to give a staccato thump when she saw it was Elsie Wilde and Harriet the maid who worked for the Wilde family at Wildewood.

Mollie ignored the lift bell ping as the doors opened and turned and walked towards the women, who both smiled as she approached.

'Mollie, how lovely I caught you just in time,' Elsie said. 'Are you free for dinner with me? I just adore this hotel. Did you know it's one of Jago's? He bought it eighteen months ago, and it's only just finished being refurbished. It's gorgeous, isn't it?'

Mollie's stomach dropped like an elevator with snapped cables. 'Jago's?' she gasped.

Elsie beamed. 'He's the silent sponsor behind the workshop. It's not his usual thing, but there you go. The things men will do for love.'

Mollie opened and closed her mouth like a fish thrown out of its bowl. 'I didn't... I mean I would never have come if I'd—' Was he behind the Cinderella ticket? Had her name been tagged on the booking system so she got in for free? She didn't know what to make of it, wasn't game enough to make anything of it. Maybe the guilt he felt about his grandfather's actions precipitated his generous actions. It might not mean anything had changed with his feelings.

'Now, about dinner. I prefer to dine in my room, if that's okay with you? We'll have a lovely catch-up, and the press will leave us alone,' Elsie said. 'Shall we say in half an hour? I like to dine early these days. I go to bed ridiculously early, especially after travelling down from Wildewood.'

'That would be lovely, thank you,' Mollie said.

Harriet gave her the room number with a smile. 'See you soon.'

Jago was staying back at work to go through the fine details of a property deal contract, but the words were blurring in front of his eyes. He had thrown himself into work just as he had two years ago when Mollie jilted him, but like then, nothing could fill the emptiness of his life now. He used to feel a sense of satisfaction when he signed off on a deal. The chase and the catch were once everything to him. Now he was left with a feeling of *Who cares how big the deal is?* Who cared what he achieved? Who cared how much money he had made? He certainly didn't. He didn't care about anything, couldn't think about anything but Mollie. She had filled the hole in his life for the weekend of his grandmother's birthday, but since she had rejected his second proposal, he was left feeling worse than he had when she jilted him. He had harboured such anger towards her for two years, anger that was now directed at his grandfather. But even that was pointless. Maxwell was hardly likely to change, and Jago had to move on with his life. He couldn't stay in this morose state forever. But he had also directed a load of anger at himself. He could have prevented this last two years if he had gone after Mollie, instead of allowing his wounded pride to stop him from pursuing her. He had gone as far as finding out where she was but did nothing to contact her after a few attempts via phone and text. She had blocked him on her phone, and he had taken it to mean she didn't want any further contact with him. He was furious and frustrated with himself for not trying harder. For not seeing what was there if he hadn't been so blinded by arrogance and pride. He was the one to blame for losing Mollie. Yes, his meddling old grandfather was a huge part of it, but Jago should have trusted her, should have trusted his own heart.

There was a firm rap on his office door, and Jack came in carrying a bottle in one hand. Typical, Jago thought. Jack wasn't one to wait to be invited; if he wanted something, he took it. Jago couldn't imagine his brother languishing for a couple of years over a woman who had left him. He would fill her place with another as soon as he could and not have a moment's conscience about it.

'Hey, got a minute for a drink?' Jack said, strolling over to plant the bottle on Jago's desk and then sat on the chair opposite the desk, legs spread wide in his customary confident pose.

'Since when do we have after-hours drinks together?' Jago asked, narrowing his eyes in suspicion.

'Yeah, I know. We're not that sort of brothers, are we?' Jack said it without any note of regret, simply as a statement of fact.

'So what's up?'

'Have you heard anything from Jonas?' Jack asked.

'No. You?'

A frown pulled at Jack's brow, and a flicker of worry moved through his ice-blue gaze. 'I know he's worked on secret commissions before, but it's been months now. Did I tell you the wedding cake designer he was dating called asking me to tell him to call her? She called me several times. I had to fob her off because before he left, he said he wanted to cut all contact with her. She didn't seem the stalker type. And I thought he had a real thing for her.'

'Since when were you an advocate for relationships? I thought you were the biggest cynic about falling in love?'

Jack gave a lopsided smile. 'Yeah, well, I see too many supposedly in-love couples tearing each other apart in a divorce to be a true believer in happily-ever-after, but Jonas dated Tess longer than he dated anyone else.' He rose from the chair in a fluid movement Jago silently envied. He hadn't exercised in weeks and felt lethargic and listless in comparison to his brother's virile and agile movement.

'Where do you keep the glasses?' Jack asked.

'Third cupboard on the left,' Jago said. 'But what are we drinking to? I'm not in the mood to celebrate anything.'

'Yeah, I got that impression.' Jack took two glasses out of the cupboard and put them on the desk then unscrewed the red wine bottle and poured two half glasses, pushing one towards Jago. 'Here. Get that into you.'

Jago looked at the ruby liquid and screwed up his nose. It was undoubtedly top-quality wine, but he had no appetite for it. 'Sorry, Jack. It's wasted on me.'

Jack took a sip of his wine, then put the glass back on the desk. He folded one ankle over his bent knee, his gaze assessing. 'You don't know what you're missing.'

What Jago was missing was being in a relationship with Mollie, but he didn't want to discuss it with his cynical older brother. He deftly changed the subject. 'How's Gran doing?'

Jack swirled the contents of his glass into a tiny whirlpool, then he met Jago's gaze. 'She's made a miraculous recovery. She's up in town having dinner with Mollie as we speak.'

Jago's jaw dropped open. 'What for?'

'Presumably to eat.' Jack lifted his glass to his mouth in an annoyingly casual manner.

'Damn it, Jack. Why's Gran getting involved? Mollie has made it clear we don't have a future together.' He shoved back his chair and stood, sending a hand through his hair in a distracted manner. 'I can do without any more meddling from either of our grandparents.'

'Listen, mate. You stuffed up your relationship with Mollie, not our grandfather. If she had felt more secure with you back then, I'm sure she would have come to you first instead of allowing Maxwell to manipulate her. You asked her to marry you and put a damn expensive ring on her finger, but the only thing she wanted—which is what most of my female clients want, and my male ones, too, for that matter—is for someone to love them and commit to them.'

Jago gave a scornful laugh. 'So you're an expert on relationships now? The playboy celebrity divorce lawyer who has never dated anyone longer than a couple of days?'

Jack gave a negligent shrug. 'I might not want it for myself, but I can see it can work for other people. You act like you're in love—you did two years ago and even more so now. It was a good ploy to get Mollie to come to Gran's birthday, but at the root of it was your desire to be with Mollie again. It was also a good plan to sponsor her conference in your hotel. You want her back in your orbit.'

Jago held on to the back of his ergonomic chair until his knuckles showed white. 'So what if I want to be with her? I'm not with her now because she doesn't want what I'm offering her.'

Jack leaned forward to put his glass back on the table, flicking Jago a glance. 'Have you told her you love her?'

'No.'

'Why not?'

Jago worked his jaw for a moment, his chest feeling like it was in an industrial crusher. He wanted to deny it, to say he didn't love her in a romantic sense, but the words just wouldn't come. He didn't want to lie to himself any more. He did love her. He had always loved her, but admitting it opened up the possibility of losing her. But hadn't he already lost her out of his stubborn refusal to own his emotions?

'I can't. It's a thing I can't seem to push past.' He shook his head and let out a whooshing sigh. 'I said it to Mum and Dad when they left for that weekend away, and look how that turned out.'

Jack rubbed at his jaw, the raspy sound of his stubble against his palm overly loud in the echoing silence. 'At least you said it to them. I never did, and I've regretted it ever since.' There was a heaviness to his tone that Jago had never heard in his brother's voice before. Jack the joker. Jack the quick-witted sarcastic one. Jack the cynical and jaded celebrity divorce lawyer who helped hundreds of clients end their relationships. Jack being gravely serious was something Jago had rarely, if ever, seen.

A light bulb went off in Jago's head, shining a light

on his mistaken beliefs about himself, about love, about allowing himself to be vulnerable. What would have been worse? Saying *I love you* and never seeing the loved one again, or not saying it and never seeing them again? At least he had told his parents he loved them. Surely Jack had a much tougher regret to weigh him down. 'I'm sorry, Jack. That must be hard to live with.'

Another shrug. 'Life sucks sometimes, hey?' Jack picked up his glass again and took another sip. He lowered the glass from his mouth and looked at Jago. 'As far as I'm concerned, Jonas is the one who missed out the most. He can barely remember Mum and Dad. At least we had a few years with them.'

'Yeah… I guess…' Jago unlocked his hands from the back of his chair.

'So what's the plan? Should I dust off my best man's suit?' A crooked smile lifted the edges of Jack's mouth.

'You mean you still have it?'

'It's a bespoke design. It cost me a freaking fortune. Of course I still have it.'

Jago smiled, a weight coming off his shoulders that made him feel light-headed and excited in a way he had never felt before. 'You'd better bring champagne the next time we catch up.'

'Will do.'

'Now, how about we have some champagne?' Elsie said as she and Mollie sat in front of a sumptuous feast that had just been delivered to Elsie's room.

Mollie gave the old lady a concerned look. 'Should you be drinking alcohol with your memory problems?'

Elsie's eyes twinkled. 'There's nothing wrong with my memory. Not since the before party.'

Mollie stared at her wide-eyed. 'Before the party? But I thought—'

'It's true I lost part of my memory for a short time, but I regained it without telling anyone. Jago, bless him, wanted to be with you, and my fall and my concussion gave him the perfect excuse to convince you to come to Wildewood with him. I was so convinced it would give you both time to fall in love all over again, but I shouldn't have meddled.' She made a regretful little moue with her mouth and continued. 'I'm sorry it didn't work out for you both. I'm furious with Maxwell for what he did to break you up. You're the first person Jago has ever fallen for, and it's so tragic you're not together. I was hoping my birthday weekend would fix everything, but I have a feeling I've only made things worse.'

Mollie reached for Elsie's hand and gave it a gentle squeeze. 'You didn't do anything wrong. It was sweet of you to try, but Jago isn't in love with me. He has never told me he loved me, not the first time around, nor the second. He just wants a marriage partner without being in love with her. I can't be with him unless I truly believe he loves me. I have craved being loved my whole life.'

'Oh, my dear girl,' Elsie said with tears glimmering in her eyes. 'You sound just like me as a young woman. I settled for financial security with Maxwell and devoted my life to our son James to make up for what I lacked from my husband. But then darling James was taken from me, and I couldn't think of leaving Maxwell, even though I was so miserably unhappy. But raising Jago and Jack and Jonas gave my life a purpose. I know this sounds deluded of me, but Maxwell does love each of us in his way. He was never taught to be open with his feelings. He finds emotions very threatening because his father was exactly the same. He punished Maxwell for showing any sign of weakness, which in those days meant showing any sort of emotion or vulnerability. And he particularly finds deep love terrifying and thinks it's more of an obsession than true love. I've tried to break the cycle, but I'm afraid each of the boys struggle with being emotionally available.'

'I can't settle for that sort of marriage,' Mollie said. 'I love Jago with all my heart, but I don't want to be always looking over my shoulder, wondering when he is going to find someone else. I need full commitment. I need to be loved in return.'

'Of course you do. Everyone does. Jago was hit so hard by losing his parents. Jack was always a tough kid, resilient and strong-willed, and he seemed to cope so much better, although who really knows what mark it's left. Jago was more sensitive and emotional, but of course, after the accident, he shut down completely. Jonas was too young to really remember much, although he must remember it on some level. Even before James and Alice were killed, Jonas was always a serious little boy. They say trauma changes the architecture of children's brains, and I can well believe it. Those darling boys all changed after losing their parents.'

'I'm so sorry. They were so lucky to have you as their grandmother.'

Elsie gave a wistful smile. 'I'd feel even luckier if you were my granddaughter-in-law. But I've done enough meddling. I can only be there for you in any way you need.'

'Thank you. You're so kind.'

There was a sharp knock at the door.

'Oh, that will be the champagne I ordered earlier.' Elsie's expression looked chagrined. 'Perhaps you'd better answer the door and cancel it. I gave Harriet the night off so you and I could spend time together alone.'

Mollie rose to her feet and went across to open the door to the room service staff. But when she opened the door, she saw Jago standing there holding a bottle of champagne and three glasses on a tray. Mollie stared at him, her mouth falling open in shock, her heart leaping to her throat. 'What are you doing here?' she asked in a tone laced with surprise and a tiny sprinkling of hope.

'I'm joining my two most favourite people in the world for dinner,' Jago said. 'Sorry I'm late. Three weeks late, to be precise.' There was a smile in his eyes, and his mouth was curved in a way that made her heart swell with renewed hope and a flood of joy.

Mollie stepped back to allow him in. 'Is your grandmother in on this visit?'

'No. But I'm happy she's here to witness my proposal.'

'Proposal?' Mollie blinked at him. 'I gave you my answer three weeks ago.'

Jago closed the door with his foot and walked farther into the suite. 'Third time lucky, as they say. Hi, Gran.' He put the tray on a side table and then turned to bend down to kiss his grandmother. 'You don't mind me gatecrashing your dinner with my future bride?'

'Not at all, my darling boy,' Elsie said, eyes shining brighter than the crystal chandeliers in the suite.

Jago turned to Mollie and took both of her hands in his. 'Will you forgive me for taking this long to realise I love you with all my heart and soul?'

Mollie's eyes stung with the threat of tears. Happy, joyous tears. 'You're the first person to ever say that to me.'

'I know, and I'm kicking myself for not saying it two years ago, let alone three weeks back. Will you marry me, my one true love? Please say *yes*. I love, love, love you and want to spend the rest of my life proving it to you.'

Mollie couldn't hold her tears back any longer. She threw herself into his waiting arms, relishing how tightly they came around to hold her close to his thudding heart. The heart that had finally unlocked to let her in. 'I love you too, so much, more than I can ever say.'

Jago tilted up her chin so her gaze met his. 'I can't wait to be married to you. I've missed you so much. I can't believe I've been so blind to my own emotions, but I've always locked them away, so terrified of allowing myself to feel anything for anyone in case they were ripped away from me. But stupidly, I allowed that to happen two years ago. I realise now if I had told you what I felt for you, things might have panned out differently. You would have trusted me and come to me when my grandfather manipulated things to get you to go away. Can you forgive me? I don't deserve it, I know. I can't believe what an arrogant prick I've been, asking you to marry me two years ago and not even mentioning how I felt about you. But I'd locked my heart away so long ago, I could hardly recognise my own feelings.

But they're real, my love, so very real. I love you and want you by my side forever.'

Mollie hugged him again, leaning her cheek on his broad chest, finally feeling safe and loved and treasured. She had waited her whole life for this moment, and it was a dream come true that it was Jago who had made her feel so loved and wanted. 'I probably shouldn't have put so much emphasis on you saying the words. Your actions were there all the time, but I didn't think they were enough.'

Jago lifted her chin once more. 'I promise to spend my lifetime showing you how much I love you.' He bent down and pressed a lingering kiss to her mouth, sweeping her away on a cloud of happiness that was unrivalled in her experience of life to date.

'Is anyone going to open this champagne?' Elsie piped up with a smile in her voice.

Jago laughed and released Mollie to do the honours with the champagne. 'Sorry to keep you waiting, Gran, but I had important business to see to.'

'Don't mind me,' Elsie said with a fairy godmother twinkle in her eyes. 'Let's have a quick toast to your and Mollie's future, and then I'll retire to bed and you can go to Mollie's room and finish your so-called business.'

Mollie could feel a blush blooming on her cheeks, but she was thrilled that Elsie was the first to congratulate them. Jago poured three glasses of the bubbling champagne and handed her one, and then one to his grandmother, before holding his against Mollie's and his gran's. 'To love and being loved.'

'To love and being loved,' Mollie and Elsie echoed and sipped from their from flutes.

'There's one other proposal I have for you,' Jago said. 'This hotel is one of my investment properties, and I've just finished refurbishing it. It's only been open a few weeks.'

'Elsie just told me about that a few minutes ago,' Mollie said then gave him a searching look. 'Were you behind the Cinderella ticket?'

Jago's eyes glinted. 'Do I look like Prince Charming to you?'

'Yes,' Mollie laughed. 'You're my Prince Charming.' She was still having trouble believing this was happening, that all her dreams were coming true. She wanted to pinch herself, but she didn't want to let go of Jago. It was so wonderful to be held in his arms and know she was there to stay there forever.

'Are you enjoying the skin care conference?' he asked.

'Very much so. It's one of the best training seminars I've ever been to.'

'Well, the proposal I have, my fourth at last count, is for you to take over the management of the day spa in this hotel. Are you interested?'

Mollie gulped back a sob of undiluted joy. 'Are you serious?'

'Perfectly serious.' Jago bent his head to press another loving kiss to Mollie's mouth, finally easing back to gaze down at her with his dark blue eyes gleaming with happiness. 'As much as I'd love to marry you tomorrow, I think we should wait until Jonas gets back from his top-secret mission. Do you mind waiting another few weeks until we hear from him?'

Mollie smiled up at him, her heart almost bursting with joy. 'I'll try and be patient.'

'That reminds me.' He released her momentarily to take out a ring box from inside his jacket pocket. He prised it open and slipped the sapphire-and-diamond engagement ring on her left ring finger.

'Is it real?' Mollie asked with a cheeky smile.

'As real as my love,' Jago said and bent his head to kiss her once more.

'*Ahem*,' Elsie said after a long moment.

Jago and Mollie pulled apart to smile at her. 'Sorry, Gran. Are we boring you?' Jago asked with a grin.

'Not at all, my darling boy, but I think I need to finish my tipple and then let you two lovebirds have some privacy, don't you?' Elsie's smile was teasing but also full of happiness that shone as brightly as the ring on Mollie's finger.

Mollie slipped out of Jago's hold to press a soft kiss on Elsie's cheek. 'Thank you for your part in bringing us back together. You are my fairy godmother.'

Jago put his arm around Mollie's waist and smiled down at his grandmother. 'You had me completely fooled, but Jack was on to you from the start.'

'Yes, well, Jack is nobody's fool, but I couldn't bear to see you so unhappy, darling,' Elsie said. 'But it all turned out brilliantly in the end.'

Jago wrapped his arms around Mollie once more. 'Yes, it did.' And he lowered his mouth to kiss her once more.

* * * * *

PRINCE SHE SHOULDN'T CRAVE

KALI ANTHONY

MILLS & BOON

To Lissanne, friend, author bestie and
fellow lover of royal romance.

Thank you for helping me stay on track and
motivated, and for being there in the hard times
as well as the fun ones.

Here's to many more royal romances between us.

CHAPTER ONE

GABRIEL MONTROY SLIPPED a monogrammed gold cufflink into the pristine white cuff of his shirt. Clipped it into place, tugged at one sleeve, then the other, adjusting them both. He glanced at a few of the more odious Halrovian tabloids tossed carelessly on a coffee table in his personal suite, the stark black headlines meaningless patterns against the dusky paper. He didn't have the time or the energy to try reading them this morning.

'What do they say today, Pieter?'

His valet sniffed.

'The same as ever, Your Highness. No worse, no better.'

That didn't bode well. Whilst the more traditional media remained staunch supporters of the Montroy royal family, over the past year something in the tabloids had turned. Morphing from overblown yet generally benign commentary to something darker, nastier. Once, he'd agreed with his parents about ignoring them, in a time where the news stories had tended to be more about titillation than truth. Then they'd evolved from being an irritating mosquito that could be quelled with a swat, to a venomous spider weaving a toxic web of lies…

Gabe did up the top button of his shirt, slowly fastening himself into place. His valet handed him a gleaming silk tie. 'The darker blue today, sir. I believe it conveys a sense of leadership, without appearing overtly intimidating.'

Gabe had no interest in colour theory, or whatever Pieter called it. He was Crown Prince of Halrovia. A position that was to be upheld with authority and confidence. His family was supposed to be the country's bedrock. Him, its fresh foundation. Instead, the press seemed intent on rumour and innuendo. More recently about his sisters, and now him. Heir apparent to the Montroy Crown. Once dubbed the Proper Prince, that moniker now used to disparage rather than to praise.

Something needed to change in the way his image was managed. Whereas his parents and their press secretary wanted everything to stay the same, he recognised that now was not the time to play safe. They—*he*—needed to take a risk. He'd known what that was like once. He'd been all about the risk and resulting reward. Gabe wasn't sure why the thought had his heart pumping as if he'd run down a football field, the opposition chasing him down. Attempting to tackle him as he made his way to the goal...

Gabriel tried to ignore the sensation, that frisson of a memory. Those days were long behind him. Instead he lifted his collar and draped the tie around his neck, tying it in a knot. Tightening it, adjusting it. Loosening it a fraction. It had begun to feel like a noose. Yet there was no point to these thoughts. He'd accepted the price he'd had to pay for those days as captain of Halrovia's national under-twenty-one's football team. When he'd lived life a little too full. Been justifiably cocky, untouchable, until he'd trusted someone who hadn't deserved the privilege.

He shrugged on his jacket, then turned to the mirror. Tugging his shirtsleeves again so his cuffs sat perfectly even, his persona firmly in place. He took a deep, slow breath, allowing himself to remember, and in some ways regret, the innocence and ignorance of his late teens.

'Read me *one*. The most egregious.'

His valet walked to the coffee table, sifted through a few of the papers as if there were something dirty on them.

'*"Are Minor Scandals Hinting at Bigger Secrets? The Nation Wonders..."*'

Any scandals were wishful thinking in the minds of the tabloid's editors. Secrets, however... He'd held on to his own since childhood. Was protected by his parents when its disclosure threatened the myth of perfection that was his family.

'That headline doesn't meet the definition of egregious.'

'In the sub-heading there's talk of a palace source expressing concerns that opinion ratings of the royal family are falling, which might lead the public to clamour for a... *republic*.'

Pieter almost spat out the word as if it were spoiled food in his mouth.

'Which is why I have a plan to reverse that alleged sentiment.'

'Then I trust the interview goes well, sir.'

Gabe nodded. Slipped in some earbuds, grabbed his mobile phone and opened the text-to-speech app, listening once again to the CV his private secretary had downloaded for him as he made his way to his palace office. Someone to manage his image, since giving his youth and his life working for the crown didn't seem to be enough.

He shut down the prickle of resentment at that thought and concentrated on the history and achievements of the person he was about to interview. Someone recommended by his sister, Priscilla. Last on the list, after he'd seen and discounted several polished but uninspiring candidates. Cilla raved about the woman who'd worked with her for around nine months on PR and the social media accounts of the Isolobello royal family, after Cilla moved there following her engagement to their Crown Prince. He wasn't so enthusiastic. Whilst her references were impressive, any tertiary studies were mysteriously absent.

Just like you.

He ignored that voice as he pushed through the doors of his office, checking the time. His situation was different. What he needed was someone to impress him. As he looked around a waiting area, he saw no one but his private secretary, Henri.

'She's late,' Gabe said.

Strike one, if he was looking for reasons not to hire the woman. He was *never* late. In Gabe's view, a lack of punctuality was a result of poor planning and lack of consideration.

'If it's any consolation, sir, she called sounding suitably panicked. It seemed genuine, and Security tell me she has arri—'

The door to the anteroom burst open. Gabe and his secretary turned as in rushed a whirlwind in black and white. A woman, grappling an overstuffed handbag as she hauled it up her shoulder and straightened her jacket, before stilling as if some forest creature caught in a hunter's sights. Her ocean-blue gaze connected with his, her eyes widening. The shock of that vivid colour trapped him, and he couldn't look away. Then he caught her scent, like hot chocolate and spice. It teased his senses, made his mouth water as if she might be the perfect dessert, which of course was nonsensical. Then a strange heat burst inside his chest, radiating outwards. He had the irresistible desire to tug at his tie and loosen it further as the room grew too warm.

What the hell? Perhaps he should get his private secretary to check the air-conditioning.

'I—I…' The woman glanced from him to his private secretary and back again.

'Your Highness,' Henri said with a quizzical kind of look on his face. 'Ms Lena Rosetti.'

Ms Rosetti seemed to compose herself. She dipped into a deep and perfect curtsey. His body's reaction was immediate and brutal, like a kick to the solar plexus. A physical blow he required all his years of royal training to not show, and that was even before his mind had really registered the full sense of her rather than the parts he'd first noticed. Her fathomless eyes. Her intoxicating perfume.

The picture then began to click into place, almost as if his brain were putting her together like a jigsaw puzzle. There was nothing outstanding about her appearance. A black suit. Shop bought, because he *knew* tailoring, but nicely fitted. Her jacket buttoned up high, crisp white shirt, dull flat shoes that looked out of place with the outfit. Black hair pulled back in a severe bun. Totally unremarkable, except for her eyes, and yet he was like a tuning fork just struck. He vibrated.

'We have a problem.'

The words simply spilled out of him with no thought to his illogical reaction to her. Her soft pink mouth opened into a perfect O. She reached up her hand almost as a reflex as if to tuck some stray hair behind her ear. Ms Rosetti had long, elegant fingers, though why that observation was of any consequence he couldn't say. Then she seemed to hesitate, as if realising there was no stray hair to be put back into place. Instead, she rustled about her handbag. Tugged something out, held it up.

'I broke a heel.'

He was assailed by her voice, its softness, like a caress. The melodic sound of her accent signalled she was from the country of Isolobello with its Latin roots, being an island state off the coast of Italy. Where his sister Cilla now lived, and would become future Queen when she married Prince Caspar in a number of months.

Luckily Ms Rosetti was oblivious to the sensations warring inside him, or that his words had been meant to convey another meaning entirely. That it wasn't her lateness, but his reaction to her, that was the real issue. Then he looked at what she held in her hand. A stiletto. Black. Patent leather. The type of shoe that would make the calves of any woman wearing it swell in a distracting kind of way. Heels seductively lengthening her legs.

The type of shoes a man might ask a woman to leave on, not take off.

Gabe tried to ignore the burn of heat that once again roared over him. Instead, he concentrated on the broken heel that was, indeed, dangling from the shoe.

A faint wash of colour drifted across her cheeks. Did something show on his face? The strange desire that hit like a kick in the gut again? He needed to rein it in. Time he'd been spending trying to quell the negative press had meant a case of all work and no play. Though for Gabe, since his early twenties, any amount of 'play' had always been intensely discreet. He'd been taught a painful lesson of what might occur if you let the wrong person get too close. The ideas that fertile imaginations could conjure. Now, he had a firm rule. Don't subject a woman to the glare of the spotlight unnecessarily if she was never going to be his wife.

'Put the footwear away, Ms Rosetti. I demand punctuality of my employees, and of myself.'

'It's why I was late. I—I twisted my ankle on the cobblestones on the way and had to find alternative shoes.' She looked down at her feet and his gaze followed. She seemed to wiggle her toes in her uninspiringly practical flat shoes, but his attention locked on her elegant slender ankles. Ones that his hands might encircle easily.

This wouldn't do. What he needed was to contact one of the few friends with benefits he kept. Women who enjoyed pleasure for the evening and would go on their way. No expectations from either of them. He knew there was a certain cache in the aristocracy with being his lover, even if it would never come to anything. All he needed to do was make a call. Engage in an evening of mutual, adult pleasure.

He had no idea why, right now, that thought held no interest. Yet the recesses of his errant brain finally registered her words. Had she hurt herself? What was he thinking? Nothing sensible at all, clearly.

'Do you require medical attention?'

She shook her head. 'No, thank you, sir.'

He strangely liked the way she called him sir, even though all his staff used the term. What would it be like to hear her say his name? Gabriel… Gabe.

Impossible.

This was meant to be an interview. An audition of sorts, but not one for a lover.

'Come into my office. Take a seat.'

He turned and led the way. Trying to ignore the prickle at the back of his neck indicating she was close.

He lowered himself into his own chair. Blue tie be damned. He clasped his hands in front of him. Fixed her with a glare. The one he usually reserved for more recalcitrant advisors of state, which people might describe as *overtly* intimidating. She was to be in charge of his *image*. One that was very personal to him. Further, anyone who worked so closely with him might come to know secrets. Some he'd prefer weren't exposed.

'One hint. I value punctuality…'

'But—'

He held up his hand. She stopped speaking. '...and preparedness.'

'So do I,' she shot straight back, then seemed to pull into herself. Adjusted her shapely jacket, which remained buttoned closed.

'I'm a reasonable employer. However, I have high expectations.'

She nodded. Short, sharp and businesslike. 'I understand.'

'Excellent. Then let's begin. I have questions.' So many questions. Whilst she came highly recommended, she seemed underqualified for the role. 'You've read the brief?'

To improve his relatability. One day he'd rule the country. Need to make hard and sometimes impossible decisions. To do that required inner strength...steel. None of it would be helped by him effectively being a 'nice guy' about it.

'Of course. I have a question of my own, if I may?'

His eyebrows rose. She liked to think she could take charge here? Something about the challenge of it all set his pulse rate thumping like he'd just taken a run.

'Be my guest,' he said, injecting a warning note of dryness into his voice.

She seemed to ignore his tone as she rummaged about her bag and pulled out a tablet. Flicked through a few screens and drew up some photographs, then slid it across the desktop to him.

'I think this is who you need to show the world. My question for you is, where is this person?'

Gabe looked at the pictures on the screen. The rapid hum of his heart stilled. Photographs of him a long time ago, from his late teens and into twenty. An ache bloomed deep inside his chest. Holding the world championship cup aloft, yellow and blue confetti in colours of Halrovia's flag fluttering down over him and his team as they celebrated their win. Shots of him out somewhere, leaving some function. Smiling for the cameras in a way that seemed totally unfamiliar. A young woman on his arm.

That woman… The press speculation had been intense but she'd wanted so much more from him than he could ever have given. A daughter of an aristocrat who clearly had expectations of a royal future, her family too, when all he'd wanted was… Gabe hadn't been sure. To be seen as something more? His difficulty reading had crippled him at school. For so long Gabe had been thought of as lazy, he'd begun to believe he would never make a decent king when it was his time. Never achieving what his parents or teachers had expected of him.

Then came the diagnosis, yet the only result from the King and Queen was steely silence. His dyslexia barely talked about, efficiently swept under the ancient rugs of the royal palace. And so he talked, not to his family, but to the person he thought of as his girlfriend, even if he hadn't contemplated any real future with her. Then, when that youthful relationship came to its inevitable end, after her tears, the threats started. That she'd tell everyone he'd be a useless king because he couldn't read. Had she and her family believed she might be Queen one day and been trying to blackmail him into reversing the break-up? He couldn't be sure. All he knew was his parents and the royal machine surrounding them took her threats seriously.

He didn't want to think about the consequences of that time because he and his family were still living them. The steps his parents took to quell the rumours. The prices paid. Some by his family, mostly by him. Forgoing the life he'd wanted for one of duty, so nobody could question his commitment to the crown. Especially if he spent all his time learning from his father how to be King.

In that time, the Proper Prince was born.

Still, these weren't conversations he would deign to have with a person he hadn't yet decided to employ.

'He grew up,' Gabriel said, pushing the tablet back towards her, dismissing the unwanted memories. 'Now for my questions.'

Time to bring this interview back under his tight control. Ms Rosetti didn't seem to be put off. She straightened herself, tugged at her jacket and her jaw firmed, as if preparing for some kind of battle.

He couldn't help but admire her resolve.

'You have no university qualifications in marketing, PR or social media. Yet you're asking me to trust you with what some see as the future of my family in the eyes of its people.' Lena Rosetti sat perfectly still. The only giveaway? The slender line of her neck convulsed in a swallow. 'What makes you believe you can provide me with value that's superior, when I have other candidates who are formally qualified?'

Lena's heart punched into her ribs. She swallowed, damp palms clutching at the leather of her handbag still sitting on her lap. Questioning some of her life choices. Why had she decided to be forward and show him those photographs of himself? Why had she shown him her *shoe*? In her defence she was a little overwhelmed because, in the flesh, Prince Gabriel looked too good to be entirely human. Sure, she'd seen plenty of photos of him during her research. But no picture could do him real justice. He was almost supernaturally handsome, in a way that turned her normally quite functional brain to custard. If gods walked the earth, she reckoned they'd look just like Prince Gabriel.

Which was her reminder, he wasn't a god but a man. Who'd apparently *'grown up'* and *'valued punctuality'*. He wouldn't care about her broken heel. It was obvious by the way he'd looked at her when she'd pulled it out of her handbag, as if that would have helped when trying to explain why she was late. The sheer intensity of his gaze had made her go all hot and cold and every temperature in between. That look in his eyes speaking of what?

Disdain. She was sure.

Lena was used to that look, back in her home country of Isolobello. Had fought against it for most of her twenty-three years. It was how so many people at her exclusive private school had looked at her for the temerity of being fatherless. Oh, she'd had a father. An absent one. A high-profile one. A man never named, publicly at least. That had been the arrangement. He'd kept her mother in a lifestyle she'd become accustomed to for all the years of their long-term affair. He'd kept his second family, the illegitimate family, in the shadows. Secret from everybody.

Then he'd died just three months earlier. Suddenly. Shockingly. Soon after, their life had imploded. The half-brother she'd never met had arrived on their doorstep stating that 'the gravy train', as he so crudely had put it, was over. Her mother could keep her jewels and whatever gifts she'd been given during her father's life and that was all. Her father hadn't recognised her family in his will. As far as the legitimate family was concerned, Lena, her mother and her brother didn't exist. The sour taste of bile rose to Lena's throat. He'd said they were a dirty stain on a great man's legacy.

Which was why she *needed* this role. Lena's whole future relied on it. To keep her younger brother in education so he could make something of himself. To support her mother so she wouldn't end up destitute, on the street. And if she didn't pull herself together, it seemed as if it might slip through her fingers.

'I'd hoped my references spoke for themselves. Each employer I've worked for showed an increase in business due to my efforts.'

Prince Gabriel narrowed his eyes. 'That may be so, yet your career didn't start in managing people's images and PR. You seem to have fallen into the role by chance rather than design.'

'There is a divinity that shapes our ends, rough-hew them how we will.'

A quote from Shakespeare, often used by one of her favourite teachers, a woman whose wisdom she missed. Especially when her mother's idea for solving their current crisis was for Lena to find a wealthy man and either advantageously marry or become a well-cared-for mistress, just as she'd been, and provide for the family. Her mother had even named possible males who might be in the market.

The prospect of this job had fallen into her lap at exactly the right time. The universe was telling her the role was hers, she just needed to secure it.

'You're correct. In my first job I was employed to wait café tables, but my employer asked me to post some pictures on social media. Their page became hugely popular and people started flooding to the café because of the vibe we showed them on the social channels.'

She was only nineteen when she started that job. One her mother said she didn't need, but Lena had wanted anyhow. To have money and something of her own, not handed to her by an absent father. Lena got a buzz from how big the café's page had become, how customers came in because they'd seen *her* posts. But what she'd said didn't seem to impress Prince Gabriel. He raised one strong, dark eyebrow. A contrast to his hair, which was a magnificent, tamed mane of burnished gold.

'And yet should you succeed in this interview you'd be managing more than my…vibe.'

His image and his 'vibe' were kind of the same thing, in her opinion anyhow, but she wasn't about to disagree with him.

'My next job was more intentional.' A florist and gift shop supporting local artisans from Isolobello. Whilst working in the gift shop there, Lena had suggested a bigger social media presence. Posting pictures of the glorious blooms. Featuring the work of various creators. 'Through my efforts, their business became extremely popular and drew the attention of your sister, who'd come into the store *because* she'd seen my posts on social media showcasing my employer's values in supporting lesser-known artists.'

'I believe the person you're meaning to refer to, Ms Rosetti, is *Princess Priscilla*.'

'Of course, Your Highness.'

Heat crept up her neck, prickling where the tag of her loathsome black jacket scratched her skin. She tugged at the collar, but that didn't seem to help much. Lena found it hard to think of Prince Gabriel's sister as a princess. *Cilla*, as she'd demanded to be called within five minutes of meeting Lena, didn't care one bit about royal titles. They'd quickly struck up an easy kind of friendship. When Lena decided it was time to move on from her job in the florist's, Cilla had suggested a role in Isolobello's palace as a junior in their social media and PR department.

'Would you care to remove your jacket, Ms Rosetti?' Prince Gabriel asked. His voice deep and rich like the hot chocolate she loved to drink as a treat when something had gone well. 'Whilst this is a professional workplace, they're not always required.'

She didn't believe him. This man looked so tightly buttoned up she'd almost bet that he'd have to be cut out of his suit each evening. Then, each morning, a new one would be stitched right back onto his fine, *fine* body.

Fine body? Where had *that* thought come from?

'Thank you, n-no. I—I'm quite comfortable.'

She was anything but. And although she wanted to accept his invitation and tear off her jacket with every fibre of her existence, she couldn't. On the way to the palace, she'd had a cup of coffee, hoping the caffeine would give her a bit of a boost. She should have known that wearing a white shirt was an invitation to spill something on it. If she took off her jacket now, His Royal Highness would see a good portion of her shirt indelibly stained, because of her clumsiness. Something her mother always complained about.

'You're as elegant as a newborn donkey. Glide, Lena. Glide like a swan.'

Lena bet her mother had never seen a newborn donkey. Yet she shouldn't be thinking about spilled coffee or stuttering or blushing. She should be answering his questions. This job was a stepping stone to securing her family's future. To even bigger, better things.

Lena took a steadying breath. She knew how to do this. She'd prepared for it, the possible questions. The answers she needed to give.

'Earlier, sir, you pointed out my lack of university qualifications. I respect a formal education.' More than respected it, she'd craved it, had seen it as a way to avoid what had befallen her beautiful, unqualified mother. Her parents hadn't seen the point of a degree in PR and marketing, suggesting something like art history which Lena had no interest in. But they'd finally capitulated after she simply applied to her university of choice and been accepted, even if she had started her degree far later than her peers. When Lena had been forced to give up her own studies after her father had died, it had been a crushing sacrifice. 'However, the job you're asking me to do requires creativity, and a deep understanding of the audience you're trying to connect with. As I assess the role, I *am* the audience. You're trying to connect with someone like *me*.'

Prince Gabriel cocked his head. Narrowed his gaze. She felt skewered to the spot. Rather like a butterfly pinned to a board by an icicle.

'Am I, Ms Rosetti?'

Lena froze. Did she really say that? Him, *connecting* with her? What was she thinking? The truth was, not much at all. Everything about him seemed so intentional and planned that he discombobulated her. His frigid blue tie matching icy blue eyes that the Montroy family were famed for. His shirt, white like hers, but unmarred by coffee. Impeccably pressed. Not a wrinkle to be seen. In fact, no wrinkle would *dare*. He was so perfect she was terrified that if she got too close her clumsiness would overwhelm her and she'd somehow manage to spill something on him, like the untouched mug that was sitting on his desk.

Yet if she allowed herself to be distracted by all of this—all of him—she'd fail, then where would she be left? She didn't want a relationship like her mother had had, or a marriage to some rich man who sought her out because of her age, her looks and—if they found out—her cursed virginity.

Lena shuddered and pulled herself together.

'That's what your brief said. That you're looking at connecting with younger people and I'm young—'

'*How* young?'

'The demographic your job description said you wanted to target is eighteen to twenty-five and I'm twenty-three. I'm at the upper end.'

'And how do you suppose I'm to…connect? You've given me no answers, only more questions as to why you're better than any other potential candidate for the role.'

Lena sat up a bit straighter. Whatever this man thought or said, she was *good* at what she did. And she'd been working informally and then formally in this type of role since her first job. In her favour, Lena also knew what it was like working for royalty. Sure, getting the job with Isolobello's royal family had been more luck rather than planning. As for this job, Cilla had said her brother *needed* someone like Lena. And she'd happily move to Halrovia permanently if it meant a step up in responsibility and income.

'You might recall the announcement of Prince Caspar's engagement. The celebration weekend. Isolobello's Crown Prince finally set to marry.'

Prince Gabriel sat back in his seat, a little more relaxed. The corner of his perfect mouth curling in what threatened to be a smile but never quite made it. She wanted to see him smile and dreaded it all the same, because if he smiled, every available and inclined woman on the planet would become utterly infatuated with him. Give him one shred of warmth and people wouldn't be able to help themselves.

She didn't know why that thought made acid churn in her gut.

'I do recall, given, as you so eloquently put it before, Prince Caspar's fiancée is *my sister*.'

She knew then that he was trying to be…princely. Lena's job was to stop him hiding behind his title and start showing the world Gabriel Montroy, even though it was clear that he wasn't at all keen on the idea.

'My colleagues wanted a more traditional approach. A few formal engagement photos. Talk of the joining of two long-term allies. I thought the moment was more important than that—'

'More important than the hundreds of years of history between the House of Santori and the House of Montroy?'

His voice was as brittle as the first winter ice cracking in spring. It sounded a warning. She ignored it.

'Yes, and Her Royal Highness agreed.'

When Lena had made her pitch about what she'd thought should happen with the royal announcement, no one had been much on board with her suggestions. Except Cilla. She'd been Lena's greatest supporter.

'The event required something more, because it was a story about love,' she said.

So clearly in Lena's mind, since everyone had believed that Prince Caspar had been going to marry Cilla's older sister, Anastacia. Princess Priscilla was a huge surprise, until you saw the couple together. Then you knew. There could be no doubt that theirs was a relationship meant to be.

Lena wasn't looking for a relationship *at all*. She had trouble trusting one. As far as she was concerned, they seemed like a trap after what had happened to her mother, ostensibly for love. Then her father, and how he'd treated his wife. In the end, he'd really betrayed two women. Sure, she'd dabbled at university with a few boys her age when they'd asked her out, but none had appealed because she'd been so focussed on her studies. Then there were the older men who wanted to possess her for no other reason than she was young, and they thought her beautiful. She'd had limited but enough experience of those sorts too. Particularly some customers in one of her jobs. The things said. Notes left for her… Her skin crawled at the memories as if there were spiders trapped underneath. Lena was looking for a future she was in control of. Not one at the behest of a man who supplied fleeting moments of himself, and money, but nothing else.

She was enough. Lena Rosetti, on her own.

All she needed to do was catch this job as if her life depended on it. She narrowed her eyes. There was a role here. She just had to convince Prince Gabriel she was the best person for it.

'Other members of the team all talked about the past. But it was also a story about Isolobello's *future*. I wanted a behind-the-scenes view of the new couple. Featuring the woman who was going to become our queen one day. The royal family's social media sites showed a significant increase in engagement but, most importantly, there was overwhelmingly positive feedback from the younger demographic.'

'I've no great story about love or any betrothal to improve the Montroy royal family's metrics. *My* future is about ensuring *Halrovia's* future.'

'But everyone has a story. You just need to know how to tell a good one.'

You need me...

Where had that thought come from? She was manifesting, that was all. Taking what his sister had said and running with it.

Prince Gabriel sat back in his chair, held his arms out. 'How would you tell mine, *better*?'

He had such an aura of authority. There was no way you could mistake this man for anything other than a leader but there was more to it than that. It almost hurt your eyes to look at him, he was so imposing, so...breathtaking. His looks alone would be enough to garner a following with the right kind of posts, if that were the audience the family were after. A few shirtless shots and...

No. She wasn't here to sell him as some kind of thirst trap. She'd done her research. She knew about his *work*. His past as a young football player leading his country to an international championship. That was the sort of thing that people could get excited about. Even her blood had pumped a bit harder and the room had got strangely warm when she'd looked at the photographs of that long ago win. But he hadn't really answered where that man had gone. Sure, everyone grew up. But a lot of people continued to celebrate their past achievements. Had he disappeared under the weight of his role? It was hard to tell. Though it was clear, the future of the royal family was this man in front of her. Still, one thing stood out to her...

'To date, the story hasn't been about you, though. It's been about your role within the royal family. People only see you as part of a whole. A cog in a wheel.'

Something about him changed with those words. She didn't know what it was, but it seemed as though the man in front of her had been wearing a mask, which had suddenly melted away. She caught a glimpse of something more. The glint in his eyes of a person excited by possibilities. Because that was the first thing that had struck her when this role had been suggested to her. The world needed to see the man, not just the prince in official photographs from the palace. Maybe he wanted that too...

Her mind began working at capturing him in a more casual way. Behind the scenes. She loved taking photographs on her phone of the unscripted moments in life. Not just shaking hands with some foreign dignitary but turning Prince Gabriel into the sort of person everyone would clamour to know. He'd been that once, in his late teens and early twenties. They just had to tap into it again.

Except she wasn't sure how. People often froze when she

held up her phone to take a photograph. Put on fake smiles. She'd checked the Halrovian royal family's social media accounts and they were *all* formality and fake smiles. Which was why her aim was to ensure that people were comfortable enough not to care about her being around them. So she tried to blend into the background, not to stand out.

Lena wondered if the man in front of her did anything less than formal, ever. He looked as if he were born in a suit. Maybe she could get him to loosen up a bit? Except there were no maybes. Her whole future depended on it. If she wasn't successful here, what was left for her?

'What changes do you propose?'

Prince Gabriel's question brought her back to the here and now. Not a future that she hadn't yet secured.

'You need your own social media accounts, to showcase *yourself* in your role as Crown Prince, not as part of the royal family.'

He checked his watch. A slender gold timepiece with a leather band. Not so showy, but something that screamed elegance and restraint. Ancient money. He was going to wind things up, she was sure. Her heart pounded a sickening, panicked rhythm. What if he sent her on her way without this job? What then? The role back in Isolobello didn't pay enough to support her and her family as it was a junior position. She needed something *more*.

Lena took a deep breath and settled her thoughts. She'd never really been to an interview like this before. Jobs had come to her because people perceived she had a talent. Yet she believed that the universe had been kind to her, given her opportunities. This was one now. Time to try being a little bold again.

'Your upcoming trip to Lauritania. May I ask what the royal family's social media team have planned?'

She'd seen the press announcing the trip. It hadn't all been positive, for some strange reason.

'It seems you've already asked. However, I'm unable to answer your question.'

'It'd be a perfect opportunity to introduce *you*, sir. Whilst I don't know the itinerary, I'm sure there'll be opportunities to show your life a little less scripted.'

Prince Gabriel narrowed his eyes. 'Let me be frank. I spend my life doing what I'm able for my country. That's the role I was born into. My consistent hard work for Halrovia should speak for itself…'

Lena's stomach dropped. He was going to let her go. What would she do now? Was a marriage of convenience to a rich man who saw her as a trophy whilst she mouldered in some grand home, dying inside every day, all that was left to her? Or perhaps a life like her mother's, mistress to a man who looked after her but didn't love her enough to *be* with her? Only catching snippets of the person you loved, yet not having all of him because that was the deal you'd struck with the devil. Her hands twisted restlessly in her lap. She tried to hold them still. Her prospective employer's face told her nothing.

'Yet it appears that my hard work and dedication doesn't mean anything at all. That I need more.'

He shuffled through some papers on his desk, straightened them. Clasped his hands on the desktop. He needed more?

'He needs you…' That's what Cilla had said.

'I'll give you a chance, Ms Rosetti, *only* because you come highly recommended by Princess Priscilla. Come on my tour to Lauritania. See what you can do. You're on probation for two months.' He fixed her with a stern, frigid gaze. 'Impress me.'

CHAPTER TWO

IF GABRIEL HAD thought that having someone managing his image would be harmless at best and an irritation at worst, he was wrong. It had only been a week and Lena Rosetti was driving him to distraction. Even worse, he was certain his parents wanted to exile her to the dungeons and order her execution, even though those kinds of punishments hadn't been utilised in Halrovia for centuries.

'Perhaps we could try the photograph with your jacket removed, Your Highness?'

Gabe wanted to pinch his nose against an impending headache. 'Why?'

'It'll make the picture feel slightly less formal. Younger audience? It'd be even better if you could roll up the sleeves of your shirt. Maybe remove your tie?'

She'd have him totally undressed soon. Would she blush if he removed more clothes? He enjoyed it when tinges of pink flushed her cheeks. Though Gabe didn't know why those thoughts entered his mind or why they seemed so enticing. He shook his head.

'You can have my jacket. The cuffs and the tie stay put.'

He stood. Shrugged out of his suit jacket under her watchful gaze. Was he mistaken, or did her eyes widen a fraction as he did? Lena came towards him with her hand held out and he passed her the jacket. As he did, their fingers brushed. It was like grabbing a live wire, the shock of sensation. Did she notice the same thing? He flexed his fingers, yet she seemed unaffected, taking the jacket and hanging it in a cupboard on the opposite wall.

'I am not removing *my* coat,' his father said.

'N-no, Your Majesty. I—I wasn't planning to make that request.'

'And why am I holding this compendium?' his father asked.

They'd been in Gabe's office for only fifteen minutes, trying to get the perfect shot as the photograph for the first social media post under his own name. For something supposed to be unscripted, this seemed to take a lot of directing.

Lena had initially asked Gabriel, his mother and father to simply talk whilst taking photographs on her phone. No photographers, she'd said. She wanted candid. That had been a disaster. Now, she was trying something else. Flitting about the office in her dark suit and distractingly bright golden yellow blouse, she looked like an overly industrious, somewhat harried, bee.

'Your Majesty, my idea is that I'll photograph you handing it to His Highness whilst Her Majesty watches on. The folder of what could be important papers signifies you "passing the baton", so to speak, to His Highness.'

Gabe's father narrowed his eyes. 'I am *not* passing the baton. The baton will pass when I do. Or should I decide to abdicate, neither of which events are in our near future.'

Lena didn't hesitate, which was a marvel in itself because his father's icy tone would have sent Halrovian courtiers scurrying. She appeared blissfully impervious or dangerously ignorant to her impending doom. The King treated the crown with deadly seriousness. In the past he'd expressed determination to be the longest-sitting monarch in Europe, if not the world. Not even Gabe would have suggested a photograph with Lena's intended implication.

'It's figurative, Your Majesty. Designed to show trust in His Highness.'

The King gripped the dark, official folder a little harder, cast a piercing glance at Gabe. The problem was, his parents had tried to keep everything under such tight control, kept so much hidden, that he wasn't sure that they did trust him. They'd never encouraged him to attend university. He'd suspected the reason was they hadn't believed he'd be successful in his studies, given his dyslexia. Wanting to avoid the inevitable questions should he fail, even though their formal excuse was that he could more easily learn how to be a good king from his father. He tried to ignore the sense that, in some ways, he was an impostor to the role of Crown Prince. But what were his years of training at his father's side, if *not* for the moment he'd finally take the throne?

Then there'd been an argument about him having an individual social media account as Crown Prince, as Lena had suggested. Managed by someone else other than the King and Queen's press secretary, not under the royal family's exclusive banner. In response, he'd fought hard for control of his own image. It had never mattered before. Gabe hadn't cared much at all, but the more control the royal machine tried to impose on him, the more he pushed back. He'd won, as he was always going to. Yet his parents weren't happy about it.

'Symbolism is important to a royal family, Miss Rosetti,' his mother said. Dressed in ice blue, her voice as frigid as the colour she wore.

Lena smiled as if impervious to the chill descending on the room. 'Which is why I would never ask His Majesty to hand over the sovereign's sceptre or the crown itself.'

Gabe knew what she wasn't saying. A folder made a statement, without really saying anything at all. It was all smoke and mirrors.

His father dropped said folder to the desk with a thud, displacing some of the supposed *important papers*. 'I don't like it.'

Lena's smile faltered. Something inside him burned with an angry heat at the look on her face. As if she'd somehow failed when, in truth, she was only trying to do her job.

She checked her phone. 'It's ten. Perhaps we could have a break for a few moments and resume with a new idea.'

'A coffee would be appreciated,' Gabe said. Preferably Irish, with a substantial swig of whisky.

'Of course, sir.' He liked the way she said that. The lilt of her accent. Her voice soft like the brush of a warm summer breeze against bare skin. 'Your Majesties?'

His father shook his head. His mother declined as well. Lena went to a carafe on the sideboard. Poured a cup, added a dash of sugar to take the edge off just as Gabe liked it. Took a little biscuit in some silver tongs and placed it on the saucer then walked to his desk. Today she was in heels, and he was transfixed by the way they made her hips sway gently as she walked. Though why he was even thinking about how she moved or how the skirt of her dark suit hugged her figure so well, he didn't dwell upon.

She was an employee, not a paramour.

Lena reached his desk and smiled as she carefully lowered the cup. The liquid inside trembled as she did, the cup overfull. As she placed it down the coffee sloshed over into the saucer, drowning the biscuit and overflowing onto the polished desktop. Her eyes widened.

'Oh, my goodness, I'm so sorry.' The words were said with such speed they almost became one. 'I—I—'

'Lena, it's all right.' He looked through the drawers of his desk and found some unused paper napkins and began mopping up the coffee whilst she looked at his parents, him, then picked up the cup and fled the room before he could provide some reassurance.

'That woman...' his mother said in Halrovian, which would have been unforgivably rude if Lena had still been with them—of course, his mother was never known for being overly polite to those significantly under her on the social ladder, who she didn't think in some way worthy '... is a hazard to the orderly running of your office.'

Lena was certainly something. A hazard to his equilibrium, the way she flitted about. Yet he felt strangely duty-bound to defend her.

'She comes highly recommended. Your private secretary endorsed her credentials. As did Priscilla.'

'Talk about handing over sceptres and crowns.' His mother sniffed.

'She was only asking Father to hand me a folder.'

'What are these important documents I'm supposed to be passing to you?'

His father picked up the embossed navy blue compendium from the desktop, opened it. Flicked over the first page. Stared for a moment. Began to chuckle. Closed the folder and handed it to Gabe. 'Indeed, most important.'

Gabe opened it as his parents looked on. Turned the page as his father had. There was a copy of a newspaper article. A headline, a picture of their greatest nemesis, masquerading as an advisor and supporter. Father to the young woman Gabriel had thought of as his girlfriend. Who'd seen fit to threaten betrayal of Gabe's trust because she wasn't going to end up as his queen. Awarding this man the position of Advisor of State was the price his parents had paid for his daughter's silence all those years ago. Except someone had scribbled on the picture in black. The man now had cartoonish horns. Dripping fangs. Flies buzzing round his head. He'd been turned into a comic villain.

Gabe shut the folder and glanced up at his father, who still looked entertained. Even his mother had a sparkle of amusement in her eyes. And there behind them, standing at the door with a faint wash of colour on her cheeks, stood Lena. Phone in hand.

Watching the scene with a look of something like guilt written all over her face.

Prince Gabriel's gaze locked on her, cold and assessing. Something about it made her shiver, but the sensation wasn't in any way unpleasant. What was he thinking? That he didn't like having his photograph taken without him knowing? Or had he seen her handiwork in the folder?

Nope, surely not. There was no need for him to look inside and when she'd snapped the winning picture the folder had been closed and everyone had been…amused. Maybe they'd been laughing about her. That his employee had all the grace and agility of a giant panda.

Heat rushed to her cheeks at the mortification of that thought. Lena cursed her clumsiness at almost spilling coffee all over her employer in front of his parents. In her defence, the King and Queen weren't an easy audience. She'd challenge anyone not to be a bumbling bundle of nerves around them, and she was *used* to royalty, given her past job. She'd despaired of getting the photograph she wanted. The one she'd imagined, an unscripted moment between monarchs and heir. If only she'd recognised earlier that all she'd needed to do was to leave the room to get the shot, it would have saved them time and a spilled drink.

Something about the realisation stung, that the only way Prince Gabriel might feel comfortable was if she wasn't there, but she was sensible enough to know that trust took time. Anyhow, she managed to get the shot she'd been looking for. The King chuckling at something and handing the folder to Gabriel. With the Queen standing on looking benevolent. It was the perfect moment. Looking warm and genuine even though the emotional temperature in the room had been about as balmy as the snowy peaks of the Alps in the distance.

'I think I have a photograph,' she said, lifting her phone and wiggling it as she came back into the room. As she approached Prince Gabriel's desk, Lena thought she heard his father mutter something that could have been *Thank God*, although she wasn't one hundred per cent certain. The King and Queen turned in unison to face her with the same assessing gaze as their son. Right now, with the three of them watching her with their matching icy blue eyes, it was rather like being trapped in a blizzard. Did she stay? Did she go? She decided to address the matter directly.

'Thank you for your time, Your Majesties. If there's anything you'd like to talk to His Highness about in private I can…' The looks the King and Queen gave her in that moment took Lena right back to her school days, when she was disdained by everyone for pretending not to know who her father was. It had stolen her confidence. Her voice. Instead of words, Lena pointed to the empty door and made walking movements with her fingers through the air. The King raised his eyebrows. The Queen watched on, stony.

'We're finished here,' Gabriel said. 'I'm sure Their Majesties have plenty to do today.'

Lena nodded. Curtseyed as his parents swept from the room without acknowledging her again.

After they'd left, her employer cocked an eyebrow. Then he lifted his hand and crooked his finger at her. 'Come here, Ms Rosetti. Sit.'

There was no question of not obeying his command. Something about the way his voice was so purposeful and stern caused another shiver to skitter over her skin, goosebumps following in its wake. Once again, the whole feeling more...needy than unpleasant. Lena moved across the thickly carpeted floor. Lowered herself into the chair opposite him. What was he going to do? The King hadn't looked upset, exactly. On the contrary, something had clearly amused him whilst she'd been dealing with the swimming saucer of coffee and drowned biscuit in the bathroom outside. Was His Royal Highness going to ask her to leave before she'd even really started this job? Her mother had always complained that she needed to comport herself better, that she was too free with her actions, didn't think about her words.

That she was too much.

So, she'd learned how to be *just enough*. But what was it about working in the Halrovian palace for their Crown Prince that made her hot under the collar? Her skin itch and prickle? As if she was *always* going to mess up, to do something wrong?

Gabriel opened the folder in front of him, and her heart froze, then dropped like an apple falling from a tree, right to her toes. He turned the page of the planner she'd begun putting together for social medial posts, to newspaper articles she'd printed, trying to get a feel for what was really going on in Halrovia. It had been difficult since she wasn't as fluent in the language as she would have wanted. Except, she'd doodled all over the picture of the man the piece featured because she hadn't liked the look of him...

Prince Gabriel took the sheet of paper out and held it up, facing her.

'Your handiwork?'

She swallowed, her mouth suddenly too dry. What could she do other than admit the obvious truth? She nodded.

'Why?'

Because the man in the picture had seemed...superior, but in a way that said he was looking down at you. Especially a person like her. One who'd come from a family with a single mother, even though it was the twenty-first century and who cared about that sort of thing any more? But she could never admit it, not to someone like a *prince*.

'I—I was just doodling. Is he a friend of yours?'

Gabriel gave what some people might have said was a chuckle, but it had a sharp, dark edge to it. Not a happy sound. He looked at the paper and back at her. 'No. He is *no* friend of the royal family's.'

Relief flooded over her that she hadn't made yet another faux pas. 'He does have the appearance of someone who likes to sit in judgement of everybody.'

'You have experience of that type of person?'

To be honest, the King and Queen of Halrovia seemed like that sort of people, but that was just another thing in a long list she couldn't say, so she told another truth instead. 'A few headmasters and mistresses I've known.'

'Ah, hence the horns and fangs.'

He said it in a chilly kind of way but with the slightest upturn of his lips, suggesting that he found her scribbles amusing, but perhaps childish.

'I'm rather proud of those. I thought the flies about his head a nice touch.'

The corners of Prince Gabriel's mouth seemed to kick up a little more, threatening a real smile this time. Her heart thumped in heady anticipation, but the smile never broke free. 'They're quite masterful. Were you a keen student, Ms Rosetti?'

Lena stilled, trying to forget the memories that assailed her. She'd been miserable at school, but she'd always known that to have a future where she stood on her own two feet, she had to do well. To excel. So she had.

But she'd also wanted to make her father *notice* her. Hoping that if she achieved good marks, he might get to know her rather than remaining a distant figure whose feelings on anything she only really heard about through her mother.

'Your father is very proud of your results. He thought the card you made for him was touching.'

Yet he never delivered those sentiments to her personally. Sure, he'd been around, when he came to the home and for a few hours they pretended to play happy families. Yet Lena always had the sense that he looked at her and her brother more as though they were perfect specimens under glass, rather than real living and breathing children. And one day she'd opened her mother's bedside drawer and found the cards down at the bottom, as if her father hadn't cared enough to take them with him. Whatever he and her mother had shared, he hadn't shared any similar affection with her or her brother. He'd provided their genetic material. She guessed from what her mother had said that he'd applauded their achievements, but he hadn't cared to truly know them.

Those memories of that time ached deep inside. Not sharp any more, but now she was an adult she didn't understand having children if you didn't have some interest in them. Was her and her brother's existence all ego? She looked up at Gabriel, his frigid blue eyes once again pinning her to the spot. There were no answers there. She'd didn't know what it was about him. The cool, impassive kind of gaze. Not giving anything much away, piercing right through her.

Lena shrugged. 'I wouldn't say keen. I believe I succeeded to spite them. And you?'

Gabriel's eyebrows shot up. Why did she ask that? This wasn't some chit-chat over coffee, this was her employer. A *prince*. The things she could learn about him came from the Internet, or years of working with a person. Not this situation where she was a week into her job, finding her way. Trying to figure out as much as she could about the rhythm and feel of the palace from other staff. His efficient private secretary. His secretive valet, who she'd bumped into in a private corridor of the staff quarters in the palace, where she thankfully had a small apartment as part of her role.

'I tried to do what was expected of me.'

It was an unusual kind of response. His school days didn't feature much at all in her online research, other than he'd studied at a prestigious Halrovian private school. She'd thought it strange that with all his advantages he hadn't attended university, announcing that his greatest education was to serve his people and learn beside the King. That had come surprisingly soon after he and his team had won the junior world football championship. He'd come home a hero. The small country in Europe overwhelming the giants of the game. It had been a triumphant moment. Lena wondered what made a young man give that all away.

'Was winning the junior world championship expected of you?'

Something about Prince Gabriel's gaze shuttered. She'd thought him closed off before, but she hadn't realised till this moment how much he showed if you cared to look hard enough. Right now, it was like a door slamming in her face. She immediately regretted her words.

'Winning was something I expected of myself, and for my team,' he said.

She wondered about the pressures of a prince and heir to the throne of his country. Working for the Isolobello royals, she hadn't much thought about it. Her royal family was loved, and their Prince had acquitted himself admirably when the King had fallen ill, guiding the country till his father's recovery. Then with Princess Priscilla, and the upcoming royal wedding, the whole country was entering the fervour of anticipated celebration, even though the wedding was still months away.

'Of course, but—'

'Those things are in the past. This is the present and where my focus lies. As should yours.'

She wanted to say that the past was what made him the man he was today, and that would help her shape the vision for his future. She didn't. Lena knew enough to stay quiet. She wasn't about to enter a full-scale argument with her employer when she was still on probation.

'Yes, sir.'

He stiffened a fraction, in almost a flinch. Then it was as if his body relaxed again. Like he was on familiar ground once more.

'You said you had a photograph?'

She nodded. She had a few to choose from on the phone they'd given her for work purposes. Luckily, none showing her offending doodling.

'Show me.'

She pulled up the album, picked the best picture and handed her mobile to him. His long fingers gently swiped the screen as he looked through. Stopping. The merest of frowns creasing his brow.

He handed the phone back. It was warm. A strange kind

of thrill shimmied through her at the thought its heat came from his touch.

'What do you think?' she asked, before she could shove the words back in. Lena didn't know why it was important, but she wanted him to like the photo she'd taken. The warmth on his face like a balmy spring day. The moment she'd glimpsed the royals as real people, and not merely the embodiment of the position they held.

'It's the picture you described you wanted.'

'And are you happy for me to post it?'

'That's your job. What I'm paying you for.'

'But as you said before, it's your image. I want to know you're satisfied with what I've captured.'

He cocked his head a fraction, as if studying her. Then the corner of his mouth curled into the merest of sly, almost wicked smiles, which did all kinds of complicated things to Lena's insides that she didn't care to dwell on.

'I enjoy knowing that a successful picture meant to depict confidence and trust in the future of the monarchy was taken at the expense of a particularly irritating advisor of state whose ideas on the future of Halrovia don't always align with my own.'

Oh, she liked that a little too much. His hint of pettiness indicating that this man could be human with all the messy frailties that went along with it. That he wasn't so proper after all. *This* was a person who might be interesting to show. Something she would love to dive into and explore.

'What do you know of what's been happening here in Halrovia?' Gabriel asked, his question loaded with unspoken tension.

Lena knew a lot, having researched him, the family, and the situation. But there was an undercurrent she couldn't quite place.

'I know Princess Priscilla's getting married soon. And Princess Anastacia's already married...' After a reported whirlwind romance and engagement on the back of what appeared to be some unfair negative press, which seemed to have stopped after her wedding. Lena hesitated, some things falling into place now she really thought about them. 'It was around the time of Princess Priscilla's engagement that things changed, wasn't it?'

'She was never meant to marry Caspar. Anastacia was. But then love intervened.'

Gabriel almost spat out the word 'love', as if it were something unpleasant.

'Then Anastacia was involved in an accident, injured, and somehow the narrative began to turn against my family. We suspect that this man—' he tapped the clipping with her doodling '—is the instigator.'

Lena frowned. 'But you said he's an advisor of state?'

Gabriel nodded, quick and sharp. 'And yet, when it comes to power, people will do anything to get more of it. The ideas being promoted in the press aren't kind to my country—they're about self-aggrandisement and filling personal coffers. Yet he still gets to drive the narrative.'

Gabriel reached over to the corner of his desk where a newspaper sat folded. Opened it out, facing her.

'Read what it says.'

She wondered why he didn't read the headline himself, but didn't say so. *"Is the Crown Worth the Cost? Critics Question Relevance of Prince Gabriel's Overseas Mission."*

His eyes narrowed. 'Each day, this is what we're facing. It's insidious, and it's not the truth. My trip to Lauritania is about increasing trade and co-operation with a valued ally. That's good for the economy.'

She began to understand the royal family's problem. How none of this was fair. Even more, she recognised the extent of the work she had to do. Especially when there wasn't an equal playing field between the truth before her and lies being told elsewhere.

'As for your "doodling",' Gabriel said, taking the offending paper between his fingers, 'I can't have anything that will cause an internal incident coming from my office.'

He stood and turned his back to her, his shoulders broad and strong. Enough to hold up the weight of his job, the weight of an entire country's needs. Then Prince Gabriel dropped the paper into a machine behind his desk. It buzzed, shredding the document.

'A few scribbles would cause a problem?'

'I'm not willing to take the chance. It seems everyone wants a piece of my family. Our special advisor is a man with an agenda. There's a small but strange push for a republic. Criticism now, where there was none before. It doesn't feel organic or authentic.'

'And if your people wanted a republic?'

Prince Gabriel sat behind his desk again, hands clasped on the gleaming wooden tabletop. 'Then they could have it.'

Lena gave a shaky kind of laugh. Surely he couldn't mean it?

'What? Give up? Just like that?'

'If I were King, my duty would be to honour and defend my people. If they didn't want my family ruling them and I couldn't convince them otherwise, then it would be my duty to stand aside.'

The way he said those words, with such strength and conviction, told her what he really thought. There was so much at stake here. If she failed... Then she'd be potentially responsible for the downfall of this man sitting in front of her, of a royal family. Lena wondered if her own shoulders were strong enough to carry the weight of her personal role here.

'But you don't want to. Stand aside, I mean.'

Gabriel shook his head. 'I'll never capitulate to this... propaganda. My family, me, *we* are the best choice.'

The morning sun streamed through the windows behind Prince Gabriel. He was lit up, magical and golden. How could anyone doubt he was the perfect prince? The king in waiting, who loved his country and would even set aside his own interests if his people wanted him to. Put a gleaming crown on his head and she could see it all laid out before her. Lena's heart quickened with excitement. She had no doubt. Gabriel Montroy *was* Halrovia's glorious future.

She just had to figure out how to show it.

CHAPTER THREE

LENA SAT AT an outdoor dining setting on a terrace, sipping a deliciously hot coffee as she overlooked the still, deep inkblot of Lake Morenberg in front of her. The snow-capped Alps soaring behind, white peaks gleaming in the early morning sunshine. They'd arrived in Lauritania's capital the night before and she hadn't had a real chance to admire the beauty of the landscape until now. The home they were staying in was one of King Rafe's former private residences. An elegant, secure modern masterpiece with expanses of glass overlooking the water on one side of the house and, on the other, views into the old town and towering Morenberg Palace they'd be visiting today.

She felt as though she'd had a kind of breakthrough with Prince Gabriel, small though it was. Their discussion over the real reasons why she'd been hired had given her more to work with. She liked to think it was some evidence of a growing trust that he'd disclosed those things to her, sensitive as they were. Giving her an insight into the true importance of her role. The challenge.

And that gave her ideas...

'Good morning, Lena.'

She startled at the deep, low voice of her employer behind her. Almost spilling her drink all over herself. She placed the mug carefully on the table and stood to curtsey and address him properly. As she did, he waved her away.

'Please. No formality, not here.'

He might have suggested no formality but even this morning he was dressed in suit trousers and a blue and white striped business shirt, which made his eyes seem even brighter. Though his hair was still slightly damp from a shower. Lena didn't know why that realisation ignited something warm in her belly.

It was likely just the coffee. She'd make a cooler cup next time.

'You talk about no formality yet here you are looking way too formal for this early in the morning.'

He took a long swig from the cup he held. 'I had a video call.'

'It's very rude of someone to organise something so early, before caffeination,' Lena said, sitting and taking another sip of her own delicious beverage.

'It was with my father.'

Lena choked, almost spitting out the mouthful. She coughed a few times, her eyes watering. 'My apologies, to His Majesty.'

'He's not here to see you, and...' Gabriel tapped the side of his nose, looking amused '... I'll never tell.'

She liked that. Someone seeing fit to protect her when no one really had. Gabriel stood for a few more seconds, staring out at the view as if lost in his own thoughts. A light breeze drifted over the terrace. She caught a scent on that breeze. Something so enticing that she wanted to simply breathe in a lungful. His aftershave, she guessed. Green, fresh, sweet, like she supposed the high alpine regions smelled. Coming from sea level and an island, she wasn't sure. Then he pulled out a chair from the table and sat down. Not *exactly* at the table itself, almost as though he was holding himself a little apart, when what he should be doing was trying to get closer to people.

Maybe he was an introvert and didn't really want to be around too many people. If that was the case, there were more ways to communicate with the world than by speaking. And after the seeming thaw between them, Lena thought it was as good a time as any to raise it. To push a little.

'Whilst I have you here…'

Gabriel cocked an eyebrow. 'Am I suitably caffeinated for this conversation?'

'I'll leave that for you to decide. I've been thinking, and I have some ideas about engaging with younger people.'

His face was devoid of expression apart from that perfectly cocked eyebrow. It remained.

'Please, enlighten me.'

Lena flicked through her phone. Pulled up a vision board she'd created. 'You're always in dark suits.'

'There's a problem with that?'

From her personal perspective, there was no problem at all. He looked impossibly handsome. Frankly, he could wear suits every day as far as she was concerned, and she could die a happy woman. Though why she was thinking like that she couldn't really tell. But she wouldn't be doing her job if she didn't suggest alternatives.

'In the right circumstances, no.'

'There's rarely a wrong circumstance in my role.'

It was as if this man didn't do anything that was fun any more. At. All.

'What about if you were…? I don't know. Judging a pet show at a local fair? With children bringing their favourite pet. And you had to pick the best one. Would a suit be right then?'

His eyes narrowed. He gave the slightest shake of his head. 'There is *never* a time I'd be doing that.'

'Well, maybe you should start. Everyone loves kittens and puppies, together with children. Totally relatable.'

'And what if a child's pet is something other than a kitten or a puppy? A snake, for example. Or a tarantula. I don't want to appear in any way relatable around those animals. I'd then wish to appear repellent.'

The sun had risen a bit higher in the sky, their little table now bathed in soft early sunlight. Lena's cheeks heated. She wasn't sure whether it was from the warmth of the sun or Prince's Gabriel's resistance to what seemed perfectly reasonable to her.

'See, Your Highness, now I think you're engaging in hyperbole.'

'There's a rule, *never work with children or animals*, for a good reason.'

'You're going to be King. If you rule out children and animals you're kind of forsaking some of the best bits of your "role", as you put it.'

'I'm not forsaking them at all, they simply haven't been in my repertoire. On the other hand, my sisters—'

'Are no longer available.'

He took a slow, and what sounded like a long-suffering, breath. 'You have a point to this conversation, I assume?'

'You're the one who took us offside with the talk of snakes and spiders.'

'And now I'm guiding us right back onside. Please get on with it. I have another meeting in fifteen minutes.'

'That's what I'm trying to do. I think you should try for a look that injects a little more colour. Something more casual. To mix things up a bit. Take a look.'

She handed over her phone to show him some of the pictures she'd found whilst trawling popular menswear blogs and social media for the latest looks. Before she'd started, she'd had no idea how much there was to learn about suits, and don't get her started on collar gaps. She had trouble looking at her employer now without analysing and admiring his impeccable tailoring. The way he moved, and the way his clothes moved with him...

'This—this—' He waved his hand over the phone as if it in some way offended him, which didn't bode well. 'No.'

Okay, so maybe some of the examples were a little out there, but she did get them from a viral men's fashion and workwear blogger who seemed to have real street cred.

'I'm just trying to show you that even if you're wearing a suit you can mix it up a bit.'

'The suit is mustard. The coat appears...shaggy.'

'But the look's stylish, even with all the colour, and shagginess as you put it. Which isn't really shaggy. It's mohair. And extremely expensive.'

He reached out and put his half-empty coffee cup down on the tabletop with a little bit too solid a thump. 'Cost *does not* equal taste.'

'But colour. A little more casual. All I'm trying to show you is that you can still look extremely stylish and...and... princely. I'm sure that your valet would be able to sort something out.'

'Pieter would resign if he thought I'd wear this. Or call a doctor to see if I was coming down with something.'

'But you can't wear suits all the time. What do you wear when you're not working? When you're in your apartments just being...you? When you're...off the clock?'

His whole demeanour rankled. Sure, she needed the job, but she was also overwhelmed with the need to keep pushing, to get a hint of who he really was. And all she could hear was a voice in her ear from her mother that a woman should be an oasis. Still and deep. Welcoming. Somewhere that encouraged a man to *stay*. Even though her mother had been calm and cool like an oasis, her father had never stayed for long. Always going back to his real family.

Being an oasis was clearly not all that it was cracked up to be.

His Highness's eyes narrowed and once again she had the uncomfortable sensation of being skewered.

'I am never "off the clock", as you put it. I'm always available to help run the country. As for the rest, that's walking into personal territory you do not have permission to tread.'

'I understand, but you gave me a job. On probation if you recall. I want to make it something permanent. But I can only do that if you work with me a bit, or at least tell me what's off-limits.'

'I'll ensure you have a list of off-limits topics by later this morning, so you can study it at leisure.'

He looked at his watch and Lena sensed that he wanted to go. Her and her darned mouth. She needed to stop arguing with the man and regroup. 'I'm guessing that's all to be said on that topic, Your Highness?'

'Yes. You're free to leave.'

So, she was being dismissed. Back to square one, then. She stood and curtseyed even though he'd told her not to, then turned and began to walk towards the door leading back inside.

'Ms Rosetti?'

She turned and her breath snagged right in her throat. Once again, he was lit up by the sunshine that seemed to love him so much.

'Sir?'

'You haven't impressed me yet.'

* * *

Whilst Gabriel understood there was a certain amount of pomp and ceremony surrounding his role as prince, there was something about today that felt off. The meeting with his father had disturbed his usual early morning routine. Even worse was the King's attempt at giving advice, which was unwanted and unneeded. A fact that Gabriel had made very plain. Still, it was as if part of him didn't slot into place. He sat in the back of a large dark-coloured car with fluttering flags travelling behind a police escort. Usually, strangers believed he wanted to travel alone. However, he saw it as wasteful in both time and resources to have a procession of vehicles, one carrying him and the other carrying staff. He liked to spend the journey to any function preparing with his team. Talking, strategising. Yet today was a private function at the palace with Lauritania's King and Queen. The only person he had travelling with him was Lena. To take more photographs.

Perhaps that was what felt off. In this enclosed space with someone still unfamiliar, whereas his other staff had been with him for years. She hadn't spoken much apart from pleasantries, especially not after their conversation earlier about his clothes, where, if he was honest with himself, he might have been a little unfair.

Still, looking at Lena now, he thought she could hardly profess to be expert in all things casual and appealing to 'younger people'. Today she was dressed in a conservative black dress. High neck, skirt below the knee. It could have looked like a nun's habit except for the three-quarter sleeves showing her golden skin, and the way the dress seemed to perfectly shape to her body. Her hair in a bun that attempted to look tidy. However, dark stray hairs fell out of it, framing her face. Making her look soft, approachable. She wasn't paying attention to him, looking down at her phone, intent.

For the first time in his life, he was at a loss on what to say. He simply watched her, nibbling on her lower lip as though she was concentrating.

As if she knew his gaze was on her, Lena blew away an errant strand of hair and looked up at him.

'I've been thinking,' she said. That didn't bode well. She'd been thinking when she suggested changes to his wardrobe as well.

'Indeed.'

'Have you ever considered having a meeting with business leaders in a more casual environment?'

Most of the time those kinds of meetings took place in a stultifying boardroom somewhere with PowerPoint presentations that flicked across the screen too fast for him to take in, and poisonously bad coffee.

'You have something else in mind?'

'I've heard you've been trying to fit in a meeting with the international youth mental health forum whilst you're here. I know you go for a run early, before breakfast—'

'How do you know that?'

He hadn't provided her with his early morning routine. It wasn't something he considered necessary. Gabriel didn't understand why he rather liked her knowing what he did so much.

'Pieter told me.'

Now *that* was a surprise. Pieter was a closed book. Not even the King and Queen could get information from him. It was always polite obfuscation. However, Pieter was also an excellent judge of character...

'When did you ask him?'

Lena tugged at the back of her bun as if adjusting the pins. 'This morning, before we left. I thought you could have a running meeting. It's early enough that people should be available. Plus, it fits because of the benefits exercise has on mental health. Afterwards you could offer everyone a free breakfast, if you wanted to.'

'And you get a photo of me looking casual...' She was clever. A simple suggestion that didn't sound manipulative at all, except he realised when he was being manoeuvred. 'What's to say I don't run in a suit?'

She snorted. 'Because that would be ridiculous, and you aren't in any way ridiculous. Plus, Pieter would never forgive you for doing that to one of your precious suits.'

Gabe couldn't help himself. He laughed. Lena's cheeks flushed a deep shade of crimson. Such a beautiful colour on her. He wondered what her plush, full lips would look like painted the same tone, rather than a neutral gloss.

'I'll see if it can be arranged.'

'I might have already raised it with your efficient private secretary.'

'Stop managing me, Ms Rosetti,' he said with a smile. Though he couldn't be angry about it. He relied on his staff being proactive. Anticipating his wishes and acting on them.

'I wouldn't dream of doing so, Your Highness.'

She had a sneaky, self-satisfied grin on her face. As if she enjoyed her little win.

'What's on the agenda today, to make me look good?'

He couldn't miss the rapid sound of her inhale. 'I think you're already looking quite...you know...'

She waved her hand about in his general direction. Did Lena think he looked good? That thought left him as satisfied as a cat given a bowl of cream. He shouldn't tease but he couldn't help himself.

'I'm not sure I do know. Please enlighten me.'

'Yes, well...you look very princely. Exactly like the description on the box.' Lena nibbled on her lower lip, the slash of pink on her cheeks darkening even further. She was terrible at trying to hide what she thought, or her own embarrassment. He decided to be kind. Change the subject.

'How was your first picture received?'

Lena blew out a long, slow breath, something like relief. 'Very well.'

'By whom?'

'The public. In the main.'

'Press?'

Since he'd been running late this morning, something entirely uncharacteristic for him, Gabriel hadn't had the time to get Pieter to fill him in on the usual news reports before work. To be fair, Pieter had told him that Lena was up and about extremely early and Gabe had wanted to give her space without her employer around. People always switched to work mode in his presence. That was all. No other reason, such as this strange sense of challenge he seemed to experience around her and enjoyed so much, rather than everyone's usual deference. Though he guessed challenging the palace status quo was what he'd hired her for.

Lena pulled up something on her phone, turned it to him.

He could catch some of the words, but he was still feeling...discombobulated. Out of sorts.

'I haven't got my glasses. Tell me what it says.'

Her eyebrows rose on her forehead. 'I didn't know you wore glasses.'

He didn't. His were a handy prop, which he put on occasionally enough to give himself the excuse that he didn't have them, should someone ask him to read something quickly. He just hadn't worn them recently. Still, Gabe didn't like to lie. For some reason, the sensation of discomfort over his untruth was especially acute with her. In the end, he shrugged.

Lena didn't question his silence. She turned back to her phone screen.

''Father and Son Moment: King's Support Shines in Prince's Online Breakthrough.''

'That's what you wanted, wasn't it?'

'It feels condescending to me. Honestly, as if you needed permission to open your own social media account. It's ridiculous.'

Something about her defence of him ignited a flicker of heat, deep inside.

'Anyhow, I prefer this one. *"Prince's Social Media Debut: Millions Follow as King Hands Over the Reins."* Though I'm guessing His Majesty will never forgive me.'

Both parts of what she'd said gave him pause to reflect, but he dealt with the one where a sound of uncertainty had infiltrated her voice.

'His Majesty has no influence here. I protect my loyal staff.'

She smiled, and it was like the sun peeping out from behind a cloud. Bright and warming for a fleeting moment, then it was gone.

'Thank you,' she said.

'As for the rest, you said…*millions*?'

Gabe hated the way that he sounded even mildly interested or surprised, when he'd never cared before.

'Millions, within the first few hours. Seems you're more popular than anyone knew.'

'There are those who disagree.'

'I'm not one of them.'

Somehow the inside of the vehicle's temperature seemed to rise, even though it was air-conditioned. Gabe adjusted his tie a fraction.

'There's much about the narrative that's unfair. My sister

Anastacia, for example. She was always thought of as the Perfect Princess. Then she had an accident. It…' Crushed her. How she'd been treated as if she'd been in some way damaged by her scarring. Even by his mother. 'It…affected her. She hid away whilst recovering. Hid her scars. Some in the press accused her of being work-shy.'

'People are cruel. The tabloids especially. But now she's married, and the press seems favourable again. Then they turned their attention to you.'

Lena's voice was quiet, sombre. As though she'd had personal experience of cruelty, which he wanted to explore. However, it wasn't his place.

'So it seems,' he said.

The car turned off onto the short but winding road that took them to Lauritania's palace. Yet somehow, he didn't want this journey to end.

'I'll do what I can to stop it.'

Lena shifted her hand, almost as if she was reaching out to touch without thinking. He held his breath for the moment her skin met his, but it never came. She drew her hand back instead. A sense of heaviness weighed down on him. Why did he crave that touch so much? He couldn't understand. Perhaps it was that his family had been in crisis-management mode for what felt like so long, he hadn't been touched recently. There hadn't been the time or the inclination. Perhaps he *should* clear a space in his diary for a night or two of adult enjoyment. Except that didn't seem to hold any interest either.

Nothing much did.

The car slowed, pulling up to a private entrance at the palace. A member of staff opened the door and Gabe exited whilst Lena followed him into the building, her footsteps clicking on the marble floor behind him. Today he was meeting his godson for the first time since his christening, delivering a birthday present for what Lena had said would be a noteworthy moment, and something that would allow him to show a softer side.

They were ushered through an oak door to the King and Queen's private quarters. As he saw them, he bowed. Unnecessary amongst friends, perhaps. But Lena was here.

Lauritania and Halrovia were close allies, and that had survived the death of most of the Lauritanian royal family in a tragic accident. Leaving their Princess, who had never been expected to rise to the throne, as Queen. Annalise and her husband, Rafe, were beloved. He could only wish for the same for himself and whoever might be his queen one day. Gabriel caught a glimpse of Lena in his peripheral vision, carrying his birthday gift for the little prince and something for his sister too, so the little girl wouldn't be jealous. That had been Lena's own insightful suggestion. Gabriel was struck by how impressive a woman she was. To garner Priscilla's confidence, Pieter's apparent trust. Managing his parents... *Him*.

'Gabriel.'

Queen Annalise reached out, giving him a warm embrace. He shook hands with Rafe. Exchanging the normal pleasantries, although he understood it was somewhat more stilted than usual with Lena in the room, since they didn't know her.

'Your Majesties, I'd like to introduce Ms Lena Rosetti,' he said as Lena curtseyed, 'who's in charge of my... PR.'

Lise smiled at Lena, always gracious. 'Welcome! Goodness, a PR manager. How long have you been with His Highness?'

'Around two weeks, Your Majesty.'

'I hope it's going well. Is His Highness doing everything you ask of him?'

Lena gave an enigmatic smile. 'I couldn't say, Your Majesty.'

'How politic of you.' Lise laughed. 'I'm afraid we're rather old-fashioned here. Perhaps we need a PR manager too? If you're ever seeking different pastures, you might get in touch…'

Those words lit something volcanic inside Gabe. He instantly wanted to shout *No!* although he had no reason to. Whilst it had only been a couple of weeks, he'd begun to value Lena in ways he couldn't explain.

'I'd ask you not to try to steal my staff right in front of me,' he said.

'No, we'll do it behind your back like any decent prospective employer would,' Rafe said with a grin. He'd been a ruthless businessman before marrying Lise. The ruthlessness remained, at least where his wife and what she wanted came into play.

That thought left Gabe feeling strangely wistful, as if looking for something he didn't know was missing. He shook it off.

Gabe turned to Lena. She stood there looking professional, impassive, although her blue eyes glittered with glee as if she was enjoying the unofficial bidding war.

'If these…poachers approach you, let me know. I'll give you a pay rise.'

Lena cocked her eyebrow. 'Sir, I believe they have already approached me. So, I'll leave that with you.'

'She's ruthless, Montroy,' Rafe chuckled. 'I like her.'

Gabe had come to realise he did too. She was fresh. Honest. Didn't pander to him. He tried not to think about the rest. Like her colouring. So striking, with her hair as black as a raven's wing, eyes like blue topaz. Skin a burnished gold.

Lena made a transfixing picture, should you take the time to notice her.

'I'm supposing you'd like some photographs, then?' Lise asked, bringing his thoughts back to the real purpose of Lena's presence.

'Yes, ma'am. I understand, whilst these are part of your private apartments, you do occasionally use this room as a formal receiving area for international guests. Is that correct? I want to make sure your private space remains private.'

'You're correct.' Lise cocked her head, her gaze on Lena intense. Gabe wondered what she was thinking. Probably how much to pay Lena to tempt her away from him. Gabe made a mental note to take that quip about a pay rise seriously. 'Thank you for being so thoughtful.'

'I was also wondering, ma'am, whether we could take a photograph of His Highness with Prince Carl. From behind, not showing your son's face. I appreciate you're careful with your children's privacy.'

Lise and Rafe exchanged a glance. 'Of course. Why don't I bring them in now? I know they're looking forward to seeing you, Gabriel. Especially as you come bearing gifts.'

For his godson, he'd brought the present he always gave children for their birthday. A book. Because reading was the greatest gift Gabe could bestow. One he'd come to finally enjoy through audiobooks, and, if persistent, by slowly reading novels when he had the time and was in the right frame of mind. Something he could never have enjoyed when he was younger.

Queen Lise left the room and returned within minutes, two squealing children running behind her, the room filling with chaos and laughter. Once again, a sensation assailed him watching the scene. Rafe, hugging his little boy. The little Princess and future queen, showing her mother something she'd drawn. He'd only ever seen marriage and family as a duty to his country. From his pre-teens he'd been told that was his role, to assure the throne with the correct partner and at least two children. It had never held an attraction as anything other than another job, securing succession.

Yet, seeing the family tableau in front of him, why did he suddenly crave for something more?

Lena melted into the background. The King and Queen made a beautiful couple. The Queen with her golden colouring and Rafe with his dark good looks. The children mirrored their parents. The little Princess Marie a whirlwind of dark curls taking after her father, and the Prince, a golden cherub like his mother.

She tried to capture it all. Gabe had been right about not working with children or animals. She had a hard time getting any shots without the children's sweet faces but she was sure that their parents might appreciate some of the photographs for their own album, so she stopped worrying and simply took pictures.

The Princess loved the sparkly fairy costume with wings and a crown they'd brought so she wouldn't get jealous. She ran about bestowing favours and wishes to everybody with a tap of her wand. Lena had almost expected Gabe to be as cool and aloof as usual, but he wasn't. Not here. She'd come to realise that his chilly persona wasn't the real man. There was someone else entirely simmering underneath his impeccable suits. Lena was sure he was hiding part of himself. She just didn't know what, or why.

It was a puzzle to sort out at another time. Right now, he sat at a little child's table opposite his godson, who was colouring in a picture with crayons. It was such an incongruous scene. Such a large man in a suit, folded into a small chair opposite a child. She picked up the book he'd brought with him and walked towards them both.

'I know you've forgotten your glasses, sir. But perhaps you could show Prince Carl the pictures?' She spread open a page adorned with colourful animals on the table between them. Gabe looked up at her as she did. She couldn't fathom the expression on his face as she stood back. It almost looked guilty.

'Why don't you draw me a fish like this?' Gabe said, pointing at the page as Carl took a blue crayon and began to scribble on some paper. Lena stood behind him, photographing as Gabe turned the pages. It was such a tender scene. The two princes. With his blond hair, Carl could almost look like Gabe's son. In that moment, a gripping sense of the future overwhelmed her. Was this what he'd be like as a father? Someone attached, interested?

She'd never had that. In truth, she hadn't really wanted it until she'd gone to school and the other students had told her it was what their fathers were like. Lena had realised, after trying to engage with her own, that he was never going to be there for her. Yet what was she seeing here? If she'd had children, it was what she'd want for them. A father who wasn't distant and aloof, but who was proud of them and their achievements. Who wanted to spend time with his children doing something as simple as looking through a book. Praising their drawings.

It left her melancholy, with a sense that she'd missed out, even though she'd had a good enough life. Been given an education. Had a mother who loved her, in her own way. Always food on the table. That was more than many had. She should be thankful. Lena couldn't say why it left a bitter taste in her mouth.

'I think I have enough now,' she said. 'I've taken lovely pictures of the children that I believe Your Majesties would like, which I can send to you. Do you want to pre-approve any before I post them?'

'No,' Queen Annalise said. 'I trust your judgement.'

'Thank you, ma'am. I feel privileged that you do.' That was the truth. Like when they'd talked about offering her a job. Lena wasn't silly enough to think it was anything serious, although she had the sense there was more to it from King Rafe's perspective, at least. Otherwise, it was all just a bit of banter between people who were familiar with each other.

More than familiar. She looked around the room. These people were clearly friends. Lena had never really had the same. Her mother hadn't encouraged it for fear that Lena would want to reveal who her father was, or that they'd search for information about him. And if she had friends, she'd probably want to spend some time without an employee hanging about. 'I might take your leave and let you catch up.'

'It's almost morning tea. I'll ask my private secretary, Albert, to meet you outside and take you for refreshments.'

'Is there anything else, sir?'

She addressed her question to Gabriel, who looked up at her with an intensity that branded skin. 'That's all. Thank you, Lena.'

Lena curtseyed, then walked out of the room. Chased by the confusing feelings she was desperate to leave behind.

CHAPTER FOUR

GABE SUCKED IN the cool morning air as his run ended. It was just past six thirty and he'd been surprised at how successful Lena's suggestion had been. Many of the highest profile participants at various mental health charities had joined him. It was a slower run than normal, along the banks of the magnificent Lake Morenburg in Lauritania's capital. They'd jogged the paved paths around the lake, followed by security at a discreet distance and some press, taking the time to talk about youth mental health and strategies for improving it. He'd missed Lena this morning, her constant presence. After a few photographs at the beginning she'd gone back to the residence they were staying in. Waiting for their inevitable arrival for a breakfast that had been arranged to continue talks in a casual environment.

Gabe hoped to make a difference. Even with all his privileges, he had some knowledge of what despair felt like. When no one could understand why he fell behind at school. Not listening to him when he said something was wrong, believing it was lack of effort rather than a true inability. It was only when he began to find sport that he'd come into his own, recognising there was something he was good at and he wasn't a complete failure. His sports teacher had also listened, suspecting the dyslexia that had finally been diagnosed.

The group jogged up the winding private path to King Rafe's home outside the palace. A perfect place to escape. It wasn't the first time Gabe had stayed here, and it was always on offer for him should he want to get away. That didn't seem enough any more. Whilst living at the palace in his own wing back home was a convenience, his time on this trip had led him to conclude he needed more. A place of his own, not something owned by the family. As he climbed the stairs to a particularly beautiful terrace overlooking the lake, Gabe made up his mind. He'd set his private secretary on the path of locating a home to purchase for himself. Whilst he was going to be King one long-off day, he was tired of having others trying to control him. Striking out on his own hadn't seemed necessary before. Now, it was somehow vital. Gabe reached the top of the stairs, where the view was most breathtaking. He wanted a place like this, with privacy and solitude. One he could staff himself, make his own choices.

Lena.

Thoughts of her came to him unbidden. He'd arrived at the expansive, tiled terrace where she was waiting, as if for him alone. What a ridiculous thought. Of course she was waiting for him. He was her employer. She was there with his private secretary, to greet the guests, which she did with charm. Gracious as always, eliciting smiles. Yet this morning, she looked different, in a way that unbalanced him.

He'd only ever really seen her in muted colours. Blacks, dark blues, making it easy for her to melt into the background. She always looked striking. However, this was something else. Not a suit, but a dress in an ochre yellow, with white flowers and burgundy accents. The colour made her golden skin glow as if lit up by sunshine. But it wasn't simply the colour that attracted him. It was the style. The dress wrapped round her body. The skirt grazing her calves with a flirty frill. The fabric skimming her curves, her body. Silky and light, fluttering in the breeze. A gust blew, hitching the front of the skirt, flicking it back. Lena smoothed it down though he knew that another gust, a little stronger, might expose a hint of her thigh.

Gabe was transfixed, he couldn't take his eyes from her, trying to catch a mere glimpse of her skin like some errant teenager. He moved from her long, lithe legs but it was almost worse, his gaze snagging on the top, the way it settled between her breasts in a vee. Wrapped round her torso, tied at the waist in a bow.

He couldn't get out of his head that she was wrapped up as if some kind of gift, just for him. For his pleasure. What he wouldn't give to reach out, tug the bow at her waist. Undo her. Unravel them both.

It was impossible. He was a prince, with expectations to marry a princess. She was his employee. Yet all he could think of was the need coursing through him. A relentless drumbeat of desire.

Why her, out of all the women he'd spent time with? Lena turned, and looked at him, her lips the same burgundy as the flower details of her dress. Another gust and her ebony hair whipped about her face. He held his breath as the corner of the skirt flicked, and for a fleeting moment he caught it, a slice of smooth, golden thigh. A powerful spike of lust struck him. He craved to—

'Your Highness?'

Lena's words dragged him out of his reverie as she walked towards him. How hadn't he noticed the sway to her gait? How her hips moved in such a hypnotic kind of rhythm? What would the press say if they could see him now?

Proper prince indeed.

'Has it been a successful meeting so far?'

'Yes. Thank you for the excellent suggestion.'

A hint of pink feathered her cheeks. He'd come to relish that colour. It was a beautiful look on her.

'I thought I might mingle. Take more photographs.'

He noticed some other men in the group admiring her. He didn't know why he was possessed with the desire to hide her away from their gazes. It was ridiculous. She was a grown woman who could look after herself. There was no need for him to be her champion in some misplaced chivalry, and yet the clawing sensation remained. He ignored it. Yet he couldn't get over the sensation that if he didn't do *something*, she'd be stolen away from him, when he had no claim on her at all.

'Whatever you need to do.'

She nodded. Her attention already on others in the group, no doubt thinking of who to approach first. These were all high-profile members of the business community. Anyone here could see her competence and professionalism, like Lise and Rafe yesterday. She made to leave, walk away from him. He was overcome by the desire to make her stay.

'Lena.'

'Yes, sir?'

Say my name. It was unfeasible. Yet he didn't know why he so badly wanted to hear it. Like it was some inevitability.

'If anyone offers you employment, tell me. I was serious yesterday at the palace.'

Her eyes opened wide. 'I—I…of course. I wasn't planning on going anywhere. I've only just begun.'

He nodded as she walked to a group, and they shuffled together as she held up her phone. Smiled for her. He marvelled at her openness, how she brought out the best in people.

How, in many ways, he felt as though he'd only just begun, himself.

***

It was clear that the breakfast was a success. When Lena had mentioned the plan, Prince Gabriel's private secretary had immediately jumped on the idea. She liked that she could contribute in a way that was more than photographs and some words on a social media site. She was beginning to feel as if she was part of a little team.

She took some more pictures, trying to ignore the prickling of awareness of her employer's presence. She'd only ever seen him in a suit and he'd joked he might wear one running, yet today he was in workout gear. It was just a T-shirt, shorts, trainers. Yet she was drawn to keep looking at him. The way that T-shirt moulded his body. Showing his biceps. His broad shoulders. The shorts, not tight, but still framing his backside. The sheen of perspiration on his skin. Had she not been used to keeping a tight rein on her emotions she might have swooned. There was a reason he'd hit the 'hottest men in Europe' lists more than once, though they'd always noted how remote he seemed, which tended to be a factor running against him most of the time.

Right now, he topped every one of her personal lists. Professional, considerate, attentive, caring, handsome. *So* handsome. He laughed at something someone said, and all of him lit up. How could anyone call him cold? Surely others could see what she could? Yet she needed to stop looking. It had become like some obsession. Instead of constantly tracking him whilst he ate or talked to his guests, she checked media alerts on her phone.

Cold No More: Crown Prince Melts Hearts as He Bonds with Toddler Godson

The headlines looked positive. Talk of his diplomacy. Applauding him showing his softer side. She was particularly proud of her photograph. Gabe, with a soft expression on his face. A warm smile, pointing out things in the book. Carl, looking on, his back to the camera. His parents out of focus in the background, but you could still tell there was an indulgent kind of expression on their blurred faces.

A slide of warmth slipped through her veins. She was glad she'd been able to show how genuine it was, because it hadn't been an act, it had been real. Authentic. A tender moment that more people needed to see he was capable of.

She was tempted to look over at him once more, before this morning's event ended and he wrapped himself in the confines of a suit again. She guessed it was his uniform of sorts. His shield. His protection. Much like her sombre professional wardrobe, which she'd decided to cast away on a whim this morning because it was a beautiful day and…she really didn't know. She supposed it was because she wasn't out in public. She didn't have to stay in the background so as not to outshine her employer. Even so, she'd got a little thrill putting on the dress and had fleetingly wondered whether he'd liked it when he first saw her. Lena tried to ignore what Gabe might think of her outfit, and instead concentrated on his social media pages.

She wished she could be analytical about it all, but she always got a bit of a buzz if something she posted did well. Underneath the photograph with him and his godson, there were so many comments.

This is the sweetest!
Such a gorgeous photo.

All reflecting the majority of the news headlines, apart from some of those in Halrovia, which still tried to put a negative spin on the post. Criticising the money spent only to show these 'homely' moments. She gritted her teeth at the unfairness of it, on Gabriel's behalf.

Lena grabbed a cup of coffee and took herself to a secluded part of the terrace in the shade and continued scrolling down. There were still a few people muttering about a republic but there weren't too many grinches today, because who couldn't help but love a picture of Gabriel being a doting godfather? The posts in response were emojis. Smiles, hearts. *Flames.* Glancing over at him standing there with his broad shoulders, narrow waist and strong thighs, she got it. She really did. Flames were apt. If the people who'd posted that could see what she saw right now, they'd want to fan themselves as much as she wanted to. They'd probably need a moment to catch their breath too, because it was as if she'd been on the run, not him, the way she couldn't catch any air.

Then there were the other posts that sent a spike of something hot and potent through her, which wasn't about attraction. If Gabriel were her boyfriend, she'd be sure the sensation was one of jealousy. It had to just be indignation on his behalf, because she didn't like being objectified, so why should he? Talk of ovaries exploding. Things like, *This picture made my heart melt, and my panties too.* Or, *Forget the book. Can I get a prince like you for my birthday?*

She tried not to judge. Who wouldn't want a prince for their birthday? Although she wasn't sure why she was thinking that, since she'd never wanted a prince before. She had no romanticism left in her, not after her parents. Still, the comments made her feel something prickly she couldn't explain, so she didn't try. She just kept reading. The sweet ones and the steamy. Unable to explain the roller coaster of her emotions as she viewed them.

'Lena.'

Gabe's voice jolted her out of her reverie. She whipped round, heel catching on the sandstone paving of the patio, hand jerking and an arc of coffee flying as Gabriel caught her, and they ended in a complicated tangle, with her somehow in his arms and him with a splat of coffee across his shirt.

He looked down at her for a heated heartbeat. Apart from the coffee she'd just spilled all over him, he smelled like the sea today, clean, salty, with an undertone. Something woodsy. It was complex. Inviting. A scent she wanted to snuggle into and stay, not moving from his strong embrace, with him looking down on her as if she could somehow answer the secrets of the universe...till she realised where she was. In her employer's arms, at an official function in front of a crowd of business people. She began to wriggle free.

'Are you all right, Ms Rosetti?'

His voice sounded somehow deeper, gravelly. Except she couldn't help notice that he was back to being formal. Putting her in her place.

'Yes, of course. The heels. I shouldn't have worn them out here. Silly me. I'm as clumsy as a newborn donkey sometimes.' Her mother's taunt was useful right now.

'Have you ever seen a newborn donkey before?'

'Well, no…' What could she do? What could she say? Her heart pounded a sickening rhythm. She'd made a fool of herself, of him, in front of all his guests. Not at all demure. She tried to shut down her mother's voice 'But, Your Highness. Your shirt!'

She untangled herself from him, grabbed a bundle of napkins and began patting away at his chest. Trying to mop up the coffee ruining the fabric of his tee. Making it stick to what she could see were the impressive muscles underneath.

The heat roared into her cheeks.

'Ms Rosetti…'

Lena couldn't stop. She was desperate to clean up the

mess she'd made. She kept patting, the white napkins staining with coffee, but it didn't seem to make a difference.

'Lena.' He put his hand over hers. She stopped, defeated, looking up at him. His pupils were huge and dark in the pale, icy blue of his eyes. Nostrils flaring. Lips parted. 'A new shirt is on its way.' She didn't know how, since she'd only just flung a coffee over him, but sure enough Pieter had arrived carrying a fresh shirt. Gabriel released her and took it from his efficient valet.

'I'm sorry,' she said, 'I—'

He held up his hand. She noticed how broad the palm was, how long and elegant the fingers. Remembered how it had felt when those hands had cradled her. Had she imagined how gentle he'd been? Yes, she must have. He didn't want her to fall, that was all.

'Accidents happen. Why don't you go and put on some safer shoes for this surface? When you return someone wants a photograph with me. They were meant to come to dinner at the ambassador's residence tonight and can't make it.'

He gave her a short sharp nod as he headed inside. She looked around her, but no one had seemed particularly bothered by her moment of clumsiness. It was only her, wanting to die inside from embarrassment, all the while unable to forget what it felt like to be in his arms.

This evening had been a long one. Gabriel strolled down the dimmed hallway of the Lauritanian home, trying to stay quiet as everyone appeared to be asleep. He understood there were people here who'd be at his beck and call should he so desire, but he didn't need anyone. Or perhaps he needed only one person.

A woman who was his employee. One who'd felt far too

good in his arms when he'd held her this morning. In that glorious dress, showing off her feminine side. Lips like wine. The scent of her, delicious, as if she'd bathed in honey and chocolate.

If he'd been any other man he might have kept on holding her. Might have tried to kiss her, even though his sensible side told him that was impossible. Yet after a long evening, he'd begun to wonder why.

He needed to get her out of his head. However, he couldn't stop thinking about their conversations. What made her different? That slight irreverence for his position she tried to hide. The sense of freedom about her that led him to consider that life might not be as constrained as his family believed. Her defence of him, her seeming belief in him as a man, and as Crown Prince. In her insightful photographs of him, showing a side of himself he'd forgotten.

He liked it, far too much. Craved it. Which was why he hated lying to her about his reading. About his glasses. Did he trust her enough to disclose what the real problem was? Would she judge him for it, for not being truthful?

He couldn't be sure. His own staff didn't care. He'd adapted, and technology made things so much easier there was no need to tell anyone outside his immediate circle because it was irrelevant. Wasn't it? Right now, he didn't have a good answer to that question whereas once, he wouldn't have thought twice about it. Tonight, it was as if the world weighed him down. He'd been to dinner at the Halrovian ambassador's home—a routine event when visiting another country, to drop in on the person flying Halrovia's flag. It had been a tedious kind of evening, because he'd seen it for what it was: conversations about the state of Halrovia, the press's views on the royal family, and the ambassador giving his own advice, because he was a good friend of Gabriel's father.

But the hints had come thick and fast about the benefits to a population's mood from a royal wedding. As if it weren't enough that Cilla was to be married in a few months, and that Anastacia had married only a few months earlier herself—although that hadn't been a royal wedding. It was a private function at her fiancé's chateau. Whilst his parents might have looked down on the occasion because it didn't meet their lofty expectations, Gabriel found something about it to be strangely satisfying. She'd married a commoner, someone she was in love with. Someone who had made her deeply happy. It was all he could ever have asked for both of his sisters.

As for himself, he'd been quietly reminded tonight of where his duty lay and, for once, he wanted none of it. He'd begun to realise that Lena's success was vital, if nothing else to ensure that more pressure wasn't put on him to marry. It wasn't that he believed he couldn't withstand it. He was his own man and wouldn't succumb to the whims of others, but over the past couple of weeks something had made him question life as he knew it.

He had rounded the corner towards his room when the unmistakable light tap of footsteps behind him made him stop and turn.

'Your Highness...' came the soft voice. 'Sir.'

It was as if the weight pressing down on him had lifted. He'd only ever seen Lena polished and professional, yet tonight she was in jeans with a soft pink top covered in butterflies. Her hair slightly damp, as if she'd just come out of a shower. He refused to dwell on that thought, on how rivulets of water would look running over her golden skin...

'How was this evening's dinner?' she asked.

The truth didn't bear mentioning. He'd done his duty—been polite, chatting to the guests, and then leaving. It had been cordial, but a pointed reminder from his parents as to what they expected from him.

'Walk with me,' he said as he set off towards his room. To remove his suit. Wash away the evening of expectation like a taint from his skin.

'How are things back home?' she asked.

He was fully aware she'd be keeping a pulse on what was going on—that was part of her job—but small talk suited him right now as the anger churned in his gut. He was an adult, and yet he was still being served missives by his parents through intermediaries.

That lack of communication irked him. He realised tonight how often so much went unsaid in his family. At least with Lena, she said what she thought. There was no guessing. In the palace and with the courtiers it was all about subtle messages you had to unravel. Reading between the lines. He was tired of it. They arrived at his suite and Gabriel walked straight to the credenza and poured himself a whisky. He held up the glass.

'Would you like one?'

Lena shook her head and held up a mug.

'Hot chocolate's my choice.'

Was that why she'd smelled like chocolate so often? Of course, it'd be improper to ask. She placed her lips round the rim of the cup and took a sip. As she did, her eyes fluttered shut as if in pleasure. The hint of a chocolate scent teased his senses. That smell of rich sweetness. Would her lips taste as sweet if he kissed her?

He slammed the door shut on those imaginings.

'The ambassador thinks an effective strategy is for me to marry.'

Lena was mid-sip when he said the words. She stopped, pulling the cup from her mouth. 'Well, people do love weddings.'

'Do you think it would be an effective strategy?' he asked.

'Spending the rest of your life with someone isn't a strategy.' The words sounded bitter in her mouth.

'Do I detect some cynicism?' he asked.

'You tell me—you're the one who's talking about getting married to improve your popularity. I can't think of anything more cynical than that.'

He shut his eyes and pinched the bridge of his nose, the pressure in his head building, because he agreed. Gabe wondered why that expectation had never really bothered him before. He'd always understood his duty, it had just seemed so distant before.

'Anyhow, who is the ambassador to say something like that to you?'

Wasn't that an excellent question? 'He's a friend of my parents, and he'd invited some suitable candidates as well.'

'Did any take your fancy?' Lena asked.

He'd realised their purpose—a few who might tempt his eye as potential brides. Whilst his parents would expect a princess, the women present were still eminently suitable members of various aristocracies. Then there were a few others who might tempt him in a different way, should that be where his inclinations lay. Once again, beautiful, polished, interesting, and yet he had no interest in any of them.

'If they had, I'd still be there.'

Lena pursed her lips, displeasure written all over her face. 'Pardon me for speaking plainly, but I find the whole thing odd.'

He took another slug of alcohol, somehow enjoying how prickly she'd become.

'So do I,' he said.

'Then why subject yourself to it? How dare people tell you how to lead your life?'

She seemed all flash and fire and he didn't quite understand why in that moment the thought of him having to marry for his role, and not for love, seemed to anger her. It was the way it tended to be done in most royal families, though the pretence of choice was still there. Put two people who met the correct criteria together, point them in the right direction with some solid encouragement and they usually got the message. Although Cilla and Ana had seen fit to break the mould...

'You're *curating* my life.'

'That's different and you know it. I'm showing people a glimpse, giving them some good news. But I'm not faking. I'm just giving people the best of you. It's what everyone does.'

Yet he was faking it in many ways. He wondered again, how she'd feel if she knew about his reading difficulties. He could share it with her, right now. She'd signed a non-disclosure agreement but, even more, he was sure she'd never breach his confidence even without that formal document. He took another sip of his drink, priming himself. Yet he couldn't find the right words. Time enough for confessions later. Instead, Gabe focussed on something easier, the desire to know what Lena thought was the best of him. *That* seemed vital. He supposed he could look at his own social media account, but he never had before. The one piece of advice he took away from his brief interactions in that public space, and warnings from Cilla when she'd first suggested Lena for the role was, *never read the comments*.

It seemed like wise advice.

'So, how do you curate your own life?' he asked.

She took another sip of her drink. He joined her with his own.

'I don't have social media in my real name. And I don't post for myself. It feels too much like work. I tend to people-watch instead.'

Something about her was shuttered. Closed off. As though there were things she didn't want to talk about, and he was treading close to them. He was assailed by a grasping need to find out why, to throw all her doors open and to peer inside. Yet he had no rights to the information as her employer. But for a woman who was happy to lay people's lives bare online, he found it surprising she wanted to keep herself hidden.

'What about your work? Surely that's all about being online?'

'Word of mouth's important. I got my job with you because of your sister. No one wants the most important person in their story to be the employee who manages their PR and social media. My job is to stay in the background, make my employer look good. As for the rest? I'm unimportant in the general scheme of things.'

He didn't know why those words seemed wrong. Was that how she thought of herself? Or was it someone else putting those thoughts into her head? He knew too well how family could cut. His sisters, particularly Cilla, had borne the brunt of his mother's disapprobation. The public's too, for not fitting a mould cast for her. Then Ana, who the press had loved as Halrovia's *'Perfect Princess'* before she had her accident, withdrew from public life and the narrative had changed. The criticisms starting.

What if, at those times, they'd had someone like Lena to show the world who they really were?

'You're not unimportant, Lena.'

She looked up at him, a gentle smile teasing her lips. Barely there, but the hint was enough. The look of pleasure at his comment. It flooded him with sensation, something warm and bright, of wanting to make her smile more often. When had he ever felt like this, enjoying the simple pleasure of making a person happy?

Never, and he craved more of it.

He looked down on her, hair long and loose about her shoulders. Her skin smooth and golden. Plush lips a soft pink. So fresh and beautiful. The collar of his normally comfortable shirt became too tight, the room too hot. Even though he knew his rooms were perfectly climate controlled, he wanted to throw open a window and let in the cool night air. Instead, he took another sip of his drink. The heat of the whisky burned, hitting his stomach.

'And you're not unimportant either—what you think, what you feel,' Lena said. 'So where does the ambassador get off raising marriage with the man who's one day going to be his king?'

There was a sharpness to her voice, a story there that he wanted to hear. And he found he wanted to know a great deal more about her. Her likes, dislikes. Her passions...

'I assume it's a message from my parents—a not so subtle hint via their friend, if you will.'

'Our parents and their desire for children to marry to solve all their problems.'

'You've had experience of this?' he asked.

The corner of her mouth kicked up. It wasn't a smile. There was sadness in that wry kind of grin of hers.

'My mother thought if I married it'd sort out her issues. It didn't seem to matter what I wanted, so I'm familiar with the sensation.'

'What did your father think?'

Something about her closed off immediately. One minute her face was open. Warm. Sympathetic. The next, it was as if she were made of glass. Cool and brittle.

'My father's dead.'

He started forward, an ache in his chest. Feeling terrible for bringing back painful memories.

'I'm so sorry.'

She shrugged. 'He wasn't much of a father. More a donor of genetic material. I'm surprised you don't know that already, what with the investigations your palace would have done to ensure I…fit.'

He guessed she was right and that she'd been investigated closely, but he hadn't bothered looking into it. If Lena had been cleared to come to an interview with him, the relevant checks hadn't shown up anything of concern.

'You'd have been vetted when you went to work with Isolobello's royal family. Priscilla recommended you. That was enough for me. But I want to know what problems your mother thinks your marriage might solve.'

If there was something he could help with, it might ease the pressure on Lena. He didn't know why he hated that thought—of her marrying someone else, whereas at the same time, he had an intense desire to see her in a wedding dress, a veil over her face, looking up at him… No, not at him. That was *not* where his thoughts were going. She was a beautiful woman, that was all, and she'd make a beautiful bride.

The air in the room seemed to get still and heated again. He shrugged off his jacket and draped it over the arm of the chair, loosened his tie and undid the top button of his shirt. Lena took another sip of her hot chocolate, then licked her lips, the pupils of her eyes wide and dark in the lower light of the room. Something heavy, palpable, weighed on him—the intensity of the situation, the desire to kiss her, to taste her. It was wrong. He was her employer. Yet, he also accepted in that moment that he was simply a man, and she was a beautiful woman. And what man wouldn't want to kiss her, wouldn't want to marry her, wouldn't want to have her for ever?

But she remained quiet, the question unanswered.

'That employment trial, your probation,' he said.

Her eyes widened, her white teeth biting into her lower lip.

'I think we both know you've passed it. I'll ask my private secretary to have the official employment contracts drawn up.'

Her mouth broke into the most beautiful smile. Whilst he'd seen her smile before, this one was pure, unrestrained joy. It lit her whole face.

'Thank you,' she said, her eyes glittering. Were those tears? 'You can't know what this means to me.'

She came closer to him, a step. Did he step towards her as well? Gabe wasn't sure. He might have imagined it, but he could almost feel the warmth from her body. His own, too hot. Everything tight, as if he were too big for his skin, as if he wanted to split in two and morph into something, somebody else. They were almost touching now, so close if he leaned down he could capture her mouth with his own. He might have imagined it, but her head tilted back. Lips sightly parted. He wanted to kiss her. Craving it more than his next breath. Did she want to kiss him?

A gentle rap sounded at the door, and the handle turned. The door cracked open, and Lena stood back. There was only one person who would ever walk in, the only other individual who had any entitlement to be in his personal quarters and space. One he'd texted after he'd arrived back at the house—his valet.

'Pieter,' he said.

'Y-Your Highness.' Gabe didn't miss the slight hesitation. 'I can leave—'

'No,' Lena said. 'We were talking work, and it's late, but maybe...' She placed her cup on a side table and reached into the back pocket of her jeans, pulling out her phone. 'We can take photographs of some unscripted moments. The public like you unscripted.'

Unscripted. He wanted to know—was that what she liked about him too? But these thoughts led nowhere.

'So what would you like us to do?' Pieter said, completely unfazed.

'What would you normally do at this time?' Lena asked.

'Get undressed,' Gabriel said.

'Oh.' She gave a low and soft kind of chuckle, a sexy kind of sound that shot through his blood more potently than any of the whisky he'd drunk tonight. 'Well, those kinds of photos would cause even more of a stir in the comments section than we have so far.'

Pieter chuckled too. 'I should read some of them to you, sir. They are quite the thing.'

Lena cocked her head to the side, studying him. Did she pick up on what Pieter had said? Who knew. Yet he wanted her to admire him, to like him. Little else seemed as important.

'What caused this?' he asked, totally bemused.

'The photograph of you and Carl. Nothing more enticing, it seems, than a man and child. But don't worry, whilst a shirtless shot would give the Internet a coronary and launch your popularity into the stratosphere, we are *not* giving them that.'

There was a sound to her voice. Something a little sharp.

Almost protective. Could it be...possessiveness? He liked that it might be.

'Just...pretend I'm not here for a bit,' Lena said. Didn't she realise how impossible that concept was? There was no way he could ignore her. Every time she was in his presence he experienced an intoxicating prickle of awareness. Something that drew his attention to her, like a compass to magnetic north.

He tried to do what she asked. Pieter seemed to have no trouble ignoring her, but that was his training. His employer was his focus, no one else. Gabe didn't know why he wanted the same focus from Lena, yet perhaps that was what he had, though always through a lens. Her eyes trying to find the essence of him.

What if she stopped seeing him through that lens and started seeing him for real?

'Did you have a good evening, Your Highness?' Pieter asked as they walked towards the dressing room where his clothes hung.

'You know how the ambassador is.'

'Of course.'

Pieter didn't need to say anything more. He'd been with Gabriel long enough to know exactly what Gabe thought of the ambassador here. Gabriel pulled off his tie, handed it over to his valet. Gabe was quite capable of looking after himself yet, somehow, talking to Pieter was like a debrief. Though he felt as if he didn't need it tonight, that he'd already debriefed with Lena...

Pieter took the tie and hung it on a tie rack.

'I'll get His Highness wearing a pink tie one day,' Lena said, the amused, lilting sound of her voice like fingers traced gently down his spine.

'I'd like to see you try, Ms Rosetti.' Pieter sniffed, although Gabe knew him well enough to glean the amusement in his voice too. Saw the merest of smiles on his usually impassive face. Gabe didn't know why he wanted his longest-serving employee to like his newest, yet he didn't dwell. A harmonious workplace was good for everyone, that was all.

In a strange way, Gabe felt adrift. Separate. As if he weren't a part of what was going on here. It was an uncomfortable sensation. He didn't know how long it had been since he'd truly felt part of something. Sure, he was a member of the royal family. He was close to his siblings, but Ana and Cilla had moved on with their lives. Some might have seen them as a close family but he'd never had an easy, warm relationship with his parents. Most of the time they'd dictated to their children, and Gabe and his sisters simply followed. Even his moniker, the Proper Prince, spoke volumes about him. It told of a person who always stood apart.

The only time he'd felt a real sense of belonging, he realised, was when he'd played football. The ease of it. He hadn't been a prince then, he'd been a team member. All with a common purpose, sure, but a camaraderie as well. He removed the cufflinks from one sleeve, then the other. Placed them on a dressing table. Looked over at Lena, glowing in the soft, warm light of the lamps. Holding her phone. Doing what? Taking stills? Video? It was such a strange sensation to be having his life catalogued like this. What did she see, or think, when she looked at him? Did she want him to undress in front of her? Something about having Pieter here seemed so clinical and cold, when all Gabe craved was heat. He'd felt that heat with her, before Pieter had arrived. Why couldn't he have it again?

Because she was his employee, and Gabe knew that their situation was impossible.

His shirt felt too rough against his skin. He wanted to be

naked, exposed to the cool night air. Not trapped in this suit that had begun to feel foreign to him. He undid the second button of his shirt. A third. Lena stilled. Something crackled in the air, a kind of electricity. It wasn't Lena in the room forgotten right now, but his valet.

She seemed to hesitate. Stopped what she was doing, looked at the screen of her phone.

'I think I have enough. Is there anything you'd like me to say on a post about your night tonight?'

'I'm sure you'll think of something that doesn't involve my telling the ambassador to keep his opinions to himself.'

Lena nodded. Gave a brief curtsey. 'Noted. Goodnight, Your Highness. I—I'll see you tomorrow, for your meeting at the palace.'

She turned and it was almost as if she fled the room, leaving her cup of hot chocolate behind. The faintest, tantalising pink smudge from her lips on the rim.

CHAPTER FIVE

LENA HAD CHECKED her compact mirror earlier, noting that all attempts to hide the dark circles under her eyes had failed. She wondered how they were shaping up now, after two hours at their morning engagement. Last night she'd barely had any sleep after her moment with Gabriel. She didn't understand it, the electric attraction that had seemed to sizzle between them. It was as if the feeling was something necessary to her very being. She craved it again. That need to simply be close to someone when she'd never really wanted it before. She couldn't shut down her mind, the memories of the feel of his embrace on the terrace, even though it had happened by accident. That moment in his room where they were so close she could almost feel his breath on her face. The way he looked down at her, eyes full of heat.

No, she couldn't think about it, yet that didn't stop the truth that she wanted him. An unsettling feeling when she'd never really wanted anyone before, not like this at least. She'd never really trusted enough, but there was something she trusted about him... It was almost as if he *saw* her, more than just as his employee, but as a person he might trust too. Lena took a deep breath to settle her racing heart. She had to keep focussed on her job.

The picture from last night had been received well. How couldn't it have been? With him, backlit in the low light of his room. Tie off, top button undone. Removing the cufflinks from his shirt. Such an intimate moment, which she hadn't thought about when she'd posted it in a fluster. She almost couldn't bear to read the comments so had asked Gabe's private secretary to scan them to see if there was anything that needed to be deleted. She was almost at the stage of needing a junior employee to help manage the account, so many people were beginning to follow. He'd said there was nothing, but was amused at the hashtag trending in the comments, *hashtag thirst-trap* as it related to their boss.

Thirst trap indeed.

She was parched dry just being around him, trying to do her job.

Now they were heading to the car to another meeting. Gabriel's shoes crunching on the gravel drive under his purposeful stride. His private secretary was planning to travel ahead to prepare. Lena almost wanted to join Henri, yet she didn't have an excuse to change the arrangements. She'd be left alone in the vehicle with Gabriel instead, with that scent of his, all fresh and evergreen. She almost couldn't breathe at the thought.

'Sir, I've loaded the documents into your reader for the next engagement. Is there anything else you need?' Gabriel's private secretary asked.

The crunch of Gabriel's shoes on the drive faltered, then quickly picked up to the same rhythm again. Reader? What was that about…?

'No, Henri. There's nothing else. I'll see you there. Lena, what are your plans for the next talks?'

Gabriel was all business this morning, not a shred of softness in him. No doubt regretting the moment between them last night. He was looking sharp in a navy suit, white shirt, and a yellow and blue tie echoing the colours of Halrovia's flag.

'I thought I'd take a photograph of you and the defence minister shaking hands in front of the countries' respective flags.'

They were attending bilateral security talks. Not that Halrovia or Lauritania had been in conflict with anyone for almost a century, but she guessed it was a show of solidarity and closeness of ties.

'Excellent,' Gabriel said, glancing down at her feet, which were in low-heeled shoes today after yesterday's debacle. Was he remembering her clumsiness on the terrace? How he'd worn a cup of coffee, and, for a little while, her? She couldn't tell, his expression hidden behind his sunglasses. Lena's cheeks flared with heat.

Before she could respond, her phone rang. She checked the number. Her mother? Lena's stomach twisted in complicated knots. They'd had some text exchanges when she'd taken this job. She'd kept in touch with her brother to make sure that he was still in university and studying. That there was food on the table and the bills were being paid, because her mother was useless at that sort of thing, never having had to worry about money in the past. Lena was tempted to decline the call, but she needed to know what was happening and her mother was terrible at texting. It would be easier to get it over with by speaking to her.

'Sir, I need to take this call,' she said as she swiped to answer. 'I'll meet you at the car in a few moments. We're ahead of schedule so you won't be late.'

He nodded, and strode on as Lena stopped in the shade.

'Mama…' Lena said. She couldn't get any other words out before her mother started.

'The landlord is increasing the rent.' Her mother's voice was tremulous, panicked. Lena's heart sank. This was bad news. She'd told her mother that she should leave her home because they couldn't afford it, but her mother had been so upset with the death of Lena's father and all that had happened, Lena had agreed to give her time. She'd given her mother and brother the money she would have spent on her own rent to cover some of the cost, topping it up with her wages. It left her with very little for herself, but she had accommodation and didn't have many needs. She could be frugal...except now, this would leave everything short.

Lena's chest tightened. She took a deep breath, wondering when it would ever end. Would she be responsible for her mother for ever? It seemed wrong. Her mother was an adult and wasn't her responsibility. Though there was her brother too... The burn of acid started in her belly as her thoughts whirred.

'When?'

'In eight weeks. What do I...?'

'You have to leave. There's *no* other choice. I'm at work now but I'll sort something out.'

'You don't get paid enough in this role. You could always—'

'No, I couldn't.'

She knew what her mother was about to say. *Marry.* Her mother claimed there were any number of men who would be interested on certain specialised dating sites for just that kind of thing. Rich men who'd look after her. Her family. The bile rose to her throat. She swallowed it down.

'I—I have had some other job offers. Maybe one will pay me more. We'll talk later, I promise. But everything will be okay.'

'You say that, and it hasn't been since your father died.' Her mother's voice cracked as she hung up.

Tears pricked at Lena's eyes. She wiped them away. She didn't believe Queen Lise had been joking about the job, should she want one, and she bet that King Rafe would offer her a premium to leave Gabriel. Yet that wasn't what she wanted. She'd committed to this job, *loved* this job. Felt as though she finally had a place.

There was more to do, that was all, and Lena never wanted to leave work half done. She was only now starting to get traction. Really achieving something. Turning the tide of press opinion as Gabriel's PR and image advisor, rather than as a junior part of a team, as she'd been on Isolobello. If she succeeded, it would make her career. A glowing reference from two royal families would mean she could go anywhere in the world for work, ask her own price. It was what she'd always wanted. Independence, security.

Wasn't it?

No decisions needed to be made right now. She could think about it a little later. Gabriel *needed* her, just as Cilla had said. Today, she had a job to do and would do it the best way she could, with dedication and focus. Lena checked her mascara and wiped away a few smudges, then began walking to the official vehicle. As she rounded the corner of the building what she saw in front of her brought her to a halt.

On an expanse of grass were a group of men kicking a football in the sunshine. Workers, she guessed, on a lunch break. They laughed as the ball was passed around, though that wasn't what caused her to stop. It was Gabriel, at the edge of the grass. Standing, watching.

To others, his expression might have seemed impassive, but she knew him better now. The corners of his lips barely turned up. The intent way he stared at the men, as if getting ready to spring into action. She stood back, watching the tableau in front of her. She'd seen him, of course, in her research. The young man leading his country to a junior world championship win. The photos then, showed a person not yet grown into himself. Still tall, yet somehow rangier. Less bulk on him.

He'd grown into himself now, in every way.

The men on the grass were clearly in competition of some sort, friendly as it was. One team manoeuvred the ball around, trying to score a goal, whilst others shouted at each other in a friendly kind of banter. They were all young, fit. Some were muscular. But Gabriel was the one who held her attention. She couldn't take her eyes from him. Yet there was something about *how* he watched. It almost looked nostalgic, the way he was so solid whilst the action swirled in front of him. In that moment she didn't think. She raised her phone, set her camera app to video, and pressed record.

One of the men aimed for the goal close to Gabriel. Missed. The ball speared towards him. His leg shot out and he stopped the ball dead with one foot, in a way that even her untrained eye could tell was with an uncommon kind of skill.

The men on the grass looked at him, and everything paused, as if the world held its breath. Then almost as if out of muscle memory, he started forwards, kicking the ball in front of him. Lena was transfixed by the brilliance of it, as he cut through the men trying to intercept him, to take the ball away. It was as if they were nothing more than mere irritations as he weaved between them, heading for the goal at the opposite end of the grass. Time slowed as she watched him dodge his assailants' attempts to tackle him. Then, in a moment almost even beyond her explanation, faced with a wall of men all joined together against him, their own teams forgotten, he lined up the ball and kicked. It flew, curved through the air in a sharp arc and hit the back of the goal net as Gabriel watched.

The men around him exploded in whoops and cheers, running towards him. Here, on this patch of grass, they were all equal. Lena forgot what she was doing, caught up in the sheer thrill of the scene in front of her. Then after a few moments it was as if he came back into himself. Gabriel turned. If she'd been asked, she would have said his expression was one of pure elation. A smile like she'd never seen before, splitting his face. Warm, true, joyous.

One that speared right into the heart of her, and in that moment, she *saw* him. Not His Royal Highness, Prince Gabriel, but Gabe Montroy, the man. It hit her as sure and true as if he'd kicked that football right into her solar plexus.

Something about him had changed. He seemed...*more*. As if he'd grown out of himself, shed an unwanted skin and somehow come alive. So unlike the man she'd met at her job interview. It was as if he'd become another person entirely. Sure, there was an ego about him. He'd be ruler of his country one day and would always carry that naturally superior demeanour with him, but this was something else.

Heat crept over her, that awareness again. Not of him as her employer or a future king, but of him as a man. Everything about him seemed larger than life. The way he fitted his clothes. His shoulders, broad and strong under his suit jacket. He seemed to become like some mythical figure. A god. His hair gleaming golden in the sunshine. All of him burnished. Beautiful. She stopped recording as he was feted by the other men. She didn't know if Gabriel could speak their language, but it didn't matter. Something about this moment seemed universal.

She took pleasure in simply watching as the men gave him the ball again and again in different positions on the expanse of grass, watching him kick goal after goal. Always the same perfect arc. Hitting the back of the net every time. She took a few still shots and some of the men had pulled out their phones too. Did they know who they played with? They had to be aware he was someone important. It was written all over him in the fit of his clothes, the way he held himself. You couldn't mistake him for anything other than a leader, yet in this moment there was a camaraderie. Prince or pauper, it didn't matter.

The game, such as it was, seemed to have wound up. Gabe shook hands with the workers, and they slapped him on the back. Made noises of disappointment about him having to go. She hadn't wanted to disturb anyone because they had plenty of time, but she still walked over to him, attracted like iron filings to a magnet. Watching as the workmen resumed their day and Gabe stood, distant and apart from it once more.

There was something about the moment that seemed poignant. Her heart beat an unsteady, excited kind of rhythm at what she'd witnessed. At the sheer *mastery* of him. He loomed so large right now, it was as if she were dwarfed. Then Gabriel focussed on her, and Lena noticed his breathing was a bit heavy, his shirt clung a little with perspiration from a workout in the bright sunshine.

'Y-you're *really* good,' she blurted out, the words spilling from her lips as the heat rose in her cheeks.

The corners of his mouth curled into a lazy smile, blinding and bright. Brimming with a magnificent kind of confidence in his own ability. He slid off his sunglasses and pinned her with his blue gaze that seemed to burn hot like a pilot light.

'I know,' he said. Winked.

And Lena went up in flames.

Gabe had always had a sense of place in the world, an awareness that he'd one day be King. Yet he'd somehow forgotten himself. Forgotten the boy he'd once been, filled with excitement at life and what lay ahead. The camaraderie of his team, whereas of late he'd felt so alone. The joy of a perfect kick, watching the ball curve and hit the back of the net. Of *winning*.

Of course, he'd won at life. He was a prince. He had all the privileges that his position entailed. Still, every day, someone wanted to carve a piece from him. The criticism, the barbs. Sometimes veiled, often not. Whilst he'd always carried a healthy sense of ego about what he could achieve for his people, he was only human. This moment just passed was simple, pure, and if he had to describe it, exhilarating. He didn't have to think, he simply *was*. It was as if he'd never walked away from the field. The memory of it came back to him. Made his blood pump hard and hot. He felt too big for his own skin. Alive again, as he hadn't been in years.

Especially with the way Lena was looking at him. He'd felt her gaze, as palpable as a caress. Now? Her cheeks carried a subtle blush, her eyes glittering. Pupils big and dark in the fathomless blue of her irises. Hair long and flowing round her shoulders like a river of dark silk that he craved to bury his fingers in to see if it was as soft as it looked.

He'd known she was watching him, and he'd wanted to perform for her. Driven to show her who he'd once been. Or perhaps, who he truly was when you stripped Prince Gabriel to his essence, and all that was left was the man.

'I—I had no idea.' That slight flush washed over her cheeks again.

The way she looked at him. He wanted to take her in his arms again, yet this time, to kiss her. Stake a claim, because he'd seen the way the workmen had looked at her. The admiration, the desire. Lena Rosetti was an exquisite woman and a man would have to be dead inside not to notice. He wasn't dead, not any more. He'd never felt more alive. As if he were King of the whole world.

'It's not hidden. I thought your research on me would have turned it up.'

'It did. It's just seeing it for real. That was...*something*. Why did you stop if you were that good?'

Because he'd been young and foolish and had felt untouchable. He'd become involved with someone he should never have trusted, and in the end that was the deal his parents had made with him. They'd dealt with the threats they never wanted to see the light of day. That he might be a hero on the football field, but he had trouble reading. In exchange, he went to work in the royal family. Who would challenge the story of a young man turning his back on everything he loved to serve his people?

If he thought hard about it and how his parents had behaved since, it was as if they didn't trust him. Neither did some of the press, not any more, though for spurious reasons. The bitter truth was that for so long he hadn't trusted himself. Questioned his own abilities because too much in his family had been unspoken. There were the frowns and thin-lipped disappointment of his parents when his school results had come in, yet they'd never asked why, only told him to try harder, as if he'd been lazy. In those times he'd wondered how he would ever be able to run a country when he had trouble making out words on a page. If he was seen as a failure…

The cut of his nails into his palms brought Gabe back from those thoughts into the present. He unclenched fists he didn't remember tightening. No. He *knew* he was trustworthy and didn't really care what other people thought of him, but deep in his soul he craved for someone who mattered to believe it. To trust him, and for him to trust them.

'I had a duty. I did what was expected of me. The burdens of my station.' Or so his parents said. Yet why did their children always have to be the ones that carried that burden for the crown?

'Was it what you wanted?'

Gabe checked the time. They needed to move to the next meeting, yet he didn't want to go. Not feeling like this. He wanted to relish the moment for a while, yet he still started walking because what was left for him but the duty to his country, which now felt like chains? He'd never been freer than on the field. It was what his sports master at school had realised after Gabe had struggled with reading and numbers and had been angry with the world because no one had worked out earlier why that was.

Then, when they had, hiding it from everyone as if it were an irrelevance when it was *everything* to him. He was tired of the dread he'd felt on entering a library. Of not being able to share the simple pleasure of sitting down and reading a book he held in his hands without feeling as though he was somehow lacking.

'What I wanted didn't matter.'

There'd not been a second's thought from his family. The utter dismissal still rankled, late at night when he lay awake, thinking of Halrovia's future and how he might shape it for the good of his people.

'It *does* matter.'

His feet crunched on the gravel beneath them, his footfalls faster and faster as if to escape the feelings swirling round him. Yet all he heard in Lena's sentence was, *You matter.* He didn't know why it hit him like a blade through the heart. An aching, needy thing that had no place in his life, and yet, he still held on to it tight, no matter the stabbing pain it unleashed.

'It's going to be years before you're King. Would it have mattered so much if you'd had an international football career?'

It had to his parents. So much about him mattered to them, but never his wants or needs. His dyslexia, his desire to play football professionally, to see what he could achieve. All meaningless. *'It's common!'* his mother had said about his request to at least try out for an international football career before his world had completely imploded with threats of betrayal.

'My parents and their private secretary felt a career in football was beneath my role as heir, and how it would be seen by Halrovia.'

A crease bisected Lena's brow as they walked past a formal garden. Clipped, restrained. Why did it remind him of himself, when all he wanted right now was colour and chaos?

Why did he want to shout out the real reason that he had to give up everything? The guilt he carried for it?

'With respect, sir, your parents' private secretary has done such a sensational job to date, I'm of the view he doesn't have a single clue about how you'd be seen by Halrovia. I mean, look at how well it's gone so far.'

The sarcasm poured hot and thick from her, though somewhat discordant with her attempt at formality. He couldn't help himself. He laughed. Around Lena, he seemed to want to laugh much of the time. What would his parents' private secretary think of this slip of a woman who had no tertiary education making that comment? Gabriel desperately wanted to see it, and see her cut him down to size. He'd bet the Halrovian kingdom that Lena would rival his mother in that skill if she really put her mind to it.

'I shouldn't have said that,' she whispered. 'I'm sorry.'

He suspected that she'd meant more than just his parents' private secretary too, that the criticism of his parents was implied as well.

Gabriel didn't much care.

'There's no need to apologise. I applaud honesty, and you're right,' he said. 'Your employment is incontrovertible evidence.'

She cocked her head, pierced him with her vivid gaze. 'Do you trust me?'

'Yes.' He didn't have to think about that answer and a sense of relief swept over him. Whilst most people around him deferred to him because of duty, she didn't. He liked the challenge of her. The way she tried to find who he was, not accept what she'd been told or shown. And, in many ways, he knew that she had his back.

'That, there?' She waved her hand behind her. 'That's who people want to see...sir.'

Something seemed to have shifted. A kind of knowing. This formality between them, it felt *wrong*.

'Gabriel. In private, call me Gabriel.'

Her eyes widened. 'Okay...'

'So long as you're comfortable with the invitation.' In her role she'd likely be witness to some of his most intimate and vulnerable private moments, and it felt wrong to maintain this false formality between them.

'I am... Gabriel.'

It was like being thrown in a blast furnace. The sound of his name slipping from her lips as she tried it out. Did she like saying it? He couldn't understand why he wanted to know so badly. He shrugged the strange sensation off. It was nothing. He'd offered the same to his private secretary, who'd politely refused because he didn't feel it was right. However, Lena wasn't from Halrovia. He wasn't going to be her king, so it mattered less.

Or that was what he was trying to convince himself...

'Excellent.'

He wasn't a man who dwelled too much on his decisions, but he was likely to ruminate over this one and, for that, he needed time.

'So,' she said as they approached the car. 'I took a video.'

'Really.' He didn't know what he thought about that, only that he quite liked that she seemed to have enjoyed what she'd seen enough to video it.

'As I said, it was...impressive.' Her vivid blue eyes seemed to darken. 'And given you said you trust me... I'd like to post it to your social media pages.'

His heart missed a beat. For a few seconds he had to think about how that made him feel. His football had been a loss. He'd tried to set it aside, even though in the end he still did some practice because he'd loved the game. Showing that side of him again? In many ways it left him exposed, reminding him of a time that was raw and painful. One he didn't really want to talk about.

'Do you want to go viral?' Lena asked, perhaps sensing his hesitation for reasons even he couldn't fully articulate. Yet, why not? It was what Lena had been employed for. She wanted to, and he believed in her judgement. She hadn't been wrong yet.

'Let's do it.'

She smiled, and it was a glorious thing. Full of warmth and happiness. Her eyes dancing with excitement. Was it because she was doing her job and was happy to be doing it well? Or was it that he'd given her *proof* that he trusted her? Gabe wasn't sure, even though he enjoyed her smile. Took it as a precious gift bestowed upon him.

'You've been working hard, and the results speak for themselves. Even my parents' secretary seems happy.' As if that were any yardstick. 'I have the state dinner tonight so you can take the rest of the day off.'

'Thank you, si— Gabriel.'

Gabe rarely second-guessed his decisions. Even though they'd failed him in the past, he'd honed his instincts on sharp and brutal experience and, now, they were invariably right. Still, hearing Lena say his name did something to him. It was like the sultriest music. It started a drumbeat of desire deep and low.

Perhaps he enjoyed the sound of his name from her mouth just a little too much.

CHAPTER SIX

LENA STROLLED THROUGH the dimly lit halls of the lake home, as she'd begun calling it. Today, she'd taken advantage of the time off Gabriel had given her. Exploring Lauritania's antique markets in the old, walled part of town. Having a lovely dinner out with a couple people from work who had accompanied the royal tour; a personal protection officer who'd had the night off too, and Gabriel's private secretary. They'd drunk a glass of champagne each, toasting the success of the trip, which was now drawing to a close. Eaten at a quaint little restaurant with red and white checked tablecloths, tea-light candles on the table, and delicious rustic food. After dinner she'd left them partying and planning to hit the clubs, whilst she'd returned home.

All the while, she had a prickling sensation of something missing. As if she shouldn't be celebrating. Was it...guilt? She had so much to think about. Her mother's situation. How to manage it on her current wage. Should she contact Albert at the Lauritanian palace and ask if Queen Lise was serious about a job? Everything about her revolted at the idea, even though it would be best for her family. But what about her? Shouldn't she be able to do what she wanted, for once, without worrying about everyone else? She shouldn't feel this way. She *should* have been able to enjoy herself like any normal young woman. Gabriel had given her the night off.

Gabriel...

She *liked* saying his name. Liked that he'd invited her to use it when in private. As if it was some secret between them. Lena knew she shouldn't be reading too much into it but something about the moments between them recently had seemed special.

He was handsome, self-deprecating. Kind, and he cared. He trusted her and she found that, despite everything, she trusted him too. He'd be a wonderful king one day. And she began to wonder, had anyone ever told him that? *Gabriel, you'll make a great king.* Lena only wished that the world could see it as she did. She felt the weight of her role, wanting to present him at his absolute best, because the public deserved to know him as she saw him. She'd do everything in her power to show them all.

It was like a fire lit inside her, that sense of protectiveness. But there was something more. Desire. A heat and need whenever she was around him that threatened to overwhelm her and burn away all common sense.

Dangerous, Lena. Dangerous.

There could never be anything between him. He was her employer, a *prince*. There was no risk of love here. She'd never much trusted the emotion anyhow, because look at how well it had gone for her mother. Spending a lifetime sharing a man, for what? But perhaps this was what made Gabriel the safest person of all, because she couldn't expect anything from him. His position wouldn't allow it, and that would protect them both.

She walked past his wing on the way to the kitchens to get a cup of hot chocolate before bed. Hesitated. Stopped. Turned around as if drawn. Her feet carrying her back along the path she'd just come, deeper into his section of the home. Wondering if he'd returned from the state dinner yet. How it had gone. Maybe he'd want to talk with someone about it?

As she approached his suite, Lena glimpsed a sliver of light under his door. She turned towards it, her feet seeming to carry her without much thought, just the sensation that she was being pulled in his direction. An itch under her skin telling her she needed to do this. Before he'd left tonight, he'd looked tired. So very tired.

She supposed trying to shore up your allies and improve your unfairly falling reputation carried significant pressures, not to mention your own ambassador suggesting you marry when it was none of his damned business. She understood being buried under the weight of obligation after her father had died. When she'd realised her whole life would have to change. The fight to find another job, the recognition that she was responsible for her family and their future. Putting aside her own dreams. What would it be like, instead, to be responsible for a *country*?

Maybe Gabriel would have preferred to come out to a simple dinner too. Sharing a glass of champagne and laughter in a little corner restaurant with no care.

Lena knocked. Waited. Listened, barely able to hear anything over the thudding heartbeat in her chest. Then one word.

'Yes.'

She cracked open the door and continued down a short entrance hall towards the lounge area of his suite, following the dim light. She almost didn't see him, standing still at the far end of the room. In a formal shirt, the top few buttons undone. Bow tie draped carelessly around his neck. His arm propped on the mantelpiece, almost negligently holding a tumbler of amber fluid. Head dropped. It looked as if the mantelpiece was the only thing holding him up. As if his glass was about to slip from his fingers.

A wiggling sensation started in her belly, like a flock

of a thousand birds taking wing. One look at him took her breath away, because he was one of the most beautiful men she'd ever seen. Although tonight, he seemed...vulnerable. Standing there as if undone. She wanted to go to him, offer comfort, offer him everything.

Though, no matter how he looked right now, what she'd come to learn over her time working with him was that his restrained exterior wasn't evidence of coldness. It was just he'd never been allowed to be himself, because his parents and courtiers wanted the best parts of him suppressed. The parts of him that people would relate to. His personality. His feelings.

Gabriel was no automaton. He was a man with passions who should have been allowed to show them.

'I... It's late.' Lena didn't know why she said it. She should have turned and walked away, leaving him to his own thoughts, but something about tonight told her that he needed some company as much as she did.

His head shot up, flinty blue gaze fixed on her. Even in the dim light of the room she could *feel* it prickling into her.

'Lena.'

The way he said her name. The rasp of it. The rough sound scraping like fingernails over her skin. If she hadn't known better, she might have thought his voice was filled with need. Maybe she needed him too.

This thing between them, it seemed to have taken on a life of its own. Bigger than both of them. The way he looked at her right now, so stark, so intense and burning as if he'd branded her, let Lena know that she hadn't imagined it.

'Gabriel.'

He took a swig from his drink. Placed the empty glass on the mantelpiece. Looked her up and down, in a way that could have been admiring. She wasn't sure. Tonight, she'd dressed to go out. Another wrap round dress. This one of soft, printed silk in jewelled colours, with beaded accents around the neck. Ruffles round the hem. It drifted about her as she walked and made her feel feminine. Pretty. Sure, the neck plunged a little lower than she normally wore but she'd never heard anyone complain before.

'You've been out.' The words sounded almost accusatory.

'It's what you do when you're given the night off by your employer.'

He almost flinched at the word, as if he didn't want reminding of who he was.

'Did you have fun?'

'Yes. Henri, Serge and I went to a little café in the old town. They wanted to continue the party. I came back here.'

'I'm glad…' She stiffened and the moment held, pregnant with possibility. 'Glad that you had a good time.'

Of course he'd want her to have a good time. It wasn't that he was glad she was back here with him. Was it?

'What are you doing here?' he asked.

'I—I saw the light. I came to see how tonight went.'

His shoulders slumped. He shrugged. 'It was a typical state dinner.'

'Well, I've never been to one of those so I can only guess. Were you seated next to anyone interesting?'

'Being the guest of honour, I sat with the King and Queen. It was a sumptuous feast with beautiful food and wine showcasing Lauritania's finest producers. The Grand State Dinner service was used. I'm told there were over a hundred candles lit for the meal.'

The whole evening sounded incredible, but he recounted what went on as if he were reading a funeral notice.

'No eligible princesses?'

That stark look returned. 'There are always eligible princesses, or daughters of dukes, marquesses, earls, counts, viscounts, barons. You name it, they're there.'

'Sounds like a fruit salad of peerage.'

'I'll never think of them the same, ever again.' Gabriel chuckled, but it wasn't a happy kind of sound. 'A veritable cornucopia, although many of them aren't as colourful or sweet as fruit.'

There was that tired sound to him again. She stepped forwards, closer. Wanting to reach out, put her hand on his arm. To touch, to comfort. To...more. Say everything was going to be okay, even though she didn't know what was wrong.

'You don't sound like you enjoyed yourself.'

'Lise and Rafe are always engaging company, but... I wish you'd been there.'

As he said it, his gaze fixed on her but this wasn't something cool and impassive. It was full of heat. That look scorched her, igniting in her core and burning outward. She shouldn't be here. This was a mistake in every way, both on his part and on hers, and yet she couldn't move.

She'd spent enough time thinking of others, worrying about what they thought of her. It all felt like a millstone round her neck because she had begun to realise what she might have been holding onto wasn't a sense of responsibility, but of fear. Fear of being criticised, fear of being seen as somehow lacking. Lena was tired of it. Holding back. Being less. Her virginity, which was another thing she realised she'd clung to in an effort to protect herself. To allow someone into your body you had to trust them, and she realised she didn't really trust much at all.

Why would she? Her parents hadn't set great examples. Her mother choosing secrecy over the welfare of her own children and her father showing how fickle he was prepared to be. For so long she'd believed if that was how people treated each other in relationships and families then she wanted no part of it. Especially when everything in her life seemed to be secrets and lies.

Except for now. There was a kind of truth in this room. This…thing that seemed to be growing larger and more palpable. She'd begun to feel as if Gabe valued her, trusted her. And in the tumult of her emotions a tiny seed of something fragile had begun to sprout and grow inside her.

She might just trust him too.

'You look beautiful,' Gabriel said, then raked his hand through his no longer neat hair, displacing it until a curl flopped over his forehead. Rubbed his hands over his face. 'That was wrong of me. I shouldn't have said it. You need to go.'

She should. Lena knew it was the sensible thing to do, but nothing would make her move backwards out of this room. She'd spent a lifetime trying to be good, be sensible, so that people would like her. Her father, her teachers, her schoolmates. And for what? That green shoot deep inside her grew leaf, blossomed. She felt so full, and so aching and empty at the same time. Instead of leaving, she moved forwards into him.

'What if I don't want to?'

He made a sound as if the air had been punched out of him. 'You should.'

'But I like that you wish I'd been with you, by your side. I like that you think I'm beautiful.'

'I'm your employer, you're my employee.'

'Before all of that I'm a woman.'

'Yes, you are unmistakably a woman. But there's a power imbalance here, and that doesn't make it fair on you.'

She put her hands on her hips, stared him down. She was tired of being seen as powerless. Right now, she was full to the brim with her sense of how powerful she truly was. An unfamiliar, intoxicating sensation.

'An imbalance? Why do you think I don't have *all* the power here? With a bad series of posts or saying the wrong thing, I could destroy your reputation irrevocably. Who has the power now, Gabriel? It seems that it's all with me.'

He pushed away from the mantelpiece and stalked towards her. Stern, intent. Goosebumps peppered her skin. A shivery kind of sensation overtook her, as if she were coming down with something, running hot and cold all over.

'You'd destroy me, would you?'

Her cheeks flushed. She wanted to protect him, not destroy him. Lena bit into her lower lip. 'Well, no, but I could.'

'What if you already have?'

A pulse started deep and low at her core. The relentless ache intensified inside her.

'Gabriel,' she whispered.

'I like the way you say my name. Say it again.'

'Gabriel.'

He clenched and unclenched his hands. Then Gabriel flexed his fingers as if itching to touch her but trying to hold back.

'A-are you expecting Pieter?' She knew if anyone walked in on them, the night would be over even before it began, and she didn't want to stop whatever might happen between them.

'No, I've given him the night off.'

They stood close now, as they had the evening before, free to see where things took them. Did she want this? The answer, clear in her head, was *yes*. She might see Gabriel, but she believed that he saw her too. Had chosen her. Valued her in a way she'd never been before. As Lena Rosetti, the woman.

The way Gabriel looked at her now. As if he were starved. As if she were the only woman left on earth. So intent... If she was going to lose her virginity, then why not with someone like him? Someone handsome, someone who stole her breath. Who thought of others. She was sure he'd take care—not that she was really planning to tell him about her virginity, but he seemed like the type of man who'd look after any woman he was with.

That thought stung. She didn't like the idea of him with anybody else, but knew that was the reality of who they both were. Perhaps she needed to reinforce it.

'I understand what this is. How it has to be.'

'Do you?' Gabe chuckled, but didn't sound very entertained. 'Because I'm not sure myself.'

'I'm not asking for promises. I realise that this is behind closed doors. And I have no expectations.'

'You sell yourself so short. Stop. You're worth more than you know.'

Her whole life she'd been waiting to hear those words. Confirmation of what she'd hoped, then believed. That Gabriel acknowledged her value as a person, when most of the time she'd felt either dismissed, or invisible. Finally, someone had given voice to an unmet need she'd carried for years. To be seen for who she was, to be seen as worthy. It was overwhelming, like a burden lifting, even if the sensation lasted for only a night.

'You have no idea what that means to me.' The burn of tears pricked at her eyes, and she blinked them away.

'I fear I do,' he said, 'and that makes the world an unfair place.'

Lena tilted her head up, and her lips parted. She craved his touch, his kiss. To do something to channel this emotion that was banked up inside her, though she had no idea how to initiate things. What to do with all the feelings threatening to overwhelm her.

'Life's unfair. We just have to snatch what joy and pleasure we can when it's offered, and live the rest the best way possible.'

Gabriel shut his eyes for a moment, took a deep, slow breath, then opened them again. It was as if something had changed. His jaw clenched, nostrils flaring in a kind of determination.

'You know what's bound to happen if you don't leave? You know where this is heading?'

'Yes.'

'Tell me you want it as much as I do.'

'I want you more than my next breath,' she said.

'Thank God.'

She wanted to lose herself in him, and his body. But she knew that she might just find herself as well. Although there were rules, she was sure. Unspoken ones, which she needed to voice.

'Gabriel, I know it's just for tonight. I know what we are—'

He placed a finger gently on her lips where it burned like a brand. His other hand settled on her waist as Gabriel slipped his arm around her, and she craved for him to touch every part of her, to kiss her, to fill the terrible emptiness gnawing deep inside.

'There's no difference between us. We're two people who want. Tonight's all we have, so I plan to give you the world for one evening,' he murmured as he dropped his head to hers, and their lips touched—his mouth soft, coaxing. The tenderness of him in this moment, as if giving thanks, as if fusing her to him. He tightened his hold and deepened the kiss. She opened for him, their tongues touching. She didn't have time to be shy. Sensation overwhelmed her. She pressed against his body, into the hardness of him, relishing his arousal, knowing she'd done this to such a magnificent man. It gave some truth to her statement that she had all the power here, though she felt the scales tipping at his masterful touch.

He pulled away. She didn't want to let him go. His breath came in heavy gusts. Gabe took her hand.

'What you do to me,' he said, and placed it on his groin. He was so hard—the feel of him made her ache inside. She clutched him and stroked through the fabric. He moaned, the sound deep and carnal, making her catch fire. Tremble with need.

'Come to bed. Let me make love to you,' he said.

There was only ever one answer for her.

'Yes.'

He swept her into his arms. This wasn't like the moment on the terrace. This was something else, purposeful, almost romantic, if she didn't know this was all they could have. He strode into the bedroom and placed her down gently at the end of the bed, looking at her feet in their strappy gold sandals.

'Shame there are no heels.'

Lena wanted to say *next time*, but there were rules and she'd stick by them. 'You just want me to fall into you so you can catch me. I know your style.'

He laughed deep and low, the sound rumbling right through her. 'I wanted to feel them digging into my back as you screamed in pleasure underneath me.'

Lena almost dissolved on the spot in a puddle of need. What could she say in response? She had nothing in her repertoire. Luckily Gabriel knew exactly what to do. He undid the tiny buttons at the side of her waist, holding her dress in place.

'You're like the most precious gift for me to unwrap.'

The front of the dress fell open. Then he moved forward

and unclipped the snap between her cleavage that kept the bodice together, trailing his lips up her neck to her ear.

'Beautiful,' he murmured as goosebumps showered over her skin.

Lena shivered with the pleasure of it. She wanted him to unwrap her, to unravel her, to pull her apart at the seams. She could put herself back together in the morning, but right now, she was thankful for his control. He reached to the other side of the dress, where ties held it together inside. Slowly, he undid one bow, then the next, until the skirt came apart, and he stood back, staring at her, his mouth partly open, looking deliciously dishevelled.

'I need to be inside you,' he said.

'I need that too.'

She didn't have any fear, even though this was her first time. He reached out and slipped the dress from her shoulders and it fell to the floor around her feet.

'Undo my shirt,' he commanded in a way that was so princely, she almost smiled. Thrilled to do as he asked. She began unbuttoning the studs on the front of his dress shirt till it was open. She'd seen pictures of him when he was younger, with his shirt off, but it was nothing like seeing him for real. The defined muscles of his pectorals, the washboard abdomen, which spoke of hard work and dedication to exercise, as she knew he applied to all parts of his life. Would apply to her. She pushed the shirt from his shoulders, resting her hands on the powerful muscles there for a moment, feeling all that strength, wondering how it would be when she was underneath him.

Trembling with the anticipation of it.

'Now my trousers.'

She reached her shaking fingers and undid the hook at the waist. Slowly undoing the zip, notch by notch, as he stood there, his gaze glassy, his breathing heavy. Once she was done, she reached inside and cupped him, feeling how hot he was, how large. She knew they'd fit. Human bodies were made for each other. But the size of him. Didn't she owe Gabriel to tell him that she'd never done this before? She squeezed slightly, testing him out.

'Temptress,' he hissed through gritted teeth, and she couldn't help but smile. She'd never seen herself that way and loved that was how he viewed her. She rested her hand on his chest, the slight dusting of hair there that bisected his abdomen and disappeared beneath the band of his underwear.

'There's something I need to tell you.'

'Contraception? I have condoms. I'm careful. I have regular health checks.'

'No.' She shook her head, 'You need to know... I've never done this before. I'm a virgin.'

'I'm a virgin.'

Gabriel stopped. He couldn't have heard correctly. Could he? But there'd been no ambiguity. This was... He'd never made love to a virgin before. The only time he thought he might have to was on his wedding night. And even then, it wasn't the sort of thing he'd ever sought out. A woman's past was her own. He'd never judge, since he believed everyone was entitled to pleasure, but this?

The sensations overwhelmed him. The privilege of her wanting him to be her first. The responsibility. Then all the questions. Such as why? Lena was a beautiful woman. Men would clamour for her, even though in this moment he might have wanted to tear each of those men apart with his bare hands.

He looked down at her and he could see in her eyes. The

way they were a little wider. The way she raked her lower lip through her teeth. Her vulnerability.

'I don't know what to say.'

'You don't have to say anything. It's not important. I just thought you should know if you wondered why I...'

Seemed inexperienced? He hadn't even thought about it, being so caught up in the moment. He took a step back to give himself space when all he wanted to do was to drag her closer.

'We shouldn't... You've clearly been waiting... You should—'

'No, I've been waiting for you.'

The heat roared over him like a wildfire. If he'd been aroused before it was nothing to how he felt now. He was so hard he could almost snap in two.

Lena wrapped her arms round her waist, another sign of the insecurity and innocence he'd not noticed before. 'I... maybe not you *exactly*...'

He wanted to chuckle, because she had a unique way of cutting him down, but feared that she'd think he was laughing *at* her, rather than at himself.

'I think you'll be nice to me. Take care of me. Make it good.'

She'd set the bar so low for herself. *Nice?* Was that all she hoped for? Part of his heart tore. Bled. He shouldn't be doing this, especially since her admission. And yet here she was, with complete power over him. Holding him in her thrall.

'Come here. Let me hold you.' He held out his hand.

She placed her own in his and he reeled her into him. Gabriel sat on the side of the bed and cradled her in his lap. She nestled into his body. He was so damned hard, desperate for her. Yet was torn between desire and doing the right thing.

She trembled in his arms. From desire, nerves or a combination of both, he couldn't tell. He stroked his hand up and down her spine, goosebumps peppering her skin under his fingertips. Gabriel kept up his ministrations. Caressing, soothing, till she melted into him.

'Why did you wait?' he asked.

'It's not important.'

'*You're* important, Lena.'

She let out a long, slow breath. 'It's not like I haven't dated a little, but I really wanted to concentrate on getting a career. Then…you know…men seemed only interested in me because I looked a certain way…'

'Beautiful, Lena. You're beautiful.'

'But they didn't really want *me*. They wanted who they imagined me to be.'

His hold on her tightened. The anger in his gut, volcanic at those kinds of men who didn't value her. Made her feel this way. He cupped Lena's jaw and she looked up at him, so open and wanting. This woman who trusted him. Who *chose* him. It was humbling.

'You deserve more than one night. You deserve to do this with a man who loves you.'

'My virginity's become this thing that hangs over me, that I don't want any more. This is *my* choice. No one else's. Anyhow, love's overrated. It seems who I want is you.'

There was a story there, but he was done. She'd entrusted herself, her body, to him for his care. He'd honour that trust, her desires. Honour her. Still, Gabriel did what he believed was the right thing, even though all he wanted to do was throw her onto the soft covers and make love to her all night.

He gave her a chance to walk away. 'Lena, are you sure?'

She nodded.

'I need the words.'

'Yes, Gabriel.'

The way she said his name, fluttering soft as a moth's wing at midnight. She wanted him. He wanted her. It was a story old as time. His hands began moving with more purpose. Not to soothe, but to inflame. One cupping her breast, the pad of his thumb teasing at her nipple through her bra till it tightened to a hard nub. She began to writhe underneath at his attention, in his lap. Grinding into him, sending darts of pleasure through his overheated body.

How much better would it be when he had her under him? Dark hair spilling over the pillow. Head thrown back in ecstasy. He was so close. Gabe had little doubt he'd be transported to heaven, but he needed to make sure she was ready. Mindless in her craving for him.

'Let's get into bed.'

He let her go. She stood and he threaded his fingers through hers, leading her to the side of the bed where the covers had already been turned down for him. She toed off her pretty gold sandals, then moved to take off her bra. Hesitated.

'Leave it on,' he said. 'I'm so desperate for you I need to slow down. Make it good for you.'

She slid between the sheets, pulled the duvet over herself, enveloped by the soft down as she watched him. Looking so innocent. Lying there, exactly as he'd imagined, with hair like black ink on the pillow.

Gabe kicked off his own shoes. Shed his trousers and tossed them onto a chair. Left his underwear on. Lena's gaze tracked him. Her eyes widened a little when his trousers came off and the corners of her mouth tilted in a subtle smile he liked to believe was one of appreciation. He stood for a few moments, admiring her right back. Her eyes gleaming in the soft lamplight. Lips the pink blush of peaches. All the while he hoped he was allowing her to take in her fill of him. To adjust to the idea of his size. Hoping that she wouldn't be afraid.

It was his responsibility to ensure that she wasn't.

Gabriel moved onto the bed beside her, reaching out. Stroking a stray strand of hair from her face. Tracing the shell of her ear with his fingertips. Her eyelids fluttered shut. Lips parting in pleasure. Then he drew her close again, into his arms. Her body soft and pliant against his own. Captured her lips with his as she moaned. Kissing long and slow and deep. Tongues caught in a hypnotic rhythm as Lena flexed against him, as if she was trying to get closer.

Gabe reached round and undid the back of her strapless bra with a practised flick. Tossed it aside. He rolled Lena onto her back and went up on one elbow, looking down at her beautiful body. Palming her left breast in his hand. Stroking then pinching her nipple, which pebbled under his touch as Lena writhed restlessly. Panting. He dropped his head and laved her diamond-hard flesh with his tongue. She began whispering his name. Over and over. Interspersed with little cries of pleasure.

'Let's get these off you,' he murmured against her burning flesh. As hot as his own. Trying to concentrate only on her when he was at his breaking point. Thank God for his foresight to keep his underwear on, because all he craved to do was to plunge into her warm, wet flesh and lose himself. Yet there was time enough for that. They had a long night ahead of lovemaking should she gift him the privilege of her body more than once. He sat up. Slipped his hands into the sides of Lena's panties and slid them down her legs and off.

In all his late-night fantasises he'd never imagined someone as enticing as her. Sprawled on the bed. Eyes glassy with desire. Golden skin and gentle curves, laid out for him. He bent down over her. Kissed her stomach. Lower. Lower.

'You're so beautiful.' Her scent was heady. A perfume of honey and chocolate with overlying arousal. Gabe reached the apex of her thighs.

'Open for me.'

Her legs fell apart and he slipped his tongue against the sweet, salt of her. Taking his time, finding the centre of her pleasure. Learning what made her gasp and cry out. The perfect rhythm. Teasing her till she was mindless. A prisoner to sensation.

When she was on the verge, the very cusp, he stopped.

'I'm going to touch you some more. Slide my fingers inside you. Get you ready for me.'

'Please, please.' Her voice was a chant. She lay before him almost wrecked. Her limbs lax. Glistening between her legs, so wet it almost undid him. Gabe climbed back up her body. Whilst he could have spent hours between her thighs holding her on edge till she begged, he wanted to be able to watch her. To make sure he could see her face so that if there was any hint of pain he could slow down, take his time.

His body ached to be inside her, but she'd trusted him with her first time and he'd ensure that it would ruin her for any other man. There'd be no one else. Something pricked in his conscience then, but he allowed himself to drown in those darkly possessive thoughts. They were fantasies, that was all. They hurt no one. Only heightened the pleasure.

And wasn't that what tonight was all about?

He dropped his mouth to Lena's nipple again. 'Let's try one finger.'

He teased her flesh with his tongue as he teased her entrance with his hand. She lifted her hips to match his rhythm. He had no doubt she ached for him to be inside her, so he slid one finger knuckle deep. She was so soft, hot, wet. Lena let out a sob. Gabe lifted his head to check on her but she lay there, eyes shut. Head arched back. A look of pained ecstasy on her face as he slid his finger in and out.

'Let's try two,' he murmured, and she moaned as he slid in another finger to join the first. Setting a steady rhythm. Working her tight flesh as he watched her lose herself to his touch.

He trembled with need like some teenager, yet refused to break his focus on her. The way a flush rose on her chest, up her neck, to her cheeks. The way her breath came in little pants. The flutter of her body on his fingers telling him she was close. Giving her time to adjust till he tipped her over the edge.

'There's a spot inside,' he said. His voice rough and unrecognisable to his own ears. 'You are going to enjoy this. Just feel, Lena. Nothing else but my hands and lips. Let yourself go.'

He curled his fingers forwards, found where he promised he would. Her eyes flew open but he wasn't sure she saw anything, the way her gaze was far away. Lost in her pleasure. He'd bring her back to him soon but, for now, he wanted to give her this. Pure bliss and nothing else.

He dropped his mouth to Lena's breast again.

'*Feel* what I'm doing to you.'

Then he captured her nipple in his mouth. Began teasing her clitoris with his thumb, his fingers deep, stroking inside. She arched her back. Stiffened. Stilled. He didn't change rhythm as Lena let out a high-pitched wail and broke around him. Her body convulsing with wave after wave of pleasure.

He continued, slowing as she began to sob. When her body relaxed, went limp, he took her gently in his arms and cradled her as she wept on his chest. Relishing the satisfaction of her first orgasm at the hands of another.

Of ruining her for ever.

* * *

Pleasure flooded over her like she'd never experienced. Lena felt broken, remade as she sobbed into Gabe's chest. He murmured gentle words that made little sense to her overwrought brain, other than recognising the tone. Gentle. Encouraging. Praising. The soft sentiments echoed by his hands on her skin. Soothing her. She'd never experienced anything like this. Didn't know how to process it. It had eclipsed anything she had ever known. She'd been mindless with it. Consciousness compressed to nothing but sensation.

'Okay?' Gabe murmured. She wanted to laugh. Just okay? This moment had changed her at an almost cellular level. A complete reconfiguration of who she'd understood herself to be. Lena wiped at her eyes. How must she appear now? Make-up a mess. Wrecked.

'I can't explain...'

He gave her a gentle smile. 'You don't need to. I understand.'

She didn't think he could.

Gabe kissed her cheeks. Her eyelids. Kissing away the tears. After what she'd experienced she couldn't imagine wanting more, but the minute his lips touched hers a wave of volcanic desire flooded over her. That need again, deep inside. For Gabe to fill her. She reached between them. Grasped him through his underwear. Stroked her hand up and down.

'Can I feel you?'

'Yes,' he said with a hiss. Sharp and pained. She reached beyond the band of his briefs, to the hot, hard skin. Marvelling at the silkiness of it. She needed to look, pushing the duvet back. Pulling his underwear down to watch what she was doing to him. Her hand moving. The ruddiness of him. A silvery bead of fluid forming at the tip. She craved to give him the same pleasure that he wrought from her. Lena looked up at Gabe's face. His eyes closed. Mouth part open. Breathing hard as if he couldn't get enough air.

As if he knew she watched him, Gabe opened his eyes, the intensity of desire in his normally cool gaze burning through her. This was a man who could have had anyone, and yet right now she literally held him in the palm of her hand.

She'd never felt more powerful, beautiful, wanted, as she did in this moment.

'I'd die to be inside you.'

'You don't have to go that far,' she said. Sliding her hands from his body and lying back, arching like a cat in the sun.

'Are you ready?' he asked. Manoeuvring out of his underwear. Tossing the briefs to the floor.

'Yes. I'm *aching*.'

His grin in response was pure wickedness. 'I can fix that for you. Make that pain go away.'

He turned to the side and opened a bedside drawer. Found protection. Rolled it on as she watched, unable to take her eyes from him. Then he was over her, his powerful body pressing her into the bed. She flexed her pelvis, rubbing herself against him. Eyes rolling back as his hardness met her soft, overheated flesh. He reached down between them. Stroked between her legs. She'd thought she'd be too sensitive but with a few gentle touches she was panting and begging for release.

'I want you. I can't wait to feel you. You're so beautiful…'

He kept up the words of encouragement as he notched himself at her centre. Began easing in with shallow thrusts.

'Lift up to me,' he said. His voice was rough and raw. Hand slipping under her backside as she tilted her pelvis and he slid deep inside.

He stilled. So did she. There was no pain, only pressure. A fullness. Their gazes clashed. She'd give everything to know what he was thinking, then he began to move and feeling took over.

'Do what's natural,' he said. 'Move. Lie there. Change position. Whatever gives you the most pleasure.'

Pleasure? She didn't know where to start. In this moment she felt complete. As though a huge part of her had been missing and she'd just found the last puzzle piece. She placed her hands on his muscular backside, relishing the way he flexed and tensed as he moved inside her. With each thrust building and building to a cataclysmic conclusion. She'd thought that her last orgasm had ruined her. This? She feared it would be world-ending. She was so open, vulnerable. The way they were joined was unlike anything she'd dreamed. He kissed her, lush and deep. Tongues moving in time to their own unique rhythm. Losing themselves till Lena was nothing but a mass of nerve endings pulsing with the anticipated pleasure of release. Then a burn started deep inside. Curling, twisting, tighter, as she raced towards the inevitability.

'Lena, I'm going to…'

Gabe's voice drifted off as their movements changed. Harder. Faster, as if running a race. Then less co-ordinated.

'Gabe!'

He moaned. 'You've ended me.' Thrusting into her one last time before stilling.

Something inside her snapped free. The ecstasy of letting go. Being cut adrift. Lena held on to Gabe tight as she fell and fell. Knowing that nothing would ever be the same again.

CHAPTER SEVEN

Lena awoke to the first sounds of birdsong. She snuggled into the warmth of the bed, wondering why she was awake so early. The sun hadn't yet risen, everything lay dark outside. She should still be fast asleep, after a night of lovemaking with Gabe. Perhaps it was that they'd planned to wake earlier than normal, so she could leave for her own room without being seen, though she still had plenty of time before the house began to stir.

Her phone pinged with a message. That had to be the reason. Usually she turned off her alerts at night so she wouldn't be disturbed. She'd forgotten last night, because she'd been otherwise…occupied. Lena smiled. Heat drizzled over her at the memories, like being immersed in a warm bath. The all-consuming pleasure she'd experienced. How she'd felt seen, desired, *wanted*. Gabriel stirred beside her, rolled over, still asleep. Even in the darkness of early morning his face was peaceful, hair flopped over his forehead in a boyish kind of way.

She grabbed her phone and turned the volume down so as not to wake him. Checked the time and almost groaned. Four. Ugh. Not fair. Another alert came in. Silent this time. That was unusual. After their conversation yesterday, she was worried it was her mother or brother. She opened her notifications and saw a stream of them.

Her heart picked up its beat. She swallowed. What was wrong? She went to the texts first. None from her mother, thank goodness. That was a problem for another day. But there were a few from Gabe's private secretary, Henri.

Have you looked at your post?

Did he mean the video? And why would he be awake now after hitting the clubs last night? Of course, he'd looked as though he'd wanted to party. Maybe he was *still* out? It didn't matter now.

She decided she'd check the alerts she'd set up for Gabe first, opening her email. A number of newspaper headlines popped up. Lena began to read.

'Oh,' she said softly.

Gabriel stirred again, and his eyes blinked open. When he saw her awake he gave her a wicked smile, full of intent, that made her toes curl.

'Good morning,' he murmured, his voice gravelly and rough. 'Why are you awake?'

'Forgot to turn off my phone notifications and they've been...something.'

'Problem?'

'No... I don't think so.'

'Then what is it?' he pressed.

'Oh, just Henri getting in touch with me...'

He snorted. 'Your job never sleeps. Neither do you, apparently. I obviously didn't do my own job well enough last night.'

'You did a superlative job last night.'

Gabriel settled his hand on her leg. His fingers tracing a distracting circle on her inner thigh.

'Then why are you looking at your phone right now?'

'Henri suggested it might be a good idea.'

'That *does* sound like a problem.'

'Not really. The press picked up my football post.'

The article showed stills from her video. The headline *From Throne to Field: Prince Gabriel's viral kick proves he's still got it.*

Gabriel let out a heavy sigh. 'What do they say?'

'Um…this one says you've still got it.'

Gabe snorted.

'I feel affronted. I didn't think I'd ever lost *it*.' He then gave her a slow smile, one that might be described as panty-melting, had she been wearing any. 'What would you say?'

She smiled right back. 'I wouldn't presume to make any assumptions, Your Highness.'

'Are you going to put down that phone now? I can think of some ways that might help us get back to sleep for another hour. Or, if you don't want to go back to sleep, ways that might be able to make us very happy for a while.'

'I just need to finish…' She waved her phone at him.

'You're detrimental to my ego. If you didn't read between the lines, I'm offering to make love to you. That you're not jumping at the opportunity is leaving me suitably chastened.'

'I think what I'm doing right now might help your ego.'

Lena scrolled through the video she'd posted. Hundreds of thousands of views. Thousands of comments. Another text from Henri, saying the international press were getting in touch.

'All I can say is, it might be good we're going home this afternoon. You don't have much on by way of official duties this morning, apart from the planting?'

It was a final farewell at the palace, where Gabe was to plant a tree to signify the enduring ties between Halrovia and Lauritania.

'No.'

'Well, I think the press might want to ask you some questions.'

'About what? Me kicking a ball?' Gabriel asked.

'With respect, you did a bit more than just kick a ball.'

She showed him the post. The numbers of views and comments climbing and climbing.

'You did say you were happy to go viral,' she said, a little breathless. She'd done well before, but never achieved anything like this.

'I'm guessing we've achieved it.'

Lena liked that he saw them as a team. For the first time in a long time, she truly felt part of something. She nodded as he lay back, hands behind his head, something like a smug smile on his face. She'd never seen that expression before. Gabriel seeming so…satisfied with himself. It was a good look on him.

'Oh, no, they're at it again,' she said.

'Who?'

'People are saying you're a thirst trap.'

'A what?' Gabe looked bemused for a moment. Shook his head. 'Don't worry. No need to explain it.'

Gabriel's phone began to ping as well.

'Why are people not asleep? Why are we not asleep? Or, even better, doing something entirely more enjoyable?' he said, reaching for his phone.

She noticed he didn't grab his glasses. In fact, she realised she'd never actually seen him in glasses before. Or really reading much at all.

'What does Cilla want?' Gabe muttered. 'And why is *she* awake right now?'

Gabe opened the text, and his phone read it aloud to him.

OMG Gabe. Exclamation mark. His Royal Hotness. I told you Lena's the best. Exclamation mark. Call me when you're awake.

That was strange. Why would he want his phone to read out a message?

Gabe took a deep breath in. Let a slow breath out.

'Did they really call me His Royal Hotness?' he asked, incredulous.

'Yes,' Lena said, sitting up. Looking down at him. Something niggling at her.

Gabriel began to chuckle, then laugh. 'None of this is real. It's ridiculous.'

'Your phone. It read that text message to you,' she said. 'Is that what you do when you don't have your glasses? Is your sight that bad?'

She found it hard to believe. He did most things without issue. Kicked a ball into the back of a net just fine. Maybe it was just a problem with reading and not long distance... Except Gabe had suddenly stopped laughing, as if the sound had been cut off. He sat up himself. Scrubbed his hands over his face. His palms scratching over his morning stubble. He put down his own phone. Took her hands in his. Looked at her. His face serious.

'My phone reads my messages because I have trouble reading them. I have dyslexia.'

Gabe didn't know why he revealed it at this point, only that he wanted honesty, because she'd been honest with him the night before. She'd told him about her virginity when she hadn't needed to say anything at all. And this morning she'd asked. He wouldn't lie. Not to her.

'Who knows?' Lena asked.

'My family. Pieter. My private secretary…'

She dropped her head, looked at where their hands were joined.

'So, the glasses?'

'I'm sorry,' he said. Meaning it. 'Not real. They have plain glass, not prescription lenses. They're a ruse. A deflection.'

'And your earbuds. Do you listen to music?'

'Occasionally. Mainly they're for listening to documents. I have a screen reader too.'

His heart rate kicked up a notch. What did she think of him on learning this? That he'd kept it hidden from her. He remembered when the word was first mentioned to his parents. Their thin-lipped, stony expressions. Yet he didn't see that with her…

Lena frowned. 'Do you have any ability to…?'

'Yes. But it takes time. When I'm stressed, or trying to do things in a hurry, it's not as easy for me. I use aids to simplify things.'

She pulled her hands away from his. Put her phone on the bedside table. He felt as though there was a distance growing between them and he craved the closeness again. Lena fixed him with her assessing gaze. Cocked her head.

'Why haven't you told anyone?'

Wasn't that the question? His parents had been the ones who thought it should be kept quiet. That people might wonder about his ability to rule, given he was still quite young with no track record. They had claimed it might cause unnecessary concern to the Halrovian people. Even though the doctor said there were numerous scions of business with the condition. Then his ex-girlfriend had happened, and the secrecy over his diagnosis had seemed to increase.

He'd wondered, much later, whether one of the real reasons was it would ruin the illusion of their family's perfection…

'I was diagnosed quite late. In my teens. People thought I was lazy at school. It turns out that wasn't the issue at all. Back then it was the decision of my parents and their advisors.'

Lena reached out and placed her hand on his forearm. Squeezed. He relished that small touch. 'This is exactly the kind of authenticity people want to see from you. Why did your parents hide it? Were they ashamed?'

He shook his head in vehement denial, even though a kind of uncertainty pricked inside him.

'No. Not ashamed…' Though they'd never really said anything much. Were they embarrassed? It was a reasonable explanation for why they didn't want him studying. Then there was the question of why they'd wanted his diagnosis buried so deeply. Deeply enough to give a manipulative, untrustworthy man a position of advisor of state, to keep his daughter quiet. 'They believed I should establish myself in my role, show I could "do the job", so to speak. Then it became something we never really talked about.'

'It's something you could talk about now. People would relate. Don't you see?'

'It doesn't seem relevant…' He had trouble understanding what difference it would make. That was in the past. Behind him. He'd found ways of adapting. Moving forwards. He still did everything expected of him. He had no limitations. He'd proven it hadn't affected him at all. There wasn't any reason to say anything any more.

'Gabe, is this why you're always holding back from people? Accused by the press of being "proper". Because you're afraid people will find out the truth?'

The comment hit straight to the heart of him. She left no prisoners.

'I'm not afraid.' He'd reorganised his life around his dyslexia, had reading aids when he needed them. These things made life easier, for him and his staff. There was no part of the job that was beyond him, no impact on his role. Telling everyone now…at the mere thought, pressure in his chest grew.

Yet Lena wasn't judging him. She looked at him, not with pity, but with softness and concern. All he saw was care and understanding, not disapproval. What he would have given to see that expression on his parents' faces when he'd received his diagnosis. He hadn't realised for how long he'd craved simple compassion and acceptance. Here it was being shown to him by this beautiful, insightful woman. That increasingly relentless pressure in his chest began to ease.

'Telling everyone might help other people. Those subjects who are just like you.'

Her words jolted him back into the harshness of reality. How would he even begin to admit what he'd kept quiet for so many years?

'Imagine the charities you could support,' she said.

Before her marriage, his sister Ana's favoured charity was one for child and adult literacy. He'd never stopped to question whether she chose it as silent support for him. It hadn't crossed his mind. When she'd left to marry, her royal Halrovian patronages had fallen vacant. They'd need to be redistributed. Perhaps he could talk to his parents about it? Show them it made sense. It was something to think about.

But for now, all he wanted to think about was Lena. Sitting up in bed, hair an unruly tousle after their night of love-making. Mascara smudged under her eyes. Making them look smoky, sultry. Her lips a deep cherry red, well kissed.

If he'd been sensible, he would have called the kitchens to make coffee, then let her go. She'd called it the evening before. One night. Yet, seeing her in his bed, Gabriel knew he didn't want this to stop. Last night had been like nothing he'd ever experienced. The passion. The need. Sex with anyone else was a distant, faded memory next to her.

He knew there were ground rules for this sort of thing. Lena didn't come from this world. She mightn't understand that if this went on there could be no hint of anything between them. That nothing about their situation could be considered normal. It wasn't fair to her, yet he didn't want to give her up. Not yet. He was sure they'd burn out eventually. Once they'd glutted on each other's bodies. They'd both become bored of each other, and it would end. But for now...

As if she knew he was staring at her, contemplating their short-term future, Lena looked up at him. 'What?'

Something must have shown on his face. 'I've been thinking.'

'Indeed.' The corner of her mouth kicked up. She'd sounded so much like him in that moment. The same imperious tone he knew he could inject into his voice. Often did, deliberately. Of course, she knew it too. 'Are you going to suggest some wardrobe changes for me that I might reject?'

There was that gentle teasing again. He enjoyed it, how natural she was. How he'd come to believe that she *saw* him. Not for what he was, but for who.

'Wardrobe? I'd have you permanently naked if I could.' He growled at the crime of ever putting clothes on her magnificent body.

'I don't know how I'd get anything done.'

'You wouldn't. But that's not what I want to discuss. This. Us. I don't want to let it go. Not yet...' he said, wondering how he could canvass the rest. 'However—'

'It needs to be kept private.'

He wasn't sure whether she was reciting what she'd assumed he was going to tell her or setting her own rules. Whatever the reason, relief flooded over him that they were both on the same page.

'I want to protect you. From any claims that you're doing this to further your career, which I know you're not, because the results speak for themselves. Also, from the press. They can be cruel to me, *never* to you.'

'I know they'd flay someone like me alive.'

Someone like her? He wasn't sure what that meant and he didn't like that she was okay with thinking that she was in some way less.

'I don't want you mobbed whenever you're out.'

'You're the story, Gabriel. I've never wanted the limelight.'

He didn't really want it either. 'Sadly it comes with being me. If I weren't a prince—'

'You'd be an international football player, and still famous.'

She showed such uncompromising faith in him. When had he *ever* had that before? 'Perhaps.'

Lena chewed on her lower lip, a look of uncertainty there. He wanted to kiss it away. 'How would it even work? I can't just stroll up to your apartments. People would get suspicious.'

'I have a way. Trust me. No one will know. Your reputation will be safe.'

'Don't keep me waiting.'

He smiled. She was going to agree? His heart pumped hard and fast. His desire once again roaring to life with a need like he'd never experienced before. Luckily, he'd texted his staff the night before, arranging a later start than usual.

He could make love to her again before she had to go back to her room. Go back to pretending, till the next time at least.

'If I promise we won't be found out, will you agree?'

'Yes,' she said with a little smile. 'Yes, I will.'

He wanted to grab her, kiss her senseless, but he also liked the game they played. The fun. The banter. All part of the seduction.

'So,' he said, intent on changing the subject so they wouldn't have to waste any more time. 'His Royal Hotness?'

'You forget. Hashtag His Royal Hotness. Hashtag thirst-trap,' she replied.

'Do you think I'm hot?'

As the sun began to hint over the horizon, a pretty blush crept up her chest. Higher. Her ears turning a soft shade of pink.

'If the hashtag fits.' A teasing smile crept onto her face. 'There was another one. Bend it like Gabriel. What does that mean?'

'It's a football term. I can show you what it means later, but do you know what I'd like to do now?'

'No, Your Hotness—I mean, Highness.'

He loved the irreverence in her tone.

'I'd like to bend you over the bed. Make love to you till you scream as the sun rises.'

Lena squealed, giggling as he wrestled her into delicious submission. Covering her with his body.

'Let me show you just how hot I am,' he growled into her ear as she relaxed underneath him. Arms curling round his neck. Threading into his hair as Lena smiled at him.

'I look forward to you living up to the promise of your online reputation.'

CHAPTER EIGHT

Lena sat in her room, her heart beating as fast and light as a butterfly's wing. It had been a few days since they'd returned from Lauritania. Apart from during their workdays, she hadn't seen anything of Gabriel after hours, as he'd had meetings and dinners, making it impossible. Yet he'd promised her there was a way and, today, she'd received a text from him:

Wait for me in your room tonight. Seven thirty. Wear flat shoes. Don't eat.

So here she was, waiting as he'd asked. She wanted to get up, pace—impatient, nervous, excited all at the same time. How were they going to do this? She'd asked for one night because that was all she'd expected. Losing her virginity and moving on. Yet the hunger. It was a compulsion impossible to ignore. Beyond mere desire, a need. She'd never expected to experience this with a man, even more, a *prince*. What would it be like to have someone actually fall in love with her? To marry? Gabe. Someone so far above her...

No. That wasn't what their agreement was. As for his status, she'd come to think of them as equals. He was funny, self-deprecating, with a wry sense of humour. He didn't seem to take himself too seriously, even though there were serious parts to his role. She felt privileged to see this side of him. The side she wanted to show to the world: the man, not the prince. But Lena had no idea how he thought they could do this secretly. Though Gabe had *promised*, and she believed him. It was an intoxicating thing, to be able to simply believe in someone. That they'd have your interests at heart, as well as their own…

Lena checked the time on her phone. Seven twenty-eight. It heightened the anticipation that she had no idea *what* she was waiting for. She amused herself with a fantasy that he'd rappel down the walls and sneak in her window, or wear some disguise to turn up at her door, all the while realising those imaginings were fanciful and ridiculous.

The time ticked over. Seven thirty. She stood and walked to the window. The sun had dipped below the horizon now, the lights twinkling in the city below them.

'Lena.'

A male voice. She squeaked, unable to help herself, whipping around, and there he was, standing in her room.

Gabe.

She wanted to run to him, fling her arms about his neck, but that wasn't the kind of relationship they had…some teenage fantasy. This was all grown up. Lena held herself back and, instead, admired him. He wasn't in a suit tonight. Dressed more casually, in tan trousers, an opennecked shirt, no jacket, no tie. His hair still slightly damp, roughly dried. So handsome, it took her breath away.

'How did you get in here without me hearing you?'

The corner of his mouth kicked up. 'This palace has many secrets, and I know them all. Ready?'

'Of course. But where are we going? And how?'

'To my room,' he said with a sly grin. 'Follow me.'

He walked through into her bedroom. She was happy she'd made her bed and that it wasn't a mess, though she'd brought few belongings with her, as she hadn't known how long she'd be staying given he'd initially placed her on probation. Now she guessed she should get more of her possessions sent from home since she was staying…

As his PR and image consultant, of course.

Gabe walked up to the wall next to her bedside table, to a panel where there was a beautiful embossed rose detail she'd admired when she'd first moved in here. He pressed, and the panel swung inwards.

'You're kidding,' she said.

Gabe winked, making her toes curl. 'Secret passageways. My sisters and I used to play in them when we were children. We were terrors, visiting each other's rooms when we should have been sleeping. In the end my parents had the doors in our rooms barricaded with large furniture to stop us exploring. But that didn't stop me. Many places in this palace are interconnected. How did you think I was going to get to your room?'

'I don't know. I was imagining all kinds of things, like a disguise or you rappelling down the side of the palace to my window.'

He chuckled. 'No theatrics or daring, I'm afraid.'

'This seems pretty daring to me.'

'Up for an adventure, then?'

She nodded.

'After you.'

He motioned with his hand and she walked through into the dark, unlit space behind her walls. He followed as she waited just inside the passageway.

'But first,' he said, easing her up against the wall in the semi-darkness. The rough stone cool against her back. The only light coming from her room. Gabe cupped her cheek. 'You look so beautiful. These past few days have been *torture*, unable to touch you. Kiss you.'

He dropped his lips to hers. Hard. Unforgiving. Desperate. She matched him. Slipping her hands into his hair. Holding him close. Never wanting to let him go, although that was just for now, not for ever. The ache at that thought fled as they reacquainted themselves with each other's bodies. Touching. Teasing. How long they stayed there, she couldn't say. Time lost all meaning. All she knew was that when they pulled apart, she was overheated, and they were both panting.

'We need to go or I'll take you up against this wall.'

'I don't mind the sound of that.'

Gabe chuckled and the sound echoed in the cavernous space. 'Noted, for another time.'

He bent down and picked up something off the floor. There was a muffled click, and a beam of light from a torch illuminated the space with a cool glow. Gabe walked to the open panel in her wall and closed it shut. Shut them in.

'Where does this lead?' she whispered.

Gabe reached out his hand, and she took it. Threading her fingers through his. He squeezed.

'To many places, including my apartments. It was lucky that your room connected to mine.'

They began walking, their footsteps echoing around them.

'How do you find your way?' Her voice was a hiss in the darkness.

'I learned exploring as a child. There are also plans. However I have a pretty good mental map of the place.'

'Does anyone else use these?' she asked as they walked through. The air was a little stuffy, warm.

'Our personal staff, rarely. Kitchen staff, when we have large functions, because there's a passage that leads into the ballroom, but most of the time they sit unused. I still walk through if I want a shortcut. I've made some marks should you want to come back to your room on your own. If you want to find mine.' He shone the torch onto the walls and Lena saw arrows in chalk. Gabe squeezed her hand again. She squeezed back.

'Very resourceful,' she said, still keeping her voice low, quiet.

'I'm not just a...what did you call me. Thirst trap?'

'That's your hashtag. Why am I whispering?' she asked.

'I don't know. No one can hear us here. It's quite safe.'

She looked at the wall again, with the chalk-marked arrows. Small but clear. All pointing to her room.

'How do I get back in?'

'I'll show you when we get to my end. There's a small latch. It's easy. The only problem is when there's furniture across the doorway. People have forgotten these passageways, or deliberately blocked them off. I can only imagine what would have been done using them,' he said, chuckling.

'A little like what we're doing now.'

'I have no doubt.'

Gabe seemed to pick up the pace. She followed his purposeful stride. 'How long will it take?'

'Shorter than walking through the hallways to get to my room, since I'm in another wing entirely,' he said. 'You're not afraid?'

'No, it's amazing! I've always wanted to walk through a secret passageway. Think of the things you could do!'

'I suspect they were used for espionage. Invite foreign dignitaries to stay, put them in the right quarters, and then you could stand in these passageways and listen.'

'Really? I would have thought the walls were too thick.'

'In certain places there are what appear to be air vents in the walls. They're not. They're listening ports.'

'Oh, that's very underhanded of you and your family. Would they be used now?'

He shook his head. 'We prefer diplomacy rather than subterfuge.'

'Isn't subterfuge what we're doing?'

Gabe chuckled again. 'I suppose it is. Must be in my blood.'

Or hers...but she didn't want to dwell. Gabe didn't have another family stashed away. They were both single, free to do whatever they wanted. She tried not to think about how they were sneaking about secret passageways to see each other. What that meant.

After a few more minutes Gabe slowed, stopped. Shone the torch on the wall, illuminating an X in chalk.

'X marks the spot,' she said. 'These are your rooms?'

'Yes. Pieter has the night off, so we won't be disturbed. Here's the mechanism to get in.' There was a complicated-looking lever in the wall. He depressed it, then turned, and the door snicked open. He closed it again.

'You try.'

She did. Once he appeared satisfied that she could get into his room from the passageway, he pulled on the handle and led her through, closing the door behind them.

Lena walked into what appeared to be a dressing room with racks of suits, business shirts—all perfectly ordered. No surprises there. It seemed as neatly ordered as himself. The space was imbued with that scent of him. Woodsy. Green. Fresh, like the cool mountain air. She breathed him in.

'Come this way,' he said, placing his hand on her lower back, the warmth of his fingers seeping into her skin as he led her into a lounge area. The light from some side lamps painting the room in gold. Glorious silks lined the walls. The furniture sumptuous, comfortable-looking, yet undoubtedly antique. An elegant room she could see he fitted into, and clearly the room of Halrovia's prince.

But what struck her aside from the opulence was something else. All around the room, all surfaces had candle holders and candles, imbuing the space with a warm, flickering light. In the corner, by what appeared to be a set of windows with the curtains drawn, was a beautiful little table with armchairs. On the table flickered small tea-light candles in holders. There was a bunch of flowers in a cut-crystal glass that glittered in the low light. Beside the table was a wine bucket, wine on ice.

Gabe stood behind her, hands on her shoulders. His body warm against hers. He leaned down, his breath brushing her ear. 'Do you like it?'

'I love it,' she said. Tears prickled her eyes at the time and care this would have taken, the organisation. She turned. 'How did you manage to do all of this without anyone finding out?'

He smiled.

'It's easy. I know where the palace stores are. It wasn't hard to get supplies. The flowers are from my terrace outside. I have a small kitchenette area if I ever want a snack without calling the chef late at night.'

'It's thoughtful. Beautiful…' Romantic, even though this wasn't a romance.

'But it's not as beautiful as you,' he said, sliding his arms around her waist. Kissing her gently this time. Long, deep and slow. She closed her eyes, relishing the attention. The care he'd taken. How would she live without this when it ended? All she'd expected was mind-altering passion. This was something else entirely.

Gabe finally pulled away and all Lena wanted to do was grab him and drag him right down again.

'We need to stop or we'll never get to eat. Come to the table,' he said, leading her over and pulling out her chair as she sat. He then went to a sideboard, opened it, and retrieved a small plate.

'The food's a little simple tonight. I said I was hungry so they'd give me more, but asked for something light that I could snack on. I hope there's something here that suits. Help yourself.'

He kept the smaller plate for himself and gave her the gold-embossed royal dinner service and cutlery. There were cured meats, cheeses, small salads, pickles, then a little cooked food. Potato rösti, some sausages. Bread with pats of butter, embossed with the royal seal. She helped herself, her stomach growling.

'Next time I shouldn't leave you so long. Would you like wine?'

She nodded, biting into a crispy rösti. It was a little cool but still delicious. Gabe uncorked and opened the wine. Poured the pale fluid into her glass and his own before raising it.

'To subterfuge.'

Lena raised her glass, touching it to his. 'To secret passageways.'

She took a sip of the crisp, fresh wine. Trying to ignore the niggle in the back of her mind that this was not where she saw her life leading. She didn't want to ruin tonight, not after the effort Gabe had gone to. Tomorrow she could give this strange feeling more thought. Instead, she'd savour the delicious food. The sight of Gabe, relaxed. Happy in front of her. Lena changed the subject, to safer ground.

'It seems one of the men who played football with you must have sold a picture of you to the press.'

Gabe's eyebrows raised. 'Good on him, if he can get some money for it. Which one was it?'

She reached into the pocket of her dress, pulled out her phone. Showed him. To her shame she'd screenshotted it.

It was the moment Gabe had winked at her. He'd seemed so alive, full of movement and passion.

The look on his face...as if he'd just rediscovered himself. She showed him.

'That's hardly interesting.'

'The press are applauding your new look, an image makeover.'

'Yet nothing's changed at all. I didn't even have to wear a mohair coat to achieve it.'

Something *had* changed though. Them. She ignored the bruised kind of feeling his comment inflicted. It's all part of how they were together. Flirtatious. Fun. Not serious. With a definite 'use by' date, even though the end date hadn't really been specified. Though what would it be like to be *chosen* for once. Enthusiastically. Openly...

They were thoughts for another time, when the possibilities were real. Not this glorious fantasy.

'You'll never let me live that coat down.'

He shook his head. 'Probably not, no.'

'It was only to show you possibilities. Anyway, here you are, almost casual.' She waved her hand in his general direction. 'You're not even wearing a tie. What would the King and Queen's private secretary say?'

'I don't give a damn about him,' he growled, almost feral. A delicious shiver ran through her at the sound. 'I only care what you think.'

Gabe fixed her with his pale blue gaze. Once she'd thought it frigid. Now she couldn't miss the heat shimmering from the depths of him. He was like a frozen lake. Cool on top, with a whole world teeming underneath the icy surface.

She placed her phone on the table. As she did, a message came in from her brother. Lena's heart rate spiked.

'You're frowning.'

'I... Do you mind if I look at this? It's my family.'

'Of course,' Gabe said, his face warm with concern.

She opened the message, saying that her mother wasn't coping with the idea of a move. She texted back, repeating that she'd fix it but for now they'd need to find somewhere else to live. There were no other options. Lena took a deep breath. Any properties her mother had suggested were the same rent or even more expensive than where they lived right now. She couldn't understand the abject denial of reality. She never wanted to be like that. Pretending everything was okay. That life didn't have to change when it so clearly did. Lena turned her phone over so she couldn't see any other messages. Tried to eat some of her meal, but it tasted like ash.

Gabe reached out and placed his hand over hers. 'Everything okay?'

She desperately wanted to say something. For most of her life, there'd been nothing she could admit about her family. So much had had to be kept secret. Her friendships were affected by it. Her life had been bound by the silence. Her mother always choosing her father's need for secrecy. What would it be like to share something of what she had to go through—the burden she carried?

Gabe had shared his dyslexia with her. He'd been honest. He'd trusted her, so surely she could trust him? She had spent so long hiding her father's identity that it was difficult to let that go. But perhaps she could give a little.

'My mother has to move out of her home. She isn't coping well with the idea.'

Gabe frowned. 'Why does she have to go anywhere?'

What could she say that didn't leave her family exposed? 'My mother and father weren't together, but he still supported the family. My brother's studying and, whilst he's on a partial scholarship, it still costs money. When my father died...'

Gabe stroked his thumb gently over the back of her hand. It was such a comfort that he just sat. Listened.

'He left no provision in his will. I had to stop studying myself. Things have been a little...tight, and now the landlord has put up my mother's rent. I've told her she has to go somewhere smaller. Within our budget.'

'Do you need—?'

'No, everything's fine.' Lena feared Gabe was going to offer money and she couldn't take anything from him. It felt too much like crossing a line that she wouldn't be able to walk back from. 'It's just difficult for her because she's lived there for so long. But the place is too big, what with me no longer there. She needs to downsize.'

'Does she? Surely if she needs support succession laws would give her some protection?'

What could Lena say to that other than a phrase that carried a multitude of possible answers.

'It's complicated.'

Something about Gabriel's gaze darkened. 'What families aren't? Are you sure there's nothing I can do? Ask some lawyers—'

'No, thank you. As I said, we'll be fine. It's just... I might need some time off work to go and help her sort it out. Maybe find somewhere else to live, show her that it'll be all right. My brother isn't as good at reassuring her as I am.'

'Of course,' Gabriel said. 'Take any time you need.'

'I'm sorry. I've only been in the role less than a month.'

'As I've said before, I look after my valued employees.' Something about the use of that word when it came to her seemed like a sharp spike to the heart. But she was what she was. They couldn't deny their respective positions.

'We have generous leave plans here. This is a family emergency. Any time will be covered.'

'Gabe, thank you. I don't know what to say.'

'There's nothing *to* say. Only promise me. If you need anything…'

Gabriel stood, held out his hand. She placed hers in it and stood too. He wrapped his arms around her and held her close, held her safe. It was the first time in so long that she'd felt as though anyone cared for her. That there might be someone who'd look after her, worry about her, who might *love* her.

No, not love. She'd seen what love had done to her mother. It was a trap that led to poor choices. She'd never succumb to the same thing. Something inside her stilled, gave her pause. Wasn't that what she was doing here? Gabe was unavailable…

No. She didn't have to think about it now. She'd go back to Isolobello, figure out her family's problems and then think about herself. Her aim had always been to secure her future and her finances first and then, maybe, consider a man in her life. Even though the idea of another man left a sour sensation in her gut. She was a loyal person, that was all. Lena didn't believe in cheating. She allowed herself this, Gabriel's tenderness. Because it was nice to know there was someone who might think about her, who seemed to care.

For a few moments, she just rested her head on his chest. Listening to the solid sound of his heartbeat as he cradled her in his arms. Letting her tears silently fall. Lena realised she'd never really cried about this before. She'd spent her whole life trying to rein in her emotions, so nobody could hurt her. She wanted to be soft and vulnerable, just for a little while. She owed herself that much.

She drew in a shuddering breath. Gabe pulled back. Lena tried to look down at the floor so he wouldn't see her tears. He placed his fingers gently under her chin and tilted her head up.

'Lena,' he murmured, his voice full of concern. 'Do you want any more to eat?'

She shook her head. Wiped her face. 'Why do I always seem to cry around you?'

'I wish you were crying because of pleasure, not pain.'

A kindle of heat ignited at her core. She didn't want to talk. She didn't want looks of pity or sympathy. He was right. He could give her something else. Pleasure sounded good. Pleasure could wipe away the pain, the fear. It was what she wanted more than anything in this moment—to simply forget.

'You'd prefer to see me with tears of pleasure rather than pain? Then there's something you can do about that,' Lena said, stepping in close to him once more. Placing her hand on his chest. 'I want you to take me to bed.'

'I want you to take me to bed.'

Lena's tears of sadness almost broke him. He couldn't bear to see her like this, yet he knew what her request was all about—avoidance. Hadn't he buried himself in a warm, willing body more than once in the past, trying to forget things in his own life? But this was different. Something about *her* was different. Whilst he could happily give Lena exactly what she craved right now, he wanted to make sure it was the right thing for her.

He knew that he could bring a look of ecstasy to her face. That he could make her forget everything that caused this sadness. Maybe it really didn't matter, allowing Lena to run away from her problems for a little while. He could do that for her, then maybe she wouldn't mind him exploring legal options with his lawyers, to see if there was any way of getting money for the family to which they had to be entitled, given her father had still been supporting them when he died. There *must* be some bequest for them, no matter how 'complicated' things were.

'I'm happy to take you to bed and make love to you till everything but us is forgotten. But I want to be sure that it's the right thing for you.'

'It's what I want. I want to forget for a little while, remember what it's like to feel alive.'

Yet somehow, it felt wrong. As if he wasn't solving any problem at all. There was a story there, and one day he'd get to the bottom of it. He had a terrible suspicion that she was holding something back from him. Still, she was entitled to her secrets in this affair they were having—though part of him rebelled at classing it as that.

Why did he feel as though that word cheapened everything, when what they had between them felt like so much more? Sure, there'd been no promises of a future, only a 'now'. He took a deep breath. 'Now' was all that he could give her, even though, in this moment, it didn't feel like enough. Still, she wanted him to pretend that everything was okay? If that was all she'd allow, that was the gift he'd grant her.

'Then come into my bedroom,' he said.

It was as if all the tension leached out of her. She seemed to slump a little before coming back into herself.

'Thank you.'

He hated that she thanked him as if he were doing her some favour. Later he'd question why she was like this. For now, he'd ratchet up the tension, play whatever game she needed to forget.

'You want me to make you scream?' he asked as she hurried after him.

'Yes.'

She stopped at the end of his bed. He couldn't wait to get her out of her dress. Tonight, a beautiful halter neck, patterned with what looked like peacock feathers. The fine fabric of her skirt drifting around her body.

'Undo the halter,' he commanded. Her pupils darkened and lips parted. She reached behind her neck and tugged. Her top fell free, exposing Lena's breasts, the perfect handful. Her skin a warm gold. He stalked forwards, cupped her breasts. Her nipples tight and dusky. Gabe stroked his thumbs over the diamond-hard peaks. So beautiful, irresistible. Her nipples tightened even further with his attention. He pinched them. Not too hard, just enough. Her eyelids fluttered shut and she moaned.

'I love how responsive you are, yet tonight, I demand silence,' he said as he kept up his ministrations. Teasing her pebbled flesh.

Her eyes flew open. 'What?'

She sounded almost drunk with desire. Lena wanted pleasure to make her forget? He'd heighten it a thousandfold.

'You might want to scream. What I want is quiet. You scream. I stop. You're silent, and I'll give you all the pleasure you need. Do you agree to my rules?'

He'd make her mindless with trying to comply. To fight her instincts. Of course he'd never leave her unsatisfied. Even if she did scream, he wouldn't stop, although he might tease. But he looked forward to her attempts to hold everything in. How she'd break under his lips and hands.

She nodded. 'Yes.'

'Good.'

He stalked to the head of the bed, grabbed his pillows and propped them up against the bedhead before returning to her.

'Turn round,' he said. Lena did. Gabe traced a finger down her spine and goosebumps dusted her skin. He drew the zip of her dress down. It fell from her hips to the floor, leaving her only in fine lace panties. Gabe placed his palm on her belly. Drew her back to him so she could feel his hardness. How much he wanted her. Then he kissed the back of her neck, the side at the juncture of her shoulder, till she squirmed, pressing her backside against his body. Inflaming him. He gritted his teeth.

'Shoes off. On the bed propped up on the pillows.'

As she obeyed he turned off the lamps. He'd spent time decorating this room with candles as well. The soft light flickered, painting her in light and shadow.

Gabe slowly undid his shirt, tugged it out of his trousers. Cast it aside. Lena propped herself on her elbows, watching as he put on a show.

'Relax back,' he said as he came forwards onto the bed, sliding her panties down her legs. Dropping them on the floor. Her gaze looked almost out of focus, but she was now nestled deep into the down pillows, as he'd demanded.

He sat on the bed next to her, his hand tracing down her stomach, fingers slipping between her legs, which fell open at his touch.

'What's my rule again?'

'You want silence,' she whispered.

He smiled, kept stroking her. Lena's hips beginning to move in time with his rhythm. She was so wet. If he kept going much longer she'd come, he was sure of it.

'And what happens if you scream?'

'You stop.' Her voice was almost a whimper.

'That's right, but you won't scream, will you? You won't make any noise at all.'

She shook her head. He stopped touching her. Lena opened her mouth as if to object, then closed it again.

'I want you to watch what I'm doing to you,' he said.

He manoeuvred himself between her legs. Lay on the bed. Her eyes widened. 'Just lie back and enjoy.'

Her legs opened further to accommodate his shoulders as

he propped himself on his forearms and dropped his head between her legs. Traced his tongue over her. The sweet salt, the scent of her arousal. He groaned. It would be a challenge to see who'd come last. He was so aroused, craving her orgasm almost as much as his own. He wanted her mindless, replete. Forgetting everything but his lips, tongue, hands. He didn't know if she watched—all his focus was on her pleasure. Her breaths came heavy and fast. Panting as he stroked her flesh with his tongue. Concentrating on her clitoris, the centre of her pleasure.

Her body trembled as she fought not to cry out. Her fingers gripping the coverlet till they blanched white. Gabe knew she needed more. He slid one finger inside, then another. Her legs shook, as if an earthquake were overtaking her body. Her back arching off the bed. His fingers slick with her arousal. He wasn't sure she was even breathing when he stopped the relentless rhythm of his tongue and sucked. She stilled. Stiffened, then broke in two. A high-pitched keening noise shattering the room. He didn't care. His plan had never been to deny her, but to give her everything. She pulsed around him as he waited for her to come down from her orgasm. Then he moved up to her. Lay on his back. Took her, lax and replete, into his arms.

Hoped, for a while, he'd allowed her to forget.

'It'll be fine, Lena,' he murmured. 'It'll all work out.'

As he said the words, Gabe wasn't sure whether he was talking about her family problems, or their time together.

CHAPTER NINE

His palace apartments felt stultifying after the freedom of his time away. Even though the building had seven hundred rooms and five apartments spread out over different wings, he still had this clawing sensation, as if he were trapped. He'd chosen his apartments to be at the opposite end from his parents and even that was too close. Nothing seemed to fit right now. His tie appeared too tight, the fine wool of his suits prickled. He was uncomfortable in everything he did. The only time he had a modicum of peace and felt he could truly *be* was with Lena. After a long day he'd let Pieter go for the evening, shut his door, and wait for the click of the secret door in his dressing room.

He and Lena would spend the evening over dinner, talking about the day. Their nights, making love. In the morning they'd wake early and Lena would leave. Then they'd start over again, to the world appearing as employer and employee until night fell and they could be lovers once more.

Only it was harder and harder to let her go as the sun rose each morning. Not reaching out to touch her in public. All things that had once seemed inconceivable, now as natural as breathing. Simple, yet impossibly complicated.

When he was with her, he wasn't thinking about a past or a future, he simply *was*. Present in the moment. He started each day with enthusiasm, evident in the headlines that were to Lena's credit. It was clear she saw something he'd thought he'd lost. Showing the world as well.

He wasn't sure what he'd do when she left to take care of her family, even though that wouldn't be for ever. She'd come back. But...what if she didn't? Lise and Rafe had all but offered her a job. No doubt they'd pay a premium for her, and her family needed the money... Those thoughts made his chest tighten. No, she'd return. There was no question of it.

But what was she returning to? There'd been no promises between them, only short term with an uncertain end date. Once, that had seemed enough. To live firmly in the present with what they had, till things burned out between them. Where the future felt like something distant and unreachable. Except things didn't feel as though they were burning out. They were burning hotter.

He looked at himself in the mirror. The same face but, in so many ways, changed. Today he was opening a library. There, he knew he'd be asked to read a book to the children, but it didn't bother him any more. He'd practised reading it with Lena till the concern that he might stumble and forget something abated. All because she had a faith in him few others seemed to hold. Gabe wanted to sit with that realisation, what it meant, for him to have someone who was becoming so vital to him. What he needed was time, to sift through these complicated feelings running through him. To work out what they meant, because he'd never been in this position before.

Time was something he'd find, except this morning he needed to button himself back into the role of Prince Gabriel, rather than Gabe Montroy. The man whose name Lena loved to scream to the room...

He shook his head with a wry smile to his reflection,

then walked into the sitting room and grabbed his coffee, which he'd taken to leaving a little later in the morning given Lena's usual presence here. Nothing had been said, it was no one's business, but Gabe had the sense Pieter's normally cool demeanour had warmed a fraction. He took the time to relish the drink, before putting on a tie and getting the day started.

His valet walked into the room. 'Sir, may I suggest no tie today? Perhaps a more casual approach, for the children.'

'Are you falling under Ms Rosetti's influence?'

Pieter grinned. 'No, sir. She suggested a tie adorned with a popular cartoon character. That would never do.'

Gabe snorted. 'No. Perhaps not. What do the headlines say today?'

He could read them himself with less trouble now his stress had seemed to ease, a revelation that gave him hope things would improve even further. Something else to thank Lena for. Still, this was a routine with Pieter he enjoyed, particularly the way his valet read the headlines with such delicious disdain.

'I quite like this—'

A knock sounded at the door of his apartment, which immediately opened. His mother striding through. He gave her a quick bow, the visit unexpected.

She waved her hand at Pieter. 'You may leave us.'

The fact she tried to dismiss his staff rankled.

'Pieter was about to tell me what the headlines said.'

Pieter didn't move.

His mother walked to the coffee table, picked up one tabloid. Whilst Lena laughed that it was 'old school' not looking at the papers online, these habits were old ones.

'Ah, yes. *"Sisters Marry. Is Prince Gabriel Next? Speculation Grows as Nation Waits!"*'

'Hyperbole,' Gabe said. 'Cilla isn't married yet.'

'Priscilla will be married soon enough,' his mother said, ominously.

He was aware he'd need to marry some day. It was just that he never gave it much thought other than as a concept. He was thirty-two. There was no rush. His father was well. He had years to take the throne. Though a vision slammed into his consciousness, of Lena looking up at him, soft focus behind a veil... They were thoughts better had at another time. He filed them for later reference.

'Too many royal weddings too soon seems excessive.'

'Let's read another headline, shall we?'

His mother's tone was prickly, but then that tended to be her default, though she usually reserved her ire for her daughters, who had never lived up to her lofty expectations.

His mother's lips pursed as if she'd tasted something unpleasant. *"From Eligible to Engaged? Prince Gabriel's New Look Fuels Bride Search Buzz!"'*

Gabe looked around and noticed that Pieter had quietly and sensibly slid from the room.

'Is there a point to your visit, Mother?'

'It seems that your makeover's working. Therefore, Miss Rosetti's services are no longer required. The role can be absorbed by others, using her formula for success.'

No!

The word shouted in his head. It was all he could do to keep quiet and not to shout the word *at* his mother. Lena's formula for success? She understood him. No one else could achieve the same because no one knew him as Lena did.

'*Others* have tried in the past, and they've failed. Lena stays.'

His mother grabbed another paper. Read it. Fixed him with her cold blue gaze.

"'All Eyes on Prince Gabriel's Change: Is Love in the Air?'"

His heart skipped a beat. Stilled. Why were they talking about love?

'The tabloid editors are being ridiculous. Royal weddings sell. Speculation about royal weddings sell even more.'

'Your father seems happy enough to allow this to continue. I know better.' His mother's voice was as cold as the first slap of a winter's wind across your face.

'I have no idea what you're talking about.'

'Save me the lies, Gabriel! You couldn't fool me when you were a child, and you don't fool me now. A dalliance is acceptable when the rules are followed.'

Gabe's blood froze. How could anyone know? They'd been careful. Whilst there was some element of protecting himself, he wanted to protect Lena from the vultures who'd descend. There was nothing wrong with what they were doing. They were two consenting adults. Whilst he'd once been sure it would burn itself out, he wasn't ready for it to stop now.

In fact, he wasn't sure he wanted it to stop at all.

'You have *no* rights to be having this conversation with me.'

'I'm *Queen*. I have every right. What's happening here is plain. A change. A new look. Words about love on the front page? Tell me, Gabriel. What's brought about that change? You have *feelings* for the woman. Heaven save us from doe-eyed commoners who seek a station higher than their entitlements. She's your *employee*. What did we tell you? Stay within your circle, where everyone understands what's possible and what's impossible. Yet here we are. *Again*.'

A fire burned inside him. He wasn't some teenager who didn't know his own mind. He was the Crown Prince of

Halrovia, the country's future, as Lena liked to remind him. Whilst Gabriel didn't want a war within his family, he'd demand to be treated like an adult. This remained no one's business other than his own. He didn't have to admit anything. Especially not to his parents.

'Your Majesty, I respect you as my mother but I'm an adult. Stay out of my business. My love life is my own. I will not be speaking about it with you. You're jumping at shadows whereas I'm here, settled in reality.'

In a reality where he no longer saw why he and Lena couldn't continue to see each other. This was supposed to be a modern monarchy. When Ana's engagement had been agreed, she'd simply left with her fiancé before they'd even set a wedding date. He'd been a commoner. Things like bloodlines didn't matter any more, not to Gabe, anyhow.

'The woman is a menace. What of her mother, her father? Do you know anything about them?'

'Conversations about parents are irrelevant. I enjoy Lena's company. Her professionalism and how she's acquitted herself are impeccable. I'm in no hurry to marry and, once again, I am an adult capable of managing my own life. You have no place there.'

His mother's lips narrowed as if preparing to spit out the next words.

'Did she tell you that her mother is said to be a notorious mistress, to a man who kept two households? One legitimate, one illegitimate. Who's to say Lena Rosetti isn't wanting the same from you? Her father's not named on her or her brother's birth certificate, yet the rumours abound about his identity. Did she tell you that as well? Lena Rosetti is unclaimed. She's a stray. And she is entirely unsuitable to be the partner of Halrovia's Crown Prince and next King.'

* * *

Lena froze in the front foyer of Gabriel's apartment. She'd forgotten her mobile when she'd left this morning and hadn't been thinking. She'd simply walked into his rooms without any care until…

Unclaimed? A stray? Entirely unsuitable?

She'd caught *everything*.

'Enough.' Gabe's voice was like she'd never heard before. Forceful. Cold, with a crack of anger. 'You will not speak of Lena, of *any* of my employees, like that ever again.'

She should leave immediately and yet remained frozen to the spot, wanting to listen to it all in some masochistic desire to hear Gabriel's responses. And yet when she had heard… The pain of it all knifed deep. He'd made it clear. No matter what they might have shared, she'd always been his employee.

What had she been thinking?

The truth was, she hadn't. It was all a blissful fantasy till reality invaded, because she wanted belonging. She wanted someone to want *her*. She wanted that man to be Gabe. Was that what had happened to her mother? Falling into a trap that she'd been unable to extricate herself from, wanting to feel wanted too? By a man as unavailable to her mother as Gabe was to her? She didn't know. But in this moment, Lena finally understood her mother a little better.

There was movement ahead of her and yet she was fixed to the spot. Not understanding why every word had been a knife to her heart. As though she were bleeding out here. There'd been no talk of a future between them. She and Gabriel had been living in the moment, hadn't they? But hearing it said out loud, *'I'm in no hurry to marry…'* made her finally face the truth, that maybe it was marriage she'd wanted all along. That she'd wanted Gabe, not for the short time they'd agreed, but *for ever*. Even if for ever hadn't been promised to her.

The Queen swept into the hall with Gabriel following, striding behind her. He cast Lena a brief glance, eyes widening for a second in surprise at her presence before a cold impassive demeanour slid over his face once more.

Any words choked in Lena's throat. She gave a quick curtsey as they passed, refusing to allow anyone to see her pain, holding it deep inside. Her Majesty didn't even deign to look at her. It was as if she simply didn't exist. Was that how her mother had always felt? Ignored? Invisible? She'd believed her only true parent had enjoyed her position, having been in it so long. Now Lena was coming to understand what might have held her mother in place, and what it had cost her.

Lena couldn't stay still now. She walked further into Gabe's apartment, found her phone. Not willing to face the Queen, or even Gabriel. She could slip out again, into the secret passageway that ran through the walls here, and melt away. When Gabe had first shown it to her, she'd thought it exciting. The thrill of walking through it from her own room in the employee's quarters, to his own. Heart pounding with every footstep as she got closer to the secret latch that opened a door into his rooms.

She'd imagined all kinds of things on those walks through the dimly lit corridors behind the walls. The thrill of two lovers, meeting in secret. Lena realised now that this was what had kept her going through the brutal walk back to her own room each morning. When all she wanted to do was to stay, not leave before daybreak and pretend until night fell again and the fantasy could begin once more. Because that was all it had been.

A fantasy.

Now, reality slapped her in the face. This hadn't simply been about 'living in the moment' or losing her virginity. She had feelings for Gabriel. She wanted *more*. Looking back, she probably always had.

'What did you hear?'

She gave a bitter laugh. 'Enough.'

Especially his mother's comments about her and her family. The ones that cut to her marrow.

'Is it true, about your parents?'

That was where he first went to? But of course. She was simply a commoner. One who'd done the unforgivable and fallen for a prince. She lifted her chin. Seeing things clearly now when she hadn't understood before. 'My mother's *only* sin was to love a man. My father's, such as he was, far greater. But they had a long relationship that lasted till he died. Most people can't say the same.'

'Why didn't you tell me?'

Part of her wanted to believe he sounded almost hurt that she hadn't disclosed the truth, but she refused to accept that he was experiencing that kind of emotion, after what she'd heard.

'Because it wasn't relevant. Because I didn't want any judgement imposed on either me, or my mother. Because I've had enough to last a *lifetime*.'

Because, Lena realised now, she could accept judgement from most people since they didn't matter. It would have crushed her if that sentiment had ever come from Gabe.

His eyes widened, yet he didn't seem chastened at all. He almost looked…pitying. She loathed pity in all its forms. She'd been pitied, disdained, for most of her life.

'*Lena*, I wouldn't have judged you, or your family.'

Perhaps that was right, but everyone else would have, and, no matter what might have happened between them,

Prince Gabriel clearly didn't want her enough to have overcome it. He was a prince, and princes didn't choose people with indeterminate backgrounds like hers.

'I suppose you did say you enjoyed my company, and that my professionalism was impeccable. But I thought you might have...*liked* me, just a little.'

She hated how that statement showed her weakness. She'd wanted to be more than liked, she realised. She'd wanted to be loved. So *very* much. To be seen for who she truly was. Someone with a good heart who was interested in people. Who cared about showing the world the truth about a person, finding the good in those who were worthy, rather than mining the bad. She'd wanted to be seen as enough, even if she'd been kidding herself, because Gabe's view of her was built on a false picture. He'd never truly seen her because he didn't have the full truth. And she had no one to blame for that but herself.

'I do, like you. And there's no reason why this should change anything.'

She'd spent her whole short life trying not to be her mother's daughter, and yet here she was. Did her mother have these same conversations with her father? A public figure who could never truly be with her, so she'd had to accept whatever shreds of himself he'd design to supply? Was that what Gabe would offer her too? That was not what she wanted. Lena shook her head. How couldn't he see?

'It changes *everything*.'

'Why? I understand this is your first physical relationship with a man so you might not realise that the chemistry we have is something rare. Something to be explored, not thrown away. My family has no part in what's happening between us.'

Yet again, there was no talk of feeling and, right now, her

whole body was awash with it. The pain of what couldn't be. Because he might have wanted her for the physical side of their relationship, but he didn't want her for anything more. He was like every other man, who coveted what they saw physically, and didn't care for anything else. She could have laughed at how she hadn't listened to lessons that her life should have taught her. Self-deception sure was an intoxicating and potent drug.

'What if one of us decides they want something more?' Though she knew there was really no 'us' in this situation. The person who wanted more was her.

Gabriel frowned, but it was so hard to read him right now she didn't know what it meant. Annoyance, frustration. She couldn't tell.

'I thought we were enjoying each other. If you're talking marriage, that's a long way off for me. I'm interested in now, which is what you said you wanted too. Time to think of futures much later.'

That might be okay if Gabriel were just any man. A commoner like her. But he wasn't. He was the Crown Prince of Halrovia. With duties and expectations imposed on him, that he'd willingly accepted. His commitment was what would make him such a good king when the time came.

'And what if one day you decided I was the woman for you? Can you imagine how it would impact your image? Because I can. Let's think up a headline…' Lena tapped her finger to her lips. '*The Prince's Shocking Romance! From Mistress's Daughter to Future Queen?* I bet it's something your family could write themselves.'

'I don't care about my image. I don't care about the headlines.'

He started forward, towards her, as if to take her in his arms. To comfort. But there was no way to make this better.

She held her hand up in a stop motion. To his credit, Gabe didn't move a step further.

'Yes, you do. I was employed to help you fix them. You enjoyed it and you changed because of it. You *do* care. To say anything else is kidding yourself.'

Lena didn't want to be the one to destroy his image. She wanted to protect him. It wasn't just her background that was the problem, but the workplace romance too. Everything about this would see him judged, even though she'd been a willing party and in many ways the instigator of her own downfall. Well, she wouldn't be the cause of Gabriel's downfall as well.

'You need to listen to me.'

'No, I don't.' No matter what she agreed to, in the end he'd come to his senses and the story would be the same. One she was painfully familiar with. Gullible woman falls for high-profile, unavailable man.

'Our positions are clear. You broke some rules and so did I.'

'Good God, Lena.' Gabe raked his hands through his hair. 'I *care* about you.'

Like. Care. They were words, sure. Once they might have been enough. But they were bland now. Mere scraps thrown from a table of emotions when she wanted the whole banquet.

'My job's never been to make your life hard, Your Highness.'

Gabe's eyes widened. 'It's Gabriel, *not* Your Highness. I don't want easy. I don't need easy. Whatever rash decision you're about to make, the answer is no.'

As much as she needed to support her family, Lena needed to respect herself more. She knew the risks if she stayed. How easy it would be to be sucked back into the vortex that was Gabriel Montroy, dying a little each day because she was showing the man she loved to the world, and he could never choose her. Then what if he met the perfect princess bride? She'd be left as an unacknowledged footnote in his history. That was something she couldn't bear. 'You don't have a choice. There's no future here. There never was. One day you'll come to realise I was right, and you'll thank me for it. But it's time to go. I resign, Your Highness, effective immediately. Thank you for trusting me, when others might not have. Given I've exceeded your objectives, I look forward to my reference.'

Before he could say anything, Lena turned and strode out of his apartment. Walked away, before she could fling herself into his arms and beg him to love her. The tears burned in her eyes and she let them fall because doing the right thing was hard, and there was no shame in that. Lena loved Gabriel, but she loved herself even more.

And sometimes the best way to love was to let a person go.

CHAPTER TEN

GABRIEL HAD NEVER wanted to look back on his life with regret, but for one so relatively short—only thirty-two years—he'd had many. Yet none was greater than how he'd treated Lena. For days after she'd left, he'd been unable to forget the look on her face. The disappointment, as if something in her had shattered irreparably. The light in her snuffed out. What wounded almost beyond description was that *he'd* done it to her, hurt her. Not realising what he was about to lose because he hadn't thought to honestly look to the future. Mired, instead, in a past and present that no longer fitted the man he'd become.

It had taken Lena's loss to make him recognise how much she meant to him. Now it was as if he walked through a haze of apathy. Nothing held any interest. He was entirely unsure how to heal the pain he'd caused, to a woman who'd come to mean everything to him. Until he could, none of this meant anything at all.

'Are you convinced this is the right course, Your Highness?' his private secretary asked.

'It's the *only* course,' Gabriel replied.

There were few people he trusted implicitly. Henri. Pieter. His personal protection officers. Lena. But she wasn't here to give him advice any more. To share all the precious moments he might have once experienced, but hadn't properly valued until they were seen through the lens of her eyes.

His failure to protect her was like a knife to the gut. She was a woman with a tender soul. Someone who said what she thought without fear. A woman he'd craved to nurture, to protect. Yet the yawning ache in his chest called Gabriel out as a liar. He hadn't protected Lena at all, sneaking her through secret passages in the palace rather than proudly inviting her through the front door of his suite, forcing his parents to accept her.

He'd gone a little way to dealing with that issue in the brutal, bleak days after she'd walked out of his life. Gabe had spoken to the King and Queen and told them they needed to take a long, honest look at themselves. Suggesting the problems with the royal family's image were more likely due to the quiet disdain in which they appeared to hold those who weren't royal like themselves, rather than anything he or his siblings had done. Then he'd walked away from them, inviting communication between their respective private secretaries until they'd properly reflected on their actions, because in the time since Lena had walked away, a single truth had glared at him.

He might have a duty to his country, which he'd carry out willingly, but he didn't want it without Lena at his side.

If he couldn't have her, how could he perform the role? He'd be miserable, and he'd make a miserable king, which wouldn't be good for the country. He'd seen how his relationship with his people had changed since Lena had come into his life. It hadn't been the photographs, the curated view of himself, that had made the difference. It had been her. She'd demanded something honest from him—not the man in hiding, not the prince, but the *real* man.

He'd spent his whole life doing what was required of him, as opposed to what he might have truly desired. Yet duty could only take you so far. It didn't make you laugh.

It didn't feed the soul. It didn't comfort or console, or keep you warm on a cold night. Lena was the one who'd offered him all those things. Encouraged him to contemplate more for himself. She'd held a mirror up to him and he finally saw himself through her eyes. That was the true gift she'd bestowed on him, recognition of the best parts of himself, the ones he'd tried to forget. That he was allowed to care but, even more, that he was allowed to show it. That he had dreams and aspirations that his people might want to see too.

Lena was the one who showed him.

Realising he was happy to walk away if it meant having her made his next task easier. He was tired of secrets. Those secrets, and a failure to address them, was what had led them here. To a place where his family was being held hostage by fear, and he was without the woman he loved. Because he'd come to realise, very soon after she'd resigned from her job and his life, that he was in love with Lena Rosetti. Now was his chance to be honest and, in some ways, atone for his personal failings.

He picked up the piece of paper that held a media release, drafted by him and his private secretary. Henri had loaded it into Gabriel's screen reader, but Gabe wanted to read the words on the page, to take the time and make the effort, since he'd written them because of Lena and in many ways *for* her. To show the woman he loved how he'd changed.

For immediate release:

His Royal Highness, Prince Gabriel of Halrovia, Adopts Patronage of Literacy Charity, sharing his personal journey with dyslexia to inspire and empower.

In a meaningful display of dedication to literacy and inclusivity, His Royal Highness, Prince Gabriel, has announced his new role as patron of the Halrovian Literacy Foundation, a charity dedicated to supporting children and adults in achieving reading confidence and fluency. In stepping into this patronage, His Royal Highness has also publicly shared his personal experience with dyslexia for the first time.

Since his diagnosis in his teens, Prince Gabriel has successfully learned to navigate the challenges dyslexia can present, allowing him to fulfil his royal duties and responsibilities. His diagnosis was kept private out of a belief that it was irrelevant to his public role. However, as he assumes leadership of the charity formerly championed by his sister, Princess Anastacia, he has chosen to share his story in the hopes of inspiring others facing similar challenges.

'Reading is something many take for granted but, for some, it's been a constant source of struggle and, occasionally, stigma,' Prince Gabriel said. 'My hope is that by sharing my story, others will feel less alone and more empowered to seek the help they need. With support and community acceptance of those with reading difficulties, we can all find ways to strive and thrive.'

With Prince Gabriel's support, the Halrovian Literacy Foundation aims to reach even more people, offering them the tools and encouragement to achieve their personal best, supporting the Halrovian community's commitment to literacy and learning for all its citizens.

Media Contact: Henri Lacoste, Private Secretary to His Royal Highness, Office of the Crown Prince, Halrovia

Gabriel wished he'd had Lena's counsel before sending the release, but she'd told him once that this was the kind of authenticity people wanted to see, and he trusted her judgement implicitly.

'Are you satisfied, sir?' Henri asked.

He wouldn't be satisfied with anything until Lena was back in his life, but, until then, this would have to be enough.

'It's time to hit send.'

Henri reached for his laptop. Tapped on the keyboard, then looked up over the screen. 'It's done. Their Majesties' private secretary will be—'

'To put it colloquially, *pissed off*, but I don't give a damn.'

If this failed as a broader strategy, he hadn't lost anything. Lena was still gone. Nothing could hurt him more than he'd hurt himself on that score, but Gabriel hoped in the process he might gain her respect. If it succeeded, then he'd freed himself and his family from a secret that had given power to a rogue advisor of state, which the man had sought to exploit through the tabloid media.

With one keystroke of a computer, Gabe had taken the power back. But that was only the beginning. He had a plan. One that had taken time and thought. Which would either be spectacularly successful or leave him shot down in furious flames. He doubted there was a middle ground in this next step, his greatest challenge of all. Making it up to Lena, fighting for her, and bringing her home to his loving embrace.

For ever.

CHAPTER ELEVEN

ISOLOBELLO GLEAMED IN perfection for the royal wedding between Prince Caspar and Princess Priscilla. The capital and every town bedecked with garlands and banners for the event. It was a magnificent morning for a celebration. The sun shone golden in a flawless blue sky. The weather, comfortably warm. Lena stood in the lounge area of her small flat. Television droning in the background to stop her racing thoughts. The churn in her belly as if it were full of snakes. She looked down again at the heavy cream card of an invitation that had come six weeks earlier, delivered to her home by courier.

His Majesty King Constantine
requests the pleasure of the company of
Ms Lena Rosetti
at the marriage of
His Royal Highness Prince Caspar of Isolobello
with
Princess Priscilla of Halrovia

After what had happened between her and Prince Gabriel, she hadn't been sure that her friendship with Cilla would survive. Yet she held the unmistakable evidence that it had in her hands. Whilst photographs she'd seen online from others displaying their invitations in excitement showed their names in calligraphy, hers had been written in the fine, elegant hand she knew to be Cilla's.

It was personal and touching. But still, Lena's heart kicked against her ribs. She took a deep breath trying to settle it. Lena slid the invitation back into her clutch purse with trembling fingers. For a while she hadn't known what to do, but as the RSVP date had approached, she'd found herself accepting the invitation. So here she was, dressed and waiting for her allotted time to leave home for Isolobello's cathedral. The guests' arrival staged to avoid traffic jams in the overflowing city, full of media and visitors wanting to celebrate what had been billed as the wedding of the year.

Yet right in this moment, she wasn't sure she wanted to go. Her teeth worried her lower lip, the fear at seeing Gabriel again almost throttling her. He'd clearly made some changes in his life. For some masochistic reason she hadn't immediately cancelled news alerts for him. The last headline she'd seen, after an important media release…

Heart of a Hero: Prince Gabriel's Dyslexia Revelation Sparks Hope for Others

He'd done it. What she believed was one of the most important things she'd ever suggested to him. It had been at that point she couldn't bear it any more and had shut the alerts down, because he was clearly moving on and so should she.

Lena rubbed at an ache in her chest, refusing to let the burn of tears spill over and ruin her make-up. How could she face him? Sure, he'd sit up front of the cathedral with the other members of royalty, but still… At least she was only invited to the ceremony. The reception was a private family-only affair. All she could do was cross her fingers and hope there was little chance of her catching any more than a glimpse of the man she'd walked away from, breaking her heart in the process.

In the distance the cheers of the crowd rose and fell like the roar of a winter's wind. Ebbing and flowing as some carriage or car paraded down the main street towards the cathedral, which she could see on the television as she'd watched throughout the day. She checked the time. Her car would be here soon enough to take her, once most of the dignitaries had arrived. She still had time to collect her thoughts, rein in her emotions. Get herself in the mood for a day to celebrate love. Something she now understood, deeply and viscerally, that she wanted for herself.

Only the man she wanted it with was unavailable, and not for her.

Lena took a deep breath. It was fine. *She* was fine. What had she expected anyway? A commoner and an illegitimate child, her father unacknowledged. Had she ever really contemplated that one day she might be Queen of Halrovia when things had started with Gabe?

The truth was, for a fleeting moment, she almost had. What she craved was for someone to love *her*, to choose *her*. To see her for who she was and not the family she'd been born into.

When she'd returned home from Halrovia, Lena had sat down to have some hard conversations with her mother. But they were also some of the most real, because of her new understanding of what her mum might have gone through. They'd spoken, and they'd cried. Both of them grieving. She'd admitted what had happened with Gabe, what she'd felt. Lena had expected her mother to berate her choice. Instead, her mother had cupped her cheek and explained to Lena how she'd fallen in love with a man and hadn't thought of the consequences till she'd been in too deep. Too far in love and too lacking in confidence to contemplate life without him. How much she admired Lena for her courage and her self-belief; having the strength to walk away. Then they'd cried some more. So many tears had fallen that day.

But she couldn't stay sad for ever. She had to keep moving. She'd been in a kind of stasis long enough. Whilst her teacher had always said, *'There is a divinity which shapes our ends, rough-hew them how we will'*, Lena realised the flaw in that quote. It removed her agency. She'd spent enough time waiting for the universe to work things out for her. Now she had to drive her own life. Which had led to her seeing a lawyer, as Gabe had suggested, to get her own advice on her father's failure to provide for them. And what she'd learned had changed her and her family's life. That they were entitled to part of the estate. A sizeable part.

So, she'd turned up to her half-brother's office and demanded their share. Not everything they were entitled to, but enough to keep her mother in her home, and her brother in university. As for her, initially she'd balked at taking any money from her father's estate but, as her younger brother had pointed out, neither of them had asked to be born, and some money, whilst not making them rich, gave her choices. She didn't have to work for anyone. She could complete her degree, start her own business. And when the dust settled, that was what she'd do. She'd have what she'd always wanted. An education. Financial security.

And yet it still seemed as if there was something, or someone, missing.

As she stood watching her country's flags fluttering in the breeze out of her window, the clatter of horses' hooves sounded in the distance. That was weird, because the path of the procession to the wedding wasn't close enough to her home to be able to hear the horses. Perhaps they were mounted police patrolling in ceremonial uniform?

'There's something you don't see every day. What are they doing?'

An announcer on the television. She turned and the two people onscreen, a man and a woman, were chuckling.

'Perhaps they've left something behind?' said the man. 'The ring?'

Lena couldn't see what they were laughing at, but surely no one had forgotten the wedding ring. She tried to listen to what the announcers were saying. Something about a carriage turning around. However, the only pictures onscreen were of guests arriving at the cathedral. The announcers said they had a reporter on the ground trying to find out what had gone on, except Lena was distracted by the clatter of hooves becoming louder on the roadway outside her apartment. The rhythm and the sound suggesting horses working in unison, rather than individually.

She went to her window overlooking the cobbled street below as the announcers mentioned something about a residential area and a carriage. In the distance she saw movement, and the reason for the sound became clear. Horses. Six. Black. Carrying three riders in full livery of red and gold and pulling a gleaming open carriage.

Her heart leapt to her throat, beating a quick and thready rhythm. She stood there gripping the window frame. The wood cool and hard under her fingertips as the carriage came closer and closer. Two men sitting in it. The broad back of one with unruly brown hair and another, whose hair was gold like the sun.

Lena gasped and pulled back. Slamming shut the windows as if trying to lock herself in. She turned to the television as they talked about members of the public calling in saying the landau carriage carrying Aston Lane and Prince Gabriel of Halrovia was travelling through the back streets of the capital to an unknown destination.

It wasn't unknown at all. They were in *her* suburb, on her street.

Lena didn't know what to do, where to go. Her thoughts whirled but none of them made sense. The sound of the hooves echoing off the buildings either side of the narrow street below became louder and louder. Lena wanted to put her fingers in her ears and pretend that this wasn't happening as the hooves clattered, slowed and came to a stop what sounded like right outside her building.

She refused to look out. She stood in the middle of the lounge area of her apartment. Waiting. For what? The building had security. No one could get in. But, she knew, no one would keep out a *prince*. Perspiration beaded on her brow. A trickle ran down the back of her neck as she tried to breathe. The television droning in the background supposing what the Crown Prince of Halrovia was doing. The whole scenario so bizarre and dissonant because she *knew* what he had to be doing.

He was coming to see her.

A knock sounded at the door. She jumped, the sound sharp and urgent. Without her thinking much, her feet took her to the door. Her hands trembling as she undid the chain. Methodically working the locks and opening it.

She gripped the door jamb to keep her upright as the man who had haunted too many of her dreams came into view, in a rush that pushed the breath from her lungs. Her Gabe.

No, *not* hers.

She might have liked to pretend but Prince Gabriel was his country's, and always would be. He'd made it clear that he hadn't considered a future with her. She'd done the right thing and set him free by leaving, as much as he'd freed her in the time they'd been together.

She couldn't look at his face. Not yet. His clothes were easier. He was as perfectly, formally attired as she'd always remembered. More so today in his morning dress. The dark coat, paler grey striped trousers. Cream waistcoat. Soft pink tie...

Oh.

Her lips almost broke into a smile because Pieter would have *hated* it with the power of a thousand suns.

She focussed on the tie of that offending colour for a while, almost afraid to look anywhere else. But she had nothing to fear, not any more. In walking away from him she had shown just how brave she could really be.

'Lena.'

Her name sounded like a benediction. She couldn't help herself. She looked up. To his full lips that had kissed and pleasured her till she'd wept. Heat crept up her throat at the memories. His eyes, the pale blue of melting snow in spring. But even though the colour might have appeared cool, it was only an illusion. Something about them, the look *in* them, blazed like the hottest of summer suns. She didn't know what to say, she could hardly remember how to breathe, so she blurted out the only thing that came to mind.

'Th-they said you might have left something behind—what?'

Gabe's Adam's apple bobbed as his throat convulsed in a swallow.

'You, Lena. Nothing else but you.'

CHAPTER TWELVE

SEEING LENA AGAIN was like a knock to the head. She stood before him, a vision in a silky dress of the softest pink, like the first hint of sunrise. A picture of such perfection that his words had failed. He'd forgotten the effect she had on him. His tongue was tied. She was inside him, had burrowed in deep into his marrow and taken up residence. One look at her in the flesh, rather than the distant and painful memories from the glorious and devastating time together, entrenched Gabe's view. There was no letting her go. He couldn't.

Every official function before Cilla's wedding, he'd known a part of him was missing. Seeing Priscilla, Caspar, Ana and Aston had solidified something he'd resolved weeks before with his press release. Marrying a princess because it was expected of him, *not* marrying for love, was something he could never do. His feelings for Lena would always come first. Even if she refused him today, he'd love her. Which was why he needed to make it up to her with everything he had. Because his life would be meaningless without her.

Lena's eyes widened as she gripped the door jamb till her fingertips paled.

'How did you find me?'

He'd always known where she'd gone. In the time since she'd left Halrovia he'd been driven to ensure she and her family had a home and weren't out on the streets. That there was food on the table, and she wasn't being forced into a situation she didn't want, like marrying. His discreet enquiries had satisfied him that she was okay, giving him time to plan.

'Finding you was the easy part. As for the rest...'

None of that had been easy, but anything was simpler than the days since she'd walked out of Halrovia's palace. Being flayed alive would have been easier than that. Yet for now he had some more pressing matters to deal with. As he stood on her stoop, some doors in the hall of her apartment building had opened. Gabriel accepted that a royal postillion landau carriage parking in the street below would cause a stir, but a few people had begun to peer out at them both. Whilst he could have a conversation with Lena in the hall if that was what she wanted, he preferred a little privacy, where he could try to say the things he needed to get her back in his arms and in his life again.

To let her know how much he loved her.

'May I come inside?' he asked.

'You're on your way to your sister's wedding.'

'And yet here I am, finding I can't go any further.'

'What if you're late?'

'I'll be forgiven.'

By his sisters at least. His parents might never overcome the theatrics, but he didn't care. He'd said enough after his world had imploded the day Lena had left. He liked to believe that his mother and father were taking the time to think about those harsh truths, though he was satisfied to continue communicating with them, private secretary to private secretary, until he had a suitable apology. It was easier, now he'd bought a home away from the palace. The purchase contracts only just settled. Soon he'd be moving.

He hoped to bring Lena home with him.

A few people began pointing phones at Lena's doorway

to film what was happening. Whilst he spent his life under constant scrutiny, he wanted to ease Lena into her moment in the spotlight. If he could convince her of the truth of his feelings, today was going to be a big day.

Lena seemed to catch herself, seeing all her neighbours peering at them. The phones pointed their way. She stood back.

'Come inside. Quickly. I don't want to be the story here.'

He stepped over the threshold, and she shut the door gently behind her then turned. In the shock of seeing her again he hadn't noticed how tired she looked. A little like himself. She hid it well under make-up, but it still wasn't enough. And there was something else he noticed about her too. The way she wrung her hands in front of her. Bit into her lip. The look on her face, troubled. He'd done that to her. Failed to realise how tender and soft her heart was. How much his rejection would hurt because of what her father had done to her. In the beginning he'd kidded himself that their secrecy was for her. To protect Lena from the bright lights of media attention when nothing was certain. But that had never been the truth. His deepest confession was that keeping her hidden was entirely selfish.

He'd been trying to come to terms with so many things. Managing the media, sure, but his own feelings. He hadn't understood those at all, when they were now clear and bright like a beacon. He'd been in love with her before he'd even realised, because she saw Gabriel Montroy. A man who wasn't proud or proper or any of those things. He simply *was*.

'Why are you here?' she asked him. 'I don't want to be responsible for holding up your sister's wedding to my future king.'

'As far as I'm concerned, the whole world can wait. Nothing's more important than this, than *you*, Lena.'

A wash of colour flooded her cheeks. 'That's not true.'

'And there lies my greatest mistake.'

Gabe would never stop regretting how uncertain he'd made her. Causing this doubt. Together, he'd not only found someone who saw him, but he'd seen her too. A woman who'd blossomed when given attention. Someone strong. Who could take over the world if she wanted to, because she'd completely taken over his. Every day, every waking thought. All his dreams.

'I have so much to apologise for,' he said. 'Most of all I want to apologise for making you believe that you hadn't become the most important person in my life. That I was in some way embarrassed, and wanted you hidden, when all I should have done was show the world what I saw. How incredible you *are*.'

'But your parents—'

'Need to learn that you were never a whim. I've had strong words with them, my mother in particular, about the things she said. But that's for another day. What I came to tell you was that you're the woman who unlocked my heart. The woman I would give up *everything* for.'

'What do you mean?'

'I have my sister's wedding to attend, but I find I don't want to go.' Lena's eyes widened. Huge pools of blue. A colour he'd missed, craving it over the last few months without her. 'Not without you by my side.'

Lena wished there were something she could hold on to. Anything. She wanted to fall over on the spot. Even though she might have hoped and dreamed, Gabriel stood in a place she'd never believed she'd see him. Her lounge room. On his sister's wedding day. And if she believed her ears, he wanted her to join him as his guest.

Impossible.

'Your parents would never accept me.'

'I don't care about them.'

'You should.'

He frowned, looking confused. But then, he wouldn't understand. He'd been accepted wherever he went.

'They're steeped in tradition, which has locked them in the past. But I've told them that until they've reflected on their behaviour and suitably apologised, there's going to be a distance between us. Though I have little doubt that if they truly came to know you, then they'd love you. As I do.'

'You what?' A sensation burst inside, like a thousand birds taking flight at dawn, singing a joyous song.

He moved forward, towards her. His face beaming like sunshine lighting up the room.

'I love you. I could never marry for duty, because it would eat away at me. I'd come to hate everything and everyone if I was forced to give up on the one person who showed me myself. Who made me better every day. Who brought colour into a world that had been grey. I'd give up everything for you, my place in succession, because you have my heart and no one else will do.'

She froze. Her brain simply couldn't compute what he'd said.

'I—wait. You can't. Give up *being King*?'

'If the only way I can have you is to give up my right to the throne, then that's what I'll do. I'll always choose you.'

'But you'd be an amazing king. What are you talking about? I don't understand.'

The corner of Gabriel's mouth kicked up in a half-smile. It looked entertained, but also sad.

'You would have understood, had I been the man I should have been. Treated you the right way. Fought my parents for you. But I wanted more time to sift through my feelings because they were so unfamiliar. I should have told them that, told you. Stood up for you, for what you meant to me. It's my greatest regret that I didn't. I treated you like your father did, when you're a woman who deserves to shine, not be hidden away. You are not my guilty secret. You're nobody's.'

All her life, she'd been told to stay in the shadows. Not to talk about her father, to say she didn't know, to protect him. To protect her mother. Now Gabe was here. Acknowledging what she'd once craved and dreamed of. Being recognised, being truly seen. Yet in all her dreams, she'd never dreamed of anything like this.

'If I haven't been clear, let me make it plain…' Gabe said, walking towards her. Standing closer. So tall and solid. A man who could take her breath away. Who might even help her shoulder some burdens, as she'd helped him. 'I love you, Lena. There's no one else in the world I want. You already rule my heart. One day, I want you to rule my country by my side. You impressed me *that* much.'

The man she loved, a man who would one day be King, wanting her to be his queen. Saying he would give it all up for her. *Her.* She'd be thrown into the world's spotlight. There would be no hiding any more.

Lena found she liked that idea, because it gave her Gabe.

'I think I'm tired of hiding. I hid my past from you because I was afraid. I didn't really trust that you wouldn't judge me like others had.'

'I hope you trust me now?'

She nodded. 'I do.'

Gabe took another step forwards, the corners of his lips quirking as if he wanted a smile to break free but wasn't yet sure.

'Then, I'll always work to honour that trust. Come join

me at my sister's wedding. Show the world what you mean to me. It seems you're dressed for it.'

Her heart leapt. 'Today?'

'Is there a better time? Cilla did say I could bring a "plus one", as she put it.'

'Where would I even sit at the reception? I have an invitation to the ceremony but you don't just walk into the formal lunch for family.'

'You are invited. You'll be with me. But you're concerned…'

He reached into his coat pocket and slid out a mobile phone. Scrolled. Put the phone to his ear. Lena didn't know who he was calling, but she could hear the murmur of a voice at the other end.

'I know, I'm running a little late. I need you to do something for me. If I bring someone to the reception, make sure there's a place for her?'

Gabe hesitated for a second. More. Lena's heart pounded. What if the answer was no? Then Gabe flinched. Pulled the phone from his ear and held it out. Lena could hear the shrieking, which sounded exuberant rather than angry. After a few moments, Gabe put the phone back to his ear, grinning.

'Yes, it *is* the best thing but don't get too excited. I haven't heard the magic word… But I hope so, too. She just needs to know there'll always be a seat at the table for her… Right. See you soon.'

He slipped the phone back into his pocket. 'It's done, if you want to join me.'

'Who did you speak to?'

'Ana, who passed the news on to Cilla, hence the collective and premature shrieks of joy.'

'Are they premature?'

'You haven't said yes. I understand why you might be

reluctant, but I can't be clearer. I love you. I want to spend my life with you. I want to show everyone the woman who found me, who saw me. Who made me a better man. Who'll one day make me a better king.'

Then Gabriel dropped to the floor, down on one knee in front of her. The sight of him so surreal she could hardly believe this wasn't all a dream.

'Would you do me the honour of joining me at my sister's wedding? Of, one day, becoming my wife? Or if you're still not sure, come with me and we can call it a trial period. Test the waters. See if you like it. See if you still like me.'

She looked at him, beaming up at her. His face full of hope. A man who saw her too. The man she loved. The man who said he would give up everything for her, and she believed him.

'Kind of a probation period?'

'Where I get to try and impress you.'

She smiled back at him. 'You don't have to impress me. You already have. And I think we both know there's no point in a probation period when we love each other. We may as well make it official.'

Gabe took her hands in his and smiled right back in a way that pierced her heart with pure joy. 'Then, Lena. Will you marry me, so that we can spend the rest of our lives together, making each other happy? Because I want you, from this day and for ever.'

'Yes. I love you, Gabriel Montroy. The answer is *always* yes.'

Gabe stood and took her into his arms, dropped his lips to her mouth and kissed her, long and deep. As if pouring all of his love into that one moment. Something passionate and endless. The heat of it ignited inside her, the slow burn soon turning into a blazing wildfire as he crushed her to him, and she plunged her hands into his hair. Time lost all meaning now they were together again. After too long and yet not enough they slowly pulled apart, both breathless. Both smiling. Lena drifted her thumb over Gabe's lips, wiping away the lipstick.

'Sealed with a kiss,' she murmured as Gabe cradled her close to his chest.

'And what a kiss it was.'

Lena sighed. It was the kind of kiss stories might be written about. Happily, she now got to write her own.

There was a loud rap at the door.

'Montroy, I don't want to interrupt but we have a wedding to get to and the horses are restless. So are the press who are now surrounding the carriage, asking why we've stopped. What do you want me to tell them?'

'One minute,' Gabe called out, then looked down at her. 'That's Ana's husband. Are you ready to join me?'

'Will Priscilla forgive you for stealing the attention on her wedding day?'

'Always thinking of others. One day I hope to teach you to think of yourself. Do you remember the squeals? As you've heard, she'll be more than happy. She wanted you there. She sent you an invitation. Cilla and Ana will probably try to steal you away from me for all the gossip. Just promise to save me a dance.'

'Every dance is yours.'

'Excellent.' He brushed his lips gently to hers again. 'So, are you ready to…go viral?'

Lena had never been so desperate to take what she wanted. To leap into the limelight, as now. She didn't want to hide any more, she simply wanted to be with the man she loved, and nothing else mattered.

'Can you imagine the headlines?'

'Yes, I can. They'll all say something like… *A Royal Fairy Tale: Prince Finds True Love with His Secret Cinderella*. The moment they see us together they'll be writing how it's the romance of the decade. One that'll enchant and captivate the nation.'

She laughed. 'I love the sound of that.'

'So do I.'

Gabe released her from his arms and took her hand. Threading his fingers through her own. His hold so strong and sure, she knew they'd weather anything so long as they were together. That he'd never let her go.

'Then let's do it,' she said, with her heart full of love. Ready to face the world as they walked hand in hand to the door. Heading into their fairy-tale future together.

EPILOGUE

Two years later

A GENTLE WARM sunshine beamed down as Gabriel and Lena sat in the royal carriage on its procession from Halrovia's cathedral to the palace. Gabe gave a final wave to the jubilant crowd that had lined the streets to celebrate their wedding, before the carriage passed through the palace's iron gates to the mews beyond. It had been two years since Gabe and Lena had returned to Halrovia in the heady days after Cilla and Caspar's wedding reception in Isolobello. On that glorious day they'd laughed and danced and showed everyone how much in love they were. Ever since, no one had doubted he and Lena were destined for one another.

Lena turned to him and smiled. Her diamond tiara, which he'd had specially commissioned for this day, twinkling in the sunlight.

'You look...' Gabe swallowed at the knot that choked his throat. Blinked away the burn in his eyes. His wife was an exquisite woman but today, seeing her walk down the aisle in her wedding dress—a marvel of a white handmade lace embossed with a pattern of Halrovia's native alpine wildflowers, a cobweb-like veil of tulle trailing behind her—his composure had cracked. She was the only person who could bring him to his knees. Perfect in every way—perfect for him.

She cupped his cheek, her eyes gleaming with tears of her own. 'I've never seen you more handsome. And I've never been happier.'

A flame of warmth kindled deep in his chest. Lena had been accepted by the people of Halrovia with joy and openness. They were simply happy to see their prince happy—nothing else mattered. As he'd promised her, the press had been mostly kind to them and their relationship. It seemed that his earlier disclosure about his dyslexia had worked. His approval had surged. Attempts by the rogue advisor to foment more discord about the royal family had been quickly quelled. He'd lost his power as Gabe had predicted. The final blow had come after a fickle media had turned on him and begun to investigate what appeared to be some questionable financial transactions, leading him to quietly resign from his role with the royal family. All the tabloids were now filled with stories of the public's support and love for the woman who'd stolen Gabe's heart. Only speaking of Lena with praise.

Gabriel took her hand in his, brought it to his mouth. Kissed it. Her engagement and wedding rings glittering in the sunlight. He'd taken time with her to design the perfect ring to honour their love. An oval sapphire the colour of her eyes and the seas around her island home. Flanked by heart-shaped, vibrant yellow diamonds. A representation of the sunshine and light she'd brought to his life. Together, the stones also represented the colours of the Halrovian flag, their life together.

In the beginning, he'd given Lena time. Allowing her to finish her studies. Steadily introducing her to the role she'd one day take up as Queen. She hadn't needed it. Whilst he'd helped her navigate the complexities of royal life, which she'd relished because of her kind and generous soul, it wasn't all one-sided. She'd helped him too, opening him to new possibilities.

'Have you forgiven me yet, for my decision last week?'

Lena pouted, but, from the cheeky twinkle in her eyes, he knew it was all for show. 'I still think you were wrong. The little black schnauzer in the bee suit should have won the pet competition.'

'I still believe the snake was the right choice. The owner had made it a *hat*. I've never seen anything like it. Anyhow, I wanted to prove my personal growth to you by that choice.'

'My darling husband, you still wore a *suit*.' Lena began to laugh. 'But you did work with children and animals and that…was impressive.'

'My darling husband.' How he relished those three words when, for a time after Lena had left him, Gabe had thought he might never be granted the privilege. 'You've always left an impression on me.'

Their carriage pulled to a stop and a member of staff in ceremonial finery opened the door. Gabriel hopped down.

'Are you ready?' he asked.

He and Lena were to be presented on the palace balcony as husband and wife. It was the moment he felt as if he'd been preparing for, for most of his life. Except it took on so much more meaning and import with Lena at his side.

She looked down at him from the carriage and beamed. His love, his princess, his future queen.

'Of course I'm ready. I'm with you.'

He helped her down from the carriage, waiting by her side as her train was adjusted, then offered her his arm as they made their way into the palace. His family and hers had already arrived.

Caspar and Aston had been his best man and groomsman today. Cilla and Ana had been Lena's matron of honour and bridesmaid. It had caused a stir to have a future queen and a princess in those roles, but his sisters were Lena's friends, as their husbands were his, and that made his heart whole.

'Hurry up, you two!' Cilla called out. 'You can't be late for the *world*.'

As far as Gabe was concerned, the world could wait a little longer.

They entered the hall leading to the balcony, where they'd soon formally greet the public as Prince Gabriel and Princess Lena. Husband and wife. As Cilla and Ana went ahead, chatting and catching up now that they lived in different countries, he saw his parents waiting to the side, talking to Lena's mother and brother, both of whom had walked her down the aisle.

It had been a slow repair to his relationship with them. Gabe had been protective of Lena, keeping her away from the King and Queen, even though they'd reached out and asked for another introduction. Small steps had finally led to acceptance; when his parents had realised that only one person would make him happy. As he'd explained, shouldn't that be what any parent wanted for their child? Of course, they'd agreed.

'We're ready when you are,' his private secretary, Henri, said. Since the announcement of his engagement to Lena, Henri and Pieter hadn't stopped smiling. He'd made many people happy with his choice, and that satisfied him to the depths of his soul.

'I'd like one moment.'

Henri nodded as Gabriel led Lena into a room off the corridor, on the opposite side to the balcony where they'd be presented to Halrovia's people. He shut the door behind them for privacy, but could still hear the rumble of anticipation from the crowd who'd packed the palace forecourt and the main road beyond. All hoping to see their Prince and new Princess, to witness the obligatory kiss.

'Come here.'

Gabe turned and opened his arms. Lena walked straight into them. He relished the feel of her in his embrace. For a few days before their wedding she'd stayed with her mother in one of the royal residences made available for them. He'd missed Lena. Their home felt empty in her absence. It reminded him of how unfulfilled his life had been before she'd burst into it.

'I wanted some time alone with you,' he murmured, 'because today, you're everybody's.'

'No, I'm not,' Lena said. 'I'm yours. Always yours—never forget that.'

'As I'm yours,' he said, smiling, his heart overfull.

'Of course you are. You promised. And I trust you.'

That trust meant *everything* to him. He'd honour it, and never betray it. Lena rested her head on his chest as he held her. She was taller today, wearing heels. He'd caught a glimpse of them in the carriage on the way back to the palace, the sparkle of crystals.

'Tonight…' he said.

'Mmm…?'

'Leave the heels on.'

She gave a low, throaty chuckle and melted further into his body. 'Do you intend to live up to your reputation, Your Royal Hotness?'

'I'll never make you a promise I can't keep.'

She tilted her head up, her pupils wide and dark in the ocean of her eyes. A hint of pink flushed across her cheeks. 'Lucky me…'

'I think I'm the lucky one but let's not argue on our wedding day. Another kiss from my bride?'

Gabe craved this private time before having to share her

with the world again. He dropped his mouth to hers, and her lips parted. The kiss tender, languid, full of reverence. Even though they had a whole future ahead of them, they took their time, reconnecting. Learning each other all over again.

Each day was an adventure of discovery with her.

A gentle knock sounded at the door. It was a reminder. For now, they were Halrovia's. At the reception tonight, and afterwards, they could be each other's again. He held out his hand and she took it as they walked back into the hall towards a room with expansive French doors opening onto the balcony, where the rest of the family would shortly gather. As they entered the space, everyone smiled.

'Let's do this,' he said, and Lena squeezed his hand in acknowledgement.

The doors were opened wide allowing the King and Queen through first, followed by the rest of the family as Gabe and Lena held back. The sound of the crowd surged in like an ocean storm, its roar ebbing and flowing.

'Oh. My. Goodness,' she whispered, gripping his hand tighter. 'Listen to everyone.'

Sometimes even he forgot what the crowds could be like from the balcony, but Lena would soon see. Realise how loved she was. It was unavoidable in the face of this.

'It's all for you,' he said as they stepped out into the morning sunshine. A sea of people spread before them, chanting their names.

Lena turned to him and smiled. 'It's for you too, never forget.'

'I know if I do, you'll remind me. Now, shall we give everyone what they've been waiting for?'

Soon, a kiss wouldn't be enough. There was already speculation about a royal pregnancy. He and Lena had spoken privately about giving up contraception for the honeymoon.

Perhaps there'd be a royal baby sooner than anyone thought. Whenever it happened, he was ready. In the meantime, he couldn't wait to start trying.

But that was for later, in the quiet of their honeymoon suite.

'I don't believe things could be any better than right now,' Lena said, her voice trembling and thick with emotion.

Gabe understood. He'd never imagined he could have what he'd gained with Lena by his side. His partner. His equal. The woman he loved. 'We've a lifetime yet to come.'

They turned to face each other. Gabe leaned down and kissed her gently on the lips. She placed her hand tenderly on his cheek and kissed back. The cheers of the crowd rushing over them in a tidal wave of joy as they shared the truth of their undying love with the world.

* * * * *

If Prince She Shouldn't Crave *left you wanting more,*
be sure to check out the first instalment in the
Royal House of Halrovia duet
Royal Fiancée Required

And why not explore these other stories
from Kali Anthony?

The Marriage That Made Her Queen
Engaged to London's Wildest Billionaire
Crowned for the King's Secret
Awoken by Revenge
Royal Fiancée Required

Available now!

MILLS & BOON®

Coming next month

KING'S EMERGENCY WIFE
Lucy King

'I'd like you to draft an announcement regarding the imminent change to my marital status.'

If Sofia was startled by his request, she didn't show it. She barely even blinked. 'Have you finally made your choice?'

Ivo nodded shortly. 'I have.'

'I understood none of the current candidates were deemed to be suitable.'

'That's correct,' he said. 'I had to think laterally. Outside the box. It turned out to be an excellent move.'

'Then may I be the first to offer you my congratulations.'

'Thank you.'

'The palace will breathe a sigh of relief.'

'I can almost hear it now.'

'I'll draft the announcement immediately and email it to you for approval,' she said, glancing down briefly to jot something in her notebook. 'It will be sent to all major news outlets within the hour.'

'Good.'

'The people will be ecstatic.'

'I certainly hope so.'

'Just one thing...'

'Yes?'

She lifted her gaze back to his, her smile faint, her expression quizzical. 'Who's the lucky lady?'

'You are.'

Continue reading

KING'S EMERGENCY WIFE
Lucy King

Available next month
millsandboon.co.uk

Copyright ©2025 Lucy King

COMING SOON!

We really hope you enjoyed reading this book. If you're looking for more romance be sure to head to the shops when new books are available on

Thursday 25th September

To see which titles are coming soon, please visit
millsandboon.co.uk/nextmonth

MILLS & BOON

MILLS & BOON TRUE LOVE IS HAVING A MAKEOVER!

Introducing

Love Always

Swoon-worthy romances, where love takes center stage. Same heartwarming stories, stylish new look!

Look out for our brand new look
COMING SEPTEMBER 2025

MILLS & BOON

OUT NOW!

THE TYCOON'S AFFAIR COLLECTION

CRAVING HIS LOVE

USA TODAY BESTSELLING AUTHOR
SHARON KENDRICK

Available at
millsandboon.co.uk

MILLS & BOON